THE BEACON

Reach for the light
in the night!

Also by this Author

THE CIRCLE SERIES

The Circle of Fire

The Circle of Duty

The Circle of Stars

SHORT STORY COLLECTIONS

Tall Tales For Dark Nights

Answers From The Darkness

THE BEACON

Owen Elgie

ISBN: 978-1-917425-49-0

PublishNation
www.publishnation.co.uk

1

Autumn was the time of year which brought the greatest range of days to enjoy.

Sure, summer came with those long days and better temperatures, and winter occasionally graced us with snow, but autumn was where you could find a lucky dip of days which could be cooler than the height of summer but still warm, but also those filled with the sharp sting of cold in the air before the true winter arrived. There was never the same amount of rain that always turned up in spring and it had always seemed that autumn was there more to look after us rather than blast us with the extremes which came with the other seasons.

Trees began to relinquish their leaves which led to the satisfying crackle underfoot when you found a particularly good one. But then thought moved to huge piles of them which you could play in, hide in, scatter about, throw at each other, and ultimately, set on fire. Far off memories of a time before, when the evenings were cold enough that you could see your breath expanding before you as all of the discarded leaf matter was set ablaze meant that winter was certainly approaching, but there was still no desperate desire to drive everyone indoors out of the cold.

Oh, how things had changed.

That heady mix of wood smoke and childish enthusiasm was an intoxicating drug that meant that adventures of any kind were open for all those who were willing to go and look for them. Fleeing from the plumes of smoke that were belched from the fires as they followed people around, seemingly sensing every time their quarry moved, or hinting that there was actually a controlling mind within the bonfire aiming them as a final act of defiance against those who were scorching them away. Familiar locations became less familiar as day time haunts were visited during the night and any and all imagined threat could have been waiting out there in the shadows.

At the idlest of thoughts, memories of far past nights, standing around fires of this kind will fill your mind and with each drawn breath, the smells and sounds would come with them. As a very young child, you remember staring in utter wonder as those flames leapt and danced in a ballet of blossoming delight. As you age, these memories are joined by all of the Halloween adventures you'd had, joining the ranks of the monsters, at least for that one night. Collecting sweets with your parents close by as you were clad in any number of different costumes.

"Come on Dad, the biggest houses are next. They've got all the best treats."

Jenna laughed to herself at the recollection of herself dragging her father and sister around the streets of her childhood home dressed as an evil witch for Halloween. She was wrapped in black bin bags from head to toe with a hat wrapped in the same material, carried a regular household sweeping brush rather than the expected broom and had her mum's purple nail polish on to really top the costume off. She'd made the costume herself and fully inhabited the role despite the flaws in her handy work.

"Can we go home yet, Dad?"

Jenna laughed again.

This time, it was her sister, Daisy, making her feelings clear. She was always the unwilling sidekick to her older sister and had been a grumpy five year old that night, far removed from the sophisticated nine years of Jenna. It never seemed to matter what they were going to be doing, as long as Jenna wanted to do it, Daisy just didn't. There'd always been arguments, and as soon as Jenna changed her mind on a given topic, Daisy would do the same and the previously detested options would become the best ever.

They'd never got on.

There'd not been anything specific about that night that had meant it would be the first thing she'd reach for but her senses filled with the far off memories of children screaming and laughing, of the smells of fallen leaves and the chill snap in the air that night from years ago. She'd done so many other things along the way in her life, but the very first thing that came to her was that night hunting Halloween sweets and treats with all of the other kids in the neighbourhood.

"We're almost finished, Daisy. Our witch Jenna's going to bring us all something sweet to eat."

Jenna had pretended to ignore her Dad's words by running off towards the nearest new house with skulls and spider decorations outside. She'd let her parents have some sweets but if Daisy didn't want to do any of the work then she wasn't going to receive any of the spoils.

Jenna climbed out of her own memories and back to the real world around her.

It may have been that Halloween the world had seen an object fall from the sky but no-one could have imagined that the world would be this different now.

Looking out over the crisp autumn morning sky, Jenna was struck by the odd shapes of the clouds. She frowned and focused her attention even harder on one particular shape which was hovering just above the level of the trees out to her right. She could have sworn that it was the perfect outline of the Starship Enterprise.

Her Dad had watched Star Trek all the time and had been doing his best to try and get Jenna to share his passion every chance he got. Jenna, for her part, thought that the funny aliens on the shows had been worth watching it for, but hadn't ever really got on with the programme. Thinking back, her early unease came from the fact that all the aliens were just humans with masks on. It had just seemed like a really huge stroke of luck that everyone in the universe basically looked the same. Of course you could get along with aliens if the only difference between you was pointy ears. Surely things would be tougher if there were no similarities at all?

Later on, that concern had proved to be bang on.

Enterprise cloud moved away from her slowly, evenly slipping behind the canopy of the shedding trees which sat at the boundary of the farm house land. Skeletal branches appeared to be reaching up and after the cloud as it went.

This was the first time in, thinking about it, she had no idea how long it had been since, she'd looked out at the world as it was now and seen anything other than threat. Halloween and Enterprise cloud had been the first time her mind had wandered away from the reality of the world she lived in now and began to run through the fields of possibilities in her mind. She had just fallen into the thought and had been able to relax just that little bit, dropping twenty pounds of imaginary weight from her back as the tension eased away for a second.

But just a second.

Sighing to herself, she resolved to try to spend more time in her own mind in the future. Just snippets you understand, not hours of carefree day dreaming. Just enough to help remind her that the world wasn't always just about the threat. Maybe that could make her life just a fraction more valuable, more of something she wanted to keep rather than being just another possession she hadn't yet lost.

Slipping soundlessly off the edge of the window, she casually brushed the remnants of the rough cracked paint from her worn jeans and eased the large wooden board back into place, completely covering the space that had once been a window, sealing herself inside, away from the dry earth and parched landscape which now lay beyond. She knew it was risky to do, opening herself up to detection from the outside but there'd been so little activity over the last few weeks that it felt like it had been worth the risk.

The world had changed so much over the years since the Arrival and although she'd been a child when it started, Jenna could still feel the memories of the world that had been as a very real thing and their tangibility made them worth fighting hard for.

The farm house was old, worn around the edges and far beyond the point of just needing a little TLC. It had been slowly crumbling before their eyes since they'd decided to move in here, or should that be commandeer, but despite the wide and varying array of people who had passed through the doors, no-one had ever attempted to maintain the place beyond the vital tasks of repairing the barricades and re-loading all of the different defences which protected them. A large perimeter had been set up to enclose the area around the house which gave the place more a feeling of being a small village now than a single dwelling but everything they had, in any and all aspects of their lives, was very well worn.

When the Ult first appeared, she remembered it all too well; there was almost a feeling that it had been a joke. It certainly felt much more like a prank than a real concern but that went away pretty quickly when the first death happened live on TV. Jenna had thought that the man's smile had been too wide as he approached the lumbering mound of meat with the grabbing appendage but the result had started the whole collapse of the world.

No-one knew where they'd come from, or how they'd got here but they just spread everywhere until cities and towns, civilian and military locations, public and private, everything, was just over-run. There had been attempts to open some form, any form, of dialogue with them to broker any kind of a peace but there had never been any response beyond attack. They didn't communicate in any way that could be fathomed; they didn't react in the way that anyone expected. There had never been even the barest acknowledgement that the human race even existed. They just swarmed, attack after attack, leaving nothing behind. Modern technology fell to ruin and with peace of any kind off the table, the ever dwindling population was forced to try and live in the cracks of the world they'd known while they hid from the invaders, surviving on scraps and making do with anything and everything they could use. Life on Earth had slipped backwards a few hundred years, and walking along the corridor, Jenna felt that point keenly as she took in the details of their home.

The house was tired and she knew exactly how it felt. Maybe it would be a good idea to give the place a lick of paint? Collect some flowers? Everything in life now was all about use and re-use, then repurpose until whatever you have is completely used up. There were no more creature comforts and just getting to the next day, week, year, was the first order of every day.

But should it only be that? If she could feel the kind of benefit from just letting her mind drift for a few seconds, imagine what the house would feel if they decorated a little.

The thought was still germinating as she moved down the bare wood stairs and slipped into what had once been the dining room. There was still a large table in the room but that was where the similarities to the place's previous use ended. Instead of the usual tablecloth, crockery and cutlery, there was a collection of maps, all covered with arrows and crosses signifying weapons caches, trade routes, and infected areas. Candles in bottles, the only light source available as technology had been eaten away during the invasion, were strewn haphazardly round the surface of what had once been a mighty oak table made for banquets more than just a farm house family meal. Wax melted down the candles sides and swarmed down the bottles, forming smiling tributaries, dripping down and onto the maps below. All of the windows into this space had been boarded and barricaded against the outside world, plunging the space into a deathly murk, a blackness which robbed the interior of their home of the concept of day and night.

They were sealed inside.

This was now where this small group of people, what felt like the final group in what had been this once prosperous farming community, now gathered to try and organize what little resistance they could against the relentless presence beyond.

This was their War Room now.

"You OK?" Chang was looking up from the table of maps, Jenna's arrival drawing his attention up and, judging by the expression on his face, he was concerned at what she'd brought into the room with her.

"Fine," she replied, and she considered that she was certainly feeling a great deal closer to it than she had done since the Arrival.

Maybe everyone needed to step away from the realities outside for a short time?

"Just thinking that the house could do with a little bit of brightening up. Everyone could benefit from a little old fashioned, pre-Arrival, normality."

Chang frowned. She hadn't even meant to say that out loud. She'd dropped her guard and without even a second thought, she'd blurted out what had been on her mind.

Chang didn't react to what she'd said but she just knew that he'd squirreled it away somewhere at the back of his mind for further inspection. Could he think that she was losing her focus from the bigger picture?

Back to the job at hand.

2

The day was a crisp cold but the open fire was doing a surprisingly good job of heating the space without there being any need to take any more severe methods. Everyone had been blazingly hot inside the farm house during the summer because every possible place even the weakest breath of air could find its way in had been very firmly barricaded. There'd been the occasional attempt to modify the boarding around the house to provide better temperatures with the installation of staggered planks, and different designs of ducts but there'd never been a solid solution created. That, in turn, meant that everyone just had to suffer the heat in the summer and the cold in the winter. The alternative of wide open windows just couldn't ever be.

"You got the lists ready?" asked Jenna flatly, her mind back into the here and now and all thoughts of Star Trek and Halloween locked back up tightly.

Chang, who was already back looking at the maps on the table, didn't even look up, but thrust out a hand with a crumpled piece of paper.

"Here you go," he replied, but without any real emotion.

"The guys are outside tanking up The Beast at the moment, the only thing you'll need to do is pack your personals," more matter of fact words.

Jenna gave a wordless sound of acknowledgement and turned to leave the room, but before she made it even two steps, Chang added,

"And Mary's coming too. Better be on your best behaviour."

Jenna barely missed her step, but that 'barely' was enough. Chang grinned and snorted a laugh while still looking at the paperwork. Jenna stomped out of the room with more purpose to her movements and her back straighter, and cursed her luck. Four days in the tractor was bad enough but add Mary into the mix and it was now going to feel more like four weeks. She needed a silver lining, any silver lining.

Maybe that laugh meant that Chang would agree with her that there was more to this place than just not dying. Maybe that laugh was his Enterprise cloud? She left the room and made her way through the house to the rear compound where the tractor was being readied.

Out in the compound, well, as outside as counted as outside these days, there buzzed mundane conversation about specific details of their impending trip or what was needed for the house. Chang may have laughed a little but by the sound of the group working here, laughter and anything to do with the true core of being human, was long forgotten. It was a usual day in that regard. The high walls around the compound always drew in the gloom earlier during the shorter days, and despite the relatively clear sky, today was looking pretty gloomy. The expedition was going to be heading out at first light in the morning but looking at the way that everyone was buzzing around the place, you'd have sworn that they were in the final countdown from ten to zero. Tension was always high as a matter of course but this seemed excessive, even for Mary.

Far across the compound, she could make out Mary holding a large blackboard which she was scratching away at, checking and re-checking the lists that were going to be heading with them to Hope. Jenna straightened her shirt to steel herself, and walked away from Mary to instead talk to Mo.

Mo was, in the terms of the way the world used to be before everything went to shit, boring. He was quite adept at a wide range of skills which made him valuable, mechanics, woodwork, some basic farming, but swore that he'd never been one of those 'preppers' who'd been running around in the woods making sure they were ready for the end of the world. Thinking about the reality of the world now, maybe a team of those guys would have been handy now that they'd been shown to be right.

"How you getting on?" Jenna asked to Mo's feet as he fiddled with something under the trailer section of their transport. Mo shifted slightly and sighed deeply, absolute frustration all over it.

"I'm getting on fine, as is The Beast here," she heard a clanking sound as he tapped something with whatever tool was in his hand, "but I've been asked to *triple* check that the under carriage linking systems are bang on because *she* thought there was a looseness the last time *she* went out in her."

Jenna frowned and shook her head. There'd been at least two further trips made since she'd last gone out without any issue but Mo was being made to look anyway.

Mary was a force of nature who was able to get things done, and arguably more importantly, was able to get people to work towards the same goal. That said, it did mean that more often than not, she had a remarkable ability to tread on toes without even trying. There wasn't an official leader of the group of people but if any of the others had been asked who they thought fit the bill, they'd have all said her.

"Four days. It's only four days," Jenna muttered to herself and closed her eyes, wishing she could be happily walking the corridors on Enterprise cloud.

"Are you prepared, Jenna?"

Jenna yelped quietly at the fright those words brought. She hadn't even noticed that Mary had been walking towards them but she swore that she'd spoken directly into her ear. She turned to face Mary without even trying to look as if she hadn't been given a fright, not seeing the point.

Mary was a tall, imposing figure who just radiated complete power. She'd done it from the very first day she'd come into the group without ever making any kind of specific push for 'leadership'. She'd never told anyone how old she was and could have easily been placed between about forty or seventy. She had straight grey hair tied in a simple pony tail and her whole bearing screamed that she was used to getting her own way.

"Just got the last bits and pieces to get together," replied Jenna, trying her best not to feel like a naughty school girl.

"Excellent. I'm looking forward to getting re-stocked. Chang should have given you the lists as well so you know what we're looking for, and indeed, it is only the four days that we have to be in the Beast together."

Jenna flushed and turned back to focus her attention very hard on a tiny fleck of paint on the side of the trailer, hoping Mary wouldn't want to say anything else.

The seconds ticked but she still hadn't said anything.

The time continued and the pressure in Jenna's whole body was almost beyond belief. The fleck of paint was filling her attention but she just couldn't stand there forever.

Eventually, she risked a slight glance over her shoulder to gauge the mood. Mary was gone. She was now back on the other side of the compound, blackboard in hand, and peering over the shoulder of everyone there. Jenna hadn't even heard her leave.

That was enough of the politics she could handle at the moment, and her body sagged as she let her tension go. Enterprise cloud was calling to her again and she could just feel that aching need for just the smallest hint of relaxation and, she hesitated to even think it, fun.

Enterprise cloud again.

"........... doesn't she?"

It was Mo's voice but his question didn't make any sense.

"What?"

"I said, 'She has the power to just make us all feel like kids, doesn't she?'"

Mo was now sat up and just taking in the view of the rest of the team, working with Mary hovering over them.

Jenna just grunted her reply, lightly squeezed Mo's shoulder, and wandered off back towards the main building. Four days wasn't long at all in the grand scheme of things but doing something awful for four days would make those four days stretch to feel like forty.

Enterprise cloud would have done it so much faster.

The next morning rushed towards them all and despite knowing she should be getting as much sleep as possible before they left, Jenna had only managed a few hours and that had just been filled with images of her family, of Mary, and of the dangers that they were likely to encounter on their journey. She'd seen the first signs of dawn showing through the house so just decided to make do with what she'd managed to get and face the day head on.

Back in the compound, the clear sky above meant that the air was sharp and despite how early Jenna was up, Mary was already hard at work, checking and re-checking anything and everything that she could possibly get her hands on. Everything was already loaded on the trailer that Mo had been working on and that had already been hitched up to complete the readiness of The Beast.

Jenna just accepted that she should have expected it, pulled her coat tighter around herself, and headed towards Mary to get the day underway.

"Morning. Up and at 'em, eh?" said Jenna as she did her best to look as enthused as possible. Positive thinking.

Mary looked up and smiled, "Very much so. We get underway earlier; we don't have to rush at the other end. You all set?"

Jenna nodded and turned to show her small back pack.

"Excellent. It's always good to see people packing light for these trips. I think some of the others could do with following your example."

Jenna didn't respond to the comment. She didn't know how to. Mary was notoriously tight lipped when it came offering praise so when she did, it tended to catch at you.

"Uhhh, thanks." Jenna stuck to the simplest option and crossed her fingers.

The silence stretched just a beat longer than was comfortable until the two women were joined by Mo, coffee in one hand while he rubbed at his eyes with the other, a yawn blossoming widely.

"Morning ladies," he practically slurred out, "didn't expect anyone else to be up this early. Thought I'd be able to do the check run through on my own."

Looked like he'd been attempting to be the first one up as well.

"By all means, come and get started," said Mary with a small smile on her face, though it didn't look like it meant she was happy.

From there, the morning unfolded pretty much as it had done every other time that they'd made the journey. Mo poked and tightened at the various different bits and pieces he was supposed to and the other members of the camp woke up and joined the bustle. The other two members of their party joined them in due course. Davis, a man who was average height, and build, was middle aged, and somehow embodied the word magnolia, and Scott, a man who had aged far beyond his twenty four years. His voice, his expression and his demeanour showed a further twenty years at least and he was someone who Jenna had taken an immediate dislike to. He always seemed to be playing 'Devil's Advocate' to everything that was ever suggested or discussed. It never seemed to matter what the point was, he just always came out against it. Even though her sister had displayed the same tendency to be awkward all those years ago, Jenna couldn't see Scott as anything more than an obstacle. Jesus Christ, he acted like she could remember her sister doing when she'd been five years old.

It was going to be a very long four days indeed.

3

Mary looked content when the final piece of preparation was completed to the level she felt appropriate and everyone climbed onboard The Beast. They were indeed going to be starting off earlier than planned.

Everyone else cleared the compound and began to seal the space around The Beast ready to open the outer gates and send them all on their way. Davis was going to be driving the first couple of hours and he was sat waiting with all systems primed to get the ball rolling.

"You'd think that we'd be better at following this whole process through by now, wouldn't you?" mumbled Scott from his seat at the back of the trailer. He wasn't even looking at anyone as he spoke, rather just giving his opinion for all to hear. Davis didn't react, either focused on his task or not interested, but Mary and Jenna both stiffened in their seats slightly.

"As long as we complete everything safely and correctly, chasing speed won't come into it," replied Mary without turning to face him. She couldn't have any nagging fears bouncing around the team from the very first day. Scott looked as frustrated as always but didn't say anything else. Clanks and hisses followed as all the words drained away, and The Beast lurched forward and began to trundle heavily away from home.

The Beast was a name that Mo came up with when he first joined the group. What had once been a traction engine of some kind, and had been ignored by everyone else for years, had been crying out to be used and it was only Mo who could not only see the value of such a contraption but also had any kind of idea what would need to be done to reach that value. Jenna still didn't know the first thing about the inner workings of it but the others with her knew enough to keep The Beast moving.

The trailer and the cab area of the Beast was completely enclosed with plastic sheeting under flat boards of wood which overlapped so there was no possibility that anyone outside could pick out any detail of anyone inside. Everyone knew by now that the silvery, mossy, mould was somehow aware when you walked too close to it but over time there'd been an evolution of the stuff so that it could move after those who it noticed. It didn't start scuttling across the ground and leap at you like a face hugger from the movie but though the movement was slow, it was far too fast for a plant of that kind. Jenna had always felt it was like a Venus Fly Trap, but one that actively went chasing after its prey.

It was easy enough to destroy, just a load of accelerant and torch the stuff, but as time passed it had been noticed that burning the patches away before they reached a certain point, that when they could actively start to move themselves, just didn't have a fully lethal effect. Jenna had speculated with Chang that it could be that the patch was deeply rooted to start with so was effectively bunkered against attacks until it became mobile and he'd liked the thought, but that had been as far as anyone had really bothered to consider after the confirmation of the weakness. That said, they would have to consider different options when the volumes of things they used to torch the patches dwindled.

The enclosure of the Beast mirrored that of the farmhouse, and the compound as a whole, and had been able to keep those inside clear of the spreading threat outside for years. The monstrous stuff had never registered that there was an object passing by or that there were people on board after the most recent changes made to The Beast. That in turn stopped the need for further study of how to better protect passengers because the problem had been overcome – so Jenna found herself sat in a large wooden box on wheels.

The three of them in the back each began to settle themselves fully into their positions, Scott was already laying flat facing away from the others, and tried to ready themselves to fight against the boredom of the slow journey towards the place for trade, Hope.

The journey was going to take two days but that didn't mean they were going to be moving all of that time. There was a way station at the half way mark so they could at least rest a while there but it couldn't ever mean that they didn't have to be hyper aware all of the time. Jenna settled herself back into as comfortable a position as she could find, though never one that really made her relax, and tried to catch up on some of that lost sleep from the night before. Mary was sat opposite Jenna with her back ramrod straight and her eyes piercingly aware of everything, but then, Mary was always going to be the one who was overseeing any and all details.

Scott was motionless so Jenna just accepted that he'd already fallen asleep, so she too gave up on being awake, and drifted off to a shallow sleep that was filled with images of Halloween all those years ago and the monsters that were all around her now.

The first day's travel to Hope was the best it could have been. The Beast kept a pace and everyone took their turn to drive while the others rested. Scott had told everyone when he came back from his latest stint behind the wheel that he'd seen movement away from the track they were following and that it had been very near to an ever growing swathe of that spreading growth. Mary wanted to know where it was so she could pick out the location from the cab but Scott shrugged back with a mumbled response about it having been miles back, and that he hadn't thought to tell anyone at the time.

Thereafter followed a short disagreement and then Scott huffed off back to his seating, again turning away from the rest of the group. Mary just kept on driving, and they were all left to ponder the idea that the movement that Scott had seen could have been from a pending attack or more painfully, from someone trapped in the open that was in need of help.

Or the patch had finally reached mobility and could be looking for a meal, or a target, or a victim.

No option sounded good to Jenna.

No-one spoke for a long time after that as that thought settled in and weighed them all down.

Sleep didn't come easy for anyone this time.

The day was still far younger than they had imagined it would be when they caught a glimpse of the station structure they were going to be using as shelter. Jenna was the one driving and she couldn't help but feel a jump in her mood at the approach of sanctuary.

"We're almost there, guys. Anybody want to come and see?" Jenna could feel that childlike enthusiasm from long journeys she'd been on with her family where the final miles were just as exciting as the actual arrival.

Mary appeared at her back but the others just grunted their opinion on the idea.

"Anything to shout about for the last leg of the journey?" asked Mary, resolutely all business despite Jenna's enthusiasm.

"Nope. Just looking forward to getting into the station and relaxing a little."

And that was the maximum amount of exuberant humanity that they could expect to see. There were no whoops and cheers for their safe arrival, not that Jenna had wanted them, but maybe just the simplest hint of satisfaction wasn't too much to ask for? Jenna considered the idea of celebration in terms of those people who used to cheer and clap when the pilot landed the plane, so maybe Mary was right after all to just get on with it.

The Beast slowly rolled up towards the structure which was going to be their sanctuary for the night and Jenna just couldn't wait to be able to at least move around outside the vehicle for a bit. Davis and Scott, who'd still wanted to sleep despite their arrival, were moving around in the space behind her, heaving and straining as they moved what could loosely be described as their door keys into place on the outer skin of the vehicle. Outside, huge pieces of thick wood were extending out in a strange display of growth over the front half of The Beast giving them an appearance of horns or antlers but Jenna slowed their pace to the very barest of crawls as she lined up ahead of the sealed entry to the way station.

Like their home compound and The Beast, the way station had started life as one thing and had morphed into something new after the Arrival. It had previously been the largest barn on a sprawling farm, set back against a small wooded grove as extra protection against the elements. Over the years that the world had been dying, the other out buildings on the farm, and the farm house itself, had fallen into disrepair as there were ever fewer people available to maintain them as more and more people were lost to the Ult.

This barn, though, had been such an important location on the way to and from so many different settlements, there'd been a specifically arranged focus on keeping it in as strong a condition as possible. From the outside, it looked akin to a very determined waste pile rather than anything that could be used for anything, so maybe it was that detail which meant the Ult didn't pay it any heed.

"You guys all set back there?" called Jenna over her shoulder as she readied The Beast to move.

"Good to go," shouted Scott and slapped on the side panelling to emphasise his point.

Jenna smiled and edged forward.

The Way Station was set up in the same way as their compound which meant that it was totally sealed against the outside world. The same materials had been used to encase the building in a skin that provided strength and safety but that meant that there was no way that the thing could be just left open to the world. There weren't enough people around to be able to keep it manned all of the time and since the Ult were apparently ignoring these kinds of buildings, it didn't make sense to maroon anyone here. The development of The Beast had given lots of people ideas about transport and that in turn gave them ideas about practical security. Evolution of thought in action.

So how to open the giant doors when there's no-one inside to do it and no-one can risk walking around outside to do it either?

As they approached the Way Station through a narrowly marked track, one of the planks outside banged against something which in turn rang a small bell. Jenna kept moving forward. Another crack sound and ring, this time from the opposite side of the cab, then another from above them and then another from near the first. Twelve more sounds rang out as they moved, each signifying a position of their makeshift combination lock, until there was a heavy thud and then a whirring as rope was pulled within the building and the massive doors began to swing open.

Jenna waited patiently until they were fully open, and then eased The Beast inside.

To say that this building had been a barn back before everything went to Hell didn't seem to be fair to it. This thing was more like an aircraft hangar. There was a mighty space that had a solid concrete base throughout and there were six bays arranged along the walls where the bulky vehicles which could arrive here could be berthed. The whole far wall of the structure had been converted into storage areas and a couple of workshops. Racking and boxes, and huge tubs, and barrels, and crates all huddled together and were filled with spare parts, tools, weapons, medical supplies and basic ration packs to allow for those who passed through to restock the basics to keep them alive until they had the chance to reach the 'proper' trading stations like Hope. There'd never been any kind of wider agreement about what was going to be left in the place but over the years that it had been used, anything that could be useful was gratefully received.

Above each of the parking bays were arrangements of seating and cots for anyone who arrived so they didn't have to sleep in their vehicles. Jenna had never known if these had been a part of the original plan here or if they'd been added later by people who wanted more than just the barest minimum for survival but it was another symbol to her that the need to do more than just exist was still alive and well in more than just her.

Jenna manoeuvred The Beast into the nearest bay station and the huge doors of the building began to close behind them. The second that they touched closed, Davis and Scott leapt from the back of the trailer and began hurriedly pulling ropes and shoving walls on runners to lock themselves in fully and maintain the sealed shell of the outer skin of the building. There'd been so little knowledge forthcoming about the Ult over the years that when anything was discovered to have any kind of positive effect on the standard of living of the human race it was immediately put to use, but without further thought of the why's and why not's of it. As long as the structure was totally tight, with no gaps under or around doors or windows, between planks of wood or metal plates, you were safe. There could be intricate piping or tunnels around the place to allow for air to flow through; just as long as there was no way that something could see you via direct line of sight.

Jenna pulled at levers and flicked switches as she set about putting The Beast to sleep and just let her mind go blank of daydreams. She had a job to do now, in the same way as the others did, and that needed to take precedence above her casual thinking about anything and everything else.

That said, she never really shook the feeling, despite herself, that Enterprise cloud would have been a damn site easier to deal with that this monstrous vehicle.

The remainder of the day was spent with the four of them steadily going about the business of readying themselves for the onward journey tomorrow, of double checking that the structure was still secure and then of picking out which cots they were each going to use. They'd made decent time during the day and they were all ready for a longer than expected lay over so the appearance of the rest areas caught them all off guard.

Scott had been the first to venture up onto the mezzanine, it was always him to finish his jobs first, and it wasn't long before he was calling down to the others.

"Guys, I need you all to take a look up here. Something's off."

His voice travelled through the vaulted building easily and the others all secured what they'd been doing and made their way towards him.

"What have you found?" called Mary as she made her way across the open space towards the stairway, happy to check what could be an issue but also recognising that Scott may not always be hugely reliable. Jenna and Davis followed close behind.

The space before them was just as they'd expected to find, the cots ready-made and the whole space tidy and waiting to be used by the next people to arrive. Everything looked thoroughly mundane. Everyone who used the place always left it tidy and ready for the next group to use, stocks used were replaced so there was always something to eat and it was as good a place to crash as any other out there.

So what was Scott worried about?

Mary asked him, but didn't fully relax. She either recognised *something* or just wanted Scott to confirm.

"I've never seen this place this dusty before," he said, and swiped a gloved hand across the nearest surface to show the covering that was now thickly caked to his hand.

"Dusty? Is that it? Jesus Scott, the place needs a spring clean but it's not the end of the world." Davis was not impressed and started back down the stairs to finish what he'd been doing, grumbling as he went.

Jenna breathed out a breath she hadn't known she'd been holding, relaxing at the idea of Scott just being Scott and looking for any possible excuse to make life even slightly more awkward.

Mary didn't though.

She just kept scanning over the room as she edged forward towards the cots to examine the fabric of the blankets. She lifted the first she came to and gave a small twitch of her wrist, which sent out diffuse clouds of dust, the motes just swirling through the light which was reflected into the room by a series of mirrors around the roof. Jenna and Scott watched as she moved around, rooted to the spot by the concern that was still holding Mary.

Mary finally arrived at the table at the rear of the area, which was also covered in a thick layer of dust, and examined a small notepad left behind to read what was there. She had to blow the dust from it beforehand too.

Silence reigned on the mezzanine as Mary read and the others waited. Davis could be heard moving things about below them but that was far from their attention.

"What's it say?" asked Jenna, keen to understand but still too scared to move from her position. Scott just shuffled his feet nervously, but didn't advance either and there was no hint that he was anything less than honest in his apprehension.

"It's just the usual note you'd expect when a group leaves. 'We used the last of the fruit protein bars but replaced them with nuts, we left four bags of mixed machine parts in the storage area and sorted what we could out, but there's some stuff that didn't fit into any of the available boxes so made an 'Odds and Ends' case.' That kind of thing." Mary was describing things in a matter of fact way, as she always did, but her face carried a much more troubled expression.

"This doesn't feel anything like that though," said Scott, picking up on Mary's clear discomfort.

"It's just that, a normal note left by the last team who used the place," replied Mary, still looking intently at the notebook.

"The part that doesn't make sense is that it's Selina's hand writing."

Uh-oh.

"It means that our people were the last ones to be here but that was just over a month ago." She dropped the book onto the nearest cot and headed back to the stairs, purpose in her stride.

Mary was halfway down the stairs before Jenna shouted after her, "That can't be right? There are too many people out there who use this place. Settlements wouldn't be able to survive without the connections with others."

Could they?

Jenna started after Mary and Scott followed after her, both looking for any kind of information which could make the sudden creeping dread they were feeling abate.

Mary didn't say anything.

The rest of the day and evening was spent checking and re-checking the whole site to try and confirm what was looking to be the truth.

Had there been no-one here for the last month?

As is always the way when confronted by an uncomfortable thought, every possible piece of evidence that they all came across became clear truth. The smell in the air was musty so it could only mean that the site was practically abandoned, though no-one was able to say confidently that it hadn't smelt that way before anyway.

Scott had used lavish amounts of sanitizer liquid on his hands and face, claiming that as they didn't know the full picture it was better to be safe than sorry. No-one else had the urge to tell him that what he was doing didn't make any sense but Jenna for one did start using some of the stuff herself, just in case.

The four person team swept through the building again, this time searching for any further clues or signs which could lead to any kind of explanation for their situation but nothing presented itself. The whole place was covered in a thin layer of dust and the parts that had been described in the note left by Selina were exactly as they'd been left. There was no way that the storage areas had been left untouched if there had been people here. The sun was almost completely gone when they all came together back at The Beast to pool their thoughts.

"There aren't any further signs that anyone has been here since Selina and the guys, so at this point, we've got to work on the assumption that no-one has and just go about our business as normal."

Mary may have sounded confident in her conclusion but none of the others shared the sentiment.

"So no problems, we just get on with things as normal?" Scott had barely let her finish her sentence before he jumped in.

"If no-one's been here, it just means that no-one's been here," replied Mary, sounding like she was trying to explain to a class of children. "It's out of the ordinary, but from what we've all seen on our way around this place, there's no bigger issue for us to be aware of."

"We can't see anything but that doesn't mean that there isn't something bigger out there," Davis pointed out, his brow furrowed and eyes hard.

Mary took a deep breath, paused, and breathed out the faintest wisp of curling steam showing the temperature was falling.

"Our situation doesn't change, regardless though. We don't know anything so what can we possibly do? All we can do is behave normally, make sure that the place is secure and get as much rest as we can before leaving tomorrow. We can't worry about the unknown simply because."

"Well I'm sleeping in The Beast," mumbled Scott and stalked away.

Jenna shared a look with Mary but it was Davis who said it.

"Sounds like a good idea. Just in case."

Just in case indeed.

4

That night was deeply cold.

All four people sealed themselves inside The Beast and settled in as best they could. There was more than enough room for everyone to fit but it was a little more cramped than any of them would have preferred. They all wrapped themselves up in what they could find inside the vehicle rather than risk bringing blankets or the like inside. Scott had made such a huge fuss about not wanting anything to do with anything from the station that Mary seemed to decide it just wasn't worth the time or effort to argue.

Davis and Scott had shared some kind of look out watch duty, again, just in case, though in the morning they were both asleep when Jenna woke up so hopefully that cemented the idea that there was nothing to see.

Mary let them all sleep in an hour or so longer than would ordinarily have been expected on a trip like this, knowing that any kind of help in keeping the collective stress levels down would be a benefit, but Scott was still sullen when he came round.

Despite the extra rest time, the speed that was thrown into the preparation for the resumption of their journey meant that they were setting The Beast ready to leave at around the time they'd originally planned. Scott and Mary had bickered about little things along the way and Davis had seemed to be ready to jump at every shadow that crossed his path, but everything was cleared away and secured for the remainder of the trip to Hope. Jenna had been sent to leave their own note for the next people to stay in the Way Station.

Climbing to the top of the stairs onto the mezzanine floor, Jenna had been slowing down with each step, as if expecting something to be waiting for her when she finally made it. When she arrived, an irrational fear of what was ahead of her fell from a great height and rooted her to the spot. She couldn't see anything out there beyond that which had been there the previous day but the way that they'd all been going about their business since then, principally driven by Scott, had left her with a hair trigger on her terror.

She stood and waited.

Nothing happened.

She waited some more.

Still nothing happened.

She waited a little more, scanning over the area for the impending attack.

Still, nothing happened.

Back at The Beast, someone dropped a large metallic object onto the concrete floor which sent shockwaves of sound bouncing through the station.

Jenna dived for cover next to the nearest chair, certain that this was the best option to avoid the obvious attempt on her life.

"Sorry," shouted Davis. "All fingers and thumbs. We're ready to go Mary."

Jenna grumbled to herself, frustrated at her own edginess, wondering how she'd been so easily spooked by Scott and Davis. She stood up and shook her jacket off of the dust it had picked up before making her way to where the previous letter had been left. She was moving with more confidence in her steps but she'd still pulled her scarf up to cover her nose and mouth.

Just in case.

She left the paper neatly folded with the original note next to it explaining who they were and where they'd come from, but most importantly, what they'd found. Mary had been keen to write nothing but the facts of the visit, knowing that even the slightest speculation about the details of how and why could just fan more flames of fear. No-one would disagree that unfounded panic was the last thing that was needed.

Mary had been the one driving as they left the station behind.

They'd all made sure that The Beast was secure and fully stocked with everything that was needed and Jenna was amazed to see a level of calm on the other faces as the huge doors clanked shut behind them, as if there was a feeling that they'd had a lucky escape from whatever or whoever had been lurking around the station. Jenna shared the nebulous sensation of relief though she was also more than a little confused about it. Her rational mind was starting to fire back up and she was looking back on their experiences with a much more critical eye. Her memories played over and over and she was becoming more and more embarrassed at her own fear. The world had more than enough to be afraid of without Scott or anyone else stoking new and dangerous paranoia.

Had they settled into such a regular routine of always seeing the same things that the unexpected was immediately a harbinger of doom? Had their collective lives moved so far to mean that tension was dialled up to eleven all of the time?

In a twist she never saw coming, leaving the Way Station behind lifted so much weight from her shoulders that sleep overcame her with no resistance. She dreamed of Enterprise cloud and of Halloween and mundanely living her life without the threat of the Ult and smiled contentedly at the relaxed joy of it all. Unbeknownst to her, Scott and Davis had done the same thing and the three of them curled into sleep like dozing mice. Mary just drove. They needed to shed the time in the Way Station and the quiet would do her good as well.

The day was going to be a long one but at least it would be quiet.

When Jenna began to stir from her sleep, she was still carrying a little of the dream she'd been having in the form of her running through an old house with her sister and parents while laughing and playing, not a care in the world. She opened her eyes slowly and sighed happily at what she'd been immersed in but her contentment was short lived.

The voices from the head of The Beast were machine gun fast and nervous. She joined the others quickly to find out what they were faced with.

The day was still young enough to have the sun high in the sky and shining happily for them but that was as far as the good news seemed to be spreading. From the driver's seat, Scott was waving his arms around wildly to emphasise the point he was making while Davis stood next to him and did the same. Mary was facing away from Jenna as she approached but just the way she was stood told Jenna everything she needed to know. The guys were on another panic but this time Mary wasn't just humouring them, she was listening intently.

"There's clearly something much bigger going on around here. We can't afford to *just* accept that it's *just* a simple oversight, can we?" Scott was holding as much inner calm as he could but his voice was already pushing towards being squeaky.

"He's right, you know? All we can do is assume that Hope, and everyone in it, is dead," added Davis, more slowly but still scared.

Jenna slid her way next to Mary, "What's happened?"

"We've arrived at Hope but it would appear that there may have been an accident."

Scott fidgeted in his seat, adding more threat to every single word.

"What kind of accident?"

Mary beckoned for Jenna to look through the periscope for herself.

Jenna hadn't been to Hope that many times over the years but she'd always kind of enjoyed the place. It had been a tiny village built around heavy industry in the time before, but since the Arrival, it had been fortified and huge walls had been built to enclose the whole place. There were look-out towers and gun emplacements standing high above the walls which looked down on open tracts of land filled with deep holes and trenches dug into the ground, barbed wire and sporadic earthworks coupled with rock and concrete obstacles and even some of those weird looking beach defences from the Second World War, the Czech Hedgehog. There was a single route to the main gates, exactly like the Way Station, with concentrations of defensive efforts bristling around it, and that road showed signs of those efforts as it had been liberally covered with blackened scorch marks and deep charring.

Inside the walls, Hope was as close to a normal town that you could possibly find. There was still a wide array of buildings housing businesses as well as people. The place had smiths of different flavours and barter spots where anything you could think of could be traded for anything else you could have forgotten. There was food, including open areas where farming was being maintained, materials, even something which had the feel of a Wild West saloon, which meant that inside, when the main doors were closed, it could be quite possible to imagine that there was no danger anywhere in the world.

Maybe that saloon was why they called the place Hope?

There'd even been a new addition to the place over the last year or so, a huge wind turbine in the centre of town, which had meant that they'd been able to generate some power of their own, much more power than anyone had had in years before. They were still working through the massive list of possible risks when Jenna had been here last but she'd been told that there was even a chance that power made could be stored and used elsewhere. You could see the turbine from miles away and it was lazily turning away as they approached. Hope had really felt like a story of the slow journey back to what could be described as normal. Beyond the Ult.

Jenna saw the problem that Mary had been referring to as soon as her eyes focused through the periscope, and the situation grew darker.

The gate was open.

5

“I knew there was something bigger at play at the Way Station, I just knew it,” said Scott, his voice beginning to tremble.

Mary looked at Jenna quickly then over to the men and sighed as she took in all of the information that was before her. She needed to get the group under control before they let their fear push them to do something really stupid, while gathering as much information as they could. Despite Scott being more than a little histrionic with his description of the state of play, he wasn’t wrong.

They needed clear thought now.

“Guys.” She only needed one word to gather the attention of the rest of the group and she didn't even need to raise her voice. Whatever Mary had been in the time before the Arrival, she’d perfected the ability of getting people to listen to her. Jenna had always thought military of some kind, like a drill instructor, but that had never been confirmed.

“It does appear that there has been some kind of incident at Hope.” Scott opened his mouth to make some comment but Mary just raised a hand in opposition and he fell back without saying anything.

“So we need to try to understand what happened in there. We can’t just turn around. We could be able to help people in there who could be waiting for medical help. We don’t know what could have happened so we need to find out as much as we can.”

Silence.

“Davis, head us into the city slowly so we can get a better picture of what’s happened.”

“There could be anything in there. It could be over-run with Ult. It could be a new nest now.” Scott was terrified.

Mary raised her hand again but this time in a much more reassuring way. Scott stopped talking again.

"We know that the Ult don't react to The Beast in any way so in here, we're as safe as is possible. All we'll do is roll in and try and understand what's happened and deal with whatever we find. I'm not going to just assume that everything has been burned down, but I'm also not going to put us into harm's way more than is needed. OK?"

The others considered that and there seemed to be a slight cooling of the mood.

Heading towards the open gates of the walled city, there was nothing out of the ordinary going on. Jenna was looking through the second scope as Davis drove and despite her senses being dialled all the way up, she just couldn't see anything that looked out of place. The view they had into the compound ahead was still mostly obscured by the angle the gates were at and the layout of the buildings beyond. They could see the gun towers were still pointing towards the landscape behind them, providing cover for the approaching Beast but there hadn't been any movement of those turrets since they'd begun their approach.

The Beast slowly moved through the gateway, pushing the gates fully out of the way, and followed the road way past the small gatehouses which clustered around the entryway. The well travelled roadway was always going to be a place that needed regular maintenance and every time Jenna had been through Hope in the past, it had been receiving some of kind of care, but as they moved slowly forward, The Beast swayed a little more than it probably should have done meaning that it was breaking down more than ever before. They could all hear water splashing as they advanced through the puddles in the road way but that was all of the sound that they could make out beyond the engine pulling them along.

"Anything?" Mary wanted to have an understanding of what was going on outside but was content to leave others at the scopes, knowing that seeing what was taking place outside would at least give them that element of control on their situation.

"Nothing at all," replied Jenna as she swept her field of vision as far as she could.

“I can’t see anything at all,” agreed Davis. “There’s no-one moving about, there’s no sign of activity in any of the buildings and everything just looks still, like it just wound down and nobody’s got round to winding it up yet.”

That didn’t sound good.

“How many people usually live here?” asked Scott from the rear of the vehicle. “Even ignoring any number of visitors like us, there should be hundreds of people here so where are they all?”

Mary turned to face him.

“We need to gather the information first before jumping to conclusions. If the main doors were left open then it could mean that the place was abandoned for some reason but there hasn’t been any sign of fighting or damage yet and no bodies etc. lying around to show that it was infiltrated by the Ult. There’s been no word to suggest that something massive took place so we just need to find out as much as possible.” She placed a hand on his shoulder and gave a small squeeze by way of reassurance but they could both feel that it was a forced gesture at best.

Davis continued to move The Beast steadily through road after road within the city, and more and more nothing happened. No movements of people going about their business, nor were there signs of defensive or military action. There was just nothing out in the open, beyond the city infrastructure, which brought to mind those 1950’s fake towns built for nuclear test sites. Jenna wondered if there was anyone hiding in a fridge to escape whatever had happened here.

After another half an hour, nothing was still all around them and an element of boredom was slowly replacing the initial panic.

“So what’s the next plan?” shouted Davis from the back of The Beast. Scott had wanted to switch him out of driving just so he could see outside. Davis had known that any action beyond his agreement would be a waste of time and energy.

Mary was thinking as she peered through the secondary scope but could only shrug.

“Why don’t we just carry on as we would on a normal run?” Jenna was clearly feeling more of that boredom than anyone else.

“Fuck that!” shouted Scott, who was clearly feeling the least.

“I’m not saying we park up and go for a beer you idiot. It’s more that on a normal run, we’d head for the Hub and get ourselves set up to deal with the place in general. Why don’t we just do that? It’s where this place is run from and it’s where we’re most likely to find anyone if they’re hiding, isn’t it?”

“What? Are you insane? We need to leave as soon as possible, not put our feet up.” Scott didn’t agree.

“But she’s not wrong though, is she Scott?” Looks like Mary did.

“All we’ve discovered is that they city is seemingly deserted but beyond that, nothing more. There’s been no movement of threats of any kind so we could be able to scoop up a load of supplies for free if everything’s just been abandoned.”

Davis nodded as he worked through the logic of the argument but Scott was still grumbling under his breath as he at least started on the journey towards the Hub station.

The Hub was just that. It was the centre structure in Hope which everything else spread out from. It had started out life as a coal mine all those years ago, and a big one at that, but over time the place had begun to shrink back as the need for coal dwindled. The buildings which had been built to accommodate train loads, and truck loads of coal being shipped out daily shrank back to just train loads, then to just truck loads and then to nothing, had been repurposed remarkably well for a massive number of people and vehicles to be berthed up as a crossing point and trade centre. Further building had taken place after the first walls had been put up as protection from the Ult until it was quickly clear that those walls would need to be expanded to fit the growing population. Hope had continued to grow behind each new set of walls though.

Scott drew them through the empty streets until they arrived at the Hub and pulled into the nearest open bay. Those streets had remained empty all of the way and now they’d parked up, there were still no signs of life.

Mary scanned round them as fast as she could but there was just nothing out there. They were alone.

"Now what?" asked Scott sullenly with his arms folded across his chest. "There's been something bad happening here so why risk anything?"

Mary sighed and just ignored him.

"Jenna, can you come with me please so we can give the place a sweep through?" Mary was speaking with authority and that simple power she'd always had. Scott being a dick about their situation had already cemented Jenna's desire to be part of the first search party rather than hide in The Beast but Mary's voice had underlined it.

Jenna started to prep their guns and then complete her tactical apparel while Mary continued.

"Davis, can you keep an eye as our lookout please? I want to make sure that if something does happen while we're away, you can see it early and then tell us about it."

Davis nodded and ran his hand through his stubbly beard as an act of concentration.

"And finally, Scott. Keep the engine running just in case we do need to leave quicker than we'd like."

Scott didn't respond but Mary hadn't bothered to check.

When the two women were ready, Jenna unlocked the different boltings and clasps around the rear of the trailer and carefully opened out the doors. Davis had been keeping a close eye everywhere before they'd declared themselves ready to leave and there'd still not been any sign of anyone or anything approaching them but they were still on edge, with guns raised as they jumped down onto the rough concrete floor.

The temperature had dropped from what they'd been experiencing in The Beast as the day had begun to retreat away from them. Their breath was already pluming in clouds with each exhalation and Jenna felt the air keenly as it reached out to touch any piece of her exposed skin. Moving as fast as they dare, Mary leading the way now, they headed towards the open door of the office block ahead of them.

Peaking through the doorway, they could see the empty office beyond but there was nothing more to report. It was the same picture as everywhere else they'd encountered, no sign of anybody who would normally have been going about their business but also no signs of any struggles or fighting. Papers were still stacked neatly in trays on desks and chairs had been pushed in behind the desks, so whoever had been the last out, they hadn't been rushing to leave.

They slowly edged into the room and there was still nothing new to find, so moved beyond into the next office only to discover more of the same. Everything was still tidy and ready to be used as a part of the normal goings on but there just wasn't anyone around to actually do the jobs.

Room by room they moved cautiously, their guns always raised and their senses alert to any and all possible eventualities. The lack of population may have been making them feel more relaxed when they'd been seeing it from inside The Beast but now Jenna and Mary were walking slowly through it, their nerves were only growing with each passing second of nothing.

And that nothing was all they found.

They worked around the main operational section of the Hub before Mary decided that there was just too much for them to look through before they lost what little daylight remained. Instead, they began backtracking and closing doors as they went, making at least some attempt to enclose themselves in an area that they knew was empty. Mary began to look through the paperwork that was in the main office while Jenna signalled to Davis that the place was clear for them to enter. The guys hadn't been overly quick to appear from The Beast but judging by the look on Davis's face, it had been Scott who'd been the one dragging his feet. Both men were carrying their rifles but Scott had makeshift bandoliers of more ammunition and at least two huge hunting knives. They both pulled up their masks before they continued which Jenna felt made them look like Wild West bank robbers. Despite herself, she smiled slightly at the idea of the two of them bursting into the office and screaming, 'Reach for the skies.'

Jenna waited for them to enter the office before her, still aware that seeing no sign of the Ult didn't mean that they weren't somewhere nearby. She still needed to be utterly switched on to possible threats. Scott and Davis, masks in place, rushed inside without looking back and Jenna pulled the door closed behind them, while lifting her own mask back into place as well.

Just in case.

Mary was sat at the Controller's desk against the back wall as she flipped quickly through any and all paper she could find.

"Is there any clue yet what happened here?" Scott again.

"We've just walked through the door. I'll need some time to do a little digging, wouldn't you agree? Maybe you could help and start looking through the filing cabinets over there and see what you can find?"

He looked around the room a single time before deciding that checking for clues himself would be an acceptable use of his time, though he did send Davis back outside to 'keep watch' for anything which may be approaching.

Jenna was feeling that maybe he was overstepping his position but feeling the cloth over her face reminded her that his fears were already rubbing off on the group as a whole. She'd never really thought about it before but it just took one voice to rub off on everyone else.

Mary didn't even look up from the papers.

They methodically worked through drawer after drawer, file after file, as day quickly descended into night. They found oil lamps and continued their reading and by the time they'd completed their work, it was well into the early hours of the next morning. Davis had come back in and had been replaced by Jenna, then her by Scott and then Davis again but there hadn't been any movement of any kind during all the time they'd been there.

Mary brought the whole team together at the desk for a briefing which she knew they all needed to have finished as soon as possible so they could get some rest.

"There's nothing here beyond the usual transit documents and logs of the cargo and people who came through town."

Scott shuffled from foot to foot, and Mary continued.

"What the logs do show though, is the volume of traffic and what types of trade stock was brought through and it's clear that over the last few months, the amount of people coming here not only dropped by journey number but also by population of each crew."

"So there's been something attacking for months?" Scott was the first to respond.

"No. All these documents show is that there has been a steady-ish decline in the number of people coming here and that the crews that were coming were also getting smaller. The why of it isn't in here, just the basic numbers of what was coming and going." Mary waved at the folders open on the desk before them by way of emphasis.

She continued,

"This information says that something has caused the usual day to day of Hope to be changed, not why, but that means that we need to find out more."

Scott shuffled from foot to foot again, his eyes darting at every possible shadow through the dusty air.

"I say we get back in The Beast and get some sleep and start up again in the morning. None of us are feeling like doing anything else now so let's get some rest while we can."

There was a quick agreement nod from everyone and one by one, they extinguished the lamps and headed out for as much rest as they could find.

6

Scott had wanted to arrange an order of guard shifts to be alert for what he called the 'inevitable attack' which would no doubt be coming during the night and took the first shift himself. The others all just agreed to his suggestion, suspecting that he'd just nod off again eventually before long, and bedded down in The Beast, wrapped up as tightly against the cold as they could. Breath was pluming now in the early hours and the pleasant day had been replaced by a sharp edged night. Winter was fast approaching indeed.

Jenna slept immediately and her head was filled with dreams again. Enterprise cloud was back but this time it was hovering over Hope, almost low enough to reach out and touch. Staring at the cloud ship, she was bathed in bright, sparkling light before materializing amongst the clouds themselves far away from the life below. Someone approached her and claimed to be the captain of Enterprise cloud and that they were here to save everyone from the Ult attack. They'd been beaming everyone from the surface and transporting them away to a far off planet to start over again safely so that was why Hope was so barren.

Jenna could feel her heart just lift at the idea that they were being rescued and taken away from their struggles, but behind the captain, she could see the other members of her group being dragged past her towards a swollen looking cloud structure. Mary looked serene as she was pulled away, her heels dragging against a solid floor, quite away from the fluffy surroundings they were located in, and it was that odd sound that made her stop and think. Her head was filled with constructs of her mind, pictures which swirled through the bizarre to the terrifying, but the more it continued, it became clearer and clearer that what she was hearing was a constant. She wasn't dreaming the sound.

Jenna snapped fully awake in a heartbeat and was rigidly still. Concentrating hard as she tried to control her breathing, Jenna listened as hard as she could for the source of that sound which had been waiting in the real world for her. Mary was asleep propped up slightly while Davis was totally buried under a mound of blankets with only his face being exposed. He was still sleeping, and was drooling ever so slightly. Neither of them had stirred at all at the sound from Jenna's dream, which was a good thing in the grand scheme of things. Mary would have heard any sound that had been made and would have just been ready for action like a coiled spring. Besides, Scott would have been all over something that was making strange noises in the middle of the night. His rattling snore from the cab of The Beast said that he wasn't going to be aware of a great deal of anything.

She remained motionless, reaching out to find that sound which had caused her to wake up, but there was nothing anywhere. Had she heard something? Had she imagined that noise in her head like every other part of the dream she'd been having and had just imagined that it was real? Had she heard one of the others move in their sleep and just filled in the gaps in her dream? Whatever was going on, as the seconds crawled before her eyes, she felt less and less confident that what she'd picked up on was real and more and more certain that her own paranoia had made her jump at the veritable monster under the bed.

Finally, she began to breathe more normally and the tightness across her chest began to unwind as she came to the happy conclusion that she'd been imagining things. She settled back in her blankets and let her mind consider where this action had come from. They'd always been hyper-aware of the risks that exist in the world around them and travelling from their home to Hope was never, ever going to be completely safe. Like everyone on the planet who was left, Jenna had seen what the Ult could do and how they'd managed to overrun all of civilization that was, and bring the human race to the brink of extinction. Everything about the lives they all lived was shrouded in awful risk and everyone knew that any failure to complete jobs and actions could be what caused the deaths of any number of people they knew, so there were never any days off for good behaviour. That was, after all, why she'd been day dreaming back at the farm house and why she'd needed to mention something to Chang. She was tired of just existing under the constant threat all of the time so any way they could create some kind of 'oasis' in the desert of their lives must be something worth doing.

Scott continued to snore and Jenna just imagined what would have happened if he'd been the one who'd thought he'd heard anything out of the ordinary. He'd have dragged them all out of their sleep while no doubt pouring gunfire in any and all directions. Him, on his own and without any real kind of plan, had started to spread panic because of his own fears without even trying. Well, if he'd been able to do that, maybe just her voice could have a more positive effect on the others when thinking about doing more than just staying alive?

Closing her eyes, she felt that she was in a better position to address any and all things that could come at them and deal with what Scott was always moaning about.

The dragging sound began again outside The Beast.

It was no more than two feet from where Jenna lay, and maybe just staying alive wasn't so bad an option after all.

An icy finger of fear ran up Jenna's spine as that slow and steady dragging noise continued from the other side of the bodywork of The Beast. She hadn't been making the sound up. She hadn't imagined something out there from her fears of the unknown. Someone or something was outside and hadn't given any kind of signal as they'd gone about their business.

As quietly as she could manage, she eased the blankets off her and manoeuvred herself into a crouched position with the barrel of her gun pointing at the spot the sound was coming from. If it was one of the Ult, they'd never even seemed to register the existence of The Beast in the past but there were still huge holes in the knowledge base of what these creatures were. Outside, the dragging paused briefly, then continued again, moving slowly towards the front of the vehicle and the cab where Scott was snoring loudly. If it was one of the creatures, was it being drawn by the sound Scott was making? There'd been testing in the past in an attempt to build up a picture of what the Ult could have possibly wanted or why they were doing what they were doing, but as time had passed and more and more people were lost to failed hypothesise, the search for a wider knowledge fell away and just keeping them at bay became the sole aim.

But what if it wasn't the Ult? Jenna began to imagine any and all other possible alternatives to try to understand what was going on. There'd been raiders in the past, not long after the Arrival, and it was becoming clear that the human race was losing. The raiders were the people who decided that the spoils should go to the strongest, so armed themselves to the teeth and began to kill and loot any people they encountered. Jenna had never understood the idea of just the smallest group surviving at the cost of everyone else so when places like Hope began to grow, it meant that raiders could either join groups and share, or they could live outside of this new society and be left to the enemies. If any raiders were here, had they been the ones to do away with everyone else here or were they just scavenging over the pieces?

The dragging continued and rounded the front of The Beast, just as Scott moved in his chair and stopped snoring. The dragging didn't change, but after a handful of seconds, there was a massive impact on the roof of The Beast's trailer which shook the vehicle and everyone inside. The others were awake in an instant and were scrabbling for weapons and any possible understanding they could find. Jenna leapt to the cab and slammed her hand over Scott's mouth before he could say anything. He was the one who'd likely do whatever it was that caused that outside thing to get in so she needed him to be as calm as possible. He partially struggled at first but recognised what Jenna was doing. His eyes were like saucers while his rapid breathing was heating Jenna's hand to a clammy mess. Above them, whatever had landed on the roof of The Beast began to slowly slither back and off the side of the vehicle before it landed again, nearer the back this time. The dragging sound continued but was beginning to increase in speed. Mary and Davis were crouched with their weapons aimed at the sound and the gravelled floor outside continued to offer up its' own horror.

"What?" mouthed Mary to Jenna, conveying every inch of the thoughts crashing through her mind in that single word. Jenna shrugged back because there was just too much that was still unknown, but they quickly had their answer.

Outside, in the cold and dark of the deserted Hope Hub, came that all too familiar guttural moan which signalled the existence of humanity's most deadly enemy. The choking, gulping noise was less a form of communication or show of intellect than it was akin to the result of a bodily process.

"ULT, ULT, ULT, ULT," gurgled from outside and there was no doubt now what they were in the presence of.

No-one moved.

The scratching, dragging recommenced as the Ult call died back.

Still no-one moved.

All the guns were aimed at the sound, the muzzles shaking under the stress of what was happening.

The dragging sound continued.

Still, no-one moved.

The dragging paused.

Everyone tensed rigid and the guns became still with murderous purpose.

No-one moved but eyes flicked to each other looking for the signal that would allow them all to start firing. Beads of sweat were forming on skin despite the cold and they all knew that this could become messy very quickly.

The dragging began again.

But it had begun to grow quieter now.

Mary signalled to Scott to risk a check of the scope.

As slowly as he could, to draw no attention to what he was up to, he turned the viewer towards the dragging sound. The Ult had never seemed to react to any noise or any movement from machinery in the past but with even just one of those hideous creatures nearby; no-one dared take any risks. He caught the final act of the nights show as the Ult bulk dragged itself around the edge of a nearby building and away from them.

Scott kept his scope aimed firmly at the spot where he'd lost sight of the Ult, expecting the worst as it made a roaring return to tear The Beast apart, but as the seconds ticked by into minutes, it was clear that it had had enough of them for the evening.

It was gone.

7

Perhaps unsurprisingly, no-one slept the rest of the night.

They all tried but the best they could each manage was just lying still with their eyes closed while they listened for the approach of the night's previous visitor. Davis had agreed that there should be someone keeping a regular check through the scope when Scott suggested it but refused to let Scott go anywhere near the job.

"We just need to have a complete view of everything around us, not the constant false alarms that you'll bring on."

Scott seemed to accept that and there wasn't another word spoken, though Jenna did feel a little sorry for him. He may have been just jumping at shadows for the most part but at the very core of the point, he'd been right. Maybe she'd been able to recognise the sound in her dream as being real because of the way Scott had been? Whatever the relative thoughts on who did what, Jenna knew that, as the first light began to creep above the horizon, the day was going to be a tough one.

Armed to the teeth, the whole group exited The Beast after one final sweep to confirm no Ult visitors, and made their way back into the offices they'd been searching the night before. Once inside, they risked a look back at The Beast to try and create a picture of what had been happening the previous night. There was a drag furrow through the grit and dust around the bay they were parked in, showing where the Ult had moved, and there seemed to been some cracking in the wood panelling on the roof where it looked to have lashed out, searching for some kind of weakness. Happily, considering the capabilities and sheer strength of the Ult, there was next to no damage.

"Maybe it just wasn't all that hungry?" joked Davis as they all took stock of the situation.

Maybe.

“I suspect that it didn’t even register that we were in there,” added Mary with a flat tone of finality. She couldn’t be sure of anything; therefore no-one else could either so there was no point speculating, therefore, they needed to turn their attention to more pressing issues.

Room by room, the team moved steadily through the Hub complex searching for anything which could possibly give them any kind of further information on what had caused the plight which had befallen Hope. Room after room gave the same picture that they’d seen the night before. All were arranged as if there was going to be a normal day taking place but without any of the people in attendance to actually complete that day. There was no mess beyond what could be called ‘the usual’ and the screaming silence within the building grew worse with each room cleared. They’d been working for over an hour when they arrived on a first aid room which gave them their first clues.

The room had been turned upside down leaving anything and everything strewn over the floor, and the bed that you’d expect to be in such a room was missing. On the floor, there were two drag marks running from the room and into the corridor they’d been moving down, before vanishing through the doors at the other end.

Mary crouched to look at the drag marks, looking for any and all information she could glean.

“Is that Ult? Is one in here with us?” whispered Scott, his voice trembling.

Mary considered the marks before replying, her tone remaining level and without any hint of doubt. “No.”

Scott sighed in relief but was still wound tight.

“The marks outside The Beast were from an Ult, which we know for sure, and they were a constant sweep, like when you drag a sack of something heavy. These,” she waved down the corridor, “are from furniture being pulled. There are two feet rather than a solid mass making the marks. See?”

They all did.

They all knew the details of what the Ult did when they moved about so the details about the tracks were far from being news to anyone but they brought a tangible sense of released tension at them being pointed out again. Jenna still wasn’t sure that the extra tension hadn't just been the result of Scott being so loud with his fears but it still felt good being told that they were OK.

"So what's the next step?" said Davis, looking much more his usual self.

Mary stood up straight and stretched her back, causing a couple of pops.

"Now, we follow the tracks."

They didn't have to go far but the checking of every room on their route did mean that it took them far longer than it would have normally done. There was still nothing of note to see anywhere beyond the empty rooms and dusty air, but the entire group was keenly aware of the risks that were potentially behind each door they opened.

Jenna was the one who opened the door with the new information behind.

The tracks led them to a large pair of double doors. It had originally been a large storeroom but there'd been a makeshift sign hung from the ceiling to signify that it had been repurposed. Opening up slowly, her gun aimed for any surprises that might come out to meet her, Jenna crept in and came face to face with something she'd never been expecting.

This was now a huge infirmary.

The bed which had caused the tracks they'd followed was pushed up against the nearest wall and it had a large man on it, partially covered by the blanket he'd been trying to pull over himself when he'd just stopped and lay back. The air smelled of something rotten and Jenna didn't want to come face to face with what it was.

The huge room had been filled with row after row of beds, laid out like she could remember seeing on TV on the news as refugees left invaded areas and fled for their lives when the Ult had arrived. Each bed also had a person in it that had all of the hallmarks of simply being asleep. Jenna felt that they could almost be said to look serene, but that idea was soon pushed down as she continued taking in the sight. Sun poured through the high windows to give the tableau before them a grim, stark image of quiet suffering.

“Looks like we’ve found the population then?” said Mary from the doorway as she scanned over what was before her.

Davis moved forward through the room checking on the people in the beds. He still had his gun raised and ready as he moved but he was clearly in business mode, holding his fear in check. Scott hung back against the wall by the doors and pulled his mask back up over his face, his own fear proving more powerful. Jenna was growing increasingly irritated by his ‘just in case’ thinking, but said nothing.

“They’re all breathing,” called Davis from the far end of the room. “Though none of them want to do anything but just lay there, even the ones with their eyes open.”

Mary frowned but made her own way down an aisle of the infirmary, checking on the people she passed. Eyes open? That didn’t make any sense. Each person she passed breathed in a steady, if shallow, rhythm as if they were just resting, but the ones who did have their eyes open, she thought about a third of them, just didn’t respond to their attempts to snap them out whatever they were in. She snapped her fingers before person after person but there was just no signal at all. They occasionally blinked lazily but not one of them gave any kind of indication that they’d even registered that there was anyone else in the room.

“Great, we’re making headway on our situation,” stated Mary in a matter of fact statement and planted her hands on her hips defiantly. Jenna nodded and considered the details of what was happening before her and was glad that Mary didn’t leave a gap any bigger for Scott to start complaining.

“We need to have a good look through any notes that can give us a picture of what struck these people down and what had been done to try and cure them. Scott, keep an eye out in the corridor for anyone or anything that might be coming this way while the rest of us go through stuff in here. I’d also suggest masks and gloves until we can say for sure what’s happened here. Thanks all, now let’s get stuck in.”

Jenna moved towards the charts hanging on the beds nearest her, putting her own mask on to go with the gloves she was already wearing, and as she lifted the first chart, even before she’d read any of the information there, the thought of how

Mary was able to lead them in such a way that they all got on with what was needed shone bright. They were focused and even Scott was feeling involved enough to just get on with his task.

Some people were just made for leadership roles.

Each of the group went about their task quickly and there was a fresh determination from all of them as they progressed. Eventually, they gathered at one of the desks that had been moved to the edge of the space to discuss where their searching had led.

Mary held up a log book which, like this room, had been repurposed due to whatever affliction was in the town.

"Whatever this is, it's been working away in Hope for weeks. It looks like it started out when a party from out east came in to trade machine parts and scrap metal and one of their guys went down with it on their second day here. He was going through some repairs to their truck and just collapsed. The notes say he fell off the roof and landed pretty heavy so they thought he was unconscious thanks to the fall but when someone else just dropped later that day, the medicals started to look more deeply."

The apparent risks of the location, which had earlier been bad enough to be causing panic in the group, suddenly took on new and terrifying features.

"So something's been infecting people at this place to such a degree that it appears that the whole population has been pretty much wiped out, Hope has pretty much totally fallen, and the Ult are freely roaming around inside the walls. Is that about a fair picture of things?" Scott listed off the problems as he saw them, without there being any wild terror to his behaviour. That seemed to make Jenna feel worse.

He continued.

"Have we all seen enough now? I think it's going to be fair to suggest that we get out of here before we catch whatever we're looking at in the others."

Jenna wanted to agree; she really did, but there was just something nagging at the back of her mind.

"I say we stay a little while longer."

The words were out of her mouth far faster than she could have been able to imagine. The three others all turned to look at her for her rationale and Jenna caught herself looking back at them all, horribly aware that she wasn't sure she knew why herself.

"Why do you think we should stay Jenna?" Mary spoke steadily but the use of her name acted like a slap to her juddering mind, snapping her away from the pause which had landed on her.

'Here goes', she thought to herself.

"Because we need to know more."

She paused after that small sentence to gather herself and try and put some kind of order on what she wanted.

"We leave now; we get back home and tell everyone that something happened out here and at the Way Station, yeah? They ask what caused it; we say 'don't know'. They ask if there was anything that we could do to help, we say 'don't know, we just left'. All we'd be left with is closing ourselves away behind our walls and sitting there until someone comes to find us because we can't ever risk going back to these places." Jenna may have been reluctant to speak about her way of thinking in the past but not here, not now.

"We can't risk taking anything from here with us when we leave, again, just in case we take this disease back with us so we just shut ourselves down to just survive?" She was on a roll now and every frustration that she'd ever had fuelled her speech.

"And how would we feel if the first people who happened to pass our home decided that it just wasn't worth the risk of getting near us? We'd be trapped behind our walls, cowering against what could be until we starved."

She paused.

"We need to find out as much as we can about all of the details of the last few weeks here to try and understand everything we can or we can pretty much kiss goodbye to our civilization. Seems worth the risk to me."

Despite all of their faces being concealed behind their masks and leaving just the eyes to gauge the mood of her audience, Jenna could feel that Mary and Davis understood what she was saying was the correct course of action. Scott didn't say anything but that in itself was tacit agreement. He couldn't pinpoint anything which could stand up against her view so he just kept quiet. Did that count as progress?

The rest of the day blurred by as the four went about their information gathering and investigation.

They headed out in two pairs in opposite directions, Mary and Scott working through the connected buildings in the Hub looking for anything else that they could possibly find as either information or potential salvage, while Jenna and Davis climbed back into The Beast and headed on a more organized route through the town to create some kind of up to date map of what was going on. They'd seen a single Ult down an alleyway but it was completely still and slumped against the wall. It made no sign of having registered the presence of The Beast as they passed by and Davis had suggested that maybe it had just been taking a leak. Jenna grinned at the very idea and began giggling far more heartily than the joke had really deserved but when you're under stress like that, any way to break the tension can go a long way.

The hours churned over through the day and a new determination fell over Jenna as she kept on to the tasks she'd set herself. In everything that she was doing, she could recognise the simple power of having a problem which needed to be solved and that spurred her on to do her very best to deliver her best work. Davis even commented that she was 'right on things' and it was having an effect on him too.

See, just one person *can* affect change.

The sun was falling low to the walls when The Beast returned to the loading dock and parked up. Shadows spilled longer and longer, almost bidding the last daylight a fond farewell, as night approached. Mary and Scott hurried from the Hub into The Beast and as the doors at the rear of the vehicle closed tightly, it was only then that the whole group finally began to feel the effects of the broken sleep the night before.

"We've found some pretty interesting stuff through the Hub," started Mary, all the while yawning and doing all she could to keep her mouth covered. "Though I think that we're going to need to do all of the full digging through back home, Hope isn't safe to be running around in."

That took Jenna by surprise.

No-one else said anything but the tension in the air climbed. Mary continued.

"We can stay locked up in here tonight and get a start on the way back tomorrow but I suggest that we get anything and everything that we can out of the place loaded up as fast as we can before we lose the last of the light. Scott and I have been bringing stuff down here ready and it's all in the office."

Jenna's senses crackled with increased power at the news and it had some effect on burning away a great deal of the previous calm she'd been feeling. She wasn't sure what was replacing it though.

"That's some big change in plan. What happened?" asked Davis.

Mary pulled a heavily stuffed folder from her bag and waved it slightly by way of explanation.

"I've grabbed stuff that paints the picture, but it would appear that the Ult managed to break through the defences here after moving through the county outside. That's why the visits had been falling over time, everywhere was being overrun."

No-one spoke despite Mary leaving a space for questions so she continued.

"More and more people fell ill like those upstairs there," she waved in the vague direction of the people they'd found, "and it left fewer and fewer people to defend Hope until the Ult were able to breach the walls."

More silence.

"We bumped into a few Ult as we went about our business today but luckily they were either dormant or all moving far too slowly to catch up with us. We barricaded them into offices where we could and did everything we could possibly think of to keep ourselves clear to continue to work. After that, we just stayed away from the parts of the building with them in."

Now Jenna felt that she could join the conversation, like the previous inertia was now burned away.

"Why didn't you call for help?" then she paused.

“Why didn’t you let us know that there were more Ult up and moving about?” It was anger which was now building to take the place of any fear.

“It wouldn’t have made any difference to what needed doing so we just carried on. There’s a big enough picture now so we can make informed choices, wasn’t that the point?” Scott was angry now as he leapt to Mary’s defence and that action made Jenna square up towards him, Davis taking a step between them as she did.

Mary just lifted both of her hands, with a hard expression which made her feelings very clear, and the aggression was halted, if not totally expelled.

“We needed to learn what had happened and now we know more than we did.” Mary sounded tired. She looked exhausted. In fact, as Jenna looked slowly across the others, she was reminded that no-one had slept the night before so they were all running on fumes.

Whatever it all meant, they weren’t going to be able to discover anything new if they were all fighting each other. Jenna’s shoulders sagged slightly as she relaxed the muscles which were bunching across her back and felt a hefty serving of her simmering anger begin to drain away.

A good start.

“Let’s get everything you put together onto The Beast and we can try and get some rest.”

The team worked fast.

The stocks that Mary and Scott had gathered were already packed in crates or boxes for the most part and there hadn’t even been questions raised about what was in them. Jenna felt that they just needed to get everything on The Beast and that superfluous conversation would add nothing of value. Christ, if she wanted to look through every crate to see what the others had scavenged she could do that far more easily inside the sealed Beast.

It took them no time to complete their task and as the doors swung into place and everything was secured from the inside, from a spot nearby, maybe two or three streets over, came that all too familiar call of their enemy.

“ULT, ULT, ULT, ULT, ULT.”

It was clear on the faces of everyone that they were just so tired they only had enough energy remaining to register the risk as a usual day to day concern. There were no histrionics, even from Scott. They all knew that they were going to have to remain inside The Beast until morning so they could travel as safely as was possible and one by one they began to settle down to get as much sleep as they could.

The continued 'ULT' calling outside became oddly soothing as Jenna couldn't help be relaxed by the steady rhythm, and she was almost fully asleep when Davis sat up with a start and blurted,

"What about all of the people in there? We can't just leave them all to just rot on their own, can we?"

"They're all fucked," said Scott from a slumped position, his head on a bundled blanket and his eyes still closed.

Jenna frowned at Mary, then Davis for snatching away the sleep she was just taking delivery of, but he had a point.

Mary sighed and propped herself up on the floor next to where Scott lay.

"They've all been up there for weeks in some cases and they're all still there. We did barricade them in and create obstacles for any Ult that happen to make it that far but the fact that they're all still there suggests that the Ult don't want to do anything with them."

Davis considered the idea.

Scott was now starting to snore so it gave a clear picture of what he thought.

"Besides," continued Mary. "Where would you like to put them all in here?"

Davis gave a small laugh and with a crooked smile, agreed.

"Good point."

The three of them lay back down and got comfortable for the night ahead suspecting that they'd most likely be awake again pretty soon anyway if there were Ult roaming near them.

No Ult did attack The Beast that night but the four of them slept so deeply, they probably wouldn't have heard them anyway.

8

The next morning greeted the still exhausted team with misty, fine drizzle and a noticeable chill in the air.

Mary was the last to wake up but by the time she had, all the requisite prep for The Beast had been completed and they wasted no time getting underway. The heavy vehicle crunched through the streets away from The Hub and as they went, they noticed at least three Ult beginning to head towards them as they passed by but fortunately they were all moving incredibly slowly so posed no threat.

As they left what remained of the once busy town, Jenna couldn't help but feel that leaving Hope behind them may be happening to them in more ways than one.

The next two days were spent driving and catching up on rest. They followed the usual route home but when they arrived at The Way Station, they parked up away from the place but next to what was left of a previous outbuilding. They were still unsure of what had been going on so didn't dare risk entering the station but being at least close to it did help them cling to the final vestiges of their normal. Everyone ate some small rations and settled down to sleep, still unsure of what had been going on, and they left quickly the following day.

Finally, with the sun almost fully set behind the horizon, Scott shouted that they were finally approaching their home, the extra weight of supplies and the softer ground thanks to autumn rain making the going harder, and therefore longer, for The Beast.

The others had been asleep but that call from Scott woke them all up and each could feel a huge relief at being home. Home was where their friends and families were. Home was where all their personal effects were. Home was where they knew that they were safe. Home was where they could have a full body wash, even if it would be cold and after the last few days, it would be a relief to expunge all the experience from their skin.

Chang greeted them as they clambered out and into the fresh air of home.

“You guys look tired. Anything we need to know about?”

“Boy, I’d say!” replied Scott as he stretched his back.

Mary gave him, and therefore anyone within earshot, the short version. The Way Station looked abandoned; Hope has fallen to the Ult, and the population of the place is either gone or in a coma.

“We’ve brought as much stuff as we could carry safely and some of their records to try and work out what happened but I’d say that there was a fair chance that we’re going to need to do some work to prepare for when it’s our turn to face whatever happened there.”

Chang just frowned as he listened but everyone knew his mind would be firing in a hundred different ways as he considered what the ramifications could possibly mean. He quickly reached a decision.

“Right then. We need to get The Beast emptied and then we need to get her prepped for her next trip. Mo?”

Mo scurried out from beneath The Beast, clearly already on the case of assessing his baby’s condition.

Chang looked at Mary and they both smiled.

Jenna and Davis began the unloading and others were soon to join them, forming a chain of people to speed the job along. Everyone could feel the importance of correct preparation on any normal day but very quickly, Jenna could see that the story of the outside world had sharpened everyone even further. Again, it had been just one person talking but the population had been affected.

The crates were cleared from The Beast and then opened and sorted further as everyone marvelled at the huge array of stuff which had been brought back from Hope. Blankets and clothing were taken to be washed, food stuffs of any and all shape and size were taken away to be put to use. There’d even been some fresh vegetables found from somewhere and Jenna just couldn’t work out where they’d come from in Hope. Machinery parts, paint, those oil burner lamps they’d used and bottles of the oil to light them, medical supplies, even an old defibrillator, were discovered as everyone worked their way through the supplies and busied themselves setting it all aside in the correct places.

It appeared that through all of the action, Mo was the only person in the whole place who hadn't dived into the new deliveries. He was still crawling all over the exterior of The Beast making an inch by inch inspection of the vehicle. Mary knew how he worked so stood over him as he went, not saying anything but being on hand to answer any questions which may come up. Mo didn't even really acknowledge her as he went on.

"Linkage with concern from before previous trip still in full working order? Good. No issue for the next trip."

"Correct Mo, you had it working bang on."

"It looks like there have been a few impacts along the side here." He smoothed his hand over the exterior wall of The Beast but kept looking lower down, trusting to his feel.

"Did you guys have any problems? Looks like the Ult came a bit too close?"

"We just had the one say hello," replied Mary. "Though it wasn't so much as hunting, it was more that it just leaned on us as it moved past."

Mo stopped what he was doing and turned to face Mary.

"One of them did this and it wasn't trying to? Jesus Christ, how big was it?"

"It was a big 'un alright. We didn't get a good look at it, we were all inside asleep at the time but it did slam something down on the roof as it went. I checked inside and there was no damage but I never actually climbed on top. Too exposed."

Mo was off like a shot and came hurriedly scurrying back with a long metal ladder, propped it up against the side of The Beast and sped up before the ladder had fully settled into place. Mary couldn't deny his enthusiasm though maybe his attention to safety could have done with some work. She followed on behind him at a more sedate pace.

On the roof of The Beast, Mo was pacing around while intently scrutinising everything he could. When Mary joined him, she could make out very clearly what his attention was being drawn towards.

"There may not have been any damage to the inner skin, but that's one hell of a crack it's got up here."

He wasn't impressed.

Mary approached the cracked area slowly and took in the damage for herself. The Ult had made contact near the edge of the roof and that impact had first caused a mighty dent but within that crater, was a jagged crack which extended about two feet and reached almost to the very edge of the vehicle.

"When did this happen?" asked Mo as he bent down to get a closer look. "It looks like the metal's already corroding quite badly, so are you sure this was recent?"

Mary looked more closely to where Mo had been inspecting, bending down herself to see what he could and frowned.

"It was only three nights ago but I can see what you mean," she replied, recognising what was piquing his interest.

The crack in the metal sheet was one thing but as Mary looked more closely, she could see a silvery build up seemingly growing from the damaged edges of the crack. Small areas of the material glinted ever so slightly in what little light was left of the day and the mounded piles just looked like piles of silver/grey sand rather than metal damage.

"Have you seen anything like this before?" Mary asked as she poked a single finger into the stuff.

Mo didn't have a chance to respond.

He'd barely had a chance to really fully register the question as he'd been watching Mary's hand approach the metallic material, but as soon as she'd made contact, the effect on her had been instantaneous. She collapsed forward like a marionette with its strings cut, every limb just folding under in no order or reason beyond gravity. Mo jerked backwards in utter shock and would later be glad that he'd been crouched where he had been as he sprawled backwards to finish spread out widely on the roof of The Beast. Almost every other point would have sent him tumbling off the side to a very sudden stop below.

Mo just breathed deeply in utter shock; his eyes wide like saucers as he tried to kick start his mind after the event which had just unfolded before him. Mary was sprawled forwards in a heap but her face was turned towards him and there was no sign there that she was even close to OK. Her eyes were still open but there was just nothing behind them. She'd just fallen like the power switch had been flicked off.

Eventually, Mo snapped out of his trance and scrambled towards Mary's crumpled form, all the while screaming for help to get up on The Beast. He rolled her onto her back quickly, as the sound of running feet and shouted questions filled the area around him, and just looked at her.

Where should he start?

He'd had some first aid training over the years, ironically that had been driven by Mary, but now he was confronted by the chance to make use of the knowledge, it had deserted him. He could see that she was still breathing and when he checked for a pulse he'd been able to find one in her neck quite easily but she was still just, stopped.

Behind him, he could make out the movement as people began to climb the ladder and he began to relax a little but there was still nothing for him to say when he was asked what had happened.

And he was asked immediately someone joined him on the roof, but he just couldn't say. The question rang out in his head again, but he didn't know who was asking it. There was someone stood next to him and he knew they were shouting for answers but he just felt like he was hearing them from under deep water. Then there was someone else on his other side doing the same and he could swear that they were starting to move around him and towards Mary without him even having said something. He just had to tell them what had happened.

What had happened?

He didn't know.

They began looking at damage to The Beast and she'd just collapsed. How could he know what had happened?

But he did know.

"Don't touch the silvery stuff. Don't get it on your skin. It's dangerous."

Mo felt kind of proud of himself for being able to get his point across having worked out what the likely cause of the problem was though the others on the roof had heard a much more slurred version of what he'd said. Everyone stopped what they were doing as he spoke and then collapsed backwards himself, hitting his head hard on the metal roof.

The panicked shouting from the open dock area of the compound had brought people from all over the buildings rushing, either in the need to help or the need to see, and that had included Jenna. She'd been in the large kitchen taking a drink of what had been packaged as tea but was more like dishwater when the call had come out. The tea was gulped down at speed and she was heading towards the commotion as fast as she could, oddly certain that she was hearing the opening salvos of some kind of attack. Arriving on the scene with a gathering crowd of people, she could see people moving about on top of The Beast with more climbing the single ladder which was jammed against her side.

"What's happened?" she asked the nearest person to her, a middle aged woman called Emily.

"Looks like Mary and Mo have been hurt. I think Mo said something about there being a dangerous chemical that had been brought in with the last trip. You'd have thought Mary would have been smart enough to not bring something like that in?"

Jenna had been crushed by a frozen, vice like grip at the thought of people being hurt, especially people she got on with, but that final comment acted like a slap in the face.

"I heard them talking up there," said another woman turning to face Jenna. "Mary had told Mo that they'd been attacked by an Ult but she hadn't fully checked The Beast afterwards and the damage had just been sat there for days."

Jenna could feel each word like a slap in the face but held tight to her composure.

"Any damage that was or wasn't there couldn't have been repaired safely. We were trapped in a place with Ult roaming around."

The second woman didn't look like she believed what was being said but she just turned back to look at events before them.

Jenna had wanted to help but when she tried to climb the ladder, she was told that there were already enough people up there and that too much weight could just make things worse.

Instead, she was forced to wait until Mary and Mo were brought down strapped to planks of wood and lowered on lengths of rope. Everyone who'd been involved in the situation had been made to wear gloves and to keep some kind of mask over their faces and the two victims had been wrapped in extra thick blankets before anyone had gone near them.

She'd heard through the rest of the evening, at least four different versions of what had happened and why people had done what they'd done but each seemed more outlandish than the last. One had been that a tiny Ult had been hiding up there and had attacked them, another that Mo had been screaming in agony as his skin burned because of contact with something but when she finally got to speak with the very first responders she learned about the silvery material and the real details. When she spoke to anyone who asked about the journey to and from Hope and what had been brought back, the truth of the events didn't seem to matter in light of the horror stories which were spreading like wild fires. Eventually, stood at the edge of what had hurriedly been transformed into a quarantine room next to their medical facilities, she just watched over the two people on the other side of the plastic sheeting who lay still on beds as others worked around them and hoped for the best.

It was late and Jenna was really feeling the weight of her tiredness from the trip acting like an anchor to everything she tried to do. She needed some sleep. Chang walked up next to her as she just watched on and was well into his first sentence before she even registered his approach. She must have shown a startled jerk as she caught up because Chang apologised profusely before starting again.

"We've had them working in there with masks on and every inch of their skin covered but without proper hazmat gear, we're still just crossing our fingers."

He placed what he hoped would be seen as a reassuring hand on her shoulder and continued speaking.

"How are you feeling? You didn't see anything like that powdery stuff anywhere on your trip did you?"

She turned to face him and just shook her head. There wasn't any more to say.

They both stood in silence as the people in the plastic 'tent' went about their business of monitoring Mary and Mo closely, and the view before them served as inspiration for Chang to fill the growing silence.

"We've burned all of their clothes, washed them down and sanitised every square inch of them so whatever that stuff was, no-one else will come into contact with it from them and there are steps being taken to get The Beast out of the compound so we can set that on fire too. Just to be sure."

That final comment was yet another slap in the face that really focused her mind out of the fog of exhaustion.

"Why are we burning The Beast? Surely we just need to make sure it isn't covered in any more of the stuff and repair any damage. A few pieces of clothing, that makes sense but we can't afford to just junk everything at the first sign of trouble."

Chang 'humpfed' but it felt like he agreed but had been over ruled.

"Look, just don't do it before we can have a decent chat about it," pleaded Jenna. "Make sure no-one goes near the thing and we can talk about it more clearly tomorrow. There's something very big going on out there and the last thing we need to be doing is cutting ourselves off behind our walls."

Chang 'humpfed' again, but didn't take his eyes off Mary and Mo.

Jenna just couldn't say or think anything more. She'd fully burned through her energy stores and was running out of any fumes which she may have had in reserve. Sighing, she just gave up and retreated to her bunk, telling Chang again that she would speak with him in the morning and not to do anything rash.

9

Jenna collapsed onto her bunk without undressing or even climbing under the covers. She just had nothing left and was asleep in seconds. The other three people who lived in this room were still up and about somewhere around the place so she was alone, and without any desire to do anything beyond sleep.

Her dreams started out mundane, the usual collection of nonsense images that just make you want to reconsider eating cheese late at night, but they quickly settled into armies of marauding Ult swarming over the landscape destroying everyone and everything in their path. She saw her sister Daisy as the child she'd been when they last saw each other, cowering before one of the creatures as it grasped out to her with that long yet bulbous arm they all had, it's rubbery fingers closing around her completely as she screamed and screamed.

Mary and Mo drifted through her mind's eye in their beds, breathing but beyond that, totally lifeless, and they were soon joined by Daisy, then her parents, then Chang, then Scott and finally, herself until she was swept through and into her own inanimate body to be locked away behind her closed eyes, aware of everything which was taking place outside her body but powerless to reach out. Sheer terror gripped her mind in the dream as she screamed and pounded against the inside of her own head, begging to be let free, all the while that all too familiar gulping call of 'ULT, ULT, ULT, ULT' just continued outside. At last, the fear grew to such a degree that she started herself awake and called out against the last remnants of the dream she was still covered in as she came to.

Sat up in her bunk, she breathed deeply and did all she could to push the memories of her dream to the back of her mind. There was enough threat to be worried about in the real world without making up new scenarios in her head. Eventually calming her breathing, she took in the detail of the room around her in the near darkness and used it to ground herself. There was a lump under the covers on a bunk on the far end of the room which she assumed was Frank, an old man who had been the most recent addition to their little rag tag family. His breathing was the familiar wet snore she'd been doing her best to get used to so at least he hadn't been woken up when she'd called out. She'd usually have been lucky to miss any kind of sound around her when she was in the house trying to get some sleep so seeing someone do it effortlessly was somewhat annoying. Oh, to be a sound sleeper.

Lucky him.

She checked her watch while considering that Frank hadn't woken her when he'd gone to bed and accepted that she must have been almost beyond tired to have slept so soundly. Her watch told her it was just past seven so the day would be beginning to crank into action around the place as she sat awake. Chang would have been up and about already, he was always an early riser but with Mary and Mo suddenly ill, he'd have been all over everything. She wondered if he'd managed to get any sleep at all.

Kicking herself out from beneath the blanket she now had over her, probably Frank so she wouldn't get cold; she must really have been tired, she slipped out of the room as quietly as she could to try and repay the favour for her sleeping colleague.

Moving through the corridors of the house, she found herself planning through the kinds of arguments she could make to stop The Beast being torched 'just in case'. People passed her as she went, and she passed people as they went, everyone clearly focused on the jobs in hand for the day giving Jenna the feeling that there was a real change in the mood of the place after what had happened.

What if something had happened during the night?

Did that mean that Mo and Mary were worse?

Were there more people who'd fallen to this same fate?

What if there was something else?

The questions just made her mind race, which in turn hurried her steps to the point that she was practically running when she arrived at the War Room and burst through the doors hoping to find Chang with answers to all of her questions.

He was stood at the head of the table with paperwork spread out before him, some of which Jenna recognised from their investigations in Hope, and had been in conversation with Selina who was sat away from the table but with more paperwork open in her lap. The two of them both snapped their gazes to Jenna in surprise at her entrance, but they weren't the only ones. Despite the early morning, the room was full of people who all wore similar expressions to Chang and Selina. Something big must have happened overnight.

"Hi Jen," greeted Chang, his expression smoothing as he did. "You feeling rested?"

"Not really but such is life. What's the situation with Mary and Mo?" Jenna was practically holding her breath as she waited to find out.

"No change I'm afraid," replied Chang.

Jenna wasn't sure what she'd been expecting him to say but that just didn't seem to be the right answer. She was glad there hadn't been any deaths overnight but she felt that there should have been something. She'd been expecting something. She'd been expecting the worst. She'd expecting something terrible so now without there being anything to be mad at, she felt a little numb.

"Cool."

Jenna's stomach knotted as she spoke that single word. She hadn't been ready to respond to that specific response from Chang but she was pretty sure that her attempt had been utter rubbish. Happily, Chang just motioned for her to join the discussion happening at the table and they all picked up where they'd left off.

"Come on then, let's get back onto the topic at hand."

His deep voice was a reassuring constant to Jenna. He was calling everyone back from the attention on her and back to the maps and that meant that there was a distinct thing which was under investigation that she could get involved in, a problem which needed solving. Back to the planning.

As all of the eyes returned to the table and murmurs of conversation started back up, Jenna took her place amongst the group and cast her gaze over what was already laid out.

It didn't make for good reading.

Every town for miles around, as far as the maps reached, and no doubt even further than that, had finally fallen. There was no-one left. Except everyone in this house. All over the map sat markers showing the locations of people and their hideouts and every one of them had been crossed through roughly with a red marker to signify its loss.

Any fleeting sensation of equilibrium was swept aside. Jenna couldn't believe her eyes. It was clear that there'd been massive changes taking place outside of their tiny existence here, the Way Station proved that even before considering what had been happening in Hope, but looking at the huge map and the now fallen settlements and caches poured ice water down her spine.

What the Hell had happened out there?

The conversations had started up again but Jenna burst into them.

"Is this accurate?" she asked, waving her hands over the map.

The entire assembled group just looked at her, but Chang spoke up with a sombre voice.

"It's what we've been able to put together from the information that you guys brought back from Hope. Obviously we can't say for certain that everything is accurate but this is the picture that's being painted by the information at hand."

Silence reigned through the room which was only interrupted by the uneasy shuffling of papers or movement of clothing as the other members of this meeting waited for Jenna to digest that most awful thought. They were alone now.

As you'd expect upon hearing that kind of information, Jenna just stood still, looking confusedly ahead while her mind juddered through the shockwaves of doing everything it could to absorb what had been said. The ramifications were massive, and represented so many huge problems that Jenna just couldn't see past them all.

If the map was true, that meant that there was only them left, but how far beyond that map was now empty as well? Were they now just an isolated pocket or were they the last remaining humans on Earth? They didn't have enough of anything to be able to survive through the winter if there was no-one else out there so what could they do? If they were the only ones left, should they just lie down and admit defeat? If they needed to travel further to find supplies, they couldn't afford to burn The Beast.

The idea of The Beast was what snapped her back to the real world from her own head. She could only deal with one thing at a time and even a tiny win at this point would be something.

"Has the talk about The Beast come up yet? Do you guys still want to burn her?" Jenna wasn't sure why she'd called the big vehicle 'her' but she'd heard Mo do it before and as he couldn't be at the table to defend her, it was only fair that Jenna stand in.

"I listened to you yesterday and had Davis move it as close to the walls of the compound and seal off the area to be sure until a decontamination effort can be put in place," answered Chang matter-of-factly, the issue clearly being one which had been dealt with some time ago for everyone else. Jenna breathed a sigh of relief that at least there'd been some kind of sense at play over night. She nodded her thanks. Emily, who'd she spoken with when Mary and Mo had been hurt, began speaking as soon as Jenna stopped.

"Now can we get back to where we were please? There's been a huge amount of reading and research done today to bring us to where we are now and this picture isn't a good one. What's our next step?"

Jenna had never really spent a huge amount of time with Emily over the years she'd been with this group and, standing there as she shot accusations at the room between the lines of her speech, she was seeing clearly why. Emily was wearing a pinched expression and she'd folded her arms across her chest while drumming her fingers on her arm. Jenna didn't know what they'd been discussing before she'd burst in but there must have been some pretty bad details beyond what she'd been told for her to be as angry as she was.

And she wasn't the only one.

There were at least two other faces which mirrored that sour expression of superior accusation that Emily was sporting and they both nodded sharply in agreement as she spoke. The others in the room all looked to be scared or at a loss to fully comprehend the situation as it was and looked to be waiting on someone, could have been anyone, to give them an instruction or order of some kind. Jenna could understand that feeling of needing to cling to anything of familiarity and structure in times of strife so it didn't come as any surprise that people were scared, but she was also feeling that the person who'd usually be the one giving these jobs and planning the response to such an event would have been Mary.

Typical.

Chang smiled gently at Emily and nodded her way which at least dialled down her displeasure a little. He hadn't agreed with her in as many words but she clearly felt like he had.

"We need to understand as much as we can before we make any choices we can't walk back from." Chang was the voice of calm as always.

"The team have brought us all of the information that they could find so we're in a position to be able to build as clear a picture as possible but we can't just panic."

Jenna couldn't really be certain, but she felt the use of the word 'panic' had been the one to light the blue touch paper. Emily's eyes blazed with righteous fire and she made her feelings very clear.

"Panic? The team that goes out on what should have been a pretty straight forward run discovers that in the time since our last trip, the entire population of our mapped area, essentially our whole world, has been wiped out by either Ult warfare or this new 'cure'. That, when the team came back, they brought that very 'cure' with them. That two people have already succumbed to this new disease they brought back. It seems like a perfect time to panic to me."

Grumbles swept the room more widely now and Jenna could see more frowns, though Emily had said something she hadn't understood.

"What's this 'cure'? Was this discussed before I came in?"

"It was," floated up from the back of the room as the person who'd spoken moved through the line of people around the table. It was Scott and he didn't look happy.

"Unlike those who were allowed to sleep all day, the rest of this group have been on the case almost non-stop."

He slipped in next to Emily, placing a hand briefly on her shoulder and squeezing gently in support.

Jenna was getting lost, but it wasn't lost on her that Scott was at this meeting with a large gun draped over his shoulder and ammunition clips within easy reach on the tactical vest he was wearing. Emily carried her own gun too. This was really not looking good.

"What are you so angry about? Who's not been doing their jobs?"

Scott and Emily just kept their eyes glued to Jenna and the War Room population appeared to show more and more threat from those she'd considered to be at least companions in the most part but there were a few true friends in there too.

Chang stepped in, seeing that the mood in the room was spiralling.

"Scott, Jenna slept as long as she needed after the assignment you all went on to Hope. You weren't woken up by anyone either and slept longer than usual. Let's keep our attention on the big picture here shall we?"

Scott didn't say anything but you could feel the anger everywhere in the room. Emily was practically snarling. Jenna was still lost but could feel that there was a great deal still to discover. Chang, though, recognising that everyone was balanced very precariously on their nerves, decided that there needed to be a break before someone did something really stupid.

"Thank you to everyone for what you've been able to achieve today and for staying on task as we've all struggled with the facts we've been finding. None of us are going to come out of this unscathed by the information here but each and every one of you has been able to keep on trawling through anyway."

The room returned to silence with only the rare tiny sound of moved feet or rustled paper. Looking around, Jenna was now able to really take in the faces of everyone else in the room and there was still that smattering of anger but now that she was taking more time to actually see what everyone else was carrying with them, she saw far too clear examples of fear, of loss, of exhaustion and of being lost and alone in the dark. Chang continued speaking.

"Everyone get some sleep and we'll continue in the morning. This is going to be a tough time for all of us but we will get through it. We'll meet back here at six tomorrow morning and get back on the job."

Everyone left quickly and in relative silence, but the voices were quick to start up when they'd reached the corridor. Finally, Jenna was left alone in the War Room with Chang and the mapped picture of their situation. Now, where to begin?

"You've been asleep all day; it's now just after seven in the evening. The map here has been compiled by the different pieces of information Mary brought back from Hope but we can't confirm anything without going to see for ourselves. The 'cure' is something new that no-one is truly able to identify but there's the feeling that it's some kind of Ult biological weapon, and Scott has been stoking the fear of the group just by being his usual wonderful self, saying that it was you and Mary not being careful enough that brought it here. Now you're caught up."

In all of our lives, we reach points where we're forced to face uncomfortable truths which smash against our views on the world. A child learning that Santa Claus isn't real stands looking back at all of the truth they thought they knew and know that feeling of being stood on sand. Their previously firm base begins to crumble beneath them as a vital plank of how they saw the world is removed. Jenna felt as if she'd had three or four of these events happen all at the same time.

Chang's voice echoed through her mind and the world swam through blurring colours as she gripped tightly to the side of the table and fought to stay upright.

"Is it the 'cure' that's responsible for the loss of all of the people? Surely we'd have heard about it before this if it was that virulent?" She wasn't sure where that question had really come from, but as she did her best to grip tightly to her own equilibrium, it seemed like an important thing to know.

"We don't know, but it looks very much like it was. It's likely that any and all movement through Hope was what meant it could sweep through the area more quickly but that is just an extrapolation. The descriptions do seem the same."

This was awful.

Jenna could see in Chang's eyes that he agreed fully but still wasn't fully sure what needed to be done in response and he'd been dealing with the problem for longer than she had. They needed to have a plan.

"So Mary and Mo have this Ult disease?"

"It looks like it. Descriptions of the first instance say that there was some kind of odd build up on the vehicle that was being inspected when the person affected fell from it but information about others just isn't there." Chang reached out and lifted a handful of pages which had been on the edge of the table by way of emphasis.

"People were found by others just collapsed so there was never any real clear picture."

Jenna and Chang just looked at each other now. There wasn't anything else to say between them at this point and they could both feel it as an oppressive force. They'd reached the point where there needed to be some kind of solution presented but there just wasn't anything to say.

Chang filled the gap.

"We've all had a busy day and everyone's at the end of their ropes so I'd suggest that you just get as much rest as possible and tomorrow morning we can have a fresh run at this, God knows, I'm out on my feet."

"You go and rest but I've only been up about ten minutes so if you don't mind, I'd like to start work on the cleaning of The Beast. I have a feeling that she's going to be important and I need to be doing something."

Rubbing his hair while yawning, Chang considered, and then agreed.

"Fine, but make sure you've got someone with you. They don't have to do anything if they don't want to but I want you watched as you're working so a decent picture of events can be laid out if something bad happens. Deal?"

She gave a curt nod in response and turned on her heel and left the War Room. She knew that Chang would lock the room so no-one who shouldn't read anything sensitive could read through things but everything would be left where they all finished off tonight, ready to be picked up in the morning. She also knew that there was an angry underbelly of sentiment which was being stoked by Scott. She wanted to believe that he wasn't doing it on purpose just because he was a contrarian and was just amplifying the fear that must be everywhere by now, but either reason sent her the same way. She was being blamed, so bringing The Beast back into play could be a good step in at least calming some people down. All she had to do now was find someone to help.

Jenna spent the rest of the night doing everything she could to reduce any exposed skin to zero as she worked over every inch of The Beast. Davis had been given an earlier finish thanks to his time on the Hope mission so had at least had some rest when he volunteered his help. He'd been doing everything he could to stick to some kind of normality amongst all of the juddering changes which had been causing upheaval around the place and that meant that he'd just assumed that his expected duties would still be the same. He'd been expecting to be working through the night so was willing to help.

To begin with, Jenna was forceful about making sure he didn't come close to the vehicle as she went about cleaning and sweeping through every surface she could reach but after him repeating over and over again that he should be doing more than just sitting and watching, she just accepted the help.

They started at the top, where they knew the Ult material had been found around the crack in the roof, and systematically scrubbed their way down. Both were draped with any waterproof clothing they'd been able to get their hands on, massive industrial gauntlets, hoods up with the draw strings pulled as tight as they could manage and goggles and sheet plastic wrapped around their boots. They'd both joked that they looked like they were preparing to deal with nuclear fallout and had a good laugh about it when they started, but any good humour was quickly washed away as they worked.

They had no real idea what the correct procedure should be to clear the material they found so stuck with the classic of soapy water, fire to burn away anything which had survived that, and then antibacterial gel for anything that was left. The wood surfaces had proved tougher but they'd still managed to get everything accounted for.

It had been a long night.

There was still a great deal of the night left to happen when they finished but Jenna and Davis both sagged as they replaced all of the supplies they'd used in the cleaning stations. Jenna hugged Davis as a sign of her thanks and they both headed off back to their respective bunks to get a little sleep before they joined up with the planning stages and the rest of Chang's gathered people. It was going to be a long day indeed if they were as hostile again but during the hours of work she'd spent on The Beast, Jenna had come up with an idea that could be just what was needed to get the masses back on side.

She quietly made her way back through the deserted corridors of the building but before she arrived at her dorm, she changed her direction and headed up stairs to that one window that she'd been looking through when she'd first encountered Enterprise cloud. It had been just a handful of days since she'd pulled the wooden panel away from the old window but so much had happened since then that she felt any positive effect from it had been washed away.

Arriving at the spot, she checked behind and ahead of her for any other presence before working that panel free again. The cold night air was sharp and a little damp and, at another time, would have felt like something to be avoided, but for right now, here at the one open window where any and all of Jenna's imagination could soar, it was the most refreshing and welcoming embrace. It reminded her just what it was to have the tiniest speck of something which was more than just the world of fear and hiding that was all around her, and it was just what everyone could do with experiencing. Closing her eyes, she just let the wind howl through her hair and smiled to herself. This is exactly what everyone needs to feel before bigger choices are made, to remind them that we need to live, not just exist.

Raising the panel back into position over the window, sealing that single link to the open air, she didn't feel any loss. She'd come up to look to confirm to herself that what she was going to do was going to be the right choice and she'd been convinced immediately. She was going to share this with everyone and it would be the first step in the journey away from the brink. Tomorrow was going to be a good day.

First, though, sleep.

10

The meeting picked up where it had left off the day before.

Jenna may have been feeling positive when she entered the room despite the only fleeting glimpse of sleep she'd had, but the others made it clear that they didn't agree with her.

The same people from the day before frowned everywhere, while others looked worried, and still more just looked exhausted, like they'd reached a point of having nothing left to give. The hope that some rest would have helped calm the group looked to have been misplaced. It also appeared that whatever concerns Scott and Emily had yesterday which made them feel the need to carry weapons into the gathering had spread to everyone else. The population practically bristled with armaments as Jenna picked out hand guns, automatic weapons and lots of spare ammunition. Everyone had clearly been listening to Scott as he made more and more play to the basest elements of their fears. Granted it was important to be switched on to possible threats but the house was surrounded by high walls which the Ult had ignored for an age. Besides, having this many people moving about armed to the teeth and expecting the worst at every turn was more likely to lead to everyone killing each other by mistake.

It was all 'just in case', but that didn't mean it was any less dangerous.

"Thank you all for coming this morning," began Chang, his political hat clearly placed on his head as he studied the weapons too.

"I'd like to pick up where we left off yesterday with the supply needs we can't afford to put off, but before we do, some positive news. Jenna has spent the night with Davis running a full decontamination of The Beast so the vehicle will be available to us as we go about our jobs."

Most of the eyes in the War Room swung to look at Jenna who was towards the opposite end of the table from Chang, and although she hadn't been looking for any kind of thanks, she hadn't been expecting what she did receive.

"Better late than never it seems," spat Emily from Jenna's right. Some of the eyes on Jenna switched to Emily but far too many for Jenna's liking remained trained on her, suggesting tacit agreement.

"We probably should have done that before we came back here but at least it's been done now. It's just a shame that it didn't take place until after the horses had bolted." That was Scott from next to Emily and although there was a very slight hint of compliment in his words, it was clear by the sharp nods from many of the others in the room that they all felt their anger just as keenly as they had last night.

Chang looked between Emily and Scott, his brow creased in impotent frustration, before he glanced over to Jenna and spoke his reassurance without words.

That was something, at least.

Chang was about to continue with the meeting but in that split second before he could move on, all of the positivity Jenna was feeling slammed against the cynicism and fear in the room and her frustration just boiled up and over before she could stop it.

"Keeping The Beast active is a good thing. It may not be the biggest and brightest piece of news that we're ever going to receive, but in terms of the here and now, it's something to be pleased with." She'd spoken before she'd been able to do any real preparation and she felt her voice shaking at the edges as she did.

More silence.

The frowns deepened on some, the blank expressions somehow deepened on others. Chang was doing his best not to just let his jaw hit the table, so shocked had he been by the statement but Jenna could make out that at least Davis and Selina, and a newer member of the group, Mark, were nodding their agreement.

Shadows and light danced across every surface, leaping from the various candles and creating images of any and all objects which were all around them, and Jenna became acutely aware that all eyes were on her and a great many were really not impressed. Candle light continually weaved and flickered, and the silence just remained resolutely oppressive.

Chang broke the deadlock.

"Thanks Jenna, for the work you did and for the positive attitude. I think we could do with any more good news we can find at the moment."

Jenna didn't blame him for the bland response. She could see that he was in an impossible position with all of the others in the room. If it had just been Scott and his new acolyte Emily, it would have been easier to accept what she'd said but as there were so many in attendance that were clearly still livid with her, he couldn't risk alienating a large swathe of the tiny population here. She even knew that he'd likely agree with her about the whole idea of home improvements but this was quickly showing itself as neither the time nor the place.

All eyes fell back on to the maps on the table and there was a shared burden which hit each and every one of them at the same time, their shoulders all sagging and heads dropping far more than just any review the maps would cause.

Everyone bar Jenna had been pouring over the information in all of the papers that had been brought back from Hope since they'd been unpacked and they'd all been just sucking that information into themselves constantly. Every new detail had been shared with the group so there was an ever growing mountain of horror being created for every member of this team to just cower before, never giving even the slightest hint that there was anything beyond death and destruction waiting for them around every corner.

Add in this new disease, The cure, and it wasn't really that surprising that everyone could feel that they'd mapped the end of humanity. Anyone who came into contact with the cure just collapsed and stopped. They had no way of moving, of speaking. Their bodies had just enough power to stay alive but there was nothing else. There had been descriptions of friends and families in Hope becoming nothing but something which breathes croakily, confined to a bed while others were forced to watch them wither. They were just gone. There was never any warning that it was in the area or was somehow going to be deployed. The invisible threat just landed on communities and that was that.

Scott broke the silence this time.

"We're out of options now, aren't we? There's nothing left out there now. We're the last of the human race and there's nothing more for us out there. Anyone have any suggestions?" He sounded angrier still.

"We can't give up now." Chang responded without even lifting his head from the scrutiny he was giving a particular segment of the cartography. He spoke with the same gentle calm which had seen him assume the mantle of leader after Mary fell to the cure, and under any usual circumstances; it would have been just what was needed. Jenna just looked at the group of people around her and missed Mary. These weren't usual circumstances and her calming influence would have kept the group from tearing itself apart.

"This disease they've all got, it's something new from the Ult and no-one's been able to do anything about it. It looks like the people we found in Hope were just left because they'd become almost dead weight to the others who'd lived there. Any survivors from Hope left those afflicted behind and struck out on their own, but considering there's been no sign of anyone who did make it out, I'd suggest they're all dead as well. "

More silence, but now, a much thicker air was draped over them all, its pressure almost painful.

"I think we need to accept that we're finished." Scott had stood up straight and folded his arms across his chest.

Jenna didn't like him. Too angry, and he was scaring everyone.

That didn't mean he wasn't right though, but she couldn't afford to fall to that idea like so many others already had.

No one spoke into the chill morning air. Everyone just considered what had just been said and by each pair of eyes it was clear that they had been thinking the same, and for some time.

Chang opened his mouth to speak but as he glanced over to Jenna, stopped himself. There was nothing to add.

“What was your favourite story growing up?” Jenna just launched into it, again not stopping to think before she spoke. Her day dreaming had had a far more powerful effect on her than she’d thought possible. The assembled people had brought what she had been feeling into sharp focus and she now realised that this wasn’t just the best time to make her point, it was the only time. All eyes turned to her and every face held a shared confusion at what had just been said. Furrowed brows sat atop faces that, in the most part, had no idea what she was on about but a couple looked like they were thinking to answer the question posed.

Still, no one spoke; each question and statement was just too far outside the realms of what had been expected that everyone was struggling to keep up. They all just looked at her trying to evaluate what she’d meant, thinking they must’ve missed a basic point of what Jenna had been trying to say.

“When you were kids. What was the story you liked to hear the most? What was it that made you most excited?”

“I don’t think this is quite the time for this Jenna. We have more important things to work out than our treasured pasts.” Scott’s voice dripped with scorn. He remained stood with his arms folded across his chest but had turned to face her fully and was practically posed like a statue, looking down his nose at her. She imagined him waiting as an artist toiled on his likeness and it helped take some of the sting out of his words.

“All we have left is our memories now.” Jenna had to make sure the conversation wasn’t snuffed out before she had made the point she needed to make. She conjured up the image of the Enterprise cloud in her head as a reminder and didn’t dare let it go. Before it had appeared she hadn’t thought of anything of the kind, but once it was there, it had taken on an almost spiritual power.

“You said it yourself, there’s nothing left for us here. Every other group of people we know about is gone, all of the supplies, weapons, food and medical tech, have been consolidated and they’re running out and the house is falling apart at the seams. The Ult took a huge amount from us but we let them take the rest of our lives by forgetting all of the good things. None of us are alive, are we? We aren’t living, we only exist. There isn't anything but pain for all of us so what does any of us need to fight for. Surely the cure has already gripped us all, the difference for some is at least we can still move."

"We really do need to try and make some kind of plan to mount some form of defence." Chang was still frowning slightly but his voice was gentle. He was talking to a friend and didn't want to just shut her down directly.

"None of us have the time to sit and waste thinking about the good old days. We need to stay focused on fighting our way to freedom." Scott's voice was now climbing register as he became gradually angrier. His hands were on his hips and he puffed his chest out akin to an overly proud rooster.

"But I think we could all benefit from remembering what we are all fighting for. A little rest should never be overlooked." Chang didn't like Scott either so was more than happy to get in his way, despite not truly believing what he was saying.

Scott huffed and his face began turning a shade of purple he was so angry. He crossed his arms over his chest again and just sulked.

Jenna smiled inside as she resumed.

"What was your favourite story as a child? Think about what you loved in the time before the Ult. We need to stop occasionally and take our fighting hat off. We can't just be soldiers. We have to be more than that and never let go of who we all were. I sat in the window at the front of the house and watched a cloud move across the sky and I remembered something I hadn't thought about for years and for the briefest time, I was away from the horror. I was back as a kid watching Star Trek, and I loved it."

"You looked out of a window? How did you manage to do that?" Scott just couldn't let it go; he had to pick at everything.

"You took the board down?" Chang spoke quickly but now his voice was steel sharp. The mood had rapidly serrated around them.

The question wasn't what Jenna had expected and she stumbled over her response. Expressions filled with wide eyed worry and there were sharp glances between all of those in the room. Chang asked again.

"The high window at the front? You took the board down?"

The tension soared even further for everyone as Jenna paused slightly as she caught on to what was being asked.

If she'd taken the board down to see out on the world which had given her such a warm fuzzy feeling, had there been anything out there to see her?

Whispers floated on the air as the assembled war council was quickly on alert to what was unfolding.

"I wasn't seen." Jenna stuck her jaw out in defiance at the suggestion. She had to keep the group on topic and not let them be distracted by paranoia.

"Are you sure? How can you be sure?" Scott spat over his shoulder as he collected ammunition for his weapon, loading fluidly as he continued.

"I'm not a child you know?" Jenna was still indignant at the merest suggestion she had made any kind of mistake and having Scott's paranoia being backed up by Chang was making her want to just push back.

Chang stood rod straight and ordered, "We need to be sure we're secure. Everyone, sweep the house and make sure there's nothing here. Strategic review of the grounds after that."

Those were the last words that were heard in the once homely dining room before the gunfire started up.

11

Gunfire is an amazing thing. Any loud noise will always make you jump if you're not expecting it but gunfire is something which doesn't pretend to be anything other than dangerous. If a gun is being fired, someone has deemed their situation to be one which has deteriorated to such a degree that violence is needed, with the very real threat of serious injury or death coming with it.

We hide from gunfire. If it's coming for us or if it's happening nearby, the end result will be the same if we get hit.

Everyone in the room dived down below the level of the table and scrabbled for any cover they could as shouting voices joined to the weapons. It only took them all a couple of heartbeats but everyone was able to work out where the firing was coming from and understand more about what could be taking place.

Their homestead had gun placements at a couple of points on the roof, at opposite ends of the walls of the compound enclosure, so the sound of firing wasn't totally out of the question but it had been a very long time since an Ult had been seen approaching the place. This sound was different though.

It was closer.

Whatever was taking place was inside their home, and it was coming for them.

"Everyone get set, I'm going to look see," said Chang from the head of the table, drawing his own hand gun while a series of clicks and clacks filled the room as each weapon was primed for use. He didn't make it further than the middle of the table when the door was flung open and two people dived in, away from an as yet unseen threat. Outside, the firing continued and Jenna, still closest to the carnage, did her best to kick the door closed despite the minimal effect a wooden door would have against the bullets. As it swung, the target of the firing became clear.

Smashing against the closing door and tearing it off its hinges to splinter across the room, , stood the misshapen frame of an Ult, its single arm reaching forward from what would have been its head if it had been human.

There was no way to know how it had been able to get into the house, if it was alone, or what it was hoping to achieve, those questions would come later if they were successful in their attempts to defend their home. Scott was the first to respond. He screamed a high pitched note of terror before his trigger finger clamped down with instinctual fear and bullets tore into anything and everything unlucky enough to be in his way.

Every other member of the 'council' was quick to start firing as well. The giant form of the Ult was an easy target this close and was chewed into by fire from every weapon in the room. There was no fear of the noise of the firing attracting further creatures so each person around the table poured out all of the brutality they could.

Jenna could only scramble along the floor as best as she could as threats exploded everywhere.

The Ult paused in response to the multiple bullet impacts, each hit causing a tiny fleck of a spark as metal hit the hide of its target. All around it, those shots which hadn't reached their intended targets had begun chewing into the doorframe, the walls and even the ceiling as ricochets pinged away as well. That pause hadn't been long lasting as, despite the hail of bullets being poured at it, the Ult began moving again and lumbered into the room.

Jenna had never seen one this close before.

They'd always been on the other side of their 'viewers,' in various compounds or using the periscope on The Beast. Those she had at least seen with her own eyes had always been quite some distance from her. She was so close to the creature that the simple detail on the hide exploded in her head in high definition. All of the knots of flesh, the fissures with raw meat within, the smell of shit coming from the filth smeared over the lower segment of its body, everything about this beast, made her feel repulsed yet intrigued. It was so unlike a human but clearly wanted to kill her. As she'd been a child when the Arrival took place, there'd always been the attempt to keep her as far away from any and all dangers as had been possible so by the time she was taking her place on the walls that protected everyone, the instances of contact had reduced dramatically. She couldn't help herself but be fascinated by the thing which was here to kill them all.

It was a mass of mobile flesh which measured about six feet in height but with that single long grasping arm protruding from the space where a head should have been. The arm swung back and forth as it stumped ahead, giving the impression that it was attempting to swat away any of the bullets it could but Jenna watched in horror as that had just been a ruse.

With terrifying speed which the Ult didn't have any right to possess, that flailing arm arrowed out far beyond the expected range of movement and the ribbon like tendrils on the end, the fingers of its hand, stretched to ensnare a man called Ozzie, a massive man who barely ever said a word. Those rubbery fingers wrapped themselves around his chest and head and despite the attempts that Ozzie was desperately employing to break free, they just tightened and tightened. Ozzie began screaming as the Ult attacked, but that sound soon became a gargle and then silence as the charred sizzling odour of incinerated flesh belched into the room. Those fingers remained tightly wrapped around what was now left of Ozzie but his unburned legs just slumped hard to the floor, spilling an ever spreading slick of blood. The fingers unwound themselves and Ozzie's gun clattered to the floor in the blood pool.

Above her, the sound of the gun fire began to pulse slightly as ammunition ran dry and magazines were replaced, everyone doing their best to keep the defensive measure going as their enemy heaved again and shifted its bulk further into the room after them.

It wasn't aiming her way but it was clear that if it decided it wanted to, it was more than capable of reaching her from almost anywhere in this room, so summoning every ounce of adrenaline fuelled energy at her disposal, she scrabbled backwards again and tried to make it to her feet to speed her removal from harm's way. Her right foot landed in the puddle of blood and as she pushed down, her foot shot backwards away from her and her balance was lost. Falling flat on her face, she didn't dare turn to look at the Ult. Any lost time would be fatal. She forced herself to stand up more steadily, though only barely, and run from the fire zone.

She took one step, and then another as more and more bullets sprang through the air, and there was a second where she even considered the sheer primal enjoyment of the fight to the death, until a deep silence enveloped Jenna.

The ongoing explosion of sound and light from every weapon in the room pouring fire at the advancing Ult must have been too much for her mind to handle. She'd reacted to the scream from Scott; a much higher sounding thing than she would have thought could come from him, and had done her best to drop below the height of the table, out of the way of the hail of metal when the attack had begun but her attempt to find more distance hadn't been that successful. She'd not made it half way to her desired point when her mind was overloaded and everything began to shut down.

First it was her hearing, flicking to a ponderous white noise of a single, high tone, but her vision followed quickly after as everything began tightening down to a singular pin point and from there to total blackness. She had no idea what was happening around her and for a second, panicked that she had been caught by a stray bullet which was passing just too close, or if she'd succumbed to the cure and this was what it felt like on the inside. Her mind raced and rushed around an almost endless array of fears and joys as her consciousness conjured up all manner of images. Enterprise cloud was back but it quickly solidified to become a rendering of the 'real' ship. She smiled to herself at the memory and wondered just how different things could have been if The Enterprise had been on hand to defend the planet from the Ult.

That idea made her happy.

It was joined by the TARDIS and then the Millennium Falcon and the three spaceships just created a feeling of support just by their existence. She was totally separated from herself as she floated through the void and those ships were there to help, they were there to give her that little fragment of herself back within all of the horror that their lives had descended into. In the black of her shuttered mind, that germinating idea allowed her to feel happy.

Beyond just happy, it warmed her to her very core in exactly the way she knew a positive thought would. She smiled again, though where her consciousness was now had no face to prove it, happy that the point she had been attempting to make to the others before all this happened had proved to be right, at least in her head.

The three ships began to whirl tighter and tighter to her point of view and the swirling soup of their familiar sounds mingled now with shattering bolts of lightning which filled her vision. Jenna tried her best to search out the source of those blasts of energy but it always seemed to just be behind her, just out of reach. The ships looped and dived in a ballet around her and she could pick out that they were defending her against whatever that lightning thing was, just like they would have done against the Ult if they'd all been real.

From behind her, more familiar and real sounds started to break through her mind again. There was the sound of wood snapping, followed by someone coughing, and then there was something heavy hitting something plastic. Her brain was re-wiring itself at last, correcting any issues from whatever had happened to her. Could that mean she was regaining consciousness? If that was the case, what had happened to her? Had she been shot?

She could hear Chang shouting her name as the other voices, she couldn't identify any of them from the stream of flowing words which all splashed on her at once, all gibbered in the background. And they all sounded serious.

Scared.

Pleading.

What was going on? What was the lone Ult doing inside their home? How had it got in?

Her own fear climbed over her quickly and she was fighting to push the fog from her mind when she felt the searing jolt of agony which heaved her back to full awareness, her spaceship attendees left behind.

Jenna coughed and groaned at the agony she was in, but was finding it hard to move. Her body felt like she'd been beaten all over rather than having a singular wound from a bullet.

"What happened?" was all she could wheeze, and then it was only those who were nearest to her who could make out the sound.

"Thank God!" It was Chang's voice and Jenna could pick out the blatant relief which rang through his words without having to see him. Forcing her eyes to focus she turned her head to pick him out. She found him slumped on his back on the floor next to her. He was breathing deeply but his face was covered in a thick sheen of sweat. Why was she still laying on the floor? She tried to lift her head but her body screamed at her in protest. Relaxing back to the floor, she was left with a growing fear that something terrible had happened to her. There was very little sound in the room around her so the Ult who'd started all the mayhem must have been dealt with but she had no clue how long she'd been out. It could have been a matter of minutes but it could have been so very much longer. Trying to move again and again, being told in no uncertain terms that that was a bad idea by every nerve in her body, she instead did her best to inventory each part of herself, making certain of what condition she was in.

Inch by inch she moved her attention from one body part to the next, checking to see if she could identify any pains or anything new she should be worried by. Aside from having the wind kicked out of her, she felt as good as could be expected but she knew something more was wrong. It was after at least another two minutes of assessment that she realised that she was now lying on the ground with her shirt torn open. She hadn't been wearing anything underneath so was now fully exposed to all of her colleagues.

Jenna was mortified at the thought of anyone seeing her breasts and tried for a third time to get moving and cover herself but it was still proving too much for her. All she had left was to grunt as loudly as she could to attract the attention of anyone else in the room to help her.

"You OK Jen?" Chang was speaking from the same position he'd been in but he was more relaxed now.

“Just wondering if you like what you see?” She was still almost silent as she spoke but the words made sense.

Chang understood immediately.

He scrambled up and took his jacket off before placing it gently over Jenna, his eyes averted all of the time he did. If nothing else from this awful day so far, that picture of Chang doing everything he could to cling to decorum and propriety after whatever had been going on made her smile. She couldn’t have asked for a clearer example of humanity for all to see.

“THERE’S ANOTHER ONE!” It was Scott again, his voice now even squeakier. Jenna realised that he hadn’t been checking on her at all and was looking for further intruders. She felt indignant at the idea he didn’t care if she lived or died but by the sounds of things, it was a good thing he had been looking.

The gunfire started up again and Jenna knew that a second Ult was in the house and was being pummelled by machine gun fire. But where was the first one?

“Go. Go. We can’t save her. Come on Chang we’ve got to move.” Scott was evilly quick to write her off.

Jenna did her best to open her eyes and croaked as loudly as she could that she was fine but her body just didn’t react in the way she wanted. Instead of the cat like spring from the floor and scamper from the invading enemy, she was left with just being able to open her eyes and speak.

She probably wished she hadn’t.

All she could see was a group of her friends retreating from her as their gunfire was hurled at the advancing Ult. It was being hit repeatedly but it was much bigger than its friend so seemed to be able to just shrug off the punishment. Whereas the first had been a creamy brown colour, this one was black and had an appendage which looked to be able to reach everywhere in the war room without trouble. And it was stumping forward with nothing between it and her.

Jenna screamed.

And screamed.

And thrashed against her body to move away from that thing which was coming for her. She managed to push through the pain that was still wracking her body and with all of the strength she could muster; she was finally able to move in a drunken lurch before face planting back to the floor.

She knew she couldn't get away from the Ult and the panic tore through her. She screamed and screamed and cried and forced her body to move but she was still slowly getting her internal systems back together. Panic flooded her body and despite the adrenaline which was now surging through her veins, everything seemed to be working in the wrong ways. The Ult was going to pounce on her and there was nothing she was going to be able to do to stop it.

But it didn't pounce.

It didn't reach out that rubbery death arm for her.

Jenna lay on the floor at its mercy and the thing heaved itself past her without giving any sign of even recognising she was there. Bullets continued to impact the Ult, sending out those small sparks more brightly against its black hide, but there was just that singular focus to reach the people ahead of it, leaving Jenna alone.

She didn't understand but took the chance she'd been given.

As the monster dragged itself past her, bringing smeared filth from outside but also dragged blood from where Ozzie had fallen, she was able to make her way to her feet and push herself flat to the nearest wall, next to what was left of a dresser unit. She had barely any cover but it was better than where she had been.

From her position she watched as the Ult lumbered forward despite all the weapons fire. The bullets seemed to be just washing off it. It reached forward with its 'arm' and grabbed out for any of the people who had been retreating into the room. Everyone knew that it would incinerate the life from them if it caught them so backed away as they continued the firing.

There was nowhere for them to go.

The windows to this room had been far too securely boarded up and the alien thing stood between the small group and the only exit. Everyone was going to die in this room. There was nothing anyone could do about that but that didn't mean Jenna was going to go down without a fight.

Picking up what was left of a giant metal water canister which was on the other side of the dresser, she forced every last inch of effort through her damaged body and smashed the canister down on the back of the Ult. It was going to be a futile effort but it was still going to do something. She could distract the beast for vital seconds and allow the others in the room to find a way out. She could strike a single blow against what had been responsible for the dismantling of her world and do it with her own hands.

Her movement was still sluggish but her systems were beginning to respond to her more normally so she was close to three quarters strength when she hit the monster.

The heavy canister impacted with a satisfying thud and Jenna smiled slightly at the now spongy sensation under the makeshift cudgel. The gun fire didn't slow as she attacked but it didn't matter to her. She knew she was far enough behind the Ult that it would give her cover from her colleagues but she had just accepted that she was going to go down swinging. Again and again she hit until the canister split open under the weight of her violence, it's now jagged edges cutting into the base of the Ult arm. She was going to make the Ult remember her.

But instead of the thing responding to her attack, it just stopped dead.

The massive bulk of the advancing horror suddenly became rigid and, after a bright pop of light and sound, collapsed to the floor, grasping arm now limp. It now looked like a meat balloon which had been partially deflated, more akin to a bean bag than any form of life.

It had been an eternity before anyone in the room dared move from their respective positions at the far wall or, in Jenna's case, standing over the now lifeless bulk. Seconds stretched on and all that filled the air was the heavy breathing of the stunned crowd.

Was that the last of them? How had they identified them here? How had they got in? What did Jenna do to stop it like that?

Slowly, gingerly, everyone edged forward and began to make their way to the side of the conquering hero and to take stock of the downed creature. Numerous gun muzzles remained trained on the mass and the tension thickened with every step.

“You OK?” Chang was by Jenna’s side, gun still on the Ult but he gripped her arm by way of reassurance.

Jenna dropped what was left of her Ult slaying weapon and nodded her response. She kept her eyes on the monster as she finally re-buttoned her shirt, though she truly felt that it wasn’t for her benefit but everyone else’s. The activities here today had been so minor in her head but she had been changed forever.

“Why isn’t it melting? What’s wrong with it?” Scott held a similar ready position to everyone else but the tip of his gun was waggling violently as he fought to control his muscles. His face was covered with sweat and he, more than any of the others there, was showing the effects of the fight.

“WHY ISN’T IT MELTING?” Scott became more insistent. He kicked the shape of the fallen Ult with his heavy boot but there was still no movement.

“Back off Scotty.” Chang soothed his comrade with equal parts kid gloves and iron gauntlet.

Throwing his weapon over his shoulder, Chang knelt down beside the creature and, after the smallest pause, dared to reach out a hand towards it. The hairs on his hand stood up as he closed the gap to the flesh of the creature, static electricity wrapped like a blanket over the corpse. That made him pause; stopping to take a look around at the group, hoping someone would recognise this sign as something. No one did.

His hand closed the distance to the bulk, down to three inches. Then two. Then one.

The jolt sent Chang tumbling backwards clutching his arm and caused Scott and Davis to fire an instinctive couple of rounds out of pure fright. Everyone else jumped at the shock. Everyone except for Jenna.

She remained motionless and just stared at the corpse.

She just stared.

Stared at the ruined mass of what had been conquering her world for so long. Stared at the meat it had just become and wondered why? The last bullets fired had shredded the flesh at point of impact and burrowed a destructive tunnel into the beast. Where they had previously bounced off, this time they had done what they did best and perforated flesh.

"WHY ISN'T IT FADING??!!??" Scott's voice was now so high that it was in danger of being audible only to dogs.

No-one answered.

There was silence, and that silence was only interrupted by the sound of Chang getting to his feet, and the cautious breaths of everyone else.

Chang was fast to drag everyone back to the here and now.

"I want everyone to sweep this house, roof to cellar, to understand how these things got in and to make sure there are no others. I also want a team of two to sweep the grounds. What defences did they trip? How did they get in here without us knowing? Complete in one hour and we meet in the southern end attic storage space for a briefing, I don't think this room will be fit for purpose for quite some time. Scott. Stay here and watch that thing. If you even smell it thinking about moving, shoot it."

It was easy to see why Chang was in charge. He was a placid man who enjoyed the quiet life but when push came to shove, he was more than willing to show he was made of iron and stone. The meetings had been descending into fractious cliques over the last couple of days and it had looked very much like there was going to be a very real split developing in the group, but now, after the attack and everyone being wired for more danger, what they all needed was someone to give them structure to get through the threat. Scott may have wanted to have his say and question every choice that was ever made, but when it came down to it, Chang would put his neck on the block.

There wasn't another word spoken, just an exchange of curt head nods and glances as people peeled from the group and made their way out to complete their tasks. Scott didn't move, the muzzle of his weapon held pointed at its target.

"Come on." Chang took Jenna's arm and gently led her from the room. Her steps were little more than shuffled attempts at dragging her feet and her whole body was turning to jelly thanks to the exertion. Jenna leaned into Chang as he guided her away from the carnage in the war room and felt a nauseating exhaustion wash through her. Whatever had happened here, she knew that everyone was going to be made to feel some kind of pain in their lives as they moved forward. All she could hope for was that the idea of embracing the tiniest sliver of humanity wouldn't be lost in the rush to avoid further Ult attacks.

She looked up at Chang as they moved slowly along but just didn't know what she could possibly say to him that would be the right choice.

Instead, that silence must have been enough for Chang to recognise what she was feeling. He just smiled slightly and hugged her tighter to him before adding,

"You need to lie down for the next hour."

12

In the smallest bedroom, perched far up and alone next to the storage space which was going to be the next meeting place, Jenna slept. She'd been so keyed up during the attack and the, whatever had happened next, that as soon as she lay down, sleep took her.

She dreamed of gunfire and bright light. Of watching the television as a child, and of Enterprise cloud. And of the Ult. She conjured up images of a sky full of attacking Ult ships that first came and began wiping out everything. Though there'd never been a single ship for anyone to see, Jenna filled the sky with fleets of them. The Arrival of the Ult hadn't been an overblown invasion from the silver screen, instead they just appeared. They'd gone from not existing one day, to then being there the next.

She could see waves of the advancing lumps of flesh and burning death that were the enemy who had made everything change for her. Her mental landscape showed her the monsters and re-ran the events of the day, each time showing her the action in a different way, a different speed. She was once herself, then Chang, then Scott, then the Ult. Each time she pictured what had taken place and did her best to understand what she was looking at but no matter what happened, the resolution just didn't come. The final piece of the jigsaw remained tantalizingly elusive.

The images continued to swirl through her head as she dreamed away the time until that giant black Ult loomed over her like a huge building forged of meat and violence. Its appendage slashed out towards her and blew her hair in every direction as the wind it created formed a hurricane.

Again and again, it made swipe after swipe to grip at her yet she leapt with agility and poise to avoid every attempt before turning and running. It followed her relentlessly, that awful

'ULT, ULT, ULT' coming from somewhere deep inside it as it pursued with the controlled determination of movie monsters who were always able to keep pace by walking when their quarry was running.

Other members of her team joined her in her dream, with Scott and Davis appearing next to her in the smoke of her mind, and with each attack, each of them was taken by that grasping arm and burned to ash, their screams filling her head with everything she wanted to run from, but the Ult kept coming.

It was never going to stop.

Since the Arrival, the Ult had been attacking all of the life on the planet. They had quickly destroyed any and all possibly strategic targets, power stations, military installations, even the largest cities as a whole were razed with a brutal efficiency. They just kept moving through all life on Earth. Humans and animals alike had been targeted by the invaders without any mercy or apparent pattern. They'd swept through the human race in rapid time but there had still been an attempt made to understand and learn about the enemy. It meant that a small database had been compiled on them by the ever dwindling group of survivors; information gleaned by contact and passed on in the hope that one day they could be beaten.

They never reacted to sound of any kind.

They made that repeating 'ULT' call but there was no idea where the sound came from.

They didn't seem to bother with movement unless it was a living creature which was doing the moving and as Jenna continued to flee in her dreams, she imagined it being able to see her body heat like another movie monster had been able to, but that idea had been tested and proved wrong.

She knew she had to wake up.

She knew she was in the midst of a terrible dream and knew she had to wake up.

She knew all of that but the Ult just wasn't going to let her escape, seemingly able to hold her so tightly with that grasping limb that she couldn't free herself from her own mind. She kept running as fast as she could before being joined now by all surrounding gunfire cracking through the quiet. Jenna screamed at the shock and joined with those who were firing the guns in their terror.

She was back in that room again and she did everything she could to find any kind of safety to dive into but the remembered experience played out just as she'd recalled.

How could they kill these things?

Looking at the creatures themselves there had been very basic research done and there were no ears or hearing apparatus of any kind. In fact there had been no sense organs discovered at all which could be identified. No-one had managed to understand the physiology of the monsters from the corpses recovered. They simply broke down to constituent parts whenever the Ult died, leaving more questions than answers. There was only a collection of rumours about the enemy of which, only a mere handful had proved to be correct.

The Ult remained a mystery to everyone.

Time and again, she re-started the dream of the action and reviewed exactly what had taken place until she played the part of herself again.

This time she started from the hail of fire at the appearance of the first creature. In super slow motion, she watched as muzzles flashed and metallic projectiles flew at and past her. She slowly forced herself to the ground as the threats of alien devastation and friendly fire warred around her, her body moving painfully slowly in her dreamscape. She made it to the ground just as her mind began to close down but this time she was able to pinpoint more detail.

From her point below the table top she was now able to make out the gun fire of at least two of her colleagues and they were now both firing downwards, closer to her and not at the previous height of the Ult. Why had they been doing that?

She pondered as the blackness closed in on this memory, preparing herself for the next step, of her waking up to a sharp pain, but as the curtains fell, at the very edge of her awareness, forgotten and unnoticed in all the action, was the barest feather light touch on her lower back. It was so light, so gentle that it was hard to decide if it had been there at all but as the film rolled on; the sensation remained and nagged at her.

The pain in her exposed chest brought her back to the action but she still considered that fleeting touch. It was still bothering her when the second Ult attacked but ignored her, all the way through to the would-be death blow from the water canister.

What was it?

She could practically see the one missing detail taunting her mind as she watched the pictures pass by again.

Eventually, Chang reached out to touch the body and Jenna was left with the hollow feeling of knowing she had almost uncovered something vital but would have to dream through the sequence again to try and make sense of it.

Chang extended his arm and this time, the bolt of shock that hit him was duplicated in her.

It smashed through her and she was heaved awake, sitting bolt upright on the small cot she had been resting on. The muffled sounds of voices could be heard coming from the next room so she must have been asleep for more than an hour. Gripping tightly to her dream, she could see the piece she'd been struggling for, the piece everyone had been struggling for. She knew what had happened and in turn, that had given her a calmness of understanding.

The meeting in the next room was well underway when she burst through the closed door. Everyone looked at her as she entered, a couple going for their guns out of pure reflex at the sudden sound.

"How long was I dead?" Jenna was speaking hurriedly, begging the others to answer with the same eagerness.

"Come and sit down," Chang soothed as he walked towards her, shaping to lead her from the room and back to her cot.

"You need to stay relaxed. You've been through quite enough already today."

She shrugged him off and repeated the question.

"I need to know. How long was I dead and how many times did you shock me?"

Silence.

Everyone looked between Chang and Jenna.

"Two minutes, and three times." It was Scott's voice who gave her the answer she had been after. She knew he'd probably done it just because everyone else had been trying to treat her with kid gloves but at least she'd been given the truth. Chang's expression showed that it was a truth he hadn't wanted her to have.

He shrugged as he did his best to draw some understanding from Jenna's expression, hoping to see an answer to her need in her features.

Jenna just frowned in concentration as she took in the details of her short lived demise. She'd died. For two minutes. She had fallen to the attack of the first Ult but her comrades, her friends, had brought her back.

"How did you know that your heart had stopped? Did someone tell you before you came in here?" Scott was quickly back into his stride of distrust. Jenna wasn't going to leave the room now, regardless of what Chang wanted. He seemed to see that as well so instead accepted defeat and brought her a chair instead.

Jenna accepted it gratefully and slumped into it, still very aware that her body wasn't anywhere close to being recovered.

"I just re-ran the attack through my mind and put the pieces together," she began and felt tightness spread through her chest as she worked for breath. She was quickly feeling VERY far from recovered.

"Besides, when I came to, I had my tits out and Chang was all sweaty next to me. It was either death or something we don't need to consider."

Despite the obvious seriousness of their overall situation, of the attack from the Ult, the possible wider threats beyond their walls, the deaths and injury which would have accompanied the attack and Jenna's death and salvation, the joke that Jenna had just cracked made at least half of the gathered crowd have to try and hide their giggles. She saw that as more proof that they were all more than just remaining alive.

Chang flushed a bright red at the unsaid suggestion from Jenna's joke and flustered his way back to his position from before she'd entered.

"Right team, enough of that," he coughed and brought order back.

"Jenna, before you arrived we'd been hearing from everyone who'd been out on their assignments around the compound and the upshot is those two Ult managed to dig a hole under the wall out at the end of parts storage. They'd been at a spot that was between the outlook posts for long enough to get the job done without anyone seeing from the outside or hearing from the inside. It's likely that they'd been there for a while what with all of the fun and games going on here since you guys got back."

Jenna nodded while taking stock of the details. It wasn't impossible but it seemed pretty unlikely that a single blind spot in their defences could be stumbled over by accident.

Lots to think about.

Chang continued.

"The damage has been assessed and there's already a team working on filling the hole in the ground and the wall. The rest of the house is pretty shot up as you'd expect but in the big picture, we didn't really lose that much."

"Try telling that to Ozzie," spat Scott from his position leaning up against the far wall, his arms folded across his chest and a sullen expression on his face.

Jenna wanted to punch him.

Prick.

"And we will mourn him Scott, but for now we need information and to keep a hold on the wins that we've had," offered Chang by way of both acknowledgement but also gentle rebuke, or at least that's what Jenna thought.

Scott continued though.

"Yeah, a great win that it was Jenna of all people who happened to be the one that felt the benefit of the defibrillator we found in Hope. Those things are rarer than rocking horse shit and it was so lucky for her."

He couldn't let it go.

"It is lucky for Jenna, but it's lucky for us all as well. Could you imagine the feeling here now if she'd died as well as Ozzie? Two deaths instead of one? How would we be feeling having to deal with that? Better? It would have been an improved position to be in?" Chang was still speaking in his usual calm fashion but everyone around the room could hear the new frost that blew in with each word he spoke. Scott didn't respond.

"Come on. Would we have been in a better position as a group if Jenna was dead?" Chang wasn't letting it go.

"You know what I meant," protested Scott, unable to meet anyone's eyes.

"No. What did you mean?"

Scott was ruffled badly by being forced into the spotlight but despite a pause, he continued,

"I meant that the choices Jenna made were likely the cause of our problems so her getting benefit beyond the rest of us doesn't seem very fair."

Chang had had enough.

Jenna had really had enough.

"Grow up Scott. You've always had a chip on your shoulder about everything that happens in your life but, Jesus man, choices that were made may have meant that we are where we are but it doesn't mean that people who made those choices should be blamed as if they had an active role. What if you'd wanted to leave Hope earlier and that had meant that you'd crossed paths with Ult out in the open and you'd been killed? Would that have been your fault?"

Scott this time kept his mouth shut and seethed at Chang in silence.

Chang nodded slightly to himself as Scott stayed quiet before turning all of his attention back to the rest of the room.

"Thank you everyone for what you all just did but I'm afraid that we're going to have to delay our further planning operations until we've got the house tidied up and liveable again. Keep your eyes open for anything out of the ordinary which could be something those Ult left behind but let's get this place back to being a home."

Everyone filed out of the room speaking quietly as they went, painfully aware of the increased horror their world was revealing to them but even despite all of those things stacked against them, there were a tiny number of laughs floating on the air. Dark humour it may have been but it was still humour after all.

She rose to leave the room as well but staggered with a wave of light headedness as her body expressed its own feelings on the idea. Chang was quickly to her side and supporting her.

“You sure you’re OK? You still look pretty pale.” He looked worried.

“I feel pretty battered but I suspect that I’m supposed to after the events of the morning, death notwithstanding.”

Chang smiled and began to walk her out of the room.

“Let’s get you down to the infirmary so someone with more idea than either of us can have a look at you,” said Chang gently, and Jenna just nodded, seeing that she needed some TLC. And that thought gave her cause to ask Chang as they made their way down the stairs.

“Why did you do it? Why did you make sure to save me and then tell everyone to go and get the place back to a home? You thinking about the humanity of the place?”

He kept walking them onwards but answered calmly.

“You’re not the only Star Trek fan you know.” His voice came out as a tender admonishment. He’d been telling her that surely she should have known this detail and that cemented in her mind that she was thinking the right way about the health of their people.

She had reached someone with her speech about living rather than existing after all.

Inside, she glowed with happiness at the thought of Chang reacting to her death by doing all he could to somehow get her revived. Maybe that would explain his slumped posture when she came to, exhaustion, yes, but also relief.

“I decided that I’d had enough of just sticking to the rations we’ve set for ourselves so just kept going. Your life was more than just an equation of reasoned parts. You’re a human being, we all are, and that’s something we need to remember.”

The slow journey through the house was painful due to her injuries but much more because of the huge damage that had been done in the defeat of the Ult invaders. The creatures had been travelling in a steady line from their entry point in the storage area towards the War Room where they’d eventually been stopped and the effects were all too clear to see. There were more bullet holes in walls, floors and ceilings than anyone could count, while there were spent shells and chewed up wood and masonry strewn everywhere making finding any kind of stable footing almost impossible. There were huge gouges in spots along the way as well but Jenna could recognise quite quickly that these hadn't come from weapons fire. The grasping arms of the Ult had been driven into the walls to rip the place apart, though as was all too familiar at this point, there didn't appear to be any reason or thought behind the actions. Maybe they were just trying to cause as much damage as they could because they liked it?

The infirmary was busier than it had ever been before when Chang led Jenna through the door. There may have only been the single death as a result of the attack but there were still other non fatal injuries that needed care. The room was filled now with the walking wounded, those who'd suffered cuts and bruises as a result of the defence of the place, but calling the wounds 'cuts and bruises' just didn't seem to convey the real level of suffering.

There were at least six people in the room, though there was a great deal of movement so there could have been a regular swapping of people, who had pristine white bandages wrapped around different parts of their bodies where that same bandage was steadily being soaked through with a stark red, blood continuing to escape. Calling these cuts and bruises conjured the picture of childhood injuries of the skinned knee or a small bump on the head which was very far from what had happened to these men. They all looked stoic in their pain, clearly far too familiar with the way triage worked but most likely also familiar with the idea of what could constitute a life threatening wound, they'd all been fighting for so long.

Was this just another day at the office for them?

One of the wounded, a man of medium height but skinny build, rose from his seat as soon as he noticed Jenna and offered it to her. His right arm was in a sling and the blood on the bandaging and sling suggested that there'd been a pretty large laceration to be dealt with. Jenna protested but his expression hardened.

"You look like you need this more than I do, now sit." He sounded determined enough that Jenna didn't even bother arguing. She appreciated the chair but knew he was never going to accept no for an answer. She thanked him and settled into the seat, feeling grateful to stop the hard work of locomotion. The man just smiled before adding,

"Besides, this is just a flesh wound. I've had worse."

Chang was off around the room looking for any of the medics who was the least busy when one happened to approach the now standing man with a small bag of tablets. Painkillers handed off, the wounded man gave his thanks before shouting to the whole room,

"Cheers all. Here's to the next time."

A small smattering of noise from the other wounded followed after him as he left.

The medic was already turned and heading back into the injured when Chang stopped him.

"Hey Artie," he greeted him as he practically threw himself into the path of the man.

"Any chance you can give Jenna the once over? There's no blood or broken bones but I think she needs to jump the queue."

Despite him having his back to Jenna, she could practically see the scepticism on his face. No blood or broken bones clearly didn't sound that serious and by the posture he took, it looked as if Artie was about to say that very thing, but instead, Chang spoke.

"She was the one we used the 'de-fib' on."

Jenna was still behind Artie but she could again understand his change in mood by the sudden stiffening of his shoulders and tilt to his head. Chang just flicked a glance over his shoulder to point him in the right direction and he turned rapidly before rushing to her side.

"You died." Artie's eyes were wide with any possible mix of fear, wonder, amazement, curiosity and likely any other emotion you could imagine as he checked Jenna's wrist for a pulse. His hand was shaking ever so slightly. It was fair to say that his bedside manner really needed some work.

"Come this way, I have a spare cot you can use while we have a better look at you." Maybe the pulse check had revealed something to him? Maybe he was just really excited? Either way, Jenna was helped to her feet and led across the room between the other people hanging around towards the large curtain which was hanging across the far end of the room.

Beyond that, leaving what was effectively the emergency area behind, they entered into what passed as a ward. There were four beds set up for longer term guests who may have needed care but there'd never been a need to use them before, what with house calls being someone just walking down a few corridors, but now two of the beds were occupied.

Mary and Mo just lay still in their beds, breathing steadily but without any further sign of life, and seeing them made Jenna jump a little. There'd been just so much going on that the first victims of the Ult here had slipped her mind and that shock seemed to make things that little bit worse. Her head swam a little and her vision began conjuring patterns of light around the two of them. She was really still feeling the effects of her near death. Or was it just her death? She didn't really know but felt it was important to know what to say. Artie didn't allow for further pause and moved her to the next bed along the wall where she lay back on the rough blanket and tried to rest.

What followed was Artie listening to her heart beat with a stethoscope he had to borrow from one of the other medics as there weren't enough to go around, recording her temperature, filling in records he was making up on the fly, and doing everything he could to try and keep everyone, including himself, as calm as he could. Chang was worried as he watched on, that was clear and you couldn't really blame him after the events of the day, but even he was throwing glances at Jenna as Artie's actions escalated his concern, his fear, his everything.

Jenna just lay back and tried to relax.

She'd always accepted that bad things could happen to her at some point along the way but there was never really that readiness for said bad things to actually take place. The risks in her life were always that nebulous knowledge that told her that she could die, just like any number of people she'd seen go the same way, but when her number finally came up, she was completely in shock. She considered that it may have been that she'd been enjoying the ideas of the good times that made her want to cling to life more tightly? Maybe it was just the basic idea that everyone seems to imagine that 'it'll never happen to me'? Whatever the reason, she wanted so badly to keep on living because it was too fucking valuable a thing to stop doing.

The light touch on her arm, followed by the slight shake, drew her attention and made her realise that during the mayhem of Artie buzzing around her and the come down from the adrenaline of the attack, she'd fallen asleep. Opening her eyes she took stock of her view of the ceiling of the infirmary while taking some time to explore how her body felt. Her chest ached, as you'd expect after the events of the day, but beyond that, everything felt OK. There was a slight buzzing in her ears and a strange taste in her mouth and as she began to ease herself into a sitting position, she could recognise that the previous noise of the infirmary had been replaced with silence and that she was now under the blanket.

Looking around the room, she was now alone, save for Mary and Mo. Chang had been stood beside her but he was nowhere to be seen now so what she'd thought of as nothing more than a snatched snooze had lasted a little longer.

"Hello?" she called out and crossed her fingers that there was someone nearby to answer. From the other side of the curtain, there was a muffled expletive, the sound of a chair scraping the floor, and the shattering of glass before Artie bustled through to answer her call.

"You're awake. How are you feeling? You must have really needed the rest." His bedside manner was a little better this time, most likely thanks to the other wounded having left the room so he had fewer problems to face.

Jenna just smiled slightly before answering with a nod and rubbed at her eyes. She was still a little blurry and she could swear that Artie was glowing. Not quite as recovered as she'd thought then.

"I'm still a bit fuzzy headed but I've just woken up so that's kind of expected. What time is it?" Jenna was going to get herself back into the world, and shoved the blanket from her before swinging her legs out.

Artie let her carry on but hovered with a concerned look on his face.

"It's a little after eight in the evening and by what I can discover, you seem to be OK but we'll have to keep an eye on you for the next few weeks. You got very lucky indeed that

Frankenstein's defibrillator worked well enough to keep you ticking."

The rest of her clothes were folded on the chair next to her cot and she was quick to get herself dressed. Despite the importance of looking after the very nature of her humanity rather than just being happy to be alive, she had to admit to herself that she had to be up and moving again and learning more about what had happened. Slipping her boots on, she stood upright and gave herself a little head rush which made that glow on Artie flash a little brighter, but she was happy to at least be up and about so didn't make a fuss and risk Artie exploding through panic. Besides, it settled down back to the original level pretty quickly.

"Are you sure you don't want to spend any more time with us down here?" asked Artie, looking like medically, he didn't know what the correct course of action should be, but that he was aiming on the side of caution, again, just in case. Jenna smiled slightly and thanked him for what he'd done in looking after her.

"I'm just really keen to get out and see what's happened to the place. I feel a bit in the dark after the attack."

Artie nodded his understanding and bustled back through the hanging curtain.

"I'll sort you out some pain killers but I'd absolutely suggest that you don't do anything strenuous for a few weeks," floated through the air as he rifled through drawers looking for whatever pills he thought could at least make things feel a little better. In no time, he was back through the makeshift barrier with a small bag of pills for Jenna.

"I was also kinda looking forward to have someone to talk to for a little while," he said as he handed them over.

Jenna took the bag and could sympathise with him.

Everyone who worked in here would have been spending their time either facing any and all suffering which could possibly come through the door, or having to watch over Mary and Mo. She didn't want to really admit it to herself, but she'd felt the weight of their presence in the room with her from the second that she'd woken up, and had been doing everything she could to not fall beneath the weight of guilt she felt at what had happened to them.

"Thanks Artie. I'll be back down here at the very first sign of trouble, don't worry." She tried to smile without letting on about how she felt and headed for the door before there were any further questions.

She was certain that it was going to take weeks to fully repair all of the damage that had been done throughout the building, though she fully expected that the outer wall had been sealed up again by now. The volume of bullet holes in walls etc. would likely need a Hell of a lot longer, while a bigger assessment of any structural damage was conducted. At least they still had The Beast, she didn't fancy trying to bring in supplies without that.

The thought of The Beast brought to mind the trip to Hope and in turn, the people who she'd travelled with. Scott was becoming a problem for everyone and she wondered what he'd been able to do while she'd been asleep. Surely there'd be the cool heads of the group who'd be able to keep him and anyone who was listening to him quiet.

She sighed as she reached the door of infirmary. Her mind was racing with worry and she hadn't even left the room yet. Artie would have had a fit if he'd known.

Taking one last look into the room, Artie pushed through from the other side of the hanging curtain and for a brief second, Jenna was able to see Mary and Mo lying still in their beds. They just looked to be peacefully asleep but Jenna's mind was rapidly forced to scramble for any further information she could glean as it became clear that there was so much more too them than just that.

Her mouth dropped open as she was confronted by a diaphanous, glowing stream of electrical light crackling slowly around them which looked as if it were spiralling upwards and on through the ceiling. They were glowing like Artie had been, but they looked more like their 'glowy' stuff was drifting up and away.

Maybe she needed longer in the infirmary after all?

13

Artie had returned to his desk and as he sat down, he noticed Jenna still staring back at the two on their beds. He just assumed she was saying a few words to herself and that she was going on her way but she instead just stood looking, her jaw working and her brow creased in thought.

"Everything OK?" he asked.

Jenna snapped out of her trance like state and looked at him hard. The expression on his face said he was concerned for her health but Jenna also expected that he could have the hope of a new companion rekindled if she was unwell, but hopefully not too unwell. He was still glowing, but that glow was beginning to becoming sharper, more detailed, and was wound all around and through his body giving him a steady yellow hue, matching the colour coming from the others.

"Uhh ....." she stammered through the confusion, not sure what she was seeing but also not sure if it meant anything at all.

Artie just looked on as his question hung between them, still unanswered.

Finally Jenna chose the best course of action.

"Just having a last look is all. Cheers Artie" and she waved while speeding out of the door.

Walking down the corridor from the infirmary, Jenna didn't know what to think. She'd seen some odd stuff in the infirmary but that could have just been down to the fact that she'd just come to and her head was still fuzzy, what with the small matter of her death and all. The light in the house in general was always low because all the possible ways for it to get in had been sealed up against the Ult so maybe she'd just seen a reflective glow from materials on Artie's clothes. That would also mean that the same small particles could have been what was around Mary and Mo as well. They'd looked different because they'd been lying down and were breathing straight up all of the time. She needed to make sure she was recovering well enough but that would lead to her eyes getting back to normal but it was likely just the room she'd been in.

Certainly nothing to worry about.

She rounded the next corner and decided to head through the wrecked section of the house towards the outside compound to get some fresh air and hoped that would clear her head.

The walls, the floor, the ceiling, everywhere she looked as she moved through the damaged section of the house, stood as a stark reminder of what just two of those things had been capable of. There was still a smell of dusty age hanging in the air and as she walked, despite the efforts of all those who'd been tasked with the clean up, and even in the low light afforded by the lanterns in the corridor, tiny specks of dust hung in the air in pluming clouds, making sure there was still proof that something terrible had happened here. Walking past what was left of the wall of the War Room, the gaping hole which had replaced the doorway had been covered by thick plastic sheeting to stop people from seeing in and as she passed it by, she shuddered at the memories that swam through her head. Ozzie being killed and then what had been left of him, the Ult monsters dragging death with them, and then her own injuries. Picking up speed, she put that place behind her and did her best to concentrate on the here and now. She couldn't help wonder what had happened to that one Ult body though.

Out in the compound, there was a steady rain drenching anyone or anything which may have the misfortune to encounter it. Puddles were forming at the usual spots and judging by the steady pour of water from a point at the centre of the canopy above, part of the guttering was blocked. Jenna stood back against the wall and hugged herself against the cold night air. Her breath fogged out clouds as she cast an eye around looking for anyone she could talk to and get a grip on what was going on. There was the usual low light out here as well but there was no glowing presence or clouds of dust to worry about and that tiny detail made Jenna smile. Her head must have been clearing.

She couldn't make out any noise to hint that people were working and considering the weather, it made sense that only the most vital tasks which couldn't be postponed would actually be happening. Everyone was inside somewhere.

Turning to head onwards with her search for people, she took her first step and walked directly into Davis who'd been coming through the door the other way. He 'Ooffed' and took a step back while Jenna shouted a handful of very meaty swear words before slapping a hand over her mouth.

"Hey. Artie said you'd left looking for action," said Davis, smiling at her startled reaction.

"How you feeling?"

Jenna just shrugged.

"Thought I was further along in my recovery but still moving, so I call that a win," she replied and rubbed at her eyes.

Davis smiled casually that at least she was on the road to recovery even if not at the final destination.

"Chang's asleep and most of the place is on down time after the attack so we've pretty much got the run of the place. So what you want to do now?" he continued, reminding Jenna very much of an old memory she had of her father when she'd been a kid. Back then, it had felt like the whole world had been a real possibility regardless of what she had asked of her father, and in the here and now, Davis was giving similar vibes of conspiratorially wanting to let her go wherever she wanted.

That tiny kernel of excitement flared ever so gently in her stomach at the idea of possibly going to places that she wouldn't normally and the possibilities that opened up were almost too many to deal with.

But only almost.

"I think we should see how the attack unfolded. I haven't been a part of any of the efforts to repair or understand so I think that I should walk through it all. Let's head to where the Ult got in and work our way back."

Davis nodded his agreement and turned to lead the way through the house. Jenna could have sworn that he seemed a little excited as well but as she watched his back as he walked, her own excitement was being tinged very badly by the long filaments of glowing yellow energy that spread all over him. His entire body was covered in them and whatever progress she may have thought had been made in her healing had clearly not been real. If anything, it felt worse now because she was seeing more and more detail in the source of the glow, tiny strings of soft light spread everywhere on Davis. Fishing out one of the tablets from the bag she'd been given, she swallowed and hoped she wasn't losing her mind.

Walking into the store room which had been the breach point for the Ult, all she could see was shelving units and boxes piled up against the furthest interior wall, opposite the repaired hole in the outer wall. It never failed to impress her when she considered the level of ingenuity that must have been on display to get to this point. The repair was certainly ragged around the edges and it was all too clear to see that there'd been acts of cannibalisation from the house to find spare material to be able to plug the gap, but deep in the very DNA of the job that had been done was that burning core of human problem solving thought. It was 'make do and mend' but on steroids and it made her feel a fierce sense of pride in the people she lived with.

The floor through the room still bore the scars of the creatures breaking in. There were scuffs in the bare concrete where the Ult dragged themselves and whatever filth they'd picked up as they moved, and despite the efforts of everyone to clean the floor fully, there were still occasional smears of dark mud. Davis lifted a lantern he'd brought from outside to give as wide a view of the room as he could and they both just stood and took in the details in silence.

"Doesn't look like there was much of anything done in here beyond them getting in. Did anyone find anything of note before they cleaned everything up?" Jenna was back on the case, her mind working more like it usually did as she took in the room before her.

"Not that I've been told," replied Davis. "Though I was only about for the earliest part of the clean up after the breach was sealed up, so beyond that there may be some new info but I haven't seen it." It was non-committal but still clear enough. Non-committal because he wanted to stick to the most cautious road, just in case. Jenna glanced at Davis as he spoke and watched on with a sense of wonder at whatever was going on with her eyes which was wreathing Davis in colour. Whatever that problem was that she had, it still looked really cool.

"Jen?" asked Davis, his head tilted and his eyes worried.

Jenna shook her head and snapped out of the tiny stare she hadn't really noticed she was falling into. Whipping her head away from him and back to the room ahead of them, she strode ahead and began to look around the space.

"Sorry, was trying to work something out."

Boxes were moved and then put back, shelving was shifted, helped greatly by the fact the units had wheels, and then put back and the repair was examined as she and Davis went about their due diligence of taking in all of the site as it was left. They found nothing of note.

Eventually, they both stopped and shared a glance which said they'd had enough, and were just leaving the room when, as Davis left with the lone lantern, the room fell into a much thicker blackness and there, above the doorway, on the wall far up near the ceiling, was a small patch of gently glowing, something. Jenna stopped rigid and couldn't take her eyes from the spot which radiated a subtle yellow shine.

What the Hell was it?

She shouted Davis back into the room as her mind whirred through any and all possibilities of what she was seeing. Whatever that was on the wall, she finally recognised that it was the first thing that she'd seen that had been giving off that glow that wasn't a person.

Pointing at the spot as Davis came in with the lantern and almost obscured the tiny glow, she was scared to ask her question.

"What's up there Davis? Right up at the top of the wall?"

He lifted the lantern closer to the spot though he was still several feet from it, and concentrated his attention.

"Nothing. Looks like a dark smudge of something but considering what came through here I wouldn't be surprised if it was just mud. Why d'you ask?"

Jenna didn't know what to think now.

She'd seen the glow from the spot up there so there had to be something going on. Or did there? Maybe it was further proof that her mind was going wonky and she was just seeing things? Maybe she needed to go back to the infirmary after all?

Recognising that his friend was clearly struggling with something and not wanting to tread on her toes, Davis passed the lantern to her and moved her further back into the room before hunting out a ladder he'd seen as they'd been searching. He fixed it in place and headed up the steps quickly towards the spot that had spooked Jenna.

From below, Jenna watched him go but couldn't pick out the glow to aim him correctly, the light in the room, though very low, was still too much.

"Hang on Davis. I'm going to put the lantern outside so I can see better, it's too bright."

Davis, who was now at the top, looked back down at her, growing more unsure of her actions. Making the room darker very rarely meant better vision. Looking up, Jenna's expression suggested she at least knew she wasn't making the best sense so that was something. Don't they say that if you think you're going crazy then that means that you're not?

Davis just stood waiting for Jenna to tell him what she'd seen and he'd go from there.

With the room again sunk back into the near total black of darkness, that area of glowing yellow was again visible for Jenna to pinpoint. It was a little way to the left and above where Davis was stood but he was easily close enough to be able to see what was going on.

"Can you see anything strange up there?" Jenna asked and Davis cast a quick look before replying that he didn't.

"Does that spot still look like mud from up close?"

"It's hard to see clearly but it just looks like a scuff mark. It looks pretty dull actually." Davis was hoping he was sounding reassuring with what he was saying but it really did look just like the most mundane little smear. He reached out a hand to see if he could rub it off but Jenna's scream from below him made him almost fall off the ladder. Wobbling wildly while clinging to the ladder with one hand made Davis look like a very low rent rodeo rider but it had at least stopped him from touching the spot on the wall.

“What the fuck was that about?” he spat out as the ladder settled beneath him. His eyes were wide and he was breathing fast so was clearly not happy.

“Sorry. I think you can come down now, and we need to keep this room shut up until I can speak to everyone.”

Davis started down, his anger quickly melting away.

“What was it up there? What did you see?”

Jenna took a deep breath to steady herself but she knew she had to speak to people about her situation.

“I think that that thing up there is the same stuff that was on top of The Beast and hurt Mary and Mo.”

Davis just looked at her blankly, hoping for more information.

“I saw a glow coming from it but when you reached out to touch it, that glow began to reach out for you as well. It was reacting to you and I could see,” she paused. There really was no turning back. “I could see that the glow in you was starting to draw towards it as well.”

Davis let his mouth loll open and managed only a ‘Huh?’ in response.

“I think I need to speak to Chang and a few others but, there’s something pretty weird going on.”

14

Jenna spent the night in the infirmary again, keen to have someone with a little medical knowledge and the right equipment on hand should something else happen but Artie had just leapt at the chance to have someone else to talk to. It had taken about an hour for Jenna to burn through her patience to his machine gun questioning about anything and everything which crossed his mind and she needed something to act as a distraction, as much for her as it was for him.

Mary and Mo were still in their beds and their glows had sharpened in detail too, making it all too easy to see the threads of golden energy being wound into funnels up, up and away from them. She still didn't understand what was happening but she was beginning to develop the first steps of an idea.

Finally, mainly to get Artie to leave her alone, she asked him if he had any books or notes on the Ult and their biology she could have a read through. She heard that there were new papers in the stack from Hope and would like to have the chance to read through them if they were at hand. Artie beamed like a delighted child at the thought that someone was keen to explore, well, if not medicine exactly it was certainly medicine adjacent. After a couple of moments of hurried movement, he deposited a pile of papers and notebooks on her bed before stepping back with a triumphant expression on his face, like a dog presenting its master with the ball they'd just thrown. Jenna was about the thank him and dive into the words when that expression cut through her mind like a knife.

He was happy.

He was excited for someone to look through things he was interested in and he was almost bursting at the sheer simple connection that this interaction was having on him. He was happy and wanted to share his enjoyment with someone and that simple connection was something that Jenna had been about to step on just to have him leave her alone. She thanked him for his help and reminded herself to try and be a bit softer with him in future.

The next few hours were spent with her head buried in the words and drawings on the rough collection of pages that had been drawn together as an information source on the Ult. There were pictures of the anatomy, as much as they could have been able to see before the things melted away at their deaths, charts of sizes, of colours, of possible campaigns they may have been running and even a speculation on their food, and even their life span. She found at least three hypotheses covering the likely point of origin of the lumbering monsters and then the possible methods which had been used to convey them to Earth since there'd never been any invading armada discovered at any point. They were so alien that they just had to *be* aliens.

Artie bid her a fond farewell as he finished his shift and was replaced by someone she wasn't sure she'd ever met before. Whoever he was, he just confirmed she was OK before setting himself up with a book of his own to read and let her get on with her work. Just like Artie and Davis, he was covered with that same yellow glowing pattern which was rapidly becoming less abnormal.

Page after page painted the most basic picture possible of what had happened since the first days after The Arrival. These things had been just relentless in their pursuit of all life on the planet and had wiped out billions of lives. They'd also caused the relative regression of human technology as cities fell and those people left did everything they could to survive while they hid rather than fought back. She didn't know what the time was when she finally grew tired enough to sleep but she took another pill from her bag before giving her new medic friend a salute and settled down for as much rest as she could manage.

Her dreams were filled with images of attacking Ult soldiers marching towards what small band of fighters she could scrape together against them, of hundreds of people being rendered utterly immobile by the Ult cure and even of Enterprise cloud being unable to beat back the real enemies of humanity. The people around her all had that same glowing structure on them and while she walked through the lines of beds in the endless wards of the still people, they all had the same funnel of yellow being sucked up and together to be formed into a huge candy floss cloud several storeys high. The gentle rocking on her arm was a welcome relief to bring her out of that dreamscape and seeing Chang looking down at her was even better.

Even if he too had that same glowing pattern on him as well.

“Morning sleepy head,” he greeted her as she rubbed at her eyes to banish the last of the sleep.

“I hear that you had a pretty eventful night.” He was concerned but was happy to be speaking with her. She felt that this whole terrible series of events had at least cemented in her mind that Chang was indeed her friend.

Smiling back at him, she pushed the blanket away and climbed out of bed so she could get dressed while she spoke. She was too energised to sit still and the words tumbled wildly from her as she spoke.

“I’m feeling fine but I think that there’s been something big happen to me. We need to get our brain trust together so I can run through what I think has been happening.”

Chang looked intrigued.

“How big is the thing and do we need to be worried? Are you in danger?” Intrigued he may have been but he was also thinking with his leader hat on.

“As far as anyone can be sure about anything medical, I’ll need to be careful for a few weeks but having your heart re-started will do that to everyone. And the big thing that happened, I think I can see what the Ult see, and I think I know what they’re doing.” Jenna fastened her boots and stood up looking eye to eye with Chang. He was still intrigued but now he was showing no little amount of worry. Not fear quite yet but he wasn’t far off.

He bit his lip gently as he considered what she’d said.

“Fine. I’ll get everyone in the meeting room upstairs in one hour and you can tell us what you think. We need to arrange for supply runs anyway so the meeting can get that off the ‘To Do’ list.” He was in leader mode as he spoke but he gave her a reassuring squeeze of her hand as well.

“And as for the brain trust,” he continued while turning to leave the room. “Scott and Emily have been whipping up the fear everywhere because they're terrified themselves, so just be careful how you go about this. Everyone's on edge."

Great!

Fifty nine minutes later, Jenna sat patiently in the new meeting room at the top of the house and waited. Chang was there and she'd explained everything to him during the time they'd been waiting. There were a couple of other people too, Selina and Mark, who smiled pleasantly at her while the seconds ticked by. Scott, Emily and whoever else was missing, Jenna just assumed were all now a part of their new faction who just wanted to close themselves away behind the walls because anything else was just too dangerous. She took a steadying breath and continued to wait. They may not all be a part of a group which is looking to overthrow the current power structure and banish Jenna because they held her personally responsible for everything. They may not want to attend for another reason all together that she wasn't aware of.

On sixty one minutes, the door to the room opened up and a column of people trooped slowly in, led by Scott with Emily close behind. They were just late then.

Jenna wasn't sure if that was better or worse.

Everyone settled themselves into the chairs, and then any available spots they could find, and waited. No-one looked happy and as Jenna scanned everyone around her, not one of them would meet her eyes except for Emily, who appeared to want to do her harm. Each was festooned with their own glowing tendril pattern that added to her certainty.

The door clicked shut finally and they were sealed inside.

"Thanks for the quick movement to get together so fast everyone. I know we're all busy but Jenna has some thoughts she'd like to share with us all about the events of the last few days." Chang spoke with the authority of a leader but the looks around the room suggested that he wasn't quite as able to keep a grip on everyone as Mary had been. Emily just 'tutted' and folded her arms across her chest.

"Jenna. Would you run through the details that you've put together please?"

All eyes turned to face her and there were many more scowls and folded arms. She didn't bother standing to explain everything and instead just carried on.

"After the attack, I've spent some time in the infirmary so I could be observed after my temporary death and I've done some reading on the Ult notes that were brought back from Hope and anything that we had on hand, and I think that I've worked out something about what the Ult are after." She paused to let the suggestion sink in for everyone around the table but no-one said anything.

"The Ult are following our electricity." Jenna started her explanation again and did her best to keep the frustration from her words.

"When they first attacked us they took out power stations and attacked big cities etc. We all thought they were just going after population centres and strategically valuable targets as part of a military attack, something like what we'd do if we were going to do the same on another planet. They were just going after the power. That's why Las Vegas was one of the first places hit. There's so much electricity coursing through that place you could probably see it from another galaxy." That was the first time she'd made a joke about one of the details of her ideas but Scott didn't react. To be fair to him, he didn't react negatively but instead remained passive to what was being said. Emily still wanted to kill her though.

Jenna continued.

"Since we started to function without the modern comforts of the twenty first century, they've been less aggressive. Every attack has come about when they had a direct view of something or someone. Think about the details we've been told by everyone who's been through here. The lightning fast attacks as they just seem to be at the right place at the right time, just grabbing people. The sieges, where they get drawn to a place, following the electrical signals of a person who'd been caught in the open, and then disappearing from their sight by returning to a hideout. All they do is just wait around until the electrical signal reappears. Sure, they've banged against walls where people may have disappeared but the sieges were always broken by people trying to fight their way out, either by trying to kill the enemy or because they'd run out of supplies."

Around her, furtive glances were being shared between everyone at what was being laid out before them. Jenna had to admit that it was going to be a tough job to, at best, get everyone on side with the new ideas about their enemy but now was the time to really go for the big twist.

"And I think that after my incident, I think that somehow, though I'm very far from certain, I've been changed so I can now see like the Ult do."

That last detail was what burst the bubble of calm.

Gasps, scraping of chairs, muttered mumbles of comment between friends, and uncomfortable movements filled the room before Emily slammed her hands down on to the table and silenced everyone.

"So you brought back a disease from Hope which puts people into a coma, then likely attracted the Ult to come here by your 'Let's all go and day dream' antics up in the high window, while amazingly being lucky enough to be saved by that battered old defibrillator, which is now out of charge and useless for the rest of us. All that and now you're telling us that through all of the fighting and repairs, you've been able to figure out something no-one else has ever managed by doing a bit of reading while you lay in bed. And you now share physical abilities with the enemy? You truly are blessed with luck, aren't you?"

The voices around the table all erupted at the same time as soon as she finished the final question. Through the cacophony of noise, all words seemed to mix together into a single soup though the occasional snippet was still clear enough to pick out.

"....... Ult ...."

".......traitor ...."

"..........careless........"

".......death........"

".........bitch......"

Jenna just sat and watched as the mob boiled with anger. She clenched her fists under the table, hoping to keep her calm in place but also to be ready to start throwing punches should the need arise. Chang was starting to try and defend her but his voice was nothing ahead of the wave of rage that was whipping around them all and eventually he sat back and just looked at Jenna with an expression of equal parts resignation and reassurance. Selina and Mark just sat still, looking nervous.

Finally, the storm winds began to recede and the voices ceased.

Chang stood up and let everyone just see him.

"Finished?" He sounded tired.

Emily shot to her feet and pointed an accusing finger at him.

"Finished? After what she's been involved in? How dare you," she screamed and flecks of spit flew as she spoke.

"Sit down Emily, please. You're not helping anything and all you're doing is shouting someone else's fears because they haven't got the backbone to do it themselves." Chang's voice was still tired but there was no way to miss the razor edge to it either.

No-one had expected that kind of response from Chang, nor the angry glare he gave Scott, and it became akin to a slap across the face for Emily, who withered back to her seat while turning redder and redder in the face.

No-one else wanted to meet Chang's eyes and Scott just kept his attention firmly on his hands.

"Jenna, will you carry on please?"

This time she did stand up, just to make herself feel bigger and therefore harder to attack.

"Whatever it was that happened with the defibrillator, I don't understand it any more than anyone else but since the attack, I've been able to see the electricity that's running through each and every one of us like it's an overlay to normal vision and I think that's how the Ult see the world."

"So it was your fault that those two Ult came here? They saw your electricity from your Rapunzel act." Scott had made his point with devastating ease. He hadn't even looked up from his hands when he'd done it. Jenna stumbled over her thoughts briefly before coming back.

"I don't think so," she replied and hoped her voice hadn't cracked.

"I think the Ult cure, the disease that's appeared, I think it was that that made them come because of what I saw in the infirmary."

Jenna's pause was a perfect place for everyone to dive on her again but this time no-one spoke. Everyone was still angry but at least they'd decided to keep their mouths shut so they could hear the entire story.

"I can see that same pattern on everyone, of the electrical charge that's running through our bodies, in our nerves and muscles, and for the most part, we all have exactly the same pattern going on, but Mary and Mo don't. When I look at them I can see a spiralling glow spreading up from them and into the ceiling. I checked the room above and it just kept going on and up. I couldn't see anything when I went outside, I reckon the light is so low that you can only see it in the dark, but to the Ult, they only see the electricity so it's likely a beacon for them."

She remained standing and felt that she was doing well.

"So the disease that was brought back because of choices you made was the cause of the attack?" Scott still didn't look up from his hands when he spoke and that seemed to make his words hit that much harder. Mumbles rippled across the crowd slowly and Jenna was getting tired of his sniping.

"I agree my choices would have contributed to the cure getting here. That would also mean that everyone of the team would be equally to blame as everyone's choices would have had a part to play. Wouldn't everyone agree?"

That did make Scott look up, and his eyes flared with fire.

"Don't try and divert the blame you feel onto anyone else. We can all see through it," spat Emily and folded her arms over her chest while fixing an impossibly smug 'shit-eating' grin on her face.

Jenna took a long, steadying breath and tried to keep her own anger in check.

"So how does your eyesight mean that the cure is anything special? Those things don't have to be connected do they?" This time it was Selina asking the question but it was a fair one. She wanted to understand the logic behind why Jenna had arrived at the point she had.

"Because I found a small patch of that same cure material down in the storage area where those Ult dug their way in, and ..." she didn't get the chance to continue further as the crowd burst forth with rushed questions about safety and further innuendoes about Jenna's motives. Chang raised his hands and let the group calm down before allowing Jenna to continue.

"And, before I was able to cordon the room off so no-one else was at risk, Davis and I investigated and discovered that the light that it was emitting, much like the electrical charges we all do, moved towards Davis when he got close to it. It suggested to me that this stuff was attracted to something rather than just being inert. It was reaching out like flowers do when they grow to follow the sun."

Selina nodded very slightly as she mulled over what she'd been told but looked very much to be understanding what Jenna had meant.

"You still haven't explained why we should imagine that your claims about what you can see mean anything more than you having had a head injury," spat Emily, again sounding every inch the petulant child.

"Because, whatever happened to me came about after contact with one of the Ult. I don't know what happened, I was in the process of diving for cover, but I suspect that I was touched by one of the attackers and it passed on the cure, but because of the defibrillator, I didn't get locked in like Mary and Mo."

Around the table there still sat a great many people who saw her as being the one most to blame for the predicament they were all in but no-one was speaking now. Jenna pushed on, crossing her fingers as she did.

"I know that there still needs to be a load of testing done to see if this is even close to being accurate and that we're in the middle of a much bigger problem than we first thought but depending on what we discover, we could be in a great position to start making advancements against the Ult, and that can mean we start living again rather just existing."

Emily grunted from behind the wall of her folded arms, though Jenna didn't care. She was aiming at everyone else rather than Scott and Emily who'd already made up their minds and would never change regardless of what was laid out before them, truth be damned.

"We are indeed in a dangerous situation and one which is going to mean a great deal more thought and, indeed, risk, but we've got to all pull together to get around this," said Chang from his seat as he looked at each person in the room in turn.

"Jenna, there's going to need to be tests carried out to determine what you can and can't do and everyone in this house is going to have to get in line as we make arrangements to survive our new circumstances. Each and every one of us is going to be doing masses of jobs but at the core, I want us to be able to hold on to our humanity. This could be the greatest advantage we've ever seen against the Ult, which in turn means that we could be a significant step closer to stamping them out. We're not going to just close the doors and cower behind them here until we all die."

He looked up and around at the group on the final word of the sentence, casting his speech out over the whole team.

"We're all in. From now on we live rather than exist."

He injected a tiny sliver of his management voice into the words and they came out as a booming rallying point. He was used to having to motivate people, and to Jenna's surprise and joy, there were more than a few faces that actually seemed to be, not fully agreeing with what was being said, but were softening their expressions of resistance.

"What about the resources we're going to burn through? Most of our food came from Hope. We could 'exist' for years by being frugal, but 'live' for only months." Scott was the first to voice the fear but, despite Chang, he hadn't been the only one in the room thinking it. Emily sat smugly next to him almost daring anyone to speak against the idea.

"We can't turn our last days into a party just because. We owe it to the next generation to create a solid base for them."

Jenna knew that he knew that wasn't what she'd meant by the whole live not exist thing but he was just wilfully ignorant. Prick.

Despite the way he'd framed his point, he did indeed still have a point.

They'd just brought back loads of supplies from Hope but it was clear that the city was now lost as a trading and meeting outpost. The information gleaned from Hope suggested that most, if not all, of the pockets of human life throughout their little corner of the world had been lost to the new Ult disease so there was no telling how they were going to be able to maintain life here if they were forced to become fully self-sufficient. There would have to be changes to give the next generation of people a chance.

"What next generation? We haven't got any kids running around here." It had been spoken quietly, barely above a whisper, but it was a dark bell that tolled into the room. Mark was a man of few words but he'd certainly made them count.

"There's no-one left."

Jenna again felt the need to drag them all back onto the path of thought she'd been walking, before everyone lost all hope.

"We're in the shit right now, we all know that," she began. "But we need to be looking at ways to move forwards rather than just stopping, and I think that my 'situation' could mean something more than just pretty pictures for me."

More silence.

"Look," and she was on her feet pacing the room as she spoke. "Why didn't the second Ult attack me when I was on the floor? It just stumped right on past and didn't even register that I existed. They've never done that before to my knowledge. They've followed on relentlessly and attacked the dying, even when they've been of no further threat. And why was I able to do whatever it was I did to it just by hitting it with a flask?" She paused and looked around at the confused faces, each which looked back like a class of children who'd been given an awful puzzle to solve and were now looking for the answer.

Another idea crossed Jenna's mind.

"Its body's still down there isn't it? Doing nothing. Not fading, just laying there, even after all this time."

"So?" Scott was asking the question but he didn't hold any real force as he spoke. Even he must have known the importance of what that fact had meant.

"The fact that it's still there means that something big has changed for it to behave in a new way. Doesn't anyone want to try and find out what it could be?"

Now those people who had been at least considering her words were starting to nod. Things were changing indeed.

15

The rest of the meeting was quickly deferred so everyone could get back to whatever they'd been doing, but mainly so a group of people could start with the exploration of the Ult corpse which was still lying where it had fallen during the attack.

Jenna had been the first to push through the black plastic sheeting which had been attached to the wreckage of the doorway into the former War Room, but Chang, Selina, Emily and finally Scott had all followed close behind.

The first thing each of them noticed as they pushed through was the smell. The mound of flesh which had once been chasing them in here was now beginning to rot and the all too familiar odour of putrid meat was thick in the air. The temperature had been pretty low so that had at least slowed the process a little but there was already staining on the floor from liquids of darkly evil colours which had begun to leak out everywhere and that stench burnt at the eyes of everyone. A small number of flies had already found their way into the room and crawled over the mass before circling the room for a short while.

This wasn't going to be a pleasant experience as they dug through the corpse looking for answers but they could only hope that it was going to be worth it.

The group slowly spread out around the mass, looking on in both awe and revulsion at the body. The thick hide was hanging loosely from frame of the Ult and it was covered with deep cracked fissures of calloused skin on its lower hemisphere, most likely from its movement.

Jenna just took in all of those details and couldn't help herself but flash back to the day that it had attacked. She'd been this close on that day as well but had only the shortest chance to see the details. Now she was staring at the monster and was able to see so much more.

The creature was still just a ball of flesh at its core but now she was really able to explore the thing, she could pick out what looked like vestigial talons on the lower surface, at equidistant points, and bizarre striations and stretch marks. The pigmentation was oddly changeable up close as well. It had appeared to be a single tone of colour but now Jenna was able to really look at it closely she could see patches of much lighter colours randomly spaced all over it.

She also noted that there was no glowing pattern of anything coming from the body so at least that meant it was truly dead.

"So who wants to go first?" Scott again with his sullen snark but, again, there needed to be a level of precaution.

"I'll do it," responded Jenna, knowing that she'd have to be the one to actually put herself in harm's way for any of the others to actually take her seriously and snapped on a pair of surgical gloves that she'd collected from the infirmary.

Moving slowly around the body, everyone else taking a step back to allow her past, she took in all of the detail she could and did her best to think of the most appropriate place to start. Eventually, she came to the conclusion that the area she'd managed to pierce the hide with the flask would be as good a place as any to start with and moved closer.

The tension all around her began to thicken the air in the room to the point that it felt to her as if someone had placed a roaring fire in there with them. Sweat began to bead on her forehead and tiny drops slid down her back, all the while the flies continued bumbling around in the air and every person locked their attention on her, but she took a breath, and slowly reached out her right hand toward the mass.

Her fingers grazed against the thing ever so slightly and all of the breaths around the room which had been held in anticipation were slowly released when nothing happened. Jenna was almost sick as she leaned more weight onto the thing as she considered that first hurdle. She was almost certain that she was right in her train of thought but right before you make that leap, that tiny fragment of risk doesn't seem so tiny any more.

Poking two fingers into the hole she'd made in the thing, she felt around inside and was able to say for certain that it felt like meat. No-one else enjoyed her attempt at humour. Moving on, she pulled out a scalpel and began prodding at the flesh to try and continue the cut she'd made and open the monster to the eyes of the world. Despite her best efforts, the hide was just too tough to separate cleanly. From behind her came a small cough and as she turned, Selina handed over a giant machete which looked to have been sharpened to within an inch of its life.

"Give this a try," Selina said while winking once. Jenna didn't hesitate and it did the job perfectly.

She carved through in smooth motions and sliced open a large hole in the outer flesh before beginning to dig through deeper structures. What appeared to be normal muscles fanned out everywhere and there was an all too familiar feel of the yellowing fat like material which sat around under the hide of the thing. Pushing through layer after layer of muscle, she was able to uncover massive cord structures which spread from a deeper point within the creature and she was able to locate rigid structures which had all the appearance of bones.

Everyone behind her had started off at a safe distance but as their curiosity grew with each cut or tug Jenna made, they edged closer and closer until they were all asking questions and pointing out areas of interest while almost pushing Jenna face first into the filth. She at least had them all holding lanterns at her back so the illumination she was working under did mean she was uncovering everything clearly. Chang had been asking questions steadily as she'd worked and was making detailed notes of every step along the way. This could be the definitive work on Ult biology after all.

"Do you think it's safe for us to touch it without gloves on?" asked Scott from his position at the back of the crowd. Jenna stopped her excavation but didn't turn to face him.

"I can't see any reason why not beyond the usual risks of handling spoiled meat," and she looked all over the body trying to hunt for any kind of signal which could show something more.

"Why don't you take a glove off and give it a go if you're that confident?" Emily was in front of Scott, still with her arms folded across her chest and her attitude in place.

Jenna had just had enough of the constant insinuation around everything she was doing and in a roar of absolute defiance; she tore away her right glove and slapped her bare hand onto the hide of the fallen Ult.

And, nothing happened, beyond the whip crack sound of her essentially, spanking it.

The rest of the group gasped and stepped away as she'd done it, clearly still not totally convinced of what she'd been saying but that slap did manage to prove that maybe she'd been onto something after all. Chang was the first of the group to risk poking the corpse with one shaking finger next to where Jenna had slapped it, followed by Selina who ran a hand over the surface, taking in all of the details.

"It's softer than I thought it'd be," was all she was able to say as the reality of what they were all doing mesmerised her. It was the first tiny steps of understanding which meant that the Ult weren't just a killer nightmare. It meant that they were able to be less afraid. Jenna pulled on another glove and picked up her machete to continue her dissection.

After a further fifteen minutes of pulling and cutting, there were pieces of flesh in small piles on either side of Jenna and the smell had continued to grow and swell around everyone but by now, there was just too much fascination to allow it to have the same effect. Even the flies in the room seemed to be wholly ignored.

"Guys, my back's knotting up so I think we need to take a break," said Jenna as she rocked back on her heels and rubbed at her spine. Chang offered to rub her back by way of encouragement.

"OK everyone, twenty minutes and then back at it."

Jenna got to her feet as parts of her body cracked and popped to signify their freedom from the constant position she'd been in, but as she moved away from the Ult, the others in the group just leaned in even closer and all of the lanterns were raised for maximum illumination. Jenna thought that it was just missing the requisite 'ooooo's and ahhhhh's' to make it the perfect attraction scene from a county fair.

Despite all of the mistrust and hostility which had been swirling through this group of people as they all entered the room, after a very short time confronted with the first glimpses beyond the outer skin of an Ult soldier, the shared curiosity had overtaken the desire to snipe and needle. Everyone was still just taking in the sight of their enemy laying before them and everything else was forgotten. Small steps.

That thought made Jenna smile and from her position leaning against the opposite wall as she stretched herself out, and watching them all harshly illuminated by the close collection of lamps, she could see that this very thing was another small proof of what she'd been thinking about. This was humanity showing that almost unquenchable thirst for knowledge as other concerns were dropped before the interest of the new. They were all showing now, as they each still gawked at the corpse, that far beyond the methodical planning or medical notes aspects of what they'd been doing, they all just wanted to wonder. Jenna couldn't help but wonder what would happen when she began to cut through that grasping arm.

And it was the arm which made her frown as her eyes passed over it. With all of the light in the room being on the other side of the mass of the Ult, the area of the grasping arm was deeply shrouded in shadow which meant that it was now dark enough to see the yellow glow coming from the tips of the rubbery fingers.

Jenna pushed away from the wall and made everyone push back from the body.

"It's glowing again."

The whole group seemed to lurch as one as they took huge, quick, steps away from the risk. The expressions on their faces told Jenna that they'd just moved at the sound of her voice and hadn't even registered the shape of the words, let alone the meaning. Curious they may all have been, but they were also still ramped up high with fear close behind it.

The shadow remained far enough over the area of the Ult in question that the faint glow was still visible and Jenna moved in closer to see what was going on.

"There's a glow coming from the finger tips here. Let me double check that there's nothing glowing anywhere else and I'll have a proper look. Can you all turn down the light please?"

They all did and the room fell almost completely dark.

“I thought you said that it was dead? If it’s glowing, shouldn’t that mean that it’s still alive? How did we touch it?” Scott was asking the questions and his high pitched tone gave away his fear, but there was no accusation in his tone, this time he just wanted to know.

Her check revealed no further signs of anything glowing so she returned everyone’s attention to the fingers.

“The creature is dead, as you’d hope considering that half of its guts are in piles on the floor.” Jenna moved as close as she dared to the hand of the monster and tried to explain what she was seeing.

“On each finger tip, there’s an area that’s full of tiny glowing motes. They’re just glowing, not doing anything else. I think it’s the cure.”

Gasps filled the room and everyone moved to that side of the corpse as, once again, curiosity flared, though no-one stood that close. It felt funnier still knowing that Jenna was the only one who could actually see the thing in question.

“Are you sure Jenna?” asked Chang from next to her, his voice showing that he was on edge for more than just his own safety.

“It looks like the stuff on the wall Davis and I found in storage, and as you leaned in closer to me, it did very slightly begin to drift towards you, so I’d say that this is where the cure comes from. It’s an Ult secretion.”

“I think I felt better with the idea that it was an engineered weapon of some kind rather than something that they make in their own bodies. Odd, huh?” Despite the words, Jenna could hear the smile on Chang’s face as he spoke. Dark humour was also pretty human after all.

“If it went after Chang,” started Emily from behind Jenna somewhere, “and that was the first sign of movement from the stuff only you can see, so we’re all going to have to take your word for. Why didn’t it move after you?”

That woman was really pissing Jenna off. Just accept that I’m not doing anything to try and kill us all, though I’m quickly beginning to change my mind on that for you.

The silence didn’t move and that gave Jenna the time to be alone with that last question.

Why hadn’t there been any movement towards her?

It didn't make any sense but it could be connected to the idea that whatever change had taken place in her meant that anything from the Ult now didn't see her, not just the creatures themselves. Reaching out a hand towards the glow, almost without any real consideration of what risks could be being posed, Jenna almost willed the glowing material to show some interest in her but the closer she got, the clear lack of anything from the material just seemed to make the idea more uncomfortable.

"I don't know." It didn't seem like there was anything more that she could really say. She didn't know, and all she had was possible suggestions.

"Fine," said Chang. "We head back to the meeting room and look through the notes and see what we have. This room will need to have a guard placed at the door to make sure no-one gets in now that we know that the thing can be touched safely, Selina can you arrange please? We'll need someone from the infirmary to work out ways of storing that collection of bits and pieces as well. Emily, can you make the arrangements with them please? We'll wait for the two of you to join us before we start."

The group didn't make any further comment, instead just heading away from the place with the understanding that there was still a lot of work to do. Jenna wasn't happy with the way that she was still in the cross hairs of the group paranoia but there had felt to have been some advancement of the thought that she wasn't just the Devil incarnate.

Standing up, a thought just grazed her mind and she called out to stop Selina before she left the room. Taking the machete back from her, Jenna hacked through the 'wrist' of the Ult grasping arm and picked up the hand near the cut. Unbidden, Chang passed her a large plastic sack which she deposited the hand within. Selina took the machete back and headed off while Jenna cast a final glance across the area of the floor where the piece of the Ult had been. There were still some small glowing specks on the bare floor but she was happy that the risk from them would be small if there was someone stopping people from getting in the room.

Now it was just back to the meetings again.

16

An hour later and, as much as Jenna could confirm the details she'd seen, along with the notes everyone else had taken, the story was spread before them all.

"How does the fact your eyesight is different make any difference to the Ult?" Scott just couldn't help but play the role of Devil's advocate to any and all suggestions made by Jenna or Chang. He was still obstinate but the venom had been steadily falling away as he did his best to work through everything. That said, he still couldn't grasp what was being put forward.

Chang just sat in the battered leather chair in the corner and did his best to keep up. He'd been listening to every re-telling of the details and had been picking up more and more each time but he still felt that there was something he was missing, a vital component that was going to resolve all of the edges to the puzzle. He'd walked into the room feeling that his scribbled notes and diagrams had been more than illuminating but as they'd all discussed point after point, he wasn't so sure.

Jenna continued.

"How did my eyes change? From the repeated shocks from Frankenstein's de-fib after being touched by that falling Ult. It and its friend were after us because it had seen that glowing tower coming from Mary and Mo, they dug their way into the building and made a direct run towards them until they encountered everyone else, where they started attacking. They were following the power signature being given off by Mary and Mo, the rest of us were most likely a big surprise when they got inside." Jenna paused and took a drink from her water, feeling that she'd been speaking for hours upon hours. No-one else spoke but the expressions appeared to show shared understanding.

She recommenced.

“After it touched me, in reality feeding in some way, it made my nervous system break. When I was shocked repeatedly by a machine which had so many questionable power sources and repairs, for whatever reason, my nervous system is now different. That’s why the second one ignored me. It couldn’t see me. Add to that the fact that it was water that spilled into the tear I made in its hide and then had the effect it did, a system wide explosion, and we are left with the revelation that, regardless of how or why it happened, I am as good as invisible to the Ult. They follow the electrical print of a person or a thing and feed from it.”

“Like I said before Jenna, I think that we’re going to have to do more work on the body while we have it and see if we can understand as much as possible. We need to be sure about what you’ve suggested today before we go ahead thinking it’s gospel.” Chang was doing his best to still sound positive with the situation but he had to sound that tone of caution before people went off doing things they shouldn’t. It made perfect sense but despite that fact, it still stung Jenna.

“Since the first appearance of an Ult, the very beginning of the attack, they’ve been gorging on the human race and all we’ve built. The problem for them is that they’ve been a little too good at it. All of our technology, all our electricity, has been destroyed leaving just the life on the planet, the animals and the people themselves. They switched to going after the population because we were their only option but they’re now running out of us too so, what do they do?”

Chang stroked his chin as he took in the latest re-telling. Despite his hard-wired desire to always remain driven purely by fact, all of the steps Jenna had taken had been well considered and followed a pathway of logic he couldn’t deny. She really had a point but there was still the fine balance of the possible factions within the camp to consider.

Despite everything that had been said, Scott seemed less than convinced.

“You’re still taking a huge amount of this on faith. You haven’t got a single piece of hard proof that what you’re saying is anything more than an elaborate fantasy spun together from the mind of someone who’s gone through a huge physical trauma. You're asking all of us to take a huge leap of faith by believing you can see all the magic colours just because you almost died."

Jenna didn't respond to anything he'd said. There wasn't anything she could say. She'd laced together a theory which explained what had taken place earlier but it was all built on if's, buts' and maybe's, which happened to fit the facts that they did have. She didn't have any real, hard proof of any of it.

"Don't believe me." Her face lit up immediately as the answer she needed presented itself.

"You're right. There isn't any concrete evidence that what I've just told you isn't anything more than a very elaborate story. It could even make a good book. We need to test the theory."

Jenna stood triumphant before the others, hands on her hips and daring anyone to say anything negative now. No-one did. Even Scott just nodded his head slowly but Emily still held firm to her hatred.

It was an hour later when they all collectively decided that the job of arranging the tests needed a break. They'd managed to agree that they needed to see if Jenna could travel unnoticed past an Ult but that's where the logistics of their predicament stopped them in their tracks. They didn't have an Ult lying around that they could use. Emily had argued that by Jenna telling them all that the cure material on the Ult was not reacting to her meant that she was taking herself out of the pool of people who could attract the things, which just wasn't fair on the rest. She still wanted Jenna to be one of the people roaming around outside the walls though, but quickly shut up when it was pointed out that creatures would be coming even without them trying to wave one down.

"We're likely to have another Ult find us on its own, what with the Mary and Mo situation," pointed out Scott. "They're going to keep shining their beacon, aren't they Jenna? Remember?"

Shit.

He was right, and within all of the back and forth recently, she'd overlooked that detail.

"Can't we insulate the room they're in? Just keep the glow from going anywhere, if the whole thing is based around electricity." Selina was a shrewd mind indeed.

"We're still having to put far too much faith onto the ideas being suggested by Jenna and it makes me feel too nervous." Scott folded his arms and slumped back on his chair, an air of defeatist haze all around him.

Next to him, Emily matched his pose completely and added, "I agree. She was the reason this disease came here so just listening to her can't be a risk we all take."

Nothing more needed saying, so the group dispersed. There was going to be a hunt for insulating materials for Mary and Mo, and Chang knew he would have to speak to the whole population of the place to explain what was happening and what had been discovered. He also saw that the sooner the word was out there from him the better, before the rumour mill that every group of people seem to set up alongside every civilisation through history, began spinning everything badly.

When the meeting took place, a couple of hours later, everyone had been there, even those who were going to be working the night shift, and everyone listened intently to everything that was said in complete silence. He risked asking the dreaded 'Any questions?' but no-one stirred. Instead, Chang was left to thank everyone and send them back to what they'd been doing, the message having seemingly been passed on perfectly.

Davis and Selina had been stood at the back of the compound watching as Chang had spoken and had watched the crowd before them, feeling very different about his efforts. They walked away feeling that the message that Chang was giving was already too late, and that Emily and Scott had already explained things to everyone, again, truth be damned.

Jenna had taken the bag containing the Ult hand down to the infirmary and felt quite reassured to see Artie there, full to the brim of that boundless enthusiasm he had shown every time she'd been around him. He'd been perched behind his desk when she'd walked in but he was totally obscured by the piles of plastic containers which had been used to house the different sized lumps of flesh that Jenna had excised. All of the containers had been sealed shut with packing tape of some kind and each of the specimens swam in a liquid of, well Jenna just wasn't sure what it was but it was clear. At the sound of footsteps entering his world, Artie's head shot up above the boxes and he beamed when he recognised who it was.

"You did all this?" He scrambled out of the chair to stand; looking to show what he felt was the appropriate deference to Jenna. She just shrugged in response, embarrassed by what other perceptions of her may be existing in the minds of people in their home. All she could do to move things forward was to reach out the plastic sack which contained the Ult hand.

"I've been holding onto the last piece as well. Be careful doing anything to this thing, it's still carrying the live cure virus."

Artie's brain just seized up at the enormity of what she'd just said and his mouth fell open limply. He glanced quickly at the sack and then back to her before burbling a handful of random sounds and pointing.

He needed to take a breath.

"Yes it's dangerous but I can help so don't worry." She'd spoken slowly and as calmly as she could and he nodded just as slowly as he tried to comprehend what was being handed to him. Finally, all the cogs in his brain rotated enough and he dived back behind his desk, before reappearing with a large plastic tub in his arms.

"Will this be enough for it?"

"Perfect."

She opened the sack and emptied the hand into it. Artie almost dropped the tub as the hand landed, clearly not thinking it was going to weigh as much as it did, but he regained his balance soon enough.

"I'd seen it was missing when I collected all of the other parts earlier but I just thought that someone had torn it off during the attack." His eyes were like saucers he was so amazed by the specimen. Jenna smiled inwardly at the beaming, child-like awe on his face.

The wonder was short lived though, as she pushed him back from where he'd been leaning over the hand as she spotted small signs of movement coming from those small glowing specks which had clearly taken notice of Artie being nearby.

"Where's the lid?" she asked as she took the container from Artie slowly. His eyes didn't leave the hand but he reached out to a spot behind a nearby wooden drawer unit to retrieve the lid and slide it into position. In next was that foul smelling liquid until the tape was finally around the container, sealing the thing inside. Finally, he stopped and looked questioningly at Jenna, looking for confirmation he could relax. She nodded curtly and he blew out a huge breath he must have been holding for the whole time.

"My God that was stressful," said Artie as he slumped back in his chair behind his wall of Ult parts.

Jenna slid the container onto the nearby drawer unit, happy to have it away from her despite the relatively low risk it had been posing to her. She took a quick look inside the sack to check for any parts which may have been left behind but there was nothing beyond a collection of those same glowing particles. She sealed it shut and knew it would have to be incinerated. They couldn't risk even the tiniest particle being free in the air to infect anyone else.

"Artie, keep that thing so incredibly well stored and away from anyone or anything that could even look at it wrong. I had it in the bag but I could see that nothing was coming out but without me to check, we need to control the risk."

From behind his wall, he just gave the thumbs up and sighed.

At least that problem was one less to add to the pile.

From outside the room, the piercing scream shattered the peace in the infirmary, making both Jenna and Artie jump. Artie added a small collection of expletives in emphasis and promptly fell out of his chair.

Outside, there were running footsteps coming down the corridor towards them and there were panicked shouts coming from deep in the property that Jenna couldn't make out beyond the clear emotion.

Scott came crashing into the room at high speed, already breathing hard, and he was wearing every inch of the terror he was clearly feeling all over his face. He looked around the room hurriedly, noticing Jenna but not lingering on her.

"Artie!" he shouted, acting like he was alone.

Artie stood up from behind the desk and smiled despite his own all too apparent fear.

"There are people down in the War Room. That Ult in there has done something to them. Come on." Scott was waving his arms and his voice was already frayed at the edges. Artie was moving slowly after him but he wasn't sure what he would be able to offer.

"Shouldn't Jenna come too? Isn't she the expert on the Ult now?"

Scott fired a look of hatred her way at the mention of her name, finally recognising that she was there with them.

"Expert indeed? She thought the room was safe," spat Scott before storming out the way he'd come. Artie just shrugged at Jenna and went after him.

Jenna didn't wait to be asked and headed out after the other two. Whatever was happening, it was going to need all hands on deck.

The War Room had the sheeting taped across the top the doorway still so everything inside was still obscured from any idle passing eyes but when she pushed through said sheets, the room beyond was a chaos which, in truth, wasn't as far removed from the original Ult attack.

There were an ever growing group of people kneeling or standing around the four who were now spread out on the floor around the remaining material of the Ult corpse. The air was still thick with that rotting odour of Ult flesh and more and more flies filled the air and explored each and every different person who came in. This had been a room of death before any single one of these people had entered but now the place was wearing death like a robe of office.

"What the fuck happened?"

Everyone turned to face the new voice entering the fray. It was Chang and he was boiling with anger at the sight before him. From somewhere within the crowd, Emily emerged with her face in a rictus of hate and jabbed an accusing finger at Jenna.

"SHE DID THIS! SHE TOLD US THIS ROOM WAS SAFE BUT LOOK AT WHAT SHE DID."

All eyes swung to Jenna and they all carried the same venom that Emily had been spitting.

"I haven't done anything. I said that it should be OK as long as no-one was coming in here. I thought there was going to be a guard to stop people." Jenna was off balance at the accusation so defended herself. This couldn't be her fault.

Emily continued,

"DON'T YOU DARE TRY TO PASS OFF THE BLAME. WE CAME IN HERE BECAUSE OF YOU," and without any further indication, she screamed and made a dive at Jenna with both arms outstretched and her fingers set and ready to claw at her face. Luckily for everyone, Chang had seen her coming enough to put himself between the two women and grasped her hands before she was able to connect and do any damage. Emily was left to sulk back to her comrades, filled with impotent rage.

More people entered the room and there came sobs as one of the newer entries fell to the floor next to one of the motionless bodies and began crying.

"Everyone. I need to understand what took place here. Artie, are they dead?" Chang was in full control mode. Artie looked up from his kneeling position next to one of the bodies with a puzzled expression.

"They're all still alive. They're just out cold." He looked at Jenna sheepishly before adding, "like Mary and Mo."

"You see?" Now it was Scott's turn to speak.

"More people have been taken by the Ult cure, which was only brought into our home because of the actions of Jenna. More of our friends and family are infected thanks to what she led us to believe."

"I didn't tell you to bring a school excursion in here, you prick." Jenna was over this now.

Chang stood directly ahead of Jenna so the crowd couldn't see her.

"Why were there any people in here at all? We discussed that this room needed to be sealed off and guarded so why are we looking at this?” Chang gestured at the tableau before them all for emphasis.

“Because these people have had to watch as their lives are being torn to pieces thanks to your star pupil Chang, and thought that maybe understanding something about our enemy could be helpful to any fight back. She did say it was safe after all.” There was anger in his voice but there was a new calm which Jenna hadn’t ever heard from him before, like he was still scared to be the position he found himself but he was more confident that he was going to succeed.

“Again Scott, this room was safe to a point but no-one was to come in. Wasn’t that clear?”

Scott didn’t answer, but instead spread his arms wide and turned to face his people, and it was clear to Jenna now that they were indeed ‘his people’, a small, sad smile on his face. When he finally turned back to Chang, his face had grown evil.

“I told you that there was no way that his ‘pet’ behind him would ever be seen as culpable, didn’t I?” All of the eyes in the group of his burned at Chang and made Artie bustle back and away to avoid what he thought was coming.

Scott rolled onwards and spoke with a voice that now had a sharp, almost serrated, edge to it.

“Could there have been different actions along the path to here? Yes. Will there ever be that acceptance for Jenna? Ever?”

He paused for effect, eating up the adulation which was coming from the crowd.

“I’m suggesting that our lives have been curtailed because of the relaxed attitude of Jenna and that all she’s been talking about is her desire to forget all of her responsibilities to the rest of us so she can daydream. And that you, Chang, are just as bad for letting her get away with putting us all at risk.”

His people all grumbled their agreement and began to change their collective postures. They weren’t mourning friends any more. They’d begun to switch to a stance of much more coiled violence, of threatened attack. It was a tiny change but everyone recognised the implication. From behind him, he felt a small bunching of his thick woollen jumper and then a gentle tug as Jenna made her feelings clear. Chang just moved a step backwards, not taking his eyes from Scott or the others, and with that tiny movement, it became clear that the dynamics within the room had shifted.

Scott had always been the same when he spoke before, petulant and just obstinate for the sake of it, but when he was challenged by someone else, he always slinked back into a hole with his tail between his legs. He'd never had the spine to back himself before but he was happy now to make his stand because he had a crowd to back him up.

"You really want this?" Chang asked as Jenna did everything she could to get them both out of the room. He wasn't finished yet though.

"I think that shows your problem there Chang." Scott was showing off.

"You think that all this is about me. I'm just the voice. We're all the words. We think that there needs to be a change of thinking around how we're going to survive and thinking about the good times wasn't ever going to be enough."

Chang jutted his jaw out defiantly, crossed his arms over his chest, and planted his feet. Scott may be feeling invincible but Chang wanted to see just how strong that formerly glass jaw of his really was.

"OK. What's your plan for all of us?" asked Chang in a flat tone.

"We need to fortify the whole location and set ourselves up for a siege. If the Ult are infecting us already, we need to isolate those affected but then head back to Hope and bring back every possible supply we can carry and then shut the doors against the world. We need to look after us, fuck everyone else." He smirked with complacency as he laid out what he felt should have been a simple idea.

Jenna knew he was prick.

Chang tapped his foot slowly as he considered the ideas, even rubbing his chin in that oh so sage fashion.

"That sounds like an interesting idea. You must have put a great deal of thought into it." Chang's sarcasm was greeted by a snarl from Emily.

"I've just got some thoughts, if I may?"

Scott nodded with his smile still set firm.

"You said you want to avoid infection by the Ult virus, which is a good place to start from, but it's already here. What's the plan for getting the virus cleared out of here?" Now it was Chang's turn to pause for effect.

"You want to go back to Hope and strip the place of supplies, but won't that just be putting the people who go into harm's way? They could bring back more of the virus." Another pause.

"And when we start to run out of supplies, what should we do then? There are still quite a few mouths to feed so we'll need ways to grow our own food beyond what we do now. How do we do that?" Chang's final pause stretched out as an invitation for Scott to fill it.

All eyes turned to Scott and despite the people being behind him both figuratively and physically, they were all looking for answers to what Chang had said.

"We cleanse everywhere which has been tainted by the virus, like Jenna managed with The Beast, and then burn anything which remains. We can't risk having the stuff in here with us and I'm sure that Jenna will be more than happy to help us root out every last molecule of the stuff, as she's the only one who can see it." Scott paused again for that fix of love but Chang stepped into the space.

"We need to cleanse every molecule? Including the bits in the victims like Mary and Mo?" He paused now to rub in the new point but also to give that extra weight for his final point.

"And these poor people here?"

The gasps were low but clear, and a handful of the people looked at Scott with a whole new fear in their eyes. Scott blinked quickly and Chang could see that his mask was slipping. Not so sure after all.

"Besides," chirped Jenna as she stepped out from behind Chang's cover. We don't understand where the virus is anyway, if someone in here has 'caught' it. I took the hand with the virus on to infirmary and it's secured there. Don't you think it'd be a good idea to let me take a look at the place to see if anything has changed since we were all last in here?"

Scott didn't answer. He'd been happily picking at the choices of others but hadn't thought beyond the most basic points of what he thought was right. Eventually, the hamster in the wheel in his head picked up enough speed and he spoke.

"That would be a very good idea. Your first step to redemption, maybe?"

Jenna was back in the cross hairs again even though Scott had been shown to not understand what he was talking about. As long as he just kept blaming everyone else for anything and everything so he could stoke the fear of the people who were now hanging on every word he uttered, he was still going to be a problem.

"Can everyone turn their lanterns all the way down please?" asked Jenna and rolled her sleeves up by way of emphasis, to everyone in the room, but also to herself. Everyone complied with her request, happy that Scott was on board so even if she was the one they all held responsible for all of the bad things happening, she was doing their bidding. Sort of.

The light fell to a deeply shrouded late dusk and the glowing of what Jenna was assuming were everyone's nervous systems, grew sharper. But that wasn't all she could see. The virus was here with them indeed.

Jenna gasped in terror as she slowly surveyed the room before her as the thousands upon thousands of lightly glowing motes of that Ult material swirled through the air. The huge tornado of bright power surged up from the four fallen people around the Ult corpse and lit up everything to Jenna. There were four people in this pyre of energy so she'd expected it to be brighter than what she'd seen in the infirmary but it seemed to be so much more. She could practically taste the static charge in the air. Looking on as the column passed upwards and through the ceiling, she felt an awful chill run down her spine. There was so much of the cure in here with them, why hadn't they all been affected when they just walked into the room?

"What's wrong?" Chang again, recognising that Jenna could see something he was missing.

"It's everywhere," was all she could stammer to him, the absolute shock stealing away so much of her thought. Chang slid close to her side and whispered so as to keep his thoughts between the two of them.

“What is?” His eyes were darting haphazardly around the room, hoping to pick out what he was missing.

“The cure. There’s clouds of the particles floating everywhere in here.”

“Then why aren’t we all on the floor?”

Jenna took hold of her panic and tried to think. Why weren’t they all ‘cured’? There was something missing from what she was thinking and she needed to work it out as fast as she could. Scanning around the room, she tried her best to ignore the flecks in the air and find anything she could use. The Ult corpse was the first to suggest something.

Spreading out from the stump on the things grasping arm was a vibrant pool of glowing material. She’d assumed that taking the hand of the thing would be enough to make it safe but it looked like the production of the stuff was deeper in the arm. Moving closer to the pile, there was still no movement from the stuff for her so she waved Chang closer.

“What is it? What have you done?” Emily watched on and was sure that whatever was taking place was going to be a scheme of some kind.

“I’m looking at the stump for any clues about what could have caused the predicament we’re in. I’ll let you know if I find something,” replied Jenna matter-of-factly.

Chang moved to her side nervously, aware that there was a risk that he wasn’t able to see, but determined to do it anyway.

The material from the Ult didn’t move.

Jenna frowned but grabbed his arm and gave him a quick look which she hoped expressed that she was going to look after him no matter what. He didn’t pull away so that was something. She edged his hand slowly towards the puddle on the floor, ready for the slightest hint that there was movement to pull him away.

Still, nothing happened.

They were so much closer than they had been before but they kept going. Finally, Jenna could see a slow stirring as the cure material recognised Chang and moved towards him, and pulled him back. It wasn’t as reactive as it had been.

“It’s still active but it looks like it’s not as active as it was before. It’s like it’s running out of power.” Jenna was still crouched down as she gave her first report and her vantage point was what made her stop in her tracks.

She'd always seen the glowing tower above those people who'd been affected by the Ult disease but she'd never paid attention to the details of the people. She could see from down here that the glowing tower which was being produced above the people was as a result of the cure material infiltrating them at the point of contact. She was looking at the nearest person, a man she thought was called Saj though she wasn't sure. He'd been a new addition to the group only a couple of weeks ago and she hadn't really had any time to speak to him for anything. Hadn't he been part of a group which had been attacked by Ult who'd then destroyed their home? She couldn't remember, and admonished herself for her lack of human compassion. They all really needed to take more time for each other.

She shook her head and dragged her attention back to the here and now. They all needed to look after one another but not at the expense of what they were doing.

The man in question, Saj possibly, was glowing in the same way as everyone else but that spidery pattern which she had decided was his nervous system, was dimmer than everyone else's who were standing around. It made sense if he was having power leeched from him, but that wasn't what had drawn her attention. All over his face was a bright, glowing smear of that cure material and there were tiny slivers of the stuff reaching through his flesh to connect to his nerves. There were other spots of the same glowing material on other areas, a major one being down the front of his jumper, but there hadn't been the same effect there.

Quickly checking the others, she found the same results. They all had gobs of the stuff on their faces. They'd taken a blast of the stuff and where it had hit their skin, it had gone to work. On their clothes had meant there'd been no effect so it likely meant that only physical contact between the cure and flesh was the dangerous part. She looked up feeling a growing excitement at what could be a pivotal discovery and as she scanned over the rest of the people in the room with her, she could see that there were small numbers of the same particles actually adhering to anyone despite the maelstrom around them all. That was all except Emily, whose hands shone out like a beacon in the dark and it was at that point that Jenna noticed that Emily had been wearing gloves.

"Everyone needs to get out of this room slowly. It looks like there are cure particles in the air and on our clothes."

The shocked gasps increased the fear on top of the news. Jenna continued.

"It looks like the material is stronger when in larger concentrations so we all appear to be OK as we are but we'll still need to be careful as we get out of here. At least the room's sealed so there's a way we could get the room clear if we open the windows up."

"OK everyone, out we go, slowly," said Chang steadily, doing everything he could to reinforce what little calmness remained in the room with them. A couple of people moved towards the doorway but most didn't.

"Then why did these people get affected when they've done the same as the rest of us? It doesn't make sense." Scott was now standing, unwilling to move. He thought that he'd picked up on something important, and his people remained motionless.

"They didn't get the same concentration. They've all got massive amounts of the material over their faces."

"Well how is that? Were they just REALLY unlucky like you were REALLY lucky?" Emily threw out, her words dripping with poison.

"Because Emily," Jenna responded but turned to face her fully. "It looks like someone picked up the appendage of the Ult and waved it about, which in turn sprayed the material all over these people in a single arc. The person who did it was lucky enough to be wearing gloves because without them the virus on their hands would have made them the fifth victim."

Emily lost all of the colour in her face and her mouth fell open. She looked down at her hands and although not seeing the danger, fully understood it all too well. Jenna hoped that would put her back in her box for a while.

"So who could have done this?" Now it was Scott's turn.

We were all here together and none of us did what you're describing. We were all here and watched as these people just fell to the floor as if they'd been shot and now you're the one presenting an idea which no-one can prove or disprove. Convenient again." His whole group voiced their agreement of what he'd said and Jenna just felt her blood boiling. They all knew the truth yet they were going to fall in line behind a lie because it was easier than accepting any personal responsibility. Emily had slunk behind Scott and was doing her best to look as angry as she'd been before but she just wasn't managing it, as she slowly removed her gloves and dropped them behind her.

There's guilt for you.

Jenna was about to roar her anger at Scott and his whole group when the hairs on the back of her neck stood up. She didn't understand what was happening but there was more than just her rage. Looking quickly around the room, at the other people and at the mass that was the Ult attacker, she couldn't pick out what was happening to her or what was making her feel the prickle of alarm.

Nothing was different.

"And now we have her acting like she can see the big boogie man that the rest of us can't, just to make sure she stays as the saviour against a problem that she created herself," spat Scott and he was back on the stage before his adoring crowd, drinking in their adulation and devotion.

"Listen, dickhead," shouted Jenna, finally at her breaking point. "I can sense something but I don't know what. It isn't anything yet because I have no idea beyond a strange feeling but I want to make sure that there isn't anything that's actually coming to kill us all. Is that OK with you and your cult?"

Scott just looked back at her with a shit eating grin and she recognised that she'd just given him a load of fresh ammunition. She just couldn't let it bother her now, there was too much else going on and she had to see if there really was something to be aware of.

The crawling tingle slithered down her spine and spread through every one of her limbs as it continued to grow in intensity. Something was about to happen but she just didn't know what it was, until the billowing tower of glowing energy began to slowly sink its peak away from the ceiling and fall towards the wall behind Scott and his people. What was it doing?

She was quickly given the answer before she reached her own conclusion though, as the outer wall of the War Room exploded inwards sending brick and stone, wood and plaster all over the room and everyone in it.

The dust hung heavy in the air and gave the room the impression of being draped in a blanket, deadening all sound, though Jenna was glad of the effect as the only thing she could make out through the high pitched ringing in her ears was the groaning and screaming coming from injured members of their party. It was only then that, from her position at the back of the room where she'd been hurled by the explosion, could she see what had caused this mess. Three giant Ult stood in what had once been a solid wall, before reaching to grip hold of any possible area of the room to drag themselves in after everyone inside.

17

Jenna couldn't see properly through the haze but now the wall of the house had been smashed in, natural daylight had poured in and given the room the feeling of being serenely within a cloud. She could see the glow of someone partially trapped beneath a large section of the wall which had been blown in but they weren't moving.

'ULT, ULT, ULT, ULT,' stamped into the room, drowning out so many of the sounds inside, and while a brisk breeze pushed its way through the hole in the wall, the dust began to clear to reveal the creatures.

They were enormous.

They were the same overall dimension as the others that she'd seen but these were orders of magnitude bigger. The grey hide carried that all too familiar appearance of calloused armour and they were all coated in slimy, muddy filth on their lower halves, proof of their journey to here.

"Everybody RUN!" was bellowed from behind her but it wasn't Chang making the call to action, it was Scott.

People moved as quickly as they could but the nearest Ult slashed out its grasping arm and scooped up someone who was nearby. The panicked screaming began immediately as that rubbery appendage wrapped steadily around whomever it was who'd been unlucky enough to be within easy reach. Behind the first, the remaining Ult began reaching out for more and more people as those in what was left of the room dived for the sheeting hanging over the doorway and whatever freedom they could find.

But Jenna didn't move.

She was in pain from injuries she had yet to fully discover but from her position amongst the rubble, she could see that she was being ignored. In the fraction of time between the explosion and where she was now, the enemies had attacked all around her, but never her. She *was* invisible.

Her attention was interrupted as the gun fire opened up from behind her as people had reacted to the crash and screams and brought any and all weapons they could get their hands on to bear. She dived flat to the floor as the bullets flew and began to smash into the Ult and anything which was in their vicinity, before starting to crawl towards the doorway.

'ULT, ULT, ULT,' continued to roll into the room as bullets hit the thick hide of the monsters and sent up more and more snaps of light as hundreds of impacts practically turned them into firework displays.

Jenna finally made it to the position of the nearest member of their defensive team and scrambled to her feet behind the wall of people. It turned out that it had been Selina she'd located and, peeking out from behind her, she watched as the Ult continued to flail against the bullets while still reaching for people to consume and she just couldn't understand such a swift attack at exactly the right point on their home. The earlier attack had come through the house rather than just through the nearest point, so why the change?

"Come on Jenna, save us all. You're the one with the superpowers aren't you?" shouted Scott from the corridor well behind the defensive effort. He wasn't even one of the people firing; he was just yelling his own brand of 'help'.

"Get me as many canisters of water as you can pump up, I've got an idea how to win this," Jenna shouted back angrily. Scott paused for a fraction of a second, his mind trying to comprehend what could be happening, before deciding that doing what Jenna had asked him would be a good idea.

Jenna moved in closer to Selina and shouted into her ear as she continued firing, "I need your machete again. When I tell you, stop shooting, I'm going to get this finished but I don't want to get killed by friendly fire." Selina nodded curtly that she'd heard her and kept the trigger squeezed as hard as she could. Jenna made her way down the line of people who were doing everything they could to keep the Ult at bay, and were certainly having more success than during the earlier attack, and told them what she needed. A couple had been people from

Scott's cabal and they had looked daggers her way at the suggestion of stopping the shooting but they'd both nodded their agreement. Maybe they'd gone through the same process of indecision as Scott but it looked like they were going to do it.

Jenna had finally spoken to everyone and was taking the machete out of the scabbard on Selina's leg when Scott reappeared at the doorway, a full bucket of water in each hand. Other people followed him with more. Jenna dragged the buckets into the room and left them lined up between the feet of the wall of people and took a deep breath to try and calm the hammering of her heart.

Now was the time for her to put her money where her mouth was.

She launched her discarded jacket into the air to fall between the Ult and the people. It arced slowly through the air, gently performing an aerial ballet until it fell into the hail of bullets that were still pouring out. That ballet became more of a violent contortion as it was ripped to bits but everyone recognised the signal and released their triggers.

The room fell into a faux silence as everyone's ears rang from the previous sound and the Ult didn't move from their position at the centre of the room. Jenna took the bucket and sped forwards, seeing the inaction of the Ult as a gift. Her footsteps must have been loud because despite her ringing ears, she was able to hear each footfall but still there was no movement from the Ult. They truly didn't hear anything but she was also not being tracked by them.

Raising the machete high, she didn't waste a second and leapt up to slash at the base of the nearest Ult's grasping limb. It made no attempt to move, still not even registering that she was even there, so was motionless when the freshly sharpened blade of the machete tore through its hide. Despite a jolt of pain through all of the muscles in her arm and a static charge making her feel like her hair was standing on end, Jenna had carved through and deftly removed the limb, which fell to the floor with a solid thud and began to spasm.

The damaged Ult didn't react in the way that Jenna had expected. It didn't react at all. It just remained still and if there had been any pain that it was going through, it gave no signal at all that anything had happened. Jenna didn't stop her movement, and instead drove the machete deep into the flesh of the stump she'd just created and opened up what rapidly became a gaping hole.

There was still nothing from the Ult.

She didn't understand what was happening but there was no stopping now. She was going to follow her plan through no matter what, even if it was looking more and more like she'd been somehow wrong about something in the Ult. With a grunt of effort, she lifted the bucket of water high and dumped the contents into the wound she'd created.

She hit the floor and was already on her way back towards Selina and the others before she risked looking back at her handy work. What presented itself was not those creatures trying to reach for her, instead, the one she'd attacked became rigid and pulsed spasmodically as something inside it was burned out and fried, before it collapsed to the floor with a deep thump. The other two remained in their positions. There was no recognition of what had just been done to their comrade and they both just remained in place. The only sign of life coming from them both was a random, twitching flare of their 'fingers' which took on the appearance of them having some kind of dream. What an idea that was.

Jenna just collected the next bucket and moved back in.

She made short work of doing the same surgery on both of the remaining Ult and they both collapsed onto the floor next to their comrade after offering no defensive effort at all. In no time, the danger was no more, and Jenna didn't understand any of it.

"Get that wall sealed back up now guys," shouted Selina to the others in the firing squad and they all headed off into the house in search of materials they'd need. Jenna just stared at what was left of the enemy which had burst into the room and felt like she was further back than she was when this whole mess had started out. They'd just stopped and let her kill them. Even if she'd been invisible to them, surely they would have at least been able to react as she did what she did? And why wouldn't they continue to go after everyone else?

The work to at least block up the hole so any electricity patterns inside would be concealed took almost no time at all. People moved smoothly and with a surety that wouldn't have been in place just a few days ago. Everyone had grown used to what was needed very quickly. Wood and plastic sheets were brought in and bolted or nailed into place while Jenna remained in the centre of the room trying to examine the Ult corpses. No-one interrupted her as she went about her business but she could already hear Scott's voice outside making sure to be the one to tell the tale of what had taken place. She didn't have the patience to deal with him so just relied on the fact that at least Chang would have her back so at least that was something.

Wait. Where was Chang?

Quickly to her feet and scanning the room as fast as she could, her eyes fell finally on the shape of the person who'd been partially buried under the masonry from the wall to see that it was her friend who'd been the one to fall.

"CHANG!" screamed Jenna and dived for him, gripping to check for a pulse as soon as she reached his side. It was still there, and it was strong despite the incident and the cuts on his head seemed to be superficial at worst.

"Chang. Can you hear me? It's Jenna?" She was aiming for that casual tone which didn't put any undue stress on the patient but she could feel the tremor in her voice anyway.

Chang's eyes flickered open slightly and he smiled gently.

"Did you save the day?" he croaked before coughing dryly.

Jenna almost slumped over on the floor next to him with the relief.

"Just a little," she replied, voice tremor and all.

"First class," Chang breathed. He was still himself despite the intervention of the wall. Christ, the wall.

Jenna stood up and began to push against the object which had pinned him to the floor. The adrenaline coursing through her made shifting the weight no chore at all and it rolled easily from Chang so he could be taken to the infirmary for any medical help he would need.

Just as she heaved and heaved against the piece of the masonry, the final wood board was eased into place in the repair, closing the tear in the wall, and for a short time before new lanterns could be turned all the way up to illuminate the area properly, Jenna was again able to see a clear image of the glow coming from everyone, the bright light from outside having dimmed it, and her breath caught in her throat.

The pattern was there for everyone around her as it had been prior to the attack, but not for Chang.

"What's the matter?" asked Chang as he recognised Jenna's expression immediately

Jenna rubbed at the back of her neck before making every possible platitude about him getting to the infirmary and that she'd even go and get him a stretcher because the big leader here shouldn't have to walk. He knew she was lying and thought he knew why.

Jenna told him to stay still but as she tried to attract someone's attention, all she could see was that glowing pattern coming from Chang which signified his nervous system and how now, it only glowed from him from the waist up. There was nothing running through his legs now.

He'd been paralyzed.

18

The rest of the day became a blur which Jenna was being swept along with rather than taking a huge active role. To move Chang as safely as they could, one of Scott's group had sourced a door from somewhere in the house and after several rounds of testing out the process, managed to fix Chang to it with cargo straps and lengths of ropes to do their best to immobilize his spine. She'd wanted to be one of the people to carry the stretcher but she just fell to the back of the group surrounding him while everyone else was about the work until she was just left adrift in the room.

Others had still been fixing and building the repairs and the single victim of this latest attack had been finally identified from the remains that had been left by the Ult who'd snatched them up. It had been Emily. A couple of people had moved around her ruined remains, appearing to confirm the identity but then not wanting to leave her alone. Jenna wasn't going to miss the woman but she would never have wished this fate on her. She was glad there was at least someone to look after her now she couldn't do it for herself. The people who'd been taken by the cure remained motionless in the centre of the room and no-one had made the slightest effort to do anything with them since the attack. Jenna just held on to the idea that they weren't going anywhere anyway.

Despite all of the action taking place all around her, Jenna couldn't stop her mind from just fogging slightly and making her feel like she was having an out of body experience. Looking around at the room didn't seem to be real to her as her mind slowed the action around her and left her feeling more tired than she had in a great long while.

Even before the trip to Hope, before she'd seen that her own humanity was being ever so slowly eroded to the point that just a simple memory of a time before was enough to give her a kind of relaxation she hadn't even recognised she was missing, she'd felt more linkage to the world that surrounded. Now though, she felt like she was just a spectator.

Shaking away as much of the fog as she could, she followed the make shift stretcher towards the infirmary and took a tight hold of her determination to push through this latest setback.

The infirmary was a swarm of activity as Chang was moved from the door and onto the nearest bed. He'd called out loudly as he was shifted, pain firing through his body at what was looking like the impact point where his back had most likely been broken. All those involved gave constant apologies and reassurances. Artie was the one leading the way and was no longer the confused and worried man he'd been previously. He was giving clear instructions to everyone in the room and was acting very much like he was totally in control. He wasn't bellowing like a demented despot, he was exuding confidence in what he was saying and everyone around him was reacting accordingly. Jenna couldn't help but be impressed.

"I need the beds with Mary and Mo in to be moved more towards the far wall. We need the extra space. Can you do it please?" Artie was in the zone and gave out assignments quickly.

"You, Sarah, is it? Can you take these canisters down to the pump room on that trolley and get them topped up with water please?" Sarah nodded and was off without further words.

"Mike, can you re-stack all of those boxes on my desk at the far end of the room with Mary and Mo please? Under their beds will be fine until we can find a more suitable place." Off went Mike and although he too didn't ask any further questions, he did look back filled with apprehension that he was moving pieces of Ult. Artie had moved onto the next issue so Mike was just left to get to work.

"Can I help somewhere?" Jenna called into the melee, needing to be active to keep that sudden tiredness away.

"Are you OK Jenna? You've gone quite grey," replied Artie who looked up briefly to see who he was being addressed by then did a double take when he saw the picture before him.

"I just feel a bit run down is all. My jumping about with the Ult must have taken more out of me than I thought." Jenna was looking for a job not sympathy, even if she did need just the smallest bit, the way she felt.

"If you're sure you're feeling up to helping, can you give Mike a hand moving the boxes of parts to the bottom end of the room and then can you inventory all of the boxes please? We're going to need to have a clear list of what we have. Thanks." He smiled and was back to his work before she could respond.

Picking up the nearest crate, she slipped past the remaining people in the infirmary and made her way to where Mike had begun his 'filing'. The beds that Mary and Mo were in were now pushed fully against the far wall of the room but that did mean that there was a great deal more space to store things but, more worryingly, it also meant that more beds could now be fit in. Jenna thought about those poor four still in the old War Room and shuddered. It wasn't going to take long to fill the space at all.

"You want me to put this anywhere in particular?" she asked when Mike looked up from his attempts at tessellation.

He didn't answer straight away and just looked at the crate, then back to her.

"Just push it under the other bed and as you bring others down, make sure to use all of the space you can."

'Thanks Mike, I never would have thought of that myself.'

She hadn't said it out loud but she was sure that Mike had read the meaning from her expression.

"You know," he began, standing up to look eye to eye with Jenna. "Why did you do this? You aren't really working with the Ult, are you?" The question stung Jenna like a slap across her face. She'd been so taken aback by the idea that she was trying to commit genocide that, for far too long, she just couldn't even begin to understand how to answer. Mike just looked confused but ever so slightly sad.

Jenna pushed the box she'd been carrying under the bed as she'd been directed and returned slowly to her position opposite Mike.

"No Mike, I'm not working with the Ult, and I haven't done any of this. Where did you get that idea?" She could feel her voice wavering ever so slightly as she replied and under the weight of her own fatigue, it was hard not to let tears flow down her face. She'd lived and worked with Mike for years. They'd never been really close but she thought that there was more than just this. She needed to understand and despite feeling that she already knew where this had come from, it was still going to be good to finally be hearing the truth. Mike shuffled back and forth and looked like he was fighting an internal battle against his own fears. Finally, his eyes dropped to the floor as he spoke.

"Emily and Scott said that you did all this on purpose because you wanted to lead this group and that you were going to take the best stuff for yourself and to Hell with the rest of us." He'd trailed off ever so slightly at the back end of the sentence, as if hearing it said out loud that one of his colleagues was going to kill everyone just so she could have the shiny toys made it very clear that it was indeed a ridiculous idea.

Jenna felt a knot constrict around her stomach which could have been hunger but felt much more like emotional shock. She'd known that Scott had been the one making all of the snide comments and it had never been a secret that he'd recruited Emily to his cause, but hearing it confirmed was a different thing all together. If you suspect something, even with all of the evidence pointing that way, there's still a chance, be it a tiny one, that you could be wrong. That chance can sustain you even in the face of so much negativity, and mean that you can keep on pushing forward. That tiny fragment of possibility is very often all that we have, but when it gets taken away by the full, ugly truth, all those awful thoughts become concrete. The horror of knowing that those were the thoughts floating around out there when people discussed you, that you were not only disliked but viewed with distrust.

And the most painful thought of them all.

What if they're right?

She couldn't stop the tears now. Her own bloody mindedness set her face like a bland mask but the water from her eyes streaked over her face like rivers rushing from the mountains to the sea. She was just so tired.

Mike looked up from his study of the spot on the floor and noticed the tears on Jenna's face. His own face seemed to collapse under the weight of what he'd said and he was finally brought back to his senses of the reality of what had been happening. He knew she wasn't doing all the bad things that had been suggested now, but for Jenna, it was just too late.

"I'm sorry. I didn't mean to make you .... It was just that Scott always .... Emily said that you and ...." He just couldn't finish any of the sentences that sprang from his lips as that truth which had been clouded from him was suddenly exposed.

"I'm not doing anything with the Ult. I'm a human for God's sake. Remember?" Her voice was soft as she fought to maintain her control. Mike looked ashamed, and for a brief second, Jenna was happy that he did. It passed quickly, though, as she remembered that he'd been on the receiving end of Scott's manipulation. He'd been scared, just like everyone else, and that had been what Scott had used by fanning those flames.

"I'm sorry. I'm so sorry," was all Mike could say now, and it repeated as he reached out slowly to place a hand on her hand by way of apology.

The second he made contact with her, Jenna felt a jagged jolt course through her whole body and with a guttural call, Mike's arm was flung back from her and sent him spinning away to collapse onto the floor, clutching his hand against the pain and moaning as he tried to pull himself together.

"WHAT THE FUCK WAS THAT?" Artie was all over the latest problem. Chang even appeared to be looking their way despite everything he'd been through.

"Uhhhhh....." was all Jenna could think to say while she wiped away the tears, hoping no-one would pay them any real attention, what with Mike on the floor. Mike eased himself to his feet back where he'd been standing before whatever had happened, happened, and flexed his hand while rubbing at his eyes, trying to shove the fuzziness away.

"Just tripped up is all. Think I knocked the wind out of myself. No biggie," Mike reassured the others, though sounding a great deal less than certain of the events himself. He looked at Jenna with utter confusion on his face, before excusing himself from the job at hand. Whatever had just happened, it was only the latest in a long list of oddities she'd just have to work out later, but whatever had caused the shock, she didn't feel as tired any more. Turning back to her task, she decided that spending as much time in the infirmary as she could, would likely be a good idea.

Time dragged for the rest of the day as she moved and logged all of the boxed pieces of the Ult, and then offered to complete any and all little jobs that Artie needed sorting so she could keep out of the grips of the rest of the people here but also make sure Chang was still OK. It was late when the next medic cover arrived to relieve Artie and as the two of them quietly discussed Chang and the changes that had been made during the day, Jenna pulled a chair up next to Chang's bed and relaxed into the worn cushions.

"How're you feeling?"

Chang smiled at her from his position on the bed and gave her a slow thumbs up.

"Living the dream."

They both chuckled ever so slightly at the idea that this was living the dream. Jenna just sat quietly and considered just how much the world had changed and how they'd finally all reached this point. The twentieth century had seen the kind of advancements in thought and technology which would make your head spin but even that would pale into insignificance next to the Ult arriving. That there was only sixty six years between the first powered flight and man landing on the moon amazed her but, the regression to the world now was just so much more powerful. It had been done to them rather than humans doing it themselves, though a great many people seemed to be keen to embrace the regression to the witch hunts.

The silence just continued between them and they both just took the time to enjoy it. Huge changes were coming for both of them and they would mean an enormous amount of hard work. They both knew that they needed to focus on tasks which would have the ability to beat them down under the weight of them, but for that night, for that short time that the rest of the house was quiet and the attacks had stopped, they were going to take a hold of that small element of being human and just sit with each other and 'be'. It didn't matter that everyone was aligned against Jenna or that Chang was probably never going to walk again. For tonight, having that air between them of just putting the weights they were carrying down and breathing in the rest, was enough.

19

Jenna didn't even notice that she'd fallen asleep.

She been listening to the steady in and out of Chang breathing next to her, had even noticed that it was changing as he himself drifted off, but her last thought had been the chances of a co-ordinated Ult attack and what they'd all need to do to be able to survive. She probably should have realised that she'd moved from there to seamlessly be at the mercy of an ever growing mass of flesh as all of those Ult combined to become one singular being that was threatening them, all while trying to suck Jenna into the mass as well.

She woke with a start as, in her dreamscape, the Mega-Ult reached out with that grotesque limb to engulf her into its whole, and as she looked hurriedly around at where she was, the blanket that someone had draped over her fell to the floor in a heap. Chang was awake in the bed next to her and was looking at her with that all too familiar worry. Jenna blew out a steadying breath as that dream finally slithered away.

"Hey Jenna," called a familiar voice from behind her, causing her fear to spike again and to turn to face what she hoped wasn't Mega-Ult again. Artie was sat at the desk in the infirmary again, his much more familiar expression of goofy exuberance sitting happily in place.

"How did you sleep?"

Relaxing again, she rubbed at her neck as she became all too aware that although the sleep she'd had had been uninterrupted, it hadn't come without the tariff of a crick in her neck.

"Had some weird dreams but feels like the sleep was pretty good. What time is it?" Jenna was waking up properly and had realised that Artie being back meant that something pretty serious was going on, or, and judging by his mood the more likely option, she'd been out cold all night.

He smiled, understanding where the question had come from.

"It's lunch time. You clearly needed the sleep."

To further emphasise the point, her stomach growled a long, bubbly complaint that was loud enough that Chang and Artie both heard it, though they did their best to hide it.

"I think I'd better get some food then," replied Jenna as she folded the blanket and left it in the chair.

"You guys want anything?"

Artie looked over Jenna's shoulder and met Chang's eyes. Whatever the look that passed between them was, Jenna felt that it was something that she needed to know.

"What?"

"It's been a pretty busy night, all things considered," replied Artie with his grin still in place but there was a darker expression leaking out from just behind it now.

"I suppose you could say that there's been a coup," said Chang flatly.

Jenna's mouth fell loose and not a single word would spring forth when she tried. What the Hell was he talking about?

"Scott had a big speech with everyone listening on where he told them all that it had been odd that Emily had been the only casualty from the last attack, when she'd been one of the people who'd seen through you." Artie had lost his grin now.

"He told everyone what had happened in the War Room and how the Ult that had attacked us just stopped and let you kill them, meaning you were given help. The Ult were there to be sacrificed but before they did they killed Emily because you wanted them to."

She couldn't believe what Artie was saying. It was utter fiction, surely no-one would believe all of this?

"It's not just you. They all think I was a part of this as well and was meant to be a sacrifice as well. I'd been protecting you so must have been in cahoots, therefore my death would look like there wasn't a link between us," said Chang with more than a little twinge of incredulity.

Jenna's head span and all she could do was stumble over to her chair and slump down without further comment. How did things get here so fast?

Artie picked up where Chang had finished, and the story got worse.

"When we all finally checked on the people who'd contracted that virus, after making the infirmary ready for the new residents," he waved an arm over towards the far end of the infirmary where four new beds had been arranged in what little space there was. Jenna got a chill seeing that those beds were empty.

"All four of them were dead, and had been that way for a while, so most likely died during the attack. Scott was happy to wave about it being people who'd been sceptical of you who were the ones to die again." Artie stopped and it felt like that was everything, finally. Chang had one more bomb to drop.

"So we're stuck in here, locked down for our own safety, with Artie as our jailer. I can't go anywhere anyway so it's pretty much just a punishment for you. Sorry."

Jenna hadn't even registered that the door to the infirmary was closed. It had always been open because if there was something serious happening, access to medical help needed to be immediate. It was there for everyone, to put them back together if they fell to bits in any way, and that simple action of shutting the door really had given it the feeling of a cell. Access was now very far from encouraged.

Jenna collapsed further into the chair as more and more of any fight she had in her melted away to the air. She understood that people were going to be scared at the new threat coming in but Scott had just taken advantage of them. She doubted that he even truly thought that she was somehow a traitor to the human race. It was more likely that he'd just done what he'd always done and taken the opposite position because he could, and when more and more people listened he just kept on going because he liked the attention. She rushed beyond having any compassion for him though, as she considered the realities of where their little society had devolved to thanks to what he'd been doing.

He'd driven them all into a spiral of terror far beyond the real threat of the Ult and the virus of theirs by just spouting whatever idea made its way into that warped little mind of his.

Anger grew and expanded to fill all of her thoughts at what he'd done. Her knuckles popped as she squeezed ever tighter on the arms of the chair, secretly wishing that it could have been Scott's neck she'd been crushing.

A metallic creak filled the air and all eyes flashed towards it. The door to the infirmary was being slowly opened by someone outside but all any of them could see was a single arm doing the pushing. Whoever was attached to that arm wasn't coming in; they were just doing the menial task. Another heart beat and finally, with just the appropriate amount of regal sweep, Scott entered like a conquering general.

Jenna's anger was a constant flame inside her now and she screamed 'PRICK!' in her head as he stood before them. The arms of the chair were crushed some more.

"Awake at last, I see," declared Scott with faux importance dripping from his words. No-one else made any effort to reply. Undeterred, he pushed on.

"We've planned out how we're going to expand the compound walls to create a home which can keep us all safe from the Ult threat, but also what we'll need to do to increase our food production and we're going to need your help to make it happen." He wasn't a huge man but he was doing all he could to stand close enough to Jenna to loom over her, as if that itself was a tacit threat against her refusal.

Prick.

"What have you come up with? Sounds interesting," probed Chang from his bed. His tone showed that despite everything which had befallen him, he was still willing to entertain the idea that there could be a positive outcome of sorts. Scott could have been able to figure a way through the list of obstacles they were facing and despite everything he'd been responsible for, the continued health and survival of the population had been what they'd all been in search of.

"You won't be involved, I'm afraid," Scott replied. That was that then.

"And if I decide I'd rather not be a part of your brave new world, what with me being a prisoner and all?" Jenna wasn't going to just go along.

"You most certainly aren't a prisoner, where could you have possibly got an idea like that?" replied Scott, with yet more performative flourish to his shock.

"No, no, no, no. We want to make sure that you're safe, is all. There have been a number of people making overt threats against you, all down to your actions allowing such access to our home to the Ult. Keeping you here means that you have someone to protect you, should the need arise." Obsequiousness dripped from every word he spoke. He knew he was talking rubbish but he wanted to do his best to put on the show.

Jenna just didn't have the strength to fight it.

She wanted to leap across the space between them and sink her thumbs into his eyes. She wanted to strangle the life from him while she watched it drip away as they were nose to nose. She wanted to explain to him just what damage he was doing and make him understand it in the most violent way possible. She wanted all of those things, and so many others, that she seriously considered just giving in to her rage and let the consequences be damned, but that wouldn't achieve anything. If anything, the second she did anything against Scott or his people, she'd just be confirming everything that they thought. The truth of where they all were had been distorted by one person to the point where everyone knew the truth even if they were wrong. It was their truth, a shared distortion of reality.

"What do you want me to do," grumbled Jenna as she accepted her position. Scott just beamed with happiness and clapped his hands together like an excited child. She couldn't be certain of it, but she could have sworn that his glowing nervous system had flashed brighter at the agreement.

"Wonderful news. All we'll need you to do to start with is carve some lines in the ground. We've planned our new home so we'll need more space to expand into. I'm sure you'll agree that seeing the plan actually on the ground will make it so much simpler to get things right and then keep everyone safe?"

It didn't sound so bad after all but that still didn't absolve Scott in Jenna's eyes.

"I'll have you sent for when you're required." That was the last Scott said before he swept out of the room and the door was creaked back closed behind him by that servant arm. Silence was left in his wake.

"That could have been worse, I suppose?" opined Chang from his bed.

"It could have been better too," replied Jenna, finally releasing her grip on the arms of the chair. Her fingers were very far beyond stiff and shouted their own displeasure at Jenna as she flexed them.

"Yeah, but at least you get to go outside for a while. The fresh air may be good for you," smiled Chang. Despite everything, he was still doing his best to look on the positive side of things. All Jenna could do now was wait for the call to come down from on high and hope that it was.

The room waited quietly for well over an hour before the door was finally opened again and Jenna was summoned. Selina walked after her in a 'guard' role but she'd winked at Jenna when no other prying eyes could see it. It gave Jenna a shock of adrenaline that there could be people who didn't think the worse of her outside of the infirmary. Maybe she wasn't being totally ostracised from the human race?

She could only hope, but there weren't any other people on her route through the house to ask. It was only when they all passed out into the compound that she encountered people who weren't guarding her, and the view was bleak. There weren't many people there, only a handful more than any other working day, but each face that she looked into contained furious malice. Time and time again, she risked a tiny smile by way of reassurance that she wasn't any kind of threat, but time and time again, stony expressions and suspicion was all she saw.

In the compound, next to The Beast, she'd been handed a blackboard with basic scratches of an outline of where she was expected to mark out, a huge duffel coat as a protection against the cold, the temperature having dropped over night so everybody's breath plumed like smoke, and a large metal rod which had been beaten flat at one end for the marking out. No-one had said a word.

"This everything?" she asked the people around her, growing more and more desperate for some kind of hint that there was at least one more person who didn't want her dead.

Everyone else just turned and left her next to the entryway. Nothing else then.

But she wasn't alone.

Selina began working the levers at the main doorway and the big inner doors swung open. Jenna just drew in a breath that she hoped would clear her mind as much as possible, and strode with her head held high, into the lock gate area and waited for Selina to seal her in. In seconds, the creaking behind her finished in a hollow thud and after a few muffled clanks and clicks, she readied herself for the outer doors to open.

"You ready?"

"JESUS CHRIST!!" screamed Jenna and spun rapidly to orient herself towards the voice, all the while dragging the metal rod up into something which could pass as a defensive posture.

Selina frowned at her, hands placed firmly on her hips, and smiled slightly.

Jenna exhaled a breath which had been utter terror and dropped the rod on the floor.

"What? Didn't think you'd be going alone, did you?" asked Selina with that familiar no nonsense tone as she made her way to the outer doors and banged on them hard. Jenna didn't respond. She didn't know what to say. She had expected to be left to her own devices so the appearance of Selina had caught her totally off guard. That thought was quickly put to one side as more clanks and clicks came from the outer doorways mechanisms and they swung open on the outer world beyond.

Inside her head, Jenna's own mind cycled through a series of clanks and clicks as she considered her next step and she quickly arrived on a terrible understanding.

"You're not going to be safe with me," she stammered while gripping onto Selina's Jacket and shaking her slightly.

"They can't see me but they'll be able to pick you out easily if you leave the compound. What are you doing?"

Selina just smiled.

"I don't think that any of the 'true believers' trusted you out here on your own but they also didn't want to be the one in the firing line should an Ult actually turn up. There's more than a few are still unsure of the whole invisible thing but, again, actually taking the risks themselves, not a chance."

"So if you believe me, why did you come out here? If I'm telling the truth, that just means that you're the worm on the hook for the Ult." Jenna appreciated the support but all she could see at this point was that a friend of hers had just put their life in her hands.

Pressure? She ate pressure for breakfast. Didn't she?

The air tasted cold to Jenna as she gingerly walked through the open doors and onto the potential battlefield that the outside world had to offer. The sky was clear but the sunlight around them carried no heat at all. The ground crunched ever so slightly with each foot fall and suggested that the job at hand was likely going to be a tough slog. Finally, Jenna located the appropriate place to start her task on the map and got to work.

The time crawled by and even with Selina helping where she could with a scrap metal bar of her own, progress was tough. The ground was frozen through and was unyielding to almost every attempt made to score through the surface, yet they continued their efforts. Occasionally, Selina would stop and scour the horizon for the approach of their enemies but each time she did, citing hunches, funny breezes, odd sounds, or even a tingling in her ears as what had warned her, there was nothing to see.

The day continued and as the sun fell below the horizon, dragging the remaining daylight with it, a cloud cover moved in over them, like the world was pulling the duvet up over itself before sleep. Selina nudged Jenna's arm by way of attracting her attention before tossing her own metal bar to the floor.

"Come on. Think we've done enough today, don't you? Let's get some coffee."

Jenna's soul soared. She was exhausted and feeling very far from ready to continue this giant art project, and the thought of a hot drink was just too good to miss out on. She slammed her metal pole into the trench she'd been working on, thinking to mark out exactly where she'd been working for the resumption of works tomorrow, but it didn't break through anywhere near far enough and just fell to the floor with an exhausted sigh of its own.

"I know how you feel," joked Jenna, and just gave up and headed back towards the still open doors of the outer wall. As the two women walked slowly back to the compound, Jenna looked into the ever darkening sky and noticed the glowing tower of light stretching into the sky coming from the main buildings. It was a stark reminder of Mary and Mo being victims of what had befallen this place. It was faint, but the cloudy sky allowed her to pick it out much more clearly. Pulling the doors closed, Jenna couldn't help herself but just stare up at the luminescence and wonder at it. She was exhausted but again, her humanity should at least recognise the beauty of what had been done to her friends, even through the horror of it.

"Problem?" asked Selina as she noticed Jenna's attention.

Jenna didn't shift her gaze but responded in an almost dreamy voice and with an expression of glazed wonder. She could pick out so many flickering sparks of energy drifting through the whole column that she could almost taste the individual nature of them, while at the same time, wrapping herself in the blanket power of the whole thing.

"It just looks pretty is all," before adding in a rush after remembering that she was the only one to see it, "The energy coming from Mary and Mo. Despite everything, I just thought it looked pretty."

Selina looked up in the vague direction of what she thought Jenna was staring at, just in case, but couldn't see anything more than the clouds.

"Cool. It looks better at night?" she asked, looking to make some kind of small talk.

Jenna nodded but as she thought about it, it occurred to her that it shouldn't make any difference. The Ult couldn't see light the same way we all did so wouldn't that mean that Jenna could see the glow in the same way? And if it was easier to see it now, had something changed to make it happen?

"You said that people still didn't believe that I was invisible to the Ult. What say we try to convince them of that fact? It could be the first step in proving each and every step of my side of things."

Selina didn't look convinced.

“I don’t think that it’ll matter that you prove you’re right any more. I get the feeling that whatever Scott sees just gets spun to be whatever he wants, the truth be damned.” Selina sounded very much like the thought had been playing on her mind for a while.

Jenna frowned and idly chewed at the inside of her cheek. Selina was most likely right but that didn’t, shouldn’t, mean that they should just give up.

She couldn’t just grovel as a part of the whole because the almighty leader wants her to.

“Fuck Scott,” snapped Jenna finally, her anger flaring.

“It’s most likely right that it won’t make a difference but that doesn’t mean that I’m not going to try. Come on.”

It was fully dark outside when they cracked the outer doorway open again. Selina had called up to someone who was on the top of the wall; no doubt prepared to ‘welcome’ Jenna back inside, and had explained what they were going to do. A voice came back down to them that Scott would have to be contacted first but Jenna wasn’t going to wait. The temperature hadn’t been high during the day but now it was falling quickly to a deep cold. The spots of clear sky above gave warning that any heat was going to be leeching away but at least that meant that moon was providing some light which was helping to illuminate the area.

“You sure you want to do this?” Selina had been asking Jenna every other second since she’d made up her mind if she really wanted to do what she had planned, seemingly begging her to reconsider, but her mind was made up.

“You got a better idea?” Jenna knew that she hadn’t, but she also knew, just knew, that she was going to be perfectly safe and would be able to step in to protect Selina if something went sideways.

“Good luck you two,” said Scott from behind them.

The two women snapped back around and looked up, trying to pinpoint where he was standing. It didn’t take long.

Scott was stood in full view of anyone or anything that was outside the walls. The walkway on the other side was built far enough below the upper level that everyone was able to move around whilst remaining wholly covered so he was most likely stood on a ladder, just to convey his magnificence to those who were watching him. Jenna and Selina traded glances regarding their feelings on what he was doing but they both recognised that they weren't the ones watching who Scott was performing for. The footsteps and voices coming from within the compound painted the picture of a fair sized crowd.

"You're happy that we do this? Couldn't this just be another ploy to attract more Ult?" Jenna had thought it but Selina was the one asking.

Scott raised his arms above his head and all of the sound drifting up from inside stopped.

"I only want all of us to be safe against our enemies. I do, though, find it odd that you're trying to undermine my choice here. A choice, which everyone knows, that came about by your request. Shouldn't I trust what you say?" If he'd been any more 'arch' he'd have been twirling his moustache.

That was that then. Selina had been bang on the money with her appraisal of his thinking and Jenna just shrugged away any ill feeling. There wasn't any point feeling angry at him for behaving in just the way that they knew he would. Selina just saluted him and they turned back to the outside world and the task at hand.

Behind them, the huge outer doors creaked and with a crack of terrible finality, they slammed shut and were locked from the inside. Selina turned and began sprinting across the open ground before the doors, hoping that they'd closed by an unnamed mistake. Had it been the wind which had pushed the heavy doors? No, there wasn't anything more than a tiny breeze. Had a mechanism broken which had let the doors go? She began pulling on them as she arrived but they didn't budge. Jenna joined her and signalled for her to look slightly away from the doors. There were two back packs, two paraffin lamps and a small cigarette lighter standing together on the ground, huddled together as if feeling their own fear. Checking inside their supplies, they found several bottles of water each.

"Looks like we made him more wary. Great." Selina snorted.

"At least he gave us the water," said Jenna briskly. "It could be that he wants to believe."

There was nothing else to add, they just had to get on with it.

Selina and Jenna instinctively retreated so their backs were pressed against the door as they lit the lamps, and despite the surety Jenna was feeling, fear was a very real thing they'd both been living with for far too long to forget it immediately.

Taking a steadying breath, Jenna hoisted her rucksack onto her shoulders and began making her way into the field before the house. Selina followed on, her own rucksack carried in one hand. Jenna carried the machete again while Selina collected the device Jenna had been using, brandishing it like a gladiatorial trident.

Walking with as much calm assurance as they could muster, they headed steadily away from the doors, and each other, until there was a huge gap between them, giving no chance that there would be any confusion around which of them was the target should they be approached. Plumes of their breath drifted on the night air and even though there'd been no contact from any Ult during their earlier time outside, they remained hyper aware of any movement. Jenna risked a glance back at the walled home she was trying to protect and picked out a huge number of glowing shapes peaking just over the lip of the defences. Everyone knew that they needed to stay well out of possible sight of any Ult outside but it would appear that the feeling of curiosity had flooded the populace inside. With all of the people adding to the towering signal from Mary and Mo it at least meant that there was as strong a target as possible for the Ult to investigate. It could help get this finished quicker than she'd first thought.

Shaking her head with resignation, she just returned to the job at hand.

The two women made slow and steady circles of the walls, doing everything they could to give as clear a target as they could should anything be watching. It was on the fifth circuit that Jenna began to notice a prickling unease crawling all over her skin which made her feel both oddly exhilarated and scared. She stopped walking as it began to reach all the way through her like a static charge and fired each of her nerve endings.

“What’s up Jen?” shouted Selina who stopped moving herself, unsure of what she should do for the best.

Jenna just held up one hand with her thumb up but didn’t say anything.

Selina assumed that she was checking out a sound or the like so began scanning around them, hoping to find whatever it was that Jenna was after. In reality, Jenna wasn’t really aware of anything beyond the space surrounding her. Every nerve ending she possessed erupted in a blaze of sensation and energy. Her whole body felt as if it was alight with energy and all of her senses bloomed with a roar of almost consciousness. Images of abstract forms and swirling sensation flew through her head, flickering snatched outlines of trees, of open fields, of rivers and of glowing patterned people running from her. She could sense every aspect of the pictures in her head as they flashed past, far beyond what would normally be felt. She couldn’t find the edges of the sensation as her head was filled with information so all she could do was just let everything rush through her.

After an age with every part of her body alive in ways that she’d never thought possible, everything began to dull around the edges while her senses were released from the grip of whatever had just happened to her. She could feel the afterglow sensation fading like the dying ring of a bell but she’d been left with a single view in her mind. She slumped to the floor in a boneless heap and was quickly aware of sounds coming from nearby yet also far away as Selina raced towards her, calling her name with frantic purpose, but that strange image remained in her head. She could see darkness mainly but flickering like static were outlines of tree trunks, bushes and movement, and there was a bright light somewhere ahead, glowing to attract her.

One half of her didn’t understand anything of this new picture but there was the other half that knew instinctively what she could sense. Selina kept calling for her but Jenna knew that there was now the need to focus all of their attention on the here and now.

“They’re coming,” gasped Jenna as she forced herself to her feet and shook the fuzzy sensation in her head away, clearing herself back to where she was. Selina didn't waste time debating her, instead turning to face away from Jenna by way of some kind of protection. From the far off woods, the sound became more and more noticeable as the seconds passed by and, bit by bit, Jenna understood that there were Ult approaching. She was going to be getting her chance to show all of the watching crowd what she'd been saying since this all started. She also understood that she'd seen the Ult approaching in her mind, and that the image she'd experienced hadn't been hers.

She'd seen the Ult approaching as if she'd been with them, looking through them.

What the hell was happening to her?

20

Selina hurried away from Jenna and brought her weapon up to a defensive position, still scanning everywhere she could while also keeping most of her attention on the approaching creatures. Jenna remained still and tried to force down the jangling inside her which just wouldn't fully stop. She held the machete but she hadn't raised it yet, her body feeling the ringing of whatever had taken place and trying to conserve her available energy.

They'd only moved a very short distance from the main doors when the Ult breached the edge of the woods, and had quickly split back to the huge space between them. When the far off tree line was breached by the misshapen horror of two lumbering Ult, they'd paused for the briefest of seconds, as if casually taking stock of the environment before them, before recommencing their advance, this time aiming at Selina. Both Jenna and Selina held their ground and just stared at the Ult, every instinct in their bodies calling out for them to turn and sprint back to the relative safety of the house, but instead, they each withdrew a single canister from their rucksacks and readied themselves for engagement.

"You ready for this or do we need to cut and run?" Selina shouted out to Jenna. She wasn't looking for an out, just checking on Jenna's condition.

Jenna shouted her response back and just sprinted out to meet the Ult, her machete now waving with intent above her head. She was very ready for this.

Jenna ran towards the two Ult but veered away as she closed on them, daring them to reach after her and pursue but there was no reaction at all as they stumped onwards. Selina was still the one they wanted. Jenna turned back towards the enemy and ran directly ahead of them, across the path they were taking forwards and again there was no signal that they'd even registered her as existing. Selina recognised it was her turn now, and began to run in the opposite direction Jenna had taken, stretching out the distance between her and the Ult again, and the instant she did, the two monsters matched her direction and began lumbering after her.

It was working.

Jenna turned again and ran back towards Selina, waving her weapon and yelling her defiance for the crowd to witness. She was going to prove to everyone that she was as human as they were. Ahead of her, Selina switched direction again and began sprinting back along the edge of the wall, her spear held in one hand and the canister of water in the other. As they crossed they both flashed wide smiles at the sheer unbridled release of what they were doing. They were daring the enemy of all of humanity to come and get them. They were taking all of the fear that they'd ever felt at the work of these beasts, and were using it as fuel to send them around and around the Ult before striking them down, the first blow for the human race in the coming fight back. The Ult followed after Selina again and just to prove her point as strongly as she could, Jenna headed directly between the two Ult and again passed by without any hint that they'd registered her.

She felt all of her senses dialled up to eleven and as she swept back round she made out a cheer going up from inside the walls. They were cheering for them. They were cheering for her. Euphoria exploded through her and she began running again, aiming back the way she'd come, knowing that Selina would be doing the same thing. She couldn't help but feel a glowing sensation of hope wrap through every part of her as she sprinted, and despite herself, Jenna let that tiny flame grow. She was proving that the Ult were indeed unable to see her and while she was doing it, she was reaching the crowd inside the compound of her home. She was going to turn the tide on all of those set up against her and she'd be able to start the return of humanity.

The flame in her roared higher as she ran and a picture of their home filled her head, a feeling of camaraderie and togetherness being just there to take hold of, but Jenna too late understood that what she was seeing wasn't just her imagination. Her mind's eye filled with a picture of a glowing Selina sprinting towards her through the darkness. She was seeing everything through the perception of the Ult again and with it, the approaching risk of where they were. Through that stuttering shared sight, a human view showed that Selina's expression looked confused as she moved on, no doubt aware that Jenna was acting or looking differently. Jenna did everything she could to shake the linking away. She needed her own point of view front and centre and knew she'd be vulnerable until it was restored.

Mentally crossing her fingers, she began to alter her line of running with the intention of bringing herself alongside Selina so they could lead the Ult away from the main doors. Her Ult shared viewpoint showed that the brightness of Selina was still the sole focus as it moved beneath the ever present towers of light of Mary and Mo.

All the while the action unfolded, another cheer went up from the other side of the wall, but this time, through the view of the Ult, people had managed to lift themselves high above the top edge of the wall to witness the show outside, presenting a radiant, shining glow of potential victims' gleaming like a halo atop the walls. One of the Ult switched its attention towards the people above it and in doing so, created another view point for Jenna to compete with.

She could see ghost images of Selina from multiple angles while also witnessing the crowd watching them. It was too much to control, and Jenna stumbled, unable to pinpoint where she needed to be moving through the mess in her head and took uncertain strides as she did everything to keep moving. She couldn't fully control herself but picked out too late that she was running directly into Selina's path.

Shit.

Pain bloomed in Jenna's back and she was able to see what had happened through the Ult. Her ragged running had sent her directly ahead of Selina without there being any chance of the collision being avoided. Selina had barrelled into Jenna with her spear held out forwards as she ran and that sharp end had been driven hard into her back, directly onto her spine. Pain shot all through her and the picture in her head scrambled back to her own vision finally, leaving her with the lasting image of her falling forwards as her pain flared brightly around her body, the glow of Selina's nervous system being joined by a millisecond long spark crackling in human form.

Had she been visible to the Ult?

The cheering beyond the wall came to a similar halt as the previous celebratory mood quickly become horror.

Selina crouched at Jenna's side, breathing hard after their running exploits but her expression showed a much greater worry.

"My God, I'm sorry Jen. I'll need to check the injury quickly to see what damage has been done but I'll get moving again and draw them away from you. Can you move?"

Jenna risked wiggling her toes in her boots and found that they seemed to be moving fine. Next were her fingers, and then her head as she risked a look up at where the Ult were. No problems. Next she risked feeling the point of impact on her back but her hand came back devoid of the blood she'd expected.

"I'm OK, just get moving and I'll look after myself until you get back," Jenna wheezed at Selina, who agreed as the single Ult chasing them was now uncomfortably close. Selina nodded and was up and away without another word, the Ult following after her, again missing the presence of Jenna. The other Ult was still grasping around at the wall towards where everyone had been stood earlier though now they'd all retreated back out of sight, so Jenna found herself free to at least sit up slowly and see what she could make out after the accident.

Sitting up, she felt oddly fine. Her back was still hurting but it was now more of an ache than any kind of sharp pain. Climbing to her feet, she stretched and moved in an attempt to find out exactly what she may have been struck with injury-wise but as she did, any discomfort drained away to the point that even her back stopped hurting.

There was being lucky but this was orders of magnitude above that. She should have had more happen to her than nothing at all, surely?

There was no further time to spend on the thought, though, as far off, from the tree line came the crashing branches and broken bushes sounds as more Ult broke through to the clearing before the house, and began moving downhill towards them all.

Panic exploded in Jenna and very quickly, she could make out the shouts and screams from inside the wall as everyone spotted the increase in the enemy force. Looking around her, Jenna quickly picked out Selina in the dark as she appeared around from the other side of the compound, having completed a full circuit to lead the Ult away and her expression showed her own panic.

"We need to get back inside," she huffed as she ran up to Jenna. "There's a wall of Ult coming towards us from the other side of the buildings, so we could do with getting indoors. FUCK ME!"

Her eyes turned to saucers as she noticed the approaching Ult on this side of the buildings and there was no question that their time running around was at an end.

Shouting up at anyone who might be able to hear them, they sprinted hard for the main doors and breathlessly began banging against them, hard. Nothing moved but there was also no sound or sign of there being anyone paying them any attention.

"COME ON – OPEN THE FUCKING DOORS!" roared Selina as she slammed her spear against the outer skin of their fortress. From another point around the perimeter, gun fire started up and light flared from nearby as flaming liquid was dumped onto the lone Ult which had been focused on the top of the wall. Molten death engulfed the mound of flesh that was attacking the wall and forced it back and away, its wild movements causing gobs of whatever burning material had been used to be flung everywhere. From deep within that enormous fire, that all too familiar call of 'ULT, ULT, ULT' boomed out and rattled through every person who was within earshot.

The meaning was clear.

It was screaming.

It continued thrashing and sending flaming missiles around at random points but there was a response from the other Ult approaching. They returned the 'ULT, ULT, ULT,' call and Jenna could have sworn that there'd been a more vicious edge when they did.

Selina continued to bang on the doors as Jenna watched on in morbid fascination, the Ult now jettisoning flaming lumps of its own flesh as it burned. Jenna was transfixed by what was happening before her and couldn't break away from a tiny voice in the back of her mind which growled and thrashed for her to cheer at the downfall of her enemy and rejoice. The grasping arm, which had for so long been the weapon that would destroy, was finally burned through and the force of the creatures flailing sent the charred and still alight appendage to crash into the wall near the very top, it coming to rest draped over the top of the makeshift battlements.

Jenna grabbed at Selina and began to haul her away from the doors with so much force that they both nearly fell sprawled onto their faces.

"The place is on fire," started Jenna, already scrabbling back to her feet and dragging Selina to do the same.

"No-one's going to let us in, they're all busy. I've got to get you hidden and I'll see what I can do to help out." They were already running again, back around the perimeter wall, with Jenna moving with a purpose that suggested to Selina that there was a specific destination. Behind them, the walls were now fully alight in a great many places. The burning liquid which had been dumped on that first Ult had been spattered in all directions when it landed and the dying creature had only added to the destruction as it thrashed.

This whole attack had been made worse by the choices from inside. Fire wasn't a weapon you wanted to use for close combat when you lived in a house made of wood. Surely there was a kids story about something like that?

Continuing hard around the wall, Jenna caught a glimpse of the advancing wall of Ult that Selina had seen earlier and felt sick to her stomach. There were just so many of them that for the short time that she stared, Jenna couldn't make out individual Ult from the mass of flesh which was approaching.

They were staging a full assault.

"Where are we going?" panted Selina, unsure of anything which could possibly be done.

"Plastic," was all Jenna said as they ran. Selina hoped that that was a good thing.

Finally Jenna slowed to a sudden stop as they reached the area of the outer wall which had been torn open by the three Ult who had broken into the War Room. The outer skin of the building had been ripped open and the repairs that had been carried out had been built up from the inside leaving access to the edges of the outer wall.

Selina looked around her at the advancing wall of alien flesh, up to the gun ports high above them where muzzles flared brightly as they spat out their defiance at the advancing Ult, and back to whatever it was Jenna was doing.

"I hope this won't take long, our friends out there are getting closer."

Jenna didn't risk a glance away from what she was working on, but hurried as much as she was able. She'd jammed an arm under the outer skin of the wall, which was made of wooden board, and was working her hand around searching for something specific. Selina could just watch on and hope that whatever was being done by Jenna as she was sunk to the shoulder into the damaged wall, would be worth it.

'ULT, ULT, ULT,' rose up in unison behind them as Jenna worked. That constant deep call from their enemy felt like an oppressive presence that they were exerting on them, and as the seconds passed by, was beginning to feel like a physical force.

"They're twenty metres from us Jen," shouted Selina with desperation beginning to bleed through her voice.

'ULT, ULT, ULT,' kept on coming.

"Got it," whooped Jenna in triumph and dragged her arm out of the wall, dragging behind it a large plastic sheet.

Neither woman said anything further and instead began sprinting away from the damaged point in the wall, Jenna draping the sheet of plastic over Selina as they went, before splitting away and aiming hard for the open space at the far end of the compound.

'ULT, ULT, ULT,' rolled on and on but checking back, Jenna saw what she'd been hoping for. The wall of advancing Ult had maintained their approach line and was still heading for their home, but they'd shown no indication that they'd registered either of the two women this time. Jenna smiled fiercely to herself before slowing and dragging Selina to the ground to look back at the warfare unfolding.

Lying on the grass covered ground, the sharp cold of the Earth embracing them both, they were able to take in deep, welcome breaths and take stock of the battle.

'ULT, ULT, ULT,' kept on booming through the night air while plumes of smoke erupted from the wall, but also now from within the structure proper. They could both smell the familiar odour of wood smoke as it drifted in all directions, and the air all around their home had begun to be cast with the tell tale orange glow of the growing flames.

"Plastic is good then?" panted Selina, now with more dark humour to her words, being further from the fighting. Jenna grinned back to her and took a second to enjoy that burning feeling of adrenaline coursing through her. It was a short lived but important 'win'.

"The Ult perceive us by our electricity. The thick plastic sheeting was able to insulate you enough to dull what they were able to pick up. I can't see your 'glow' so it made sense they wouldn't either."

Selina nodded her appreciation but that positivity quickly receded before the view of the house.

The line of advancing Ult had reached the wall near where Jenna had removed the plastic sheet, and had begun reaching those long appendages up towards the gun ports as they picked out the people within who were firing out. Jenna could also make out that, most likely as a response to the tactical error of the poured burning liquid, there were now people heaving out smaller burning missiles which were at least making the damage happen further from the walls therefore lowering the risk of collateral damage.

"So? Now what do we do? We can't get back in and the Ult are surrounding the place." Selina was coming to the same conclusion as Jenna and they both knew deep down that the battle was taking an awful turn. Scott and his people would be calling the shots and none of them were going to be able to fill Chang's shoes.

Jenna had to do something fast or their home was going to be overrun.

'ULT, ULT, ULT.'
'ULT, ULT, ULT.'
'ULT, ULT, ULT.'
'ULT, ULT, ULT.'
'ULT, ULT, ULT.'
'ULT, ULT, ULT.'

"You stay put, I'm going back in to try and cause as much damage as possible to those bastard creatures. If you try to approach now, there's too big of a risk that they'll spot you and I don't want to see you eaten by monsters."

Selina looked angry but any complaint was kept to herself. Despite her burning need to play a part in the defence of her home she accepted the reality of what they were facing. Jenna was right.

Jenna took out the machete and took the spear from Selina.

"Stay out of sight under that sheet and I'll be back for you when I can."

Without another word, Jenna set off back towards the melee which was unfolding before her eyes, hoping beyond everything that she wasn't already too late.

21

Jenna approached the battle as fast as she dared; not wanting to risk a wayward shot from inside greeting her, and did her best to formulate some kind of strategy.

Nothing was forthcoming.

The fire at the front of the compound was spreading further and further, chewing through any and all possible fuel it was encountering. So much of the building work had been completed using wood that the fire was being incredibly well fed as it gnawed its way through the defences. On the wall close to the burning, Jenna could make out the brightly glowing patterns of people who were shooting down at the Ult pushing ahead into the flames. Those flames meant nothing to the Ult though as they were seemingly happy to ignore their own safety for the chance to breach the wall.

'ULT, ULT, ULT.'

'ULT, ULT, ULT.'

'ULT, ULT, ULT.'

The gathered Ult from the opposite side had begun to spread out around the full perimeter of the compound as they searched for any kind of weakness that they could exploit to gain entry.

Did that mean that they couldn't break through from the areas they'd used before?

More gun fire crackled through the air and she just knew that the advancing monsters would be still moving forwards. Scanning the Ult for any clues to their possible plan, nothing presented itself as clear proof of anything yet, they still just kept advancing. Through the belching smoke she could make out a scattering blue spark around some of the Ult, one which appeared to leap from one and then onto another, all the while still more burning missiles were being launched from inside. Her heart sank as she pinpointed another Scott mistake.

The Ult were now all directly next to the outer skin of the house.

Blooms of light danced through the night as each missile reached a target but Jenna could see that although the Ult were indeed being burned away, that same fire was behaving just as the first load had. There appeared to be at least three more towers of flame coming from different points around the buildings and the shouting coming from inside was starting to turn into screams.

'ULT, ULT, ULT.'

'ULT, ULT, ULT.'

'ULT, ULT, ULT.'

'ULT, ULT, ULT.'

There was no use trying to develop any wild strategy now. It was too late. All she could do now was attempt to kill as many of them as she could and hope that she could make a big enough impact that everyone inside would be able to repel what was left.

Balling all of her courage and determination into as tight a mass as she was able, Jenna climbed fast into a sprint directly at the nearest creature and gripped tightly to her machete ready to inflict as much destruction as she was able.

She approached fast and did her best to appear visible to anyone who may have been aiming her way from inside. She'd kind of made peace with the idea that this could be where she died but during daring defiance of the Ult rather than the dumb luck of being picked off by friendly fire.

The Ult ahead of her, slightly smaller than the others she'd seen recently and a dark colour, had begun to thrash against the wall with its arm, landing concussive blows which sounded destructive more than they appeared to be doing any real damage outside. Jenna wasn't going to let it be successful.

Dropping her spear to clang on the hard ground, she angled her run to bring herself into position to sprint past her intended victim and poured on all of the speed she could muster. She could feel that animal surge in her whole body as she approached the dullard creature and her blood blazed with a killer fury at what she was going to do. As she closed towards the kill she leapt into the air with her machete held high.

She was passed the Ult in a flash, hitting the ground beyond without breaking her stride, with her hand still tightly gripped on to the machete but now with it having completed its savage arc to carve cleanly through the Ult arm and separate it from the body to leave it a stuttering mess on the ground.

Wasting no time, Jenna pulled a flask free from her back pack and headed back at the jerking and damaged Ult where she leapt again and dumped water into the sputtering stump on the top of the creature. As she'd hoped, the Ult convulsed once and fell still, before slumping down and rolling onto its side, all the energy driving it now gone. None of the other Ult, the nearest of which would have been able to 'see' what she'd just done, gave a single hint that they'd been aware of her.

Excellent.

Baring her teeth in an animalistic snarl, Jenna set off towards the next Ult in line.

With decisive strokes every time, Jenna struck down five more of the Ult as she worked her way methodically around the perimeter of the buildings. She wasn't sure exactly how many of the things there were but she was going to do everything she could to chip away at them. Gun fire, which had become more sporadic as she'd been moving on her killing spree, began to resume in more focused bursts, and for a handful of heartbeats, Jenna felt the hope kindle inside her again that inside the walls, people were registering what she was doing and were climbing back into the fight with a renewed sense of resistance.

Her hope was quickly discarded as she came to a skidding halt before her sprint onto her next victim.

She could still hear that gun fire.

There was that almost metronomic call of 'ULT, ULT, ULT,' coming from the invaders, along with the screams and shouts coming from inside the walls.

She'd been surrounded by the sharp odour of burning wood and the sting to her eyes reminded her that she'd been running through the ever billowing smoke from those fires, and even the seared and severed flesh of the Ult was becoming common place but a raised wind brought a terrifying fact to light.

Above her, driven on by that advancing gust, came a blanket of thick and heavy cloud which cut away all of the moon light which had been helping her see more clearly. It hadn't made an enormous change to the conditions that they were all fighting under but it gave Jenna a brief second to recognise what the Ult were doing.

The fire continued to burn, sending out that huge plume of smoke but as it had been destroying more and more of where they called home; it had been kicking out tiny burning fragments to tumble and spin through the night air. Jenna had seen so many of them as she'd been moving that she was sure that there would be precious little time for her to put her fight back into action, but as the cloud cover rolled in, robbing them of the moon light, it became clear that she'd been horribly mistaken.

The vast majority of what she could see flittering around weren't remnants of the fire.

They were motes of the Ult cure.

Looking back over the route she'd taken, her mouth fell open as she could now pick out the massive smears of 'cure' which were all over the walls, the ground, and were still leaking out of the monstrous corpses.

The Ult weren't trying to break in. They were just going to dump their disease everywhere. They'd been able to smash their way in before, but this time they were acting like they'd been doing for years, setting a siege, though now with an added sting in the tail of a new biological weapon.

Another gust of wind rose and swept the clouds onwards again, revealing another break and freeing the light from above. The smears of cure dulled to almost nothing again and Jenna was snapped out of her thoughts.

What were they trying to do?

Why had they changed how they behaved after this long of going about things the same way?

The questions were swirling in her head and it was making her feel like she was drowning under the flood of new possibilities. Her skin prickled and the wind cast along the ground, sending any and all of those free motes tumbling through the sky, but her chest tightened and her whole body shuddered at the stark realisation of what the Ult were doing.

She had to get inside. She had to at least let them know what was happening so everyone could at least try to defend themselves.

Jenna considered heading back to Selina to bring her into the action for any kind of help, but each time she considered the options, Selina ended up incinerated, 'cured', or dead in a thousand hideous ways which in turn meant that Jenna would likely be killed because she wouldn't just let her friend head off without any protection.

'ULT, ULT, ULT'.

Her mind just wouldn't find a way to do anything of worth and her whole body was beginning to feel like a plucked string on a violin, ringing out under the tension she was under.

She had to do something.

The bolt of energy which came out of the sky, burning the irregular shapes of light onto her eyes, brought her back to the here and now.

Falling back hard under the impact wave of whatever blast had landed nearby, Jenna blinked her eyes and rubbed at them, doing anything she could to force away the glowing blob shadows from her vision. The energy still crackled all over her whole body as if she was still holding a charge and her teeth all felt as if they'd been super-charged, practically dancing in her mouth.

The shouts and screams coming from within the walls were still floating out on the night air while the gun fire was still clack-clack-clacking. Looking around her as best she could, Jenna couldn't see any sign of nearby Ult or impact damage from whatever had made the bright light and explosion, but the fight was still raging. Above the compound, she could still see the tower of glowing energy coming from this end of the buildings so that at least meant that Mary and Mo were still alive, if you could still call it that, but now there was a second tower beaming towards the sky at the other end. It meant that there was another person fallen victim to the 'cure' inside. Or more than one?

It was rapidly joined by another beam as the cure claimed another victim.

Jenna just couldn't think of the possible fallen and instead gripped tightly to her purpose, but that was soon shaken as her mind fell in on itself and she was treated to an overlapping of visions from a multitude of locations. There'd been no overt sign that something was about to happen in her head but she was utterly engulfed by the pictures of the striking colours of energy coming from people inside the walls, she could see sparks of blue light exploding like insane fireworks before her face and reflexively flinched away from them despite knowing they were coming from an Ult somewhere else.

Randomly cycling over and through the images, she was treated to a complete vision of the fight and could see that there were at least two of the monsters inside the walls who were stumping their way around in search of victims.

Their home was falling.

The slap to her face dragged her rapidly back into the clarity of her own perspective and the searing burn on her cheek suggested that something bad had just happened to her. Her hand instinctively flew to her face and checked for blood or other sign of injury before she could register that Selina was now crouching before her, wincing slightly as she rubbed her hand.

"You back?" Selina was all business and with an urgency to her voice.

Jenna wasn't sure.

The empty look that she gave Selina put that point across.

"You want a fresh one?" asked Selina and raised her hand, ready to strike again.

Jenna understood and raised a hand to placate her friend, seeing that she really meant to do what she was threatening.

"Good," said Selina as she grabbed at Jenna's arm and hauled her to her feet, her need for action making Jenna panic again. They sprinted hard for the main doors of the compound and Jenna did everything she could to shake away the cloying sensation in her head.

"We've got a chance to get back inside but we can't hang about," shouted Selina as she dragged Jenna hard behind her. The words were almost lost to the warring melee of sounds around them but Jenna was able to catch it. Inside her head, flashes of barely remembered imagery kept rising to remind Jenna that the fight was going badly but she pushed on.

Reaching the doors, Selina wasted no time and began smashing her fist against the wooden surface and screaming out for anyone inside to notice them. The doors were showing signs of widespread burning and charring but they were soaking wet and still standing. Jenna began banging against the doors as well, though without any of the urgency that Selina was exhibiting, her whole body still limping back to full speed.

From the other side of the doors, more and more words were becoming intelligible for both women and they kept doing everything they could to draw any attention their way. Finally, after what felt like an age, there was a response.

"Who's there?" squeaked a male voice from inside. Selina sighed her gratitude, but neither of them recognised who was speaking.

"It's Selina. Open the fucking doors, there's Ult everywhere out here."

There was no response from whoever it was on the other side.

Jenna's whole body prickled with a static electricity and her muscles began to seize and tense spasmodically, causing her to collapse backwards away from the doors. The screaming inside was fast to start up next and it was accompanied by more and more crashing and shattering of wood and concrete. Selina grabbed Jenna and began to drag her away from the doors as the ground began to shudder under the impacts of something huge.

The explosion which erupted from within the boundary of their now dying home sent billowing plumes of glowing fire into the night sky and in doing so, framed the monstrous shape of the gargantuan Ult which was smashing through the buildings and people.

Panic rose in Selina and Jenna alike at the scale of the thing.

It was the size of a three storey building with an over sized and over muscled appendage which was slamming through any and all of the buildings which were in its path. What little gun fire remained was being hurled at this new foe but Jenna could see that there was no effect. Tiny specks of flashing blue energy were erupting briefly where the bullets met their target but they just didn't travel any further than the creatures thick hide.

"I saw that lightning hit a load of the Ult on the back wall and burned them all down," said, Selina, her voice trembling as it cracked under the weight of what was becoming clear to her.

She began to weep silently but then kept speaking.

"I thought it was nature saving us, I really did. I thought that it had been the turning point we'd needed, I mean, you hear in stories that just at the last minute, something happens and the heroes are able to save the day. I saw the mass of Ult moving in spots but just thought that it was them dying after the lightning." Her voice trailed away from any further attempt to comprehend and she slumped to the floor next to where Jenna was laying.

That was why she'd been so desperate to move when she'd slapped Jenna.

That's why, thinking about the time since she did, there were no Ult actively attempting to chase Selina. Her plastic sheet had been discarded yet there was still no sign of attack, and it was because some of?, all of?, the Ult had been amalgamated into this giant creature.

There was nothing left to do now.

They'd have to run but there was nowhere to go. Every settlement around them had been lost to the Ult in one way or another and any survivors from here wouldn't have any protection from future attacks.

They'd be open and visible to every Ult that crossed their path.

They wouldn't be able to rest properly.

There wouldn't be enough food or water.

Jenna shuddered at the realizations and sagged under the gravity of them all.

Maybe those who died here were the ones who were getting the best deal?

From inside, the giant Ult began to roar that all too familiar 'ULT, ULT, ULT' call as it swung back and forth with that enormous grasping arm, scattering anything in its path, left and right. The gunfire had stopped now and as Jenna just stared up at the sky above what had once been her home, she could see that there were now more of those towers of glowing light but they were now all aiming squarely at the giant Ult rather than just the sky above.

Jenna thought it odd but didn't care anymore.

Why bother?

Everything was coming to an end before her eyes and there was just nothing more to say.

The piercing whistle from inside the walls shocked Jenna out of her pit of despair, reigniting more curiosity, and that shock dragged her mind fully back into the game as the doors of the compound were smashed open to a splintered mess as The Beast barrelled out through the space which remained. That screeching whistle became a clarion call for both Selina and Jenna as they stared on in wonder. It wasn't moving fast, but in terms of what the old girl was capable of, she was practically sprinting.

Selina was first to her feet and was again dragging Jenna behind her as she made for the trundling vehicle.

"Come on. We can get inside and they won't see us," shouted Selina, instantly buoyed by the faintest hope of survival and the knowledge that there was someone driving so therefore there was someone else who was alive.

Behind The Beast, the opened doors showed the clear picture of the devastation which had been visited upon the fractured settlement. Fires raged at so many points throughout the ruined estate that the glare of the fire was turning the night into day, the orange incandescence blooming everywhere.

The two women raced to the head of the vehicle and began to make as much noise as they could while waving their arms around for anyone inside to be able to see if they were looking through the periscope. The searching eye of the periscope, which had been swinging back and forth hunting for any possible points of attack while also maintaining their route, snapped hard to focus on them both and remained aimed at them.

"They've seen us," yelled Selina as she bounced around the far side of The Beast to reach the rear doors. Jenna followed and hoped that they were going to be let in. The doors were already opening when they arrived, and bathed in the light and radiating heat from their home, a single arm was outstretched to offer assistance climbing aboard.

Jenna shoved Selina forwards to take Artie's hand first, knowing that even if the Ult weren't paying them any attention, Selina was the only one who was going to visible if they did. They needed to keep their escape as quiet as possible. Selina understood the situation so gave no disagreement before being heaved inside.

Artie's hand was quickly offered again for Jenna and the expression on his face, a face which had looked so young when she'd first met him, now carried the haunted expression of the soldier who'd witnessed the very worst of what the universe had to throw at them. His whole face was covered in blood though Jenna had no way of knowing if it was his or someone else's. The hair on the right side of his head had also been plastered down to his scalp and the cloying liquid was congealing into a solid mass.

Jenna jumped, gripped his hand tightly, and was dragged inside The Beast.

She recognised that there were other people in the vehicle with her but she had no idea how many or who they were as she turned back to catch site of their home before the doors were slammed shut and they could make their getaway.

Artie scrambled for the door and pulled it hard to slam shut but in the cramped confines of The Beast, Jenna had been standing too close to the doorway when he did and it smacked hard into her before shutting. Jenna was flung backwards into The Beast where she landed sprawled across some of the others in there with her. There were quickly words swarming over her as others checked on her condition and all she was able to do was respond with robotic words as she tried to understand what had happened to her.

She was fully aware of the details of the impact but she'd seen a huge blue eruption of energy where the door had hit her but there had been no pain at all. Even her landing on the others had felt like nothing.

The world was staggering again as her mind worked through what had been taking place all through the skirmishes and now invasion and she realised that she was showing the same ability as the Ult in another area. She could see like them, but she'd moved to being a part of some kind of shared hive mind ability they had as well. Now she was resistant to impacts which meant that the Ult had evolved that same ability.

Laying there, The Beast rocking as she steadily put more and more distance between them all and the destruction, Jenna watched as Artie finally began to drag the door closed but before it closed, the world outside erupted in a detonation of booming thunder and the darkness of night was banished in a super heated and super charged eruption.

Whatever had happened, their home had just been wiped off the map.

Jenna closed her eyes and let herself be rocked by the movement of The Beast as it pushed onwards. Outside, fires raged through the obliterated ruins of what had once been a secure place to live and the giant Ult convulsed heavily against the flames which wrapped themselves around it. The Beast was long gone when the Ult monster finally fell, crushing large sections of the building which were still upright, but through the smoke which was growing thicker and blacker with each passing second, if Jenna had been looking on she would have seen that all but one of the glowing towers of light from 'cured' people had been extinguished.

There was no way of knowing who it had been, but the fire finally chewed through something structural near to them and whatever was left of the buildings above them shuddered and finally collapsed inwards.

If Jenna had been there to see it happen, she would have been able to see that final column of weak light flicker, before quietly winking out.

22

The Beast kept on moving through the night, steadily traversing the open ground which spread out before it. Some of the survivors were able to get some sleep but there was a terrible feeling of fragile loss which was travelling with them all as well, and it appeared to be having an effect on most people.

Jenna managed to get some sleep as they travelled but every time she drifted off her mind treated her to swimming images of Ult attacking people in so many ways that she ended up deciding that just laying with her eyes closed was going to be the best form of rest she was going to get. Selina was wedged in close next to her, squeezed against Jenna and on the other side, the wall of The Beast. Regardless of the potential discomfort she may have been feeling, or any mental trauma the loss of her home had caused, Selina was deeply asleep with her head back and mouth open, snoring with an almost casual abandon that practically shook every fibre of all of the people around her. Jenna was jealous that sleep had come that easily, her own exhaustion being a constant companion, but she was also just a tiny bit impressed that Selina was able to switch off so readily.

Time wafted past and no-one spoke a word as it did.

Haunted expressions greeted her whenever Jenna cast a look around her, yet not a single person acknowledged her when she met their eyes. The low lamp light, cast from a battered oil burner swinging from the roof, was barely above the blackness of night but it showed all too clearly that every single survivor remained locked inside their own minds, trapped unmoving behind their empty eyes which saw nothing of the here and now.

After an eternity of metronomic movement, The Beast was brought to a halt.

Jenna had no way of knowing how long they'd been moving but just assumed they'd put as many miles between them and their ruined home as possible.

Glancing up from her position amidst the bodies, she picked out Davis and Artie as they peaked through from the cab section and cast an eye over who was left. Quickly enough, Davis noticed the snoring form of Selina and then met Jenna's gaze through the darkness. His smile made it clear that he was happy that she was OK but that it was clearly the smallest bright spot in what had been a very dark night. Jenna pushed herself slowly up on her elbows, wanting to go to him and learn what had unfolded inside the walls, but he raised a hand quickly to halt the movement. His eyes explained everything that Jenna needed to know.

He was exhausted, Artie too. Despite the darkness, she was able to see that Artie had at least wiped the blood from his face but in doing so, had just removed any disguise of his loss. There were no bandages on his head that she could see so it would likely mean that the blood on him had come from someone else. That much blood from a friend would be a memory that wouldn't dull quickly.

They all needed rest so any meeting would have to wait.

Conversation would rouse others, from either sleep or fugue.

So would the movement of her climbing out of her position next to Selina.

They were safe inside The Beast so could afford to rest now. There'd be plenty of time to discuss the events of the previous night and there were a great many things that would have to be discussed, just not right now.

Jenna smiled weakly back at him and settled herself back flat. The talking would start tomorrow and there was likely going to be some very hard decisions to make.

The morning arrived without fanfare.

Sleep had been attempted by everyone but not everyone had been successful. Jenna had given up on the idea of any truly fulfilling rest but that seemed to have been what had made it possible for her to finally drop off. She came to with a start as she recognised that she was no longer awake. Quickly taking stock, Selina was no longer wedged in next to her, the number of other people around her was greatly reduced, and most tellingly, the back doors of The Beast were flung open and a cold breeze was sending a spattering of the falling rain in to land on those who were left.

Panic bloomed at the sight of the open doors, but was quickly tempered by the thought that she was functionally invisible to their enemies. No-one else was though. Easing herself towards the exit, Jenna braced herself to be confronted by the worst possible scenario she could imagine, before she gingerly edged to look around the edge of the doorway.

"Morning Jen," came from behind her.

Jenna jerked herself flat to the wall of The Beast as she spun to face the voice. It was Davis, and he looked awful.

"Sorry. Didn't mean to make you jump." His voice sounded as if it had been hammered flat of any and all emotions and the dark circles beneath his eyes showed that he'd been suffering without rest. Jenna didn't give any thought at all and just dived across the space between them and wrapped Davis in an all encompassing hug. He staggered under the impact but hugged Jenna back hard, enfolding her in an embrace that felt so vitally important for both of them.

Not a word was said between them as the embrace continued, but there was just nothing that needed to be added. They both soaked in the warmth, the sheer life of the other as they stood and after what had been visited upon them in the recent past; it reaffirmed that most precious element that Jenna had been exploring. Their humanity.

Finally breaking apart, Jenna looked up at Davis and did everything she could to fix the lid onto her emotions.

"You wanna run through how we ended up here? What happened inside last night? And where are we?"

Davis gestured to follow him and jumped out of The Beast and into the open air. Jenna followed.

Outside, the day was sharply cold and the rain which fell was soaking everything with that fine, hazy efficiency which meant that if they stayed outside, they'd be soaked through in minutes. Jenna didn't recognise the location and did her best to get her bearings.

They were in a relatively small space which had high stone walls all around them, though no roof over head. The Beast had been reversed in through a huge collapsed hole in one wall and large pieces of wood and metal had been placed into position to plug the gap from any passing Ult.

"We're about a mile away from the Way Station," said Davis in answer to one of Jenna's earlier questions.

"It was most likely some kind of old farm house or out building back in the day but like so many other things, after the Ult, it was either repurposed or just abandoned. It's off the usual route we all use so it wasn't something which regularly appeared on anyone's radar. Mary decided that we needed to have more ways to get to the safety of the Way Station and we stumbled over it by accident. She thought that it was no use because it needed too much work to make it secure but when needs must, we find a way, eh?"

Jenna looked back at the material serving as a door and only then noticed that they were actually doors. They were the doors from The Beast, and some other panels too, which had been re-used. Looking back to Davis, he just shrugged as he understood what she'd just seen.

Against the back wall of the space, a large plastic sheet had been pitched as a sheltering tent for the survivors and when Jenna poked her head around the edge to see beyond, the number of people she found was horribly small. Selina was talking with a couple of people, one being Artie, the other being a woman Jenna didn't recognise. There were three others.

"This can't be all that's left, surely?"

Davis's expression told her what she needed to know before he even spoke.

"The few still in The Beast as well, but yup, this is all we managed to get out."

"So everyone else is dead? What happened when the Ult attacked?" Jenna just couldn't understand what could have unfolded that would have given the Ult such a powerful victory in as little time as they took.

Davis's eyes hardened.

"Scott happened."

Of course he did.

"He was the one who ordered the burning liquid be dumped out. He was the one who just told people that they were all safe behind the walls. He was the one who eventually sent 'his' people to barricade themselves into the stores to wait out the attack. He was the one who didn't ask for help from people around him who wanted to help but were just left and ignored." Davis had become granite with each word spoken and he clenched his fists tightly in impotent rage.

"It was only after they'd all left the rest of us to fend for ourselves that Chang made the plan he did."

Chang.

Jenna had seen the small number of people who'd made it out but she'd totally overlooked the ones that hadn't.

Chang was gone.

Davis squeezed her hand, again knowing where her mind had gone.

He got us to set up fuel dumps, and what little explosive material we had, all around the main compound and through the buildings where that massive Ult sprang up. He was the one who told us to get The Beast moving because even though he'd missed all of the fighting, he could tell that we'd lost. He stayed behind and waited for us to get far enough away."

Davis stopped still and paused the memory. He didn't show it on his face, but anyone who knew him would be able to see that he was screaming with rage in his head.

"Chang was the one who detonated everything."

Jenna and Davis didn't speak.

Jenna and Davis didn't move.

For a time which spread for eternity, Jenna and Davis just stood with their eyes on one another. Both had lost a friend. In truth, they'd both lost a great many friends thanks to the attack but it was all too clear to them that it had been the choices of those who'd followed behind that lunatic Scott and his spouting of seductive idiocy.

Scott had killed everyone, including himself, because he just wanted to be the one in the spotlight.

The glowing image of Davis's nervous system exuded proof of life to Jenna and through the silence of their locked eyes, she just let herself watch the power which was running back and forth through him and truly marvelled at the hypnotic patterns.

It was all she could do – to cling to something which was a bright spark in the darkness.

Every one of any tiny move he made drew her attention around him and did everything it could to calm the enormity of the fury she had inside her. She'd been aware of the rain falling on her but the longer she stood drinking in the dancing patterns that Davis was projecting, the less and less she was aware of the sensations.

Seconds continued to tick by and Jenna could feel herself sinking deeper and deeper into those broiling shapes of roaring energy and with each step she fell, she cared less and less about what may have been happening all around them. That energy was hypnotic and the calm that she was calling out for began to extend through all of her body. She needed rational thought to be a part of the group's next steps but, for now, she was glad she was able to feel this.

Finally, that glacial calm enclosed her and she could feel herself lost in the swirling clouds of an embrace which she could now finally see was what had been missing from, not only her, but from everyone else on the planet. She felt like she was finally being embraced into the complete removal of threat, of danger, of risk. She could feel the fear drifting fully away and it left behind nothing but so much freedom and calm that she knew she wouldn't need to worry any more.

The lightning blast rattled through her perception and made the clouds judder, snapping her mind hard enough that some of that calm vanished.

What was that?

A second blast followed and the fear she'd been holding for so long was returned to her, and the third blast made her eyesight blur.

It was the fourth blast which dragged her back to the tiny, soaked, ruin but now, she wasn't staring at Davis.

"THEY WERE ALL RIGHT ABOUT YOU. WHAT THE FUCK ARE YOU?"

The shouting startled Jenna and she jerked herself away from wherever it had come from, and stumbled herself into one of the stone walls which enclosed the area. Disorientation ran riot through her as she tried to understand what was going on. All around her, there were angry faces and everyone had some kind of weapon raised with their intentions very clear.

"What happened? What's wrong?" Jenna couldn't understand.

Selina, who was previously deep in conversation in that tent was now stood nearby with a heavy truncheon raised, though her stance suggested she wasn't about to just dive at Jenna.

"What do you remember?" she asked.

"About what? Guys what the Hell are you on about?" Somehow, Jenna felt more lost.

"We were talking about last night," chimed Davis from the other side of the compound.

"We were talking about Chang. Do you remember that?"

"Of course I remember that, it was two minutes ago." Jenna was finding a tiny piece of level ground now.

"And then what?" it was Selina again but her eyes were narrowed, focused.

"Then I calmed down after wanting to kill Scott all over again before being yelled at and threatened. Does that sum things up about right?"

"Not quite," said Davis as he took slow steps forwards. He held his neck as he approached, like he was reacting to a bee sting and as he closed the gap; Jenna could see a new pattern of glowing energy spreading under where his hand was.

"We were talking about Chang but what you called calming down didn't feel that way to me." Davis removed his hand and revealed reddened skin with blisters and scrapes all over one side of his neck.

Jenna didn't understand, but more importantly, she so badly didn't understand that she just couldn't decide on a possible response.

"You started to chant like them and when you touched me, you burned me. I pushed you away but you chanted and chanted and began to follow me with your hand out trying to grab me." Davis spoke into the silence and the tension all around them was cranked and cranked higher.

"I tried to keep you away from me, and then Selina tried. You just chanted and kept coming. Eventually; look I was out of ideas and just wanted you to stop, but I punched you. Hard. In the face."

Davis hung his head in apparent shame at what he'd done to his friend. The silence around them all just grew and grew at every chance it was given and that lack of interjection felt like it was making threats or demands of those around it, daring them to fill the gaps.

Jenna couldn't meet anyone's eyes as she ran through what was being suggested to her. There wasn't any pain in her face from being struck by Davis and that in itself felt like it should have been enough to pour cold water on the idea that she'd hurt someone.

Davis continued.

"You just kept moving at me and there was nothing that I could say or do which was stopping you. I hit you a couple more times but all I got for my troubles was a static shock. Selina was the one to break you out of your trance and she did it with her truncheon."

"What's happening to you Jen?" asked Artie from the rear of the gathered people.

"I don't know. I have no memory of doing any of what you said. Why would I try to hurt people and how could I have been able to burn you? And most importantly, if Selina had smashed me with that truncheon, surely I'd have been unconscious at best. Not a scratch and no pain anywhere."

Jenna paused.

"Look at my hands. There's no way I could have done what you said, I'm just a human being after all," and she raised her palms to the others by way of proof.

Each and every person in that tiny sanctuary gasped as one as Jenna did so. Some placed hands to their mouths in shock, a couple stumbled backwards in instinctual recoil and there were a couple of shouted threats from others. Jenna examined her hands for herself and the fear exploded in her as it had in the others.

Her left hand looked like a left hand. She was still muddy from the events of the previous night and there was a healthy covering caked over her palm and fingers, but outside of that, she was seeing a left hand that had always been her left hand. Her right hand was the one to force all of the air out of her lungs.

It was still hand shaped in that it had five digits radiating from that central palm but although the muddy covering was the same, it bore no resemblance to her left. Her fingers were now unnaturally long, as if they'd doubled in length overnight, and her whole hand was now covered in a darkened and thick hide like elephant skin.

Jenna shouted out in surprise at the sight of her altered appendage and thrust it away from her, wanting it to be as far away from her as possible. The hideous form was utterly alien and shouldn't have been in any way attached to her.

How could it be that way?

No-one else spoke around the compound, and Jenna just stared helplessly at her hand as she cautiously flexed and moved, working the fingers to further understand what was happening to her. She hadn't wanted to show any emotion during the accusations but the sight of that revolting flesh limb carved through her defences without a care and tears began to fall over her face.

Her fingers still felt like they were her fingers, even down to a tell tale stiffness in the joints of her index finger thanks to a childhood fracture, but they moved now without any form of jointed hesitance. They had become more fluid, more expressive, in how they moved and Jenna felt sick when those same fingers showed themselves able to bend the 'wrong' way and even from side to side.

What had happened to her?

It was only when she focused her attention onto her finger tips that she began to understand what was going on, and in that instant there was a flicker of hope in Jenna. If she could understand this, it meant that she could be able to undo it.

"I need to explore an idea about this," shouted Jenna out to anyone who'd listen to her, brandishing her hand forward and hoping that people wouldn't just kill her without a second thought. Selina and Davis edged forward, Selina still ready with her truncheon, while everyone else kept to a decent distance.

“What do you need,” asked Davis.

“I need to check some details about this thing but I think I’ve got an idea. Grab Artie and we can run through what I think.”

Selina and Davis traded looks which showed the warring concerns of safety and concern for their friend, but eventually agreed.

Five minutes later, the small group were sat together in The Beast with a plastic sheet pinned up to keep the ever falling rain water out. The few people who’d been still asleep in The Beast had been woken by the earlier commotion so were more than willing to make way, throwing sideways glances at Jenna as they did.

The single lamp which hung from the ceiling was turned up as high as it could go and despite their friendship, Selina stood primed with her truncheon ready to defend everyone else should Jenna do anything out of the ordinary.

“OK Jen, we’re listening. What do you want to do?” Davis was speaking with a slow and measured tone, keeping everyone calm.

Jenna took in a deep breath and mentally crossed her fingers.

“I don’t know how or why, but I think I’m either taking on more and more of the Ult abilities, or that I’m actually turning into one.”

Everyone recoiled a step from Jenna and terror flushed over all of them.

“Easy, easy, please.” Jenna raised her hands hoping to show no threat. No-one moved but the tension around them was almost rigid.

“I will be more of a threat to the group if I don’t start to understand what’s happening, so I need your help. I also think that I can break free of the Ult and really strike back against them, so it’s going to be worth the risk of tracking through my thinking.”

The silence was back and stretched as the four of them considered what could be the correct next step. Could Jenna be able to really hurt the Ult? Would they listen to Jenna or just decide the risk was too great?

Jenna didn't want to wait for them to decide against her so just started up making her case.

"We know that I can see everyone's electrical system and that I can see the 'cure' material, right?"

Nods were returned but there was an edge to the feeling.

"OK, I know that I have to accept that you'll be taking my word for it but, please, I can."

More nods.

"Well, as I've said about that, I think it's what the Ult are able to perceive, the electricity of everything. That all came about after my near death experience where Chang shocked me." She had to pause for a second to keep a hold on her emotions at the mention of Chang. He'd hung everything on the idea that Jenna was telling the truth when it would have been so much easier not to.

She was always going to miss him.

"What if I was 'cured' when that Ult touched me, and the de-fib was able to get me going again. This," she gestured at herself, "collection of changes is from that. The charge that got me awake could have done something to the cure and we find ourselves here."

"OK." It was Artie.

"Makes sense. How?

"I don't know, we're kind of stuck making educated guesses from the facts at hand. We only had a very small pool of knowledge about the Ult to start with and that was burned up in the fighting last night."

Artie perked up and headed into the cab area out of sight. There was a small crash, followed by him swearing, but he eventually came back with a massive grin on his face.

"No it didn't."

In his arms was a large plastic container which was filled with all of the paperwork and notes they'd found in Hope and added to with their own efforts.

Jenna felt that small flame of optimism grow in her chest.

"Artie, you genius."

This meant they had all of the information to compare as they worked through what was happening here. The educated guesses were likely to be getting a little more educated.

Jenna continued.

"I think that the cure is more than just a way of killing us or feeding off us." Her speech quickened as the urgency of possibilities filled her mind.

"All of the notes in the box there say that the cure kind of appeared in Hope one day and from there, it just grew and grew. Davis, we saw the massive ward that they'd set up where all of the people who'd been infected could be cared for. What if the Ult were feeding from them all like they were a buffet? The Ult who broke into the farm would have been able to see the beacons from Mary and Mo from miles away but that would have been the only thing to suggest that there were any people there. The Ult all aimed for those beacons because they saw them, but also, I think, because they were hungry."

"During the second attack, the Ult stopped after they'd first broken in, didn't they?" Artie was frowning at his memories as he moved pieces of the puzzle around.

"They did," added Jenna, gaining more clarity of her own.

"They were all just stood still around the bodies and didn't put up any fight when I hacked and slashed. Maybe they needed to shut down lots of themselves to be able to feed?"

"But they didn't grab anyone when they were feeding," pointed out Selina.

Jenna had been mulling over her conclusion from all of the data that she had at hand and as the conversation had moved forwards, she'd been growing more and more confident in her deductions.

"They didn't need to touch anyone now. That's what the cure is. It's a process to give the Ult," she paused, searching for the right words. "Wi-Fi."

Artie still looked confused as he went about fitting that piece of information into the picture he was building. Selina frowned a stony expression which, at first glance, could be seen as threatening but she chewed steadily on the inside of her cheek while she tried to understand. Davis was nodding slowly with a small grin on his face. Was that a good or bad thing though?

"Wi-Fi?" he asked flatly.

"The Ult have the internet now?"

“Not quite.” Jenna grinned a little herself despite their situation.

“It’s just a way for them to feed without having to expend energy going out hunting. The cure stops a person and the Ult can just wander near it and get stuck in.” Jenna’s internal flame of enthusiasm was growing further.

Selina coughed to attract attention.

“Why give them this ability if they’re then that vulnerable when they eat? We’ve just agreed that they let you kill them when you said they were eating. Why would they accept such a massive flaw?”

Jenna’s flame fell back a little.

It was a fair point.

The Ult had just stood there while she did her thing. Why didn’t they defend themselves?

“They didn’t know they were being attacked!” yelped Artie, in a Eureka moment, before padding out his idea.

“Jenna, you said that the Ult couldn’t see you so wouldn’t that mean that the only people they could see were the other people in the room and none of them were making any kind of attempt to get near them.”

Jenna’s flame was growing again.

“But just standing still while they feed, even if they could see that everyone else was still far enough away, still isn’t that smart a move.” Selina again.

“We could have just torn them to pieces with gun fire from a safe range so why make their Wi-Fi so reliant on them being stationary?”

The four of them looked back and forth between themselves as they struggled against that idea. Selina had asked the questions which had broken the idea being put forward by Jenna but she wasn’t doing it the way that Scott had done. She wanted to understand, to move towards the truth, not just be a dick about everything. It was becoming clearer by the second that everyone in The Beast was relaxing into the problem solving process and any implicit threat was being burned away.

Everyone considered their own memories of the different encounters they’d had with the Ult over the years and did their best to integrate the new information as they searched for the next step.

It wasn't looking good.

The Ult *had* just stopped still when they were supposedly feeding.

They had just let Jenna attack them but even if they hadn't been able to see her, surely they would have known that something was happening?

Time passed them all by and the container of notes was handed around so any and all tiny details could be double checked, cross referenced, or investigated. Despite everything that they'd been able to discover, they still had so many assumptions built into their work.

Outside, the smell of a fire drifted around as hunger was dealt with in the rest of the group population but those inside The Beast didn't move. They could all feel it as they worked. They could all feel that they were closing in on that tiny thread of information which, once pulled, would unravel all of the mystery they were facing so the idea of giving up for any reason, even food, would never be entertained.

Rain continued to beat a steady refrain against the sheeting which had been hung over the end of The Beast, it having moved from fine misty spray to fully grown downpour, but even that wasn't enough to break the smell of the cooking. Stomachs were gurgling as they worked and Jenna could see on the faces of everyone else that they're need for refuelling was becoming more acute.

Finally, that most basic of human needs, food, couldn't be ignored any longer.

"Come on guys, we need a break and something to eat," said Davis, dropping the notebook he was reading haphazardly back into the container on the floor and stretching his arms above his head. Despite still feeling that they were all just on the cusp of something, there wasn't any disagreement.

Selina was first to her feet so she was the one who pushed the sheeting away from the back of The Beast, giving the heavy rain drops access to them.

"Jesus. It doesn't look good out there," added Artie.

"Yeah, but I'm too hungry to care," responded Jenna and leapt into the open air, squelching muddy water over her legs as she landed.

"Besides, we're only going to be getting wet on the way over there, so stop being such a baby." Selina smiled as she joined Jenna and lifted her face to the sky and, for just a short second, let the rain just wash away the fuzziness her mind had been feeling.

Artie and Davis joined the women, Artie mimicking Selina with the look to the skies while he ran his hands through his hair. It may have been a way to clear his mind, just like Selina, but the tiny streams running from his hair were quickly being stained red as more and more blood was washed free, a stark reminder of the events which had brought them all there and taken so much from everyone.

Jenna didn't feel quite so upbeat with that thought, so turned and headed for the tented area where the others were huddled against the rain. It was coming down harder and harder and would have made life much more difficult if they'd all been forced to stay inside The Beast. The tent was a good way to get everyone out of the confines of The Beast but still keep them all dry.

Jenna grimaced at the idea of having to eat without the protection of that tenting.

The lightning bolt that hit Jenna wasn't the same as the one that she'd witnessed the night before but there was no less effect. This one had been a bolt of understanding rather than real energy but she'd just figured out the piece they were missing.

The Ult had a way of protecting themselves while they ate as well but it wasn't only used at meal times.

"THEY'VE EVOLVED PROTECTION!!" Jenna shouted, which in turn startled everyone within earshot. A few heads poked out from under the tent and looked around the surrounding walls in search of the invading creatures they'd assumed were attacking. Selina waved to signal that there was no threat and they all slinked back under the cover.

"What protection?" Artie was channelling that ordered medic, take change part of his brain and stood close to Jenna in anticipation of what she could explain.

"It's that blue spark," stammered Jenna, her mind having to work overtime to get the tracks down in time for her train of thought to travel towards the answers.

"What blue?"

"Selina's spear couldn't do it and the blue was there as we left."

Artie looked sideways at Davis hoping that he had had more luck translating what was being said. Davis's expression again said that he was struggling as well. Jenna kept her stream of thought going.

"We've seen that the Ult have attacked us and there hasn't really been a massive change in the way they've gone about things but they've been a damn sight more durable recently, haven't they?"

That made sense.

"We've poured bullets into them since they first appeared but it's only now I stop to look at the bigger picture that I can see what we all overlooked in the house. There was the usual terror and wild firing at the first sign of an Ult but after that, we've all been looking the wrong way about changes taking place."

"What wrong way," asked Selina while she absent-mindedly tightened her grip of the handle of her truncheon.

"What changes did we miss?"

The rain was forgotten as Jenna understood where her brain was taking her.

"We all kept looking at me being the big problem because I was the one with the new abilities. There was so much attention on me that we didn't notice the abilities the Ult were showing us. Our guns did pretty much nothing to them ever since we got back from Hope but Scott and his mob just kept everything being about whose fault anything was. The cure was a new worry, yes, but Scott kept the story all about who'd done what to mean we were all at risk. We were all looking at each other rather than trying to understand the Ult and we missed that they've developed some kind of ability to fend off attacks."

Jenna looked around at the others expectantly and willed that they'd seen what she had.

"So they're bullet proof?" Davis asked tentatively.

"Potentially. It's the sparks we've been seeing coming off the Ult when we shot them. It's a new development and that blue colour which spread out from any impact point was just too exciting to just be a trick of the light."

"OK, they're bullet proof," began Selina, folding her arms as she tried to fully comprehend what was being said.

"If bullets don't hurt them, how did we manage to shoot that first Ult that dug its way in? The one that 'cured' you? And for that matter, how were we able to stop any of them at all? If they're bullet proof I'd have thought they'd have been 'Jenna proof' as well."

Jenna grinned wildly and beamed with excitement, clearly having seen the questions coming.

"That first one was smaller than the others we've seen so it's possible that it was just weaker than the others, and the amount of fire it took was enough to, I don't know, wear its shield down. As for being 'Jenna proof', I've been slicing and dicing but only after the initial attack. I think that I'm sharing their abilities so I can pass through what they have as protection. They all look like they've been disconnected from the mains when I've dumped water into them so why wouldn't they be using electricity for their defence?

"But you aren't bullet proof. Are you?" Artie spoke with a surprising lightness as he probed, his absolute amazement taking over at the idea of what was basically a super power.

Jenna smiled again.

"Everyone take a swing at me, it should be a pretty cool show."

What followed drew gasps from everyone. People crawled out from under their tent and watched agog as Jenna was struck over and over again.

The attacks started out gingerly as, one by one, Selina, Artie and Davis hit out at Jenna, connecting with her arms, her shoulders, so as not to cause any damage that may be too much should her assertion of protection not pan out.

“Come on, do it like you mean it,” yelled Jenna as the opening blows washed off her. There had to be a decent test to prove that she was going to be safe.

Selina was the first to really throw a punch in anger. She slammed her fist hard into Jenna’s stomach with all of the power she could muster, only for Jenna to be forced back a single step as she balanced herself. Selina was amazed by the lack of affect her strike had but had been shocked by the sensation which had greeted her effort. Her hand had felt as if it had hit a solid object, but one which was more akin to a gelatinous mound than a human body. It had absorbed her impact and she’d felt her hand sink into that surface before being flung out painfully under the shocking charge of power. Said power which then shot up her whole arm, turning all of her muscles to a static channel.

Davis was next, slamming a shot into Jenna’s kidney, and met with the same effect. Stepping back, he shook his hand in pain as his arm too caught all of the charge. Finally, Artie tried, and despite his solid connection to Jenna’s jaw, was dealt the same reaction.

For Jenna, each blow had been resulting in ever growing blooms of blue light spreading out over the protective layer that was surrounding her. The others hadn’t seen the blue but their faces told Jenna that they each believed what she’d told them.

“You see what I mean?” she grinned at the others and that flame of possibilities grew inside her again.

The three of them rubbed at their numbed muscles and nodded in awe of what was being suggested.

“Each Ult has this shielding or protection or whatever you want to call it, but because I’ve grown one as well, it means that I can pass through without any trouble, and that includes weapons that I might be carrying as well.”

Davis was next to speak up.

“So what does that mean we can do now, outside just letting you go and do all of the slaughtering?”

The growing silence from everyone told them that no-one really knew.

23

The next week was spent inside the ramshackle compound with everyone doing their best to catch their breaths after such concentrated attacks over the previous days. The rain had continued intermittently during this time while the temperature continued to drop. What little food had been hurriedly thrown into The Beast before they all left the farm was now almost completely gone and the available material they could use to burn and keep warm was growing harder and harder to come by. Jenna had been outside the walls to bring back sticks and logs from the wooded areas around them but being the only person who could safely complete the task was meaning that she was growing more and more tired by the day. She'd even been as far as the Way Station on one occasion, hoping that there'd been some kind of proof of further human presence since their last visit but it was still untouched. She'd brought some food back but she hadn't been able to carry much and the idea of everyone moving there was still greeted with utter terror after the stories Scott had been more than happy to tell.

The Beast was their fortress inside the compound but that meant that effective rest and good sleep were in very short supply for anyone.

Each day, the unofficial war council in hiding would meet up and comb through all of the pages and notes concerning the Ult and did their best to formulate some kind of strategy which would give them all the best chance of survival. Davis, Selina, Artie, and Jenna would resolutely refuse to admit defeat but, with each gathering, the others could see that Jenna was beginning to show just how hard she was finding everything.

"You need to rest, you're exhausted," demanded Selina as Jenna climbed back into The Beast with her shoulders slumped. Jenna just slid into a seating position leaning against the wall, rested her head back and closed her eyes. Inside her head, far away from the world outside, Jenna was flying through a clear blue sky while Enterprise cloud swept along behind her, mirroring her sweeps and swoops in a balletic display of aerial synchronicity. She could feel the wind rushing through her hair, and its chill biting at her skin as she arrowed onwards through the empty sky, looking down upon a world, and its inherent dangers, that were so far away, and she smiled widely at the absolute feeling of release.

"Jen," shouted Davis when Jenna didn't respond to Selina. She didn't answer him either.

The call of her name had broken through to the mindscape that Jenna was exploring, but it became nothing more than a whispered suggestion out at the edges of her awareness and while she flew, there were already so many of those little voices that she just tuned it out.

"Leave me be. I'm busy flying." Jenna slurred and garbled her response to all of the voices in her head and did her best to grip onto the flight. She was aware at the very centre of her mind that she was just imagining the time in the sky but she reasoned that she was just doing what she'd been talking about from the very beginning, taking a time to just wallow in the sheer joy of what it was to be human. She was tired, no, she was exhausted, and was feeling the stresses of their lives acutely, so this most simple joy was something that was greatly needed.

The others must have understood the subtext of her short response and instead, just moved to start their work without Jenna. Snatching any time for yourself had been shared among the others in the tiny band of survivors, as a method of clinging onto the joys of humanity, so every person had been doing their bit to keep the fires of old humanity alive. Jenna could only hope that everyone else was feeling just as euphoric as she was when they did.

Jenna just kept on soaring through the air with her cloud ship companion following close behind and watched as the fields and woods, the buildings and towns, all passed by underneath her and she began to pick out areas and locations she recognised. As she flew, she could see the farm that they'd all called home, nestled in the slight dip in the landscape but as she smiled down on it, it jagged from the fortress it had previously been to become the smoking crater it now was. Jenna did her best to put the reality out of her mind as she flew on but that update remained unaffected by all of Jenna's attempts.

Below her, she was fast approaching the Way Station and, far away from her own minds control, she shot downwards to being no more than twenty metres from the ground. Her stomach lurched as she descended and she continued her best efforts to slow herself and then return to a greater altitude but her mental image had other ideas.

The Way Station appeared through the hazy low cloud and jutted out into the landscape, looking like an ancient obelisk of long lost purpose, and as Jenna closed on it, still trying to tear her mind away from what she was seeing, her attention was drawn out to her right by the very tiniest of suggestions. Turning her gaze towards the miniscule attraction, Jenna didn't understand what was pulling her attention but she soon noticed their current location rendered in complete detail as it had been before they'd arrived, empty and shattered. But like their old home had done, that image jagged through static and colour and was populated with The Beast and, oddly, tiny moving figures.

Jenna had seen enough of her floating break from the real world. She'd been enjoying it to begin with but her mental landscape was now hurriedly retreating below her as she shot to a much greater height, again without her giving any guidance to what was happening. The map below her was showing a huge area of their home county, with the destruction of their home still awfully visible and their present hideaway directly below her, but as she stared down, tiny bolts of blue energy began to appear at different points all over the map. There were a total of around thirty of the things from what she could make out but she was far too high up to be able to see what was happening.

What were they?

She was clearly asleep and dreaming but what was her sub-conscience trying to tell her?

Jenna needed to be out of this but her eyes wouldn't open and the whole landscape she was within didn't recede. She was trapped in her own mind and for the smallest time, felt that maybe she'd actually gone completely mad, but as she continued to hover in the sky, she became aware of those whispered voices out at the edges of her perception again. They were all around her but whenever she turned to follow the closest thread as it drifted by her; they seemed to just scuttle away through any and all nearby clouds. One by one, the voices pushed against her mind and each of them brought with it a deep urgency to be heard, to be a part of a conversation, and that they all wanted to speak to Jenna.

The whispering was growing in intensity, if not volume, and was starting to make Jenna feel as if the owners of the voices were crowding around her, all wanting to make contact with the information which was so vital they just had to get it to Jenna. That increased intensity brought with it an ever growing, buzzing, weight which coursed throughout her body and made her feel as if she were a can of fizzy drink which had been shaken, filled with pressure enough to burst.

It was growing to such a pitch that Jenna could feel her ears and eyes be dialled to a blank and her mind closed down in on itself. All that remained was her desire to do nothing beyond just listen to the voices as they began to force her away from the controls of her thoughts.

Jenna was left sat at the very back of the bus of her mind as all of the thoughts that had been pushing against her came thundering in. She was sat outside herself, looking down at her mental avatar, somehow feeling like she was having an out of body experience, only the feeling had been multiplied. There were no spoken words within those thoughts, and there was no aspect that Jenna could truly say that she could explain to anyone on the outside, but as she watched down on the map below from her position far away from the controls of her own mind, she was treated to an incandescent glow erupting far off around Hope which bathed it in a corona of electric blue energy, all the while that same energy suffused the whole landscape with its light, reminding Jenna of a film she'd seen once as a child and the far off city in Oz being bathed in emerald. Despite her distance from the picture of Hope, she was able to see that it was achingly beautiful, and all she wanted to do was reach out to that place, to rest under the slowly spinning blades of that huge turbine in the centre of the mental model, that she should have been there, that she belonged there.

She swirled and danced through the shared conversation and shared thoughts coming from Hope, and screamed out in terror at what was suddenly happening to her.

Detonation after detonation filled her mind from very far away, but they were just so far away that Jenna's calls of terror didn't feel as if they'd be enough to reach out for whatever they were. Jenna needed to reach those explosions and knew that she had to do everything in her power, and even anything beyond, if she could, to break out of the dreamscape she was trapped within. The voices that were still all around her became angry at what she was doing, though still not venturing beyond just her inner knowledge of what they were trying to convey, but Jenna wasn't going to stop.

"JENNA! WAKE UP!"

The words wobbled to her from very far away but it was a voice that Jenna recognised. It was Selina. That drove her to scream and strike out harder at what was holding her captive and in a blast of huge light, Enterprise cloud swooped by close overhead and opened fire at anything and everything all around her.

The giant ship swept past and under the barrage from its weapons banks, the forces holding her tightly inside her head lost their grip and with a huge screaming deep breath, Jenna was returned to the real world where she collapsed onto her side due to the vast exertion.

Panting deeply, Jenna's skin felt suddenly cold as a breeze from beyond The Beast skipped over her sweat soaked flesh, shocking her more awake. Her head swam at the multiple layers of confusion that she just couldn't fight away and she tried to get herself back to the real world, all the while, her body was screaming at more and more new pains it had developed. It took a few deep breaths to help clear the fog and she was slowly able to make her way to a seated position, again leaning back against the wall of The Beast, but what she was faced with scared her.

The others were all stood back and away from her and each held some kind of weapon high above their heads ready to start swinging, again. Each of them had an expression which suggested that they'd just seen something horrifying and Jenna suspected that she now knew exactly what it was likely to have been.

"You OK Jen?" Davis asked the question with the care of someone who was ready for the worst, all too familiar with having to deal with a volatile person. Jenna noted that his knuckles were white on his club.

Raising her hands slowly, Jenna tried to calm everyone.

"I'm back from wherever I went. Are you guys OK? What did I do?"

No-one relaxed their posture.

"You started to shout," replied Selina, her own grip on the bat she held as taut as could be.

"You were shouting the Ult call, but not like we would. You were calling out with a different voice, like your voice had broken and a new deeper, more alien, one had replaced it. You were using the voice of an Ult."

"Well it's gone now," replied Jenna, rubbing at her neck carefully and clearing her throat a little by way of proof that the other voice was gone, assessing what could have happened to her. Her hand didn't have to travel far in the search for something out of the ordinary, and quickly found the bulbous and hard mass which was now forcing its way against the skin in her neck, suggesting that her Ult features were beginning to accelerate their propagation.

The others watched as Jenna's hand fell back to the floor but the full significance of what had just happened was only now dawning on Jenna herself. Her mental flight over the map of their tiny part of the world had been one thing but the full events of that experience had explained the final piece of the puzzle of the Ult that they'd all been looking for. She looked down as she flexed her more Ult hand and only under the greater scrutiny, was she able to recognise the difference in the sensation that was coursing from it.

Looking outside, Jenna witnessed the clear sky, utterly devoid of clouds of any kind, and for the first time really noticed just how dark everything was out there. The sun was high in the sky but there was just so little light coming from it that you'd swear that there was a thunder storm raging up there. Slumping back again, her whole body just sagging at what was taking place; Jenna knew that there was likely nothing that she was going to be able to do to stop what was happening to her. Selina was the first to register the change in Jenna as she sat looking blankly into space and lowered her bat before kneeling close to her friend.

"Jen? What's happening?"

The words came in the tiniest whisper but they sounded like a giant gong to everyone.

"I saw inside the Ult and they saw inside me. I was a part of them all."

The plastic sheeting fluttering meekly in the low breeze was the only sound around them all now, with even the whole outside world falling silent at what had been said. Jenna continued slowly.

"I think that we're running out of time before I'm not me anymore. My changes seem to be accelerating so I think we're going to have to consider the practicalities of how you guys are going to function after I 'go'."

Silence reigned and the utter shock of Jenna's bluntness sucked away all of the fear the others had been feeling. Weapons were lowered and fear was replaced with concern for a friend. When no-one else said anything to break the silence, Jenna just barrelled ahead.

"It's not all doom and gloom though. I think I've figured out that final piece of the puzzle that we've been looking for so there's a pretty decent chance that we're in a position to really hit the Ult hard, maybe even kill them off." She smiled weakly at the thought of destroying the Ult, of giving them a serious bloody nose at the barest minimum.

Even if she wasn't going to be around to see it.

"How do you think that the change is getting faster and why does that mean that you're going to die?" Artie asked the question and it made Jenna's heart warm. The first thing that he wanted to know was about her rather than the much bigger situation they all found themselves within.

"The changes taking place now are much more far reaching in terms of physicality. I appear to be growing a new 'organ' in my throat which is hugely different to what I've already got in place. Whatever changes happened for my eyesight were likely just in my brain and that defensive ability is likely to be coming from a more diffuse structure all over my body but that new voice you all heard," she pulled her jacket and jumper away from her neck to fully expose the misshapen mass, "is coming from something much bigger and which would have taken a great deal of effort to grow."

She replaced her clothing before starting again.

"And I think the piece that I was always missing in the way that the Ult go about what they do is that they're not an invading army as such. Since the very beginning, from the very first time that the Ult appeared to anyone, the word was always that they were this sweeping force of alien creatures and as such, they were strategized against like they were an army like humans would define." Jenna adjusted her seated position and grimaced at the pain which was creeping through her. She must have been sat down for too long.

"Every idea about them was wrong though. They aren't an army; they're all off shoots of a single mind, a single Ult. The individuals, the ones we've all seen, have limited autonomy but there's one that directs the others to do what it wants them to."

More silence followed and mouths fell open.

"In my mind, when you heard me 'speaking fluent Ult', I could feel all of the individuals, but I was overpowered by that central mind. It kicked me out of the driving seat of my own brain and I had to watch on as it took over."

Selina gasped.

Davis could be heard grinding his teeth.

"It's even worse than that. I think that it was able to update what it was capable of perceiving of the world by looking through me. I saw an awareness focus on our little hidey hole here and I suspect that it's now able to send any and all of the wandering monsters our way because it's had a glimpse of a more complete picture of its environment, thanks to me. Sorry."

From outside The Beast, the shouts from the remaining members of their group leapt up with terribly perfect timing. Selina didn't hesitate and rushed for the periscope in the cab of The Beast and began to sweep it back and forth, hunting for the source of the fear growing outside. She pinpointed her targets quickly.

All around the ruined compound, still far away from them but on all sides, were approaching Ult.

24

Outside The Beast, panic exploded and the people began screaming and shouting and started to rush to climb into the vehicle in search of safety. Artie and Davis forced everyone to stop their surge and started to organise the efforts to bring as much of the material which had been taken from The Beast, back.

Selina joined in with those efforts and Jenna kept her eyes pressed hard to the periscope to keep that focused view on the approaching creatures. She'd seen this very thing in her mind's eye, the hordes of advancing Ult zeroing in on their current location, and seeing that bizarre landscape become rendered in reality made her feel as if she were standing with sand shifting beneath her feet. Swivelling to check on all of the Ult, Jenna could feel a dizziness rising in her head in response to her hurried circling movements. She tried to slow her jerky action but her attention just screamed out for more and more knowledge of the approaching Ult. The far off whispers in her mind rose in volume as she became rapidly aware of multiple perspectives forming as a diffuse collection of dancing colours before her eyes and even as she snatched her eyes away from the viewer, she could feel that same Ult consciousness pushing against her.

In a fit of panic, Jenna screwed her eyes shut and pushed her way through the other people in The Beast and threw herself outside and to the ground, wanting the hard impact to be enough to act as a large enough shock to break her free of what was happening to her.

She landed hard on her right side and an explosion of pain ripped through her body, severing the connection with the outside force. As she slowly opened her eyes, Artie was already at her side, checking for a pulse.

"They're trying to take me over again," gasped Jenna before her breath caught in her throat, an instinctual response as her tiny movement sent a blossom of agony out from her right shoulder.

"Well you've dislocated that pretty well," replied Artie, registering Jenna's pain.

"Hold still, I'll get it back in now and we can get you back inside."

He began to manipulate her arm, doing his best to avoid causing Jenna any undue discomfort, and Jenna winced with each adjustment, until, with a deeply satisfying 'thunk' and a snap into place, Jenna's shoulder joint landed where it was supposed to be and all of the pain that she'd experienced evaporated.

"Thanks Artie, but I don't think it's going to be wise to have me come with you all."

Artie didn't look up from what he was doing with her arm.

"Rubbish. When I get this shoulder of yours back in position you'll be ready to go just fine. Besides, a dislocated shoulder, even one as badly dislocated as this, isn't cause enough for a gallant sacrifice."

He'd continued to rotate and pull her arm with ever growing force as he'd spoken. Jenna hadn't thought that much of what was being said though, instead being more than content that the terrible pain in her shoulder had been doused and the infiltration of her mind had been thwarted. It was the sharp jolt he gave her arm which made her pay full attention again.

"Artie, you got it. You can't fix something once it's been fixed so stop with the pulling."

They locked eyes, with both parties clearly not understanding what the other was thinking, before looking down at Jenna's shoulder.

It soon became clear what each had been missing.

Jenna had felt all the pain stop as her shoulder had dropped into place and she'd flexed her arm wildly to prove the point, yet Artie had still been trying to affect some change in the joint because of the position it was now in. Jenna's right arm may have felt like it was back in the socket but it was now in a greatly elevated position towards her neck, almost like it was growing out of the top of her shoulder rather than the outer end.

"Fuck me!" yelled Jenna as she began to move her arm in its new configuration and Artie scrambled back and away from her.

"My God Jen, doesn't that hurt?" Artie was still looking on from the world that said that only serious injury could result in what he was seeing, but Jenna knew that for her, that world was a distant memory.

"Like I said, my changes are accelerating."

"Guys, we need to get the doors on The Beast. Jen, can you .... JESUS CHRIST!" Davis had been all business until he registered what Jenna was looking like and shocked panic took over.

"I'm fine, trust me, now get everyone in The Beast," replied Jenna and didn't give any chance for there to be any kind of dissent as she ran for the doors in place at the mouth of the walled compound. Artie was about to follow her but she reached them first and with barely a hint of effort, lifted the doors from their place and began to return them to The Beast. Recognising that his help wasn't required, Artie, who'd been the last member of the team outside, dived for cover as Selina gunned the engine to start The Beast moving slowly forward.

The whispering started again at the very edges of Jenna's mind as she took stuttering step after stuttering step, and her focus began to drill down to a single point as she could sense the assault from the Ult-mind outside. The whispering was growing in intensity with each step but she wasn't going to let her friends be taken by these monsters.

The world outside her was now almost completely shadowed but still she pushed herself to a point where those on The Beast would be able to take the doors from her, holding that singular task at the very centre of her mind as she pushed on.

'ULT, ULT, ULT.'

She could hear the sound but there was no way for her to identify if it was from far away, from the force in her mind, or from her own new voice, but she just tried to hold herself to the task at hand against the growing voices all around her.

Despite everything she'd been attempting, despite every effort of concentration she'd been trying, with a tiny effort of thought, her whole body felt to be falling apart with rapid energy as her mental protection buckled under the weight of the outside consciousness.

Her mind was filled with the multitude of voices under the control of a much greater whole. That mind had been so huge before that it had taken acts of violence to break its hold on her, but this time Jenna was just held powerless before the absolute vastness of what was invading her head.

'ULT, ULT, ULT.'

The whole world opened before her and Jenna was forced to watch on as the Ult-mind explored through her thoughts and probed at the depths of what made Jenna who she was. Images floated before her eyes, unbidden, as the Ult-mind accessed her memories and explored through them. The whole power of the Ult-mind poured into her head and she swore that there was a physical discomfort coming along with it as recollections of her family at Halloween from all those years ago, of the home she'd shared with the rag tag group of humans trying to survive in the wasteland of the Ult, of Hope and that giant spinning turbine at the centre of the town, and of her ability to see so much more than either of the two species alone were able. The bright colours from her memories added to the spinning blades of the turbine, becoming hypnotic in their delivery of energy, and for just the slightest second, just barely there but unmistakably so, the grip and power of the Ult-mind wavered.

Everything that Jenna was experiencing reacted to that tiniest of sensations and all of the memories the Ult-mind had been toying with melted away to nothing. Jenna found herself unexpectedly back at the helm of her own thoughts and the Ult-mind was retreating from her rapidly, skittering away, a sensation of fear and uncertainty all through it.

All around her, she could feel the other Ult begin to rapidly increase their speed as they raced towards the compound, that fear from the Ult-mind triggering a vital urgency to grow in each of them.

As the Ult-mind continued its disengagement from her, Jenna was returned to her body in the here and now, and found that The Beast was now well away from her, with its doors fitted firmly in place. Sprinting after it, she didn't want to risk the others having to expose themselves by opening the doors, so instead yelled as loudly as possible as she ran alongside.

"I'll stay here. Get the others to safety and come back for me after it gets dark. We can finally go after the thing controlling the Ult. See you soon."

Without any further word, Jenna peeled away from The Beast and headed into the nearby woods as fast she was able to move. Her gait had changed thanks to her arm being in a new position but she was still well away from the edge of the woods when the Ult arrived at the compound. Climbing a nearby tree, all Jenna had to do was stay out of sight and wait for The Beast to come back when the coast was clear. She knew for certain that the Ult mind had pushed through her defences and had taken giant bites from her mind but that in doing so, had accidently shown a little of its own to Jenna.

And that little piece had been the location it was hiding.

When The Beast finally lurched back into view, Jenna felt as if it was so far past night fall that it was nearly day break.

The Ult, which had been approaching the compound when everyone left, had quickly reached the walls which had been a protective embrace for the small group of humans, to find nothing inside that they could use to even prove the existence of their enemy. There were crowds of the things bumping into one another for well over an hour as they explored the area with those hugely versatile grasping arms before Jenna was able to pick out that some of them had begun to drift away.

As she'd watched from her hiding spot in the trees, the voice of the Ult-mind and its comrades swam through the air all around Jenna, still whispering in their non-language that she was feeling all too familiar with, but there was no further attempts made to apply any kind of force to her. The individual Ult moved steadily at the behest of the Ult-mind but there was never any attention thrown anywhere near Jenna. She couldn't be wholly sure that the Ult-mind was unable to pick her out so she remained motionless but that gigantic mental presence was always a good enough distance from her to make her entertain the idea that it had actually been avoiding her. She'd watched as smears of the cure were secreted from the Ult and marvelled at the hypnotic swarm of the burning motes as they danced through the inky black of the night, allowing herself the chance to admire the beauty they held despite their danger.

Hissing to a stop, The Beast pulled up at the edge of the tree line and waited. Tension filled the air around Jenna and she could guarantee that the same thing was happening inside the vehicle. Everyone was understandably being hyper cautious before breaking their respective covers but the longer that held breath of tension remained held, the more tense everyone was becoming. The periscope on The Beast span round in every direction, checking and double checking for the smallest suggestion of an Ult lying in wait and every sweep which presented no risk was being triple checked before action.

Jenna decided that she'd have to make the first move.

Breaking cover, she shambled across the open ground ahead of The Beast and raised her hands in mock surrender. Her body was now hurting everywhere, most likely thanks to both the changes taking over her system but also from being wedged into place up a tree for hours on end, so each step felt stiffer and more brittle with each footfall. The periscope snapped onto her and tracked her as she moved, but there was still no movement from anywhere else on The Beast.

Finally, a hatch on the roof of the cab was unlocked and eased open to allow Davis to push himself into view, a bottle with a rag fuse in his hand.

"Hey. Are you still you?" Davis had never been one for flowery exposition, and the wavering creak to his words made it all too clear that he was terrified.

Lowering her hands, Jenna smiled despite her discomfort.

"Still me," she croaked, sucked in a deep breath, and began walking unevenly towards The Beast. "You ready to go kill the big boss?"

Inside The Beast, Jenna slumped back to the spot on the floor she'd been using previously and fought to find the most comfortable position. Eventually deciding that the best she would be able to manage would be half propped up against a pile of crates and a collection of mounded ropes, Jenna did her best to relax but was accepting that she was fighting a losing battle.

Around her, the other members of their much smaller War Council watched her with fresh anxiety. Selina had her machete raised again, Artie wielded a bat, and Davis still carried his Molotov cocktail though that seemed to be a pretty drastic idea given their surroundings. That thought at least made her smile weakly.

"Are you sure you're going to be safe for us?" Davis, again, with that blunt question.

Jenna didn't move, she was in too much discomfort, but her eyes reached him. She was sad that there was so much fear from her friends but it made sense. She knew if it had been someone else on the other side of this equation, she would have been just as suspicious as Davis.

"I'm only going to get worse so I'd suggest that certain measures are taken to keep you all safe, but I don't think that the Ult-mind wants to risk reaching out to me until I've fully become one of them."

The four people, all brought together under the attack of a brutal invader, just took in the enormity of the words that Jenna had thrown out there, devoid of the requisite emphasis. Jenna understood that there was a great deal more going on between herself and the Ult but her own delivery of the information showed everyone, including her, that there couldn't be anything beyond the simple facts. For the others, talk of the Ult-mind represented the perfect rendering of the human existence since the Ult had arrived. Humans had always been on the back foot of the story of the Ult, with information concerning the enemy being limited and seemingly always just out of reach. To everyone else, Jenna embodied the sheer gulf in knowledge of the Ult for the rest of the human race. Through Jenna, humanity were receiving the very first glimpse beyond the most strongly built protective wall in existence, and what they were seeing was just proving that there were volumes still to uncover.

"So what's the next step?" Artie this time.

"Hope. We need to get back to the turbine in Hope. I think that the Ult-mind has been feeding from it."

25

Davis drove while the others rested and discussed options.

Following the description of the Ult-mind and what it was seemingly able to do to Jenna, the consensus had been to have Jenna tightly bound with rope and chain so she was as immobile as they could manage. There had been some attempt made to make Jenna as comfortable as possible but the best that was managed seemed to only go so far as not being painful, but that was better than nothing.

Time dragged along with them all and the discussion quickly turned to what, if any, plans would defeat their enemy.

"The turbine was still turning when we were in Hope last and I never even considered that it was doing anything. I thought it had just been forgotten about when everyone who could had left the place behind." Despite the discomfort of her situation, Jenna couldn't keep the flare of excitement from her voice.

That excitement didn't travel as far as anyone else in The Beast.

"So that Ult brain is under the turbine and it controls all of the smaller ones. We kill the big one, does that mean the others are toast?" asked Davis from the driver's seat, clearly keen to be involved despite being away from the others.

"It's what I think will happen, but you can never be certain."

Jenna wanted to be honest but maybe she could have sugar coated that a little better.

She tried again.

"The way the Ult work means they have certain weaknesses which we've been able to exploit so although the Ult-mind is something no-one has seen before doesn't mean that it won't share those same weaknesses." She felt that covered things with a little more positivity at least.

“So what’s the plan then? How do we go about actually doing this?” Artie was all business and his demeanour made Jenna compare him with Mary and Chang. He was going to be a great leader some day.

Jenna smiled.

“We bring the turbine blades down on it like spears while dumping the contents of one of the water towers with them. It’ll kill the Ult-mind in a bigger version of what we’ve done already. There are water towers everywhere in Hope so there’s got to be one nearby. Factor in the dwindling number of people taking water out and it’s guaranteed that we’ll have enough to do the job.”

Artie considered the idea and his face showed him running through possibilities, Davis was silent so was likely doing the very same. Selina, though, was different. The grin spreading across her face made it clear that she was convinced.

“So we’ve got the rest of the journey to sort out the details then? Excellent.”

Very convinced indeed.

As the hours passed by and The Beast was driven towards Hope, pieces of the plan were steadily nudged into place until, with the sun now well passed early morning and filling a clear blue sky, they arrived at the top of a hill overlooking Hope. The idea was to get some rest before heading into the city and setting their plans into motion and the juddering halt made everyone look forward to some down time, but Davis called back from the cab to come and join him, his intonation suggesting that their rest wasn’t going to be as easy.

“I think our target knows we’re coming,” stated Davis, his brow creased into a deep frown.

Confused glances were exchanged before Davis signalled to the periscope.

From her shackled position in the back of The Beast, Jenna was forced to wait on the information.

“What’s happened? Guys? Davis, what can you see?”

Selina returned from the cab and had her own frown now.

“Jesus, what is it?” Jenna was getting more and more frustrated at the not knowing.

“You said that there were only a small handful of Ult in Hope the last time you were there.”

“Not just me, Davis too.”Jenna hadn’t meant to sound so defensive but it just slipped out.

“Well it looks like your Brain-Ult had a great idea and brought in reinforcements. Come and have a look.” Selina worked the various locks and knots quickly and freed Jenna but still kept her machete drawn and ready. Jenna acknowledged the threat but Selina just shrugged as she replied.

“Just in case.”

The Ult metamorphosis hadn’t taken any massive leaps forward for Jenna but she could just feel her whole body being twisted and pulled in wrong directions as she moved. She was in pain and recognised that as more and more time passed, that pain was only going to get worse.

Finally entering the cab, the two men backed away from their friend to give her the space to check the periscope, they too wearing that same concern as Selina. Rubbing at her eyes to try to alleviate some of the fatigue there, Jenna peered through to firstly see the giant turning blades of the turbine wheeling away before she scanned down to the outer walls of Hope and the huge gates of entry. There were hundreds of Ult milling around along the base of the walls and the numbers spread out onto the ‘no man’s land’ circling the city. There were several fires burning at different points in the open space where booby traps had been triggered and had destroyed whatever it had been that had tripped them but the effect was barely a scratch on the surface of the Ult numbers.

Jenna sagged back from the viewer and just didn’t know what to do.

There were hundreds of the creatures in the one place that they needed to access to finally strike back against an enemy that had been driving the human race to the point of extinction.

She was still aware of their plans and of how they needed to go about them but seeing that many of the enemy creatures in such a concentrated area was so far beyond the realms of comprehension as to become like starting the conflict afresh. There hadn’t been this many of them together since the very start of the invasion and Jenna could just feel that they’d all been growing too familiar with the way their lives had fallen into a new routine of settled evasion of the Ult.

All of their previous thoughts about what they'd be able to accomplish had effectively gone up in smoke and it was all too clear that the Ult-mind had been making plans of its own.

They needed to change the plan.

"So now what?" asked Davis as Jenna made her way back into the trailer section of The Beast and he slipped back into the driver's seat.

Artie stroked his fuzzy chin by way of showing he was trying to find a solution, though it was still eluding him. Selina followed Jenna back to her spot and refastened all of the ropes and chains and didn't say anything until everything was secure.

"You got any ideas?"

Jenna just shook her head and did everything she could within her bonds to get comfortable. It didn't work.

"I say we get some rest before we even consider doing anything else," called Davis from the cab. Artie joined them in the trailer and agreed. Selina tightened her grip on her machete, the grip creaking under the pressure, and just stared at Jenna.

Everyone was silently hoping that one of the others would be the one to make the ultimate decision and as glances were exchanged, it became clear that everyone was trapped in a loop of uncertainty.

Jenna finally broke the stalemate.

"We rest. We all need some sleep before we consider any kind of attack and they can't see us in here. I say that we make the most of the quiet. Five hours should be enough"

Just the action of saying it out loud finally made it OK for everyone to feel, but more importantly admit to, the reality of the drain they were all fighting against. Shoulders slumped slightly and following a series of clanks and clicks from the cab Davis joined them all, The Beast having been 'parked'.

"Are you sure that we're still invisible to them?" asked Artie quietly, appearing to need to find out, but also aware that the question itself would make others worried. It seemed to Jenna to be more proof that Artie was going to be someone that their survival could be built around.

"The Ult-mind is avoiding me because it knows I could see back when it looked through me. It's set up defences because it thinks we're coming for it so I doubt it'll want to risk giving any more secrets away."

Artie nodded and lowered himself into as restful a position as he could manage, happy that at least the smallest reassurance had been given.

Against the expectations of all of them, everyone was able to get some decent rest.

The five hours flew by but when the alarm did sound, the faces that greeted them all were those of people who were ready for what was coming. Davis set about powering up the engine while the others checked and re-checked the materials they were going to be using and readied themselves for the off.

Selina checked the view through the scope to see that there was still just as thick a population of Ult through the open space before the walls of Hope. Almost every single one of the creatures was stationary and, Selina thought, looking relaxed, as if the idea of any kind of attack coming against them would be futile. She ground her teeth at what she saw as her anger flared to life.

"No change?" asked Jenna from her 'imprisonment' seat.

"They're all pretty much still. Looks like the Ult-boss has set its defences and is waiting." Selina sat down opposite Jenna and stared at her.

"Are you still going to be able to do this? We're going to need to untie you so the last thing we want is you switching sides."

"I can feel the Ult-mind out there so I'd suggest that it can sense me as well, which is likely why the troops are out on display, but I also know that it's keeping away from me. I've reached out to it a little and it's backed away whenever I did."

"You've been trying to talk to it?" Artie was fierce in his question.

Jenna shifted slightly under her bonds.

"Just kind of seeing what was visible for me, I never tried to go directly after the central mind. Think of it more like having a look around than trying to actively attract someone's attention."

Artie didn't look happy.

"It was a tiny action but it showed me that it either doesn't understand what happened to it when I saw behind its curtain or it does and it's worried that I'll do it again. Both of these mean that I'm still human me."

Artie stood silently, looking hard at Jenna and weighing up what she'd said. Eventually, Selina leant forwards and began to undo the ropes and chains holding Jenna in place before looking up at Artie and delivering, "She's part of what we're doing so we need all hands on deck. There aren't any other options."

Choice made.

Jenna smiled and began to move herself to her feet, every joint crackling its own protest as she did, telling Jenna that they needed to get moving if this plan was going to work. Not long after, The Beast began to move forwards along the rough dirt road towards Hope and the fields of Ult fighters, meaning the fight they'd been preparing for almost all of their lives was finally here.

The Beast moved slowly at first but as the slight gradient was reached, the speed increased. Davis was sticking to the roadway and was aiming to go through the main route that was always used into Hope and even after the Ult takeover, the surface was still smooth. The surrounding areas were going to have been far too risky to use. It may have been open space but the ground was pitted and far more treacherous than it looked. That, and no-one fancied being felled by one of the very defences that had been set up to keep them all safe. As they approached, they collectively held their breath in silent prayer that no Ult began to move in their direction.

None did.

The Ult force around Hope was vast but Davis had noticed earlier that there was no apparent mass plan behind what they were doing. There was one entrance into Hope and it had always been kept to that single opening because it meant that anyone wanting to make it inside would have to come through the same point, so defensively, the big guns could be concentrated there. The Ult forces weren't doing the same thing though. They'd been spread out all around the city evenly to protect everywhere against the possibility of attack.

Selina kept her scope tracking around to the nearest Ult to The Beast as they edged onwards and Davis made the tiny amendments to their course to avoid the two Ult which happened to be stationed on the roadway they were using.

Still, none of the Ult moved to signify that they'd seen them.

Eventually, The Beast passed through the huge open doors to Hope and moved slowly into the city proper.

Inside the walls, Hope was deserted. The huge display of force outside stood in stark contrast to the ghostly streets that The Beast was now traversing and that fact just made the tension worse.

"Where are they now? They can't all be outside, can they?" Selina was pressed hard to the scope, still pivoting hard to cover as much of the environment as she could. Artie flashed a look at Jenna, hoping that she would be able to shed some light on things but she just shrugged back as best as her mutated body would allow.

"It doesn't matter really," pointed out Davis as he drove. "As long as they can't see us we could be surrounded by them and still be safe."

Artie's shoulders unknotted a little, as did Selina's and Jenna smirked to herself ever so slightly. Davis knew there was more to it than that but he'd certainly taken the steam out of any fear which could have been building too fast.

"We just aim directly for the Hub station and get started with our attack. Let's get this done." Jenna just wanted to be all business despite the reassurance she was giving out. She was just like the others in that she was nervous, as you'd expect for any group infiltrating an enemy stronghold during war time, but the flutter in her chest and stomach couldn't just be written off by that. She could have sworn that something had shifted inside her since they'd started their journey to Hope, such that it had left her with a sensation of something very real now being missing.

The Beast continued on its slow and steady route through the deserted streets of Hope. Selina and Davis gripped tightly to the scopes, always reviewing for threats, expecting that each second which passed without incident was only there to act as some kind of decoy. The tension in The Beast was thickening but still there was no response from the Ult. When The Beast rounded the final corner of their route and the Hub came into view and there'd still been no movement, Selina's call of "We've arrived," came as an almost anti-climax.

As calmly as he could, Davis reversed The Beast into place into the closest bay to the entryway to the building proper. No-one spoke but they all recognised that they'd reached the point of no return. No words were exchanged as everyone prepared themselves for what was going to unfold. Each of the four knew that they needed to concentrate fully to complete their part of the process, but more importantly, they each understood that anything that they said at this point was going to be of no use to anyone. After a further half an hour, they were all ready.

Davis and Artie were clamped to the two scopes, searching out any possible sign of Ult approach, while Selina and Jenna prepared to open the back doors of The Beast.

"You still feeling OK?" Selina asked Jenna.

"Never better," replied Jenna and gave a thumbs up by way of proof. Selina couldn't help herself, as her feelings were splashed across her face, her response was instinctual. Jenna's hand was now very far away from being the good old human image that everyone would have expected. The fingers which had been expected as a show of her readiness to start the fight for humanity were now hugely stretched, covered with a grotesque thickened flesh, and horrifying proof of the distance Jenna now stood from the others. It was an Ult appendage now.

Selina tried to apologise but the damage had already been done for Jenna. She couldn't really blame Selina for her reaction, she hadn't noticed the full detail of her transformation to the point it had now reached either and it'd been happening to her own body. An uncomfortable silence squatted between them but Jenna recognised what it was telling her, and that solidified her determination. She'd been banging on about doing more than just living and how being a human being was more than just eating, sleeping and fighting and she knew that she wasn't going to stop until she'd struck out against the creatures who'd taken all of their lives from them. She was going to make the Ult pay.

Narrowing her eyes and flashing a wolfish grin, she pushed through the doors at the back of The Beast and headed into the main hub building, pushing the doors closed as she left. Inside, Selina started her countdown and made her way to the others who were still scanning everywhere. They had ten minutes and then it was their turn.

26

Jenna moved with as much speed as she could muster but her gait was being steadily ruined by her metamorphosis. She was still inside her clothes but she could pick out where there were new masses growing to push against seams which had been previously loose.

The office area was very much as it had been the last time she'd been there but the doors leading deeper into the Hub were now hanging loosely from their hinges and had been cracked and splintered by a heavy impact from the other side which had thrown them open. Quietly, at the very back of her mind, she hoped that the damage had been caused by people, maybe even survivors from the ward deeper in the building, as they blazed their escape, but as she loped down the hallway, the smears and drag marks on the floor gave light to the much more likely fact that a great many Ult had passed through here.

She just hoped that they'd all been heading out or she was going to have a tougher job than she first thought.

Making the slow turns required to send her deeper and deeper into the structure while also giving her as much chance of locating any threats before she barrelled into them, Jenna risked the slightest extension of her mind as she could to see where the Ult-mind was but yet again, that giant consciousness was maintaining a large buffer zone between them. Despite her physical position with the mass making up the Ult-mind being closed down by the second, that mental separation was always held in place far beyond the real world. She could sense the lighter presence of the other, smaller, singular Ult which had been stationed as guards outside the walls of Hope but there was so very little to them it was again as if there was a determined effort to keep away from her.

Did the apparent fear from the Ult-mind mean that it hadn't registered that she was actually already beyond the defences it had erected?

It was enough of a positive to make her grin.

After an age of ever more uncomfortable movement, Jenna finally reached the doors of the infirmary. Stopping for the smallest rest, she dragged all of the air she could find into her lungs, willing the burning which had blossomed in her chest to shrink away.

Nothing changed.

Concentrating now, she mustered as much focus as she could and tried to keep her breathing steady. The burning in her chest was continuing and there was just no way for her to breathe deeply enough. The panic would be next, snapping at her mind as she fought off her exhaustion, so she screwed her eyes closed and just breathed, shutting out everything else and keeping her thoughts blank. The minutes ticked on and without even trying, she pictured Enterprise cloud again, soaring through the emptiness she held in her head. The giant starship exuded a calmness which just washed over her and finally, without any further effort or concentration, her breathing finally caught up with the demand which had been generated.

Jenna slowly opened her eyes, again wishing deep down inside herself that they'd had their very own Enterprise cloud ship which could have fought back against the Ult, she returned to the here and now and checked around her for any changes or threats. Thankfully, she was still alone.

Pushing into the infirmary, she'd been expecting to find the room in a very different condition to their previous visit but even with everything which they'd all seen and experienced over the recent days, the tableaux inside was sickening.

Jenna just gasped and covered her mouth to stop the scream which had been close behind.

The rows of hospital beds, which had previously been arranged with an almost obsessive level of control, had mostly been scattered to any and all locations. The vast majority of them now lay empty of their previous occupants and the smeared filth all over the room suggested that the Ult had been the cause of the carnage.

Had they all been taken by the creatures?

Edging slowly into the room, Jenna kept her hand clamped over her face to ward off the smell she could still identify despite her efforts. It was rotting flesh, shit, damp and all of the worst possible things for a human to encounter and she didn't want to risk a full inhalation. The tiled floor was slimy with that effluence so Jenna took the tiniest steps as she aimed for the back of the ward and the windows looking out.

Bile rose in her throat as she eased her clumping steps into the room as the haze of rotting filth forced its way past her defences. As she continued to scan the room for any sign of either Ult or human presence, she slipped on the slick tiles before regaining her balance. This place was ruined.

Clomping onwards with her unbalanced gait, she made her way deeper into the wreckage of what had been laid out previously. Equipment was discarded with the casual lack of care that came from acts of malice or utter indifference and that level of horror caused Jenna to miss that which was so much worse.

There'd been dead bodies on some of the beds when they'd first found this place, and from whatever had happened here, no-one had wanted to do anything with them so they all remained, but half buried under a pile of hospital beds near the window was a body which gave Jenna something of an answer to questions she still had.

It was a body.

It wasn't moving.

The rictus expression on his face, Jenna thought it was a man but the body was so badly deformed that she couldn't get any more certain, was fixed to a single scream of pain but it was all too clear that he was dead, even discounting the lack of electrical glow being produced. And he'd been becoming an Ult when he died, his body being brutally misshapen in a similar way to her own.

The realisation, as much as the assault on her senses, quickly became too much for her and Jenna threw up. She didn't attempt to move or arrest the process; she just convulsed and emptied at what she was seeing.

The transformation before her had been one that, unlike what was happening to her, had exploded in ferocity. The person who'd been there to start with would have been immobile on one of the beds when the cure effect was activated and rather than any kind of slow and controlled metamorphosis, whatever power the Ult-mind had had shattered every possible system in the human form and began the change toward Ult.

She threw up again.

And again, though now there was a tiny volume being expelled as her stomach was completely voided.

Staggering, Jenna moved as fast as she could towards the windows and began to smash the glass out enough for her to enact her part of their plan, while also letting fresh air in. The brittle sound of the glass rebounded through the empty streets below but there was no fear of the Ult being able to register it. The pain in her abdomen continued as she moved and she retched and retched as she worked, though nothing was coming up. She'd been given a direct glimpse of the more glacially paced process which had been taking place in her and that had made her understand exactly what had unfurled at Hope.

All of the Ult that were now surrounding the city had come from this room.

They'd all been human before the cure had reached them.

She retched again at the thought of not only seeing the human race killed by the Ult, but by the taking of all of them as slaves, but this time, the drawing need to vomit didn't abate. Instead, her stomach spasmed and exploded in a blinding pain which sent Jenna sprawling to the floor as her legs turned to water. Wave after wave of agony surged and Jenna gagged and retched, utterly lost to what was happening to her.

Until, with a blazing, white hot agony, she retched for a final time and expelled a misshapen, meaty mass from her mouth, leaving behind a trail of bloody fluid which dribbled down from her mouth and began to pool on the floor.

Jenna lay still and just breathed, her body exhausted after the effort of what had just happened. The pain she'd been experiencing was gone but she felt as if she'd run several marathons, such was the tiredness.

Looking at the mass on the floor that she'd thrown up, she just didn't understand what had happened to her. At the most base level, she couldn't remember ever eating that so how had it been in her stomach? And what was it anyway? If it was a new Ult structure, why was it on the floor? If it wasn't, what was it she'd thrown up? Surely it couldn't have fit into her stomach. Reaching out with her Ult hand, she risked poking the lump and instead of any movement or attack, it simply drained a thickening liquid from an opening on the back side. The smell in the room was still just as fetid as it had been previously, the imagery just as brutal, but now Jenna didn't feel the need to throw up, even with the sight of what she'd brought up, and it was that sudden lack of revulsion which made her come to an awful conclusion.

She'd just thrown up her own stomach.

Time wasn't going to force her to give it any more thought though as the tinny ring of the alarm clock she'd stored in her coat pocket broke her concentration, and slapped her back to the reality of the movement of the plan they were putting into action.

The others were setting off.

Inside The Beast, their alarm had also gone off.

Artie traded looks with Selina, and Davis quickly scanned the area through the scope to double, triple check that the coast was still clear before, with a curt nod, he pushed the doors open, and the three of them jumped out and star burst away. Each had a role to play in the execution of the plan and there was a burning concentration in all three.

Despite the apparent lack of Ult threat, each of them was wrapped in pieces of the plastic / rubber sheeting which Selina had used around their home to avoid detection. None were going to be perfect at providing the ability to disappear from the enemy completely but it would certainly make their detection as hard as possible.

They hoped.

Pouring on as much speed as he could, Davis sprinted away to the far left streets from the Hub and headed off towards the giant building with 'Almighty Save Us' painted in fading white letters across the upper walls. None of them knew what this place had been used as before the Arrival but Davis was convinced it had been storage and workshops, his logic being that there was no way that somewhere that size near to what had been a mine complex could be anything else. Inside the building, taking over the top two floors, was his target, one of the massive tanks which stored water for the city. Taking the stairs up two at a time, he piled on all the speed he had available to him and rationalised that if he did meet an Ult coming the other way, that same speed would let him get out of harm's way before it could do anything about him.

Eventually, he reached the top of the stairs and stopped before the closed door to the tank room. His heart was hammering in his chest and the free flowing sweat was running down him everywhere it was able. There was no way to know what was happening on the other side of that door but he knew that there was the weight of the world standing on him being successful. There were precious few alternatives.

A couple more steadying breaths, and there was nothing else he could do.

Pushing the door open, he checked all around the place beyond as fast as he was able to try and pick out threats but as each and every second ticked past, nothing showed itself. There were no signs of the Ult being anywhere up there, but also, there wasn't any sign of them having been in the building at all. Did that mean he was safe? Or at least as safe as you could get?

Pushing the idea away, he hurried to his target area on the far wall of the building and began unloading items from the bag he'd slung over his shoulder. He still had enough work to complete that he was already up against the clock but he dived in with real vigour.

Selina and Artie surged out of The Beast together and ran away from the Hub, back along the roadway they'd used coming in. Both carried back packs of their own though they both also had large calibre weapons slung over their shoulders as well. This meant that neither was going to be able to reach the highest speeds they were capable of so they both hugged the edges of buildings as they moved, doing all they could to hunt out possible cover they could. Each turn in their journey took on a massive threat but as they travelled, no Ult appeared to strike out at them.

After what felt like a marathon, the two of them rounded the final corner before their target and took stock of their situation. The road opened out into a wide, empty courtyard which was sheltered on all sides by the high buildings. Their target was on top of the building opposite them and both took a second to marvel at the hypnotic calm of the slowly rotating blades of the massive turbine.

"What do you fancy then Selina? Through the front entrance or risk it in the back door?" Artie was sucking down gulps of air but, despite his tiredness and the fear that each of them would have been carrying with them, he actually sounded quite chipper. Selina, dealing with her own fatigue, smiled at his attempt at calming her with his stab at humour.

"I think that it looks clear enough that the front will be the easiest way in. Jenna said that the Ult-mind wouldn't be able to sense that we were here beyond our electrical signals so as long as we keep away from the edge, we should be fine." Selina didn't wait for any reply and instead strode out with as much confidence as she could muster to be able to pass the gaping hole in the ground which covered around half of the floor space available in the courtyard.

There was more than enough space for the two of them to walk comfortably out of the view of what they'd been told was below them but just knowing that the creature they were fighting against was at the bottom of the giant pit made the walk several orders of magnitude worse.

The courtyard had always just been this empty area between all of the buildings and as such was pretty unremarkable. Jenna had explained what she'd been able to recognise from her sharing of the Ult-mind and so gave the others the understanding of what they were likely to discover there, but knowing something as a concept and then confronting that same thing in reality are two very different things. As close as they dared approach the opening, there was nothing that they could identify within. There was nothing more than muddy walls to see and the chasm in the ground became a yawning, screaming gulf with a brutal evil within, no matter how much calm thought was used.

Selina and Artie moved quickly past the hole and approached the doors into the building supporting the turbine. They were open, and that somehow made the idea of passing through them worse. It didn't matter that there were just the usual things that you'd expect to find in the lobby area of some kind of official building beyond those doors, the deep quiet which was all around them made that doorway into something much more threatening.

Why had the doors been left open?

Had the Ult been able to set a trap of some kind?

Artie paused, that seed of doubt rapidly expanding, but Selina just surged forward, sure that if she stopped, she'd be at risk of never starting up again. Artie caught up quickly, deciding that in or out, he was in danger so he'd rather be with someone else if he was going to be fighting for his life.

Inside the building, there proved to be no waiting Ult and that flared a new burst of confidence for both Artie and Selina and they made their way to the stairs without any hesitation, their route fixed in their minds. After a breathless climb, they reached the door which led out to the roof and the massive base of the turbine.

The turbine had been built on the top of the building at the centre of town because it was nearest to the Hub so if they'd been able to successfully generate any power, they wouldn't have to transfer it very far. Walking out onto the roof, a wind of much greater power than they'd expected swirled and roared around them and Selina just stared up at the giant blades as they thundered past, just marvelling at the amount of work which would have been needed to go into the construction. Artie kept moving forward but his mouth just hung open at the enormity of what they were about to do, but also with an amazement of just how close to them the blades actually were as they turned. It may have been stunted in height compared to turbines built before the Arrival but it was still amazing. It was only the sound of the door behind them slamming shut which broke their trances.

"Come on then Artie. Let's get this thing stopped and get our 'spears' ready," said Selina with that familiar determination, patted his bulky backpack, and headed to the door which had been cut into the body of the giant turbine. Artie, feeling his own fears as a chasing force, scurried afterwards.

At the three locations, the three arms of the attack worked hard and fast to ready themselves for the next alarm to go off which would signify the time to throw their plan into motion. Everyone checked around them regularly in search of new threats but there was never even the barest hint of movement from any Ult. In the old infirmary, Jenna struggled to manipulate the explosives she was preparing as her body became more and more cumbersome. Her Ult limb thrashed as she attempted to complete what would have been simple for her as a human and alongside all of the frustration, all of the horror and rage she was feeling, there was always that circling force of the Ult-mind just relentlessly trying to keep out of her range.

It took her almost all of the time that was available to her to actually finish what she needed to do but as she finally primed the device and checked the clock again, she took a deep breath, or as deep a breath as she was able, and closed her eyes against the world outside. She wished she'd done this more often when she'd had the chance, back through all of the long days since the Arrival and the Ult, and let her mind wander.

That Halloween memory was the first thing that slipped into focus and the way that she'd felt on that night about how her sister was just getting in the way and how her dad was doing his best to encourage the two girls to get along, but rather than dwelling on her anger at her sister or the need for sweet treats, she just let the memory of their faces hang at the very centre of what she was thinking. Jenna tried to summon all of the tiniest details that she could but the more that she pushed, the more clearly she was able to realise that the sought after clarity was forever lost to her. She'd spent so long doing everything she could possibly imagine to survive that she hadn't thought back to the very reason why she was trying to survive.

It hadn't been long after Halloween that the Ult had attacked her home town and it hadn't been long after that that she last saw her father and her sister. Their faces looked back from her subconscious but they were just the broad strokes of memory that had been worn down by the intervening years of non-use.

A single tear fell and ran down what was left of her face but she remained locked inside her head with those most simple memories of being human. Enterprise cloud didn't make an appearance this time. Instead, she watched on at the complete, full, mundane, humanity of it all and hated the Ult even more than she had before. She was physically broken now but her human experience had been destroyed years earlier and she hadn't even been able to see it.

The ringing of her alarm snapped her back to the task at hand and she scooped up her explosive gift with her giant Ult hand and readied herself to hurl out her revenge.

At the same time, an alarm sounded with Davis and he lit the long fuses leading to his piece of the puzzle, and Selina and Artie waited to do their part, hovering at the doorway to the stairs with their own explosive device set with a timer.

Davis sprinted away from his efforts, the fuses burning through without any further help needed from him, and knew he had to do everything he could to get out of this building and back to The Beast before any of the Ult outside the walls recognised what was happening behind them.

The plan they'd come up with had been pretty simple when all things were said and done. Jenna had explained that the Ult-mind was just a larger version of all the other Ult that they'd faced so they were going to need to think bigger to kill it. It had been at the centre of Hope, at the base of the turbine where it had been able to feed on any electricity that was being produced by the still spinning blades so they'd need to not only stop its food supply, but also do enough damage to kill it off.

They'd all agreed that they couldn't risk all going together so they created the three arms of attack. They needed water to really do the damage and short out the creature so Davis would be the one to set the charges to blow the supports out from under the tank and get it to cascade down onto the Ult-mind below, controlling the fall in much the same way as a logger would orchestrate the felling of a tree.

When the first detonation went off, Jenna would take up a position in the infirmary across from where these buildings were located and throw her explosives at the very centre axel of the turbine. The bomb goes off and the blades all come crashing down on the Ult-mind. No human would have been able to get the package anywhere near to the target without a complicated launching mechanism but Jenna had been more than happy to point out that as she'd been slipping further and further towards the Ult, she'd developed a much greater physical strength. She'd even demonstrated the fact before they began their journey into Hope by launching a basketball sized rock as far as she could while the others had been watching from inside The Beast. There'd been no measurement but the consensus had been at least one hundred and fifty yards.

The final team, Selina and Artie had the most important role and while Selina just accepted it, Artie seemed less than ecstatic. Firstly, they were the ones who'd be cutting off the power supply to the Ult-mind by stopping the turbine as soon as they could but they'd also be arming the blades to do the most damage. One of the boxes inside Artie's pack contained part of the remains of the Ult that had been dissected back at their farm and it was that material which was going to give the blades the chance to breach any shielding that the Ult-mind could have.

"Compared to the others, that thing is enormous so any strengths it has will no doubt be just as enormous," said Jenna when they'd been planning.

"We need those blades to do as much damage as possible so can't afford to just assume that the extra weight of them will be enough. If the Ult can get through the shielding of the Ult, then we use something of the Ult we have at our disposal."

The box of Ult meat had been left in The Beast but there'd been no specific planning that meant it came along with them. Jenna had been supremely pleased that it had though. The pieces could give the blades enough coverage to have them pass through to the enemy below.

Selina had fixed a piece of the flesh onto each of the three blades of the turbine, effectively giving their 'spear' poisonous tips so when Jenna blew the head of the turbine apart, they'd all go firing down at the same time as the water that Davis had released, and the Ult-mind would be nothing but a memory.

"But what happens if Jenna can't complete her part of the plan?"

The question had brought everyone to a standstill.

Davis had asked it and they all knew that he hadn't meant to be anything other than mission focused but that didn't stop Jenna wincing as the words stung.

"I don't think that it's going to risk coming to grab my mind again but if I can't hold the Ult-mind away from me and I don't do my part, just assume that I'm now a danger to everyone and get the blades down any other way you can."

Selina had worked it out that she'd be able to cover if Davis and Jenna couldn't do their bit but hoped that it wouldn't come to that.

The alarm was still ringing as the first popping blast came from under the water tank. The second and third blasts were much greater and every inch of the world shuddered in response. Jenna didn't waste any time and began her run up to the smashed windows, her explosives in her Ult hand, and drew it back ready to send the bomb towards the head of the turbine. She reached the open space and with a huge effort and accompanying roar of fury, she hurled her device out towards its target.

Her increased Ult strength meant that the device she'd put together travelled like a missile from the infirmary toward the turbine, almost as if it was being laser guided to its target and Jenna just watched on as the tumbling explosive flew to strike back for the human race. More pops and several cracks echoed up from the water tank building as it flew and just prior to it hitting the blades, the whole side of the water tank building finally shattered, sending masonry and pluming clouds of dust into the air as the massive volume of water was pitched out and directly into the crack in the ground where the Ult-mind was ensconced.

There was no time to marvel at the destruction that was unfolding before the next explosion erupted.

Jenna's missile reached its target and the blast wave from the elevated position was strong enough to shatter glass in windows nearby. Billowing clouds of smoke and flame flew upwards and Jenna watched on from her position away from the destruction with a wolfish grin spreading across her face. Her vision was still human enough that she could enjoy the colours of the fire as they blossomed and with more huge cracking sounds, the whole bladed section collapsed and fell perfectly where they'd been aimed, into the torrents of water which were cascading onto the Ult-mind.

Jenna roared with triumph and smashed her hands against the frame of the window. It was the absolute release of the pressure that they'd all been under but was standing as a celebration of everything that was the core of the human spirit. They'd all been beaten back and beaten back over the years until there'd been a real fear that the entire human race was going to go extinct before the ever growing waves of Ult, but even at what could have been the moment their collective fire was going to be snuffed out, they'd been able to turn the tide. Humanity had prevailed, even if it meant that she was doomed to death.

More explosions went off from the turbine building and Jenna was treated to the remaining skeletal structure of the tower collapsing and being sent down after the blades. It clearly meant that whatever Selina had been planning should Jenna not have been able to hold up her end had been set off to put the icing on the cake of their plans.

Now to see if it had had the desired effect.

Davis was already back in The Beast, starting the process to get her moving, when the turbine fell. He'd recognised the different sound of the new detonation and risked a pause in his work to strain his hearing to check on the progress. Shattering concrete and broken brick mingled with the water he'd released, quickly followed by the clanking and breaking sounds of the falling turbine blades, and he knew that they'd done the best they could. There was no way for them to be able to check what had happened until Jenna made it back and began to explain what she'd seen but he didn't want to miss the moment that everything actually went off, even if it was only the sound of it.

He was back in action when he made out the sounds of running footsteps from outside, which were quickly followed by calls of his name and then banging on the rear doors of The Beast. Opening the doors revealed Selina and Artie who clambered in while they sucked in deep lungfuls of air with sweat streaming down their faces caused by their own rushed retreat.

Davis returned his attention to warming up The Beast while Selina took up position to scan everywhere she could through the top scope, hoping with everything she had that Jenna would be quickly joining them.

There was no sign of her.

The sounds of cracking and breaking were still swirling up and away from the site of their attack but even they were draining away to nothing.

"Do you think it did the trick?" asked Artie from his prone position on the floor, still breathing hard.

"No way of knowing yet. We'll just have to wait for Jenna," said Selina, voice tight and her attention fixed through the scope.

There was still no sign of her.

Seconds ticked by.

Still no sign.

Seconds became minutes.

Still nothing.

The pressure to act grew and grew inside The Beast. Should they go looking for Jenna or should they wait longer? Should they leave? Everyone was fighting the same battle in their own minds, but before further questions could be asked, Selina called out a bellow of elation as Jenna came into view exiting the Hub and making her way towards them.

The elation didn't last for Selina though.

She could recognise Jenna but there was now almost nothing human left of her. Since she'd entered the Hub her body had gone through more stages of metamorphosis to have pushed her almost completely over to the Ult. It could technically be said that she was walking but her legs had become nothing more than stubs with flat pads where her feet had once been. Her body was swollen and misshapen and had lost almost all tell tale features of her humanity. Her Ult limb was now fully set at the top of her bulk while the more human limb was now hanging limply and withered at her side. Her head and face were the final truly human signs that gave the smallest hint of her human origin and even from through the scope lenses, Selina could see her expression being wide eyed terror.

"She's coming but she's not looking good," warned Selina and stepped towards the doors of The Beast to let her in. Artie was on his feet next to her ready to offer any and all help he could, while Davis made ready to get moving.

Selina cracked the doors but from outside, a force slammed them shut.

Pushing again, the doors didn't move this time and regardless of the effort she used, Selina couldn't do anything. From outside, Jenna's voice began to limp towards them.

"It didn't work," she slurred in a crackling tone much deeper than that she'd had previously.

"Leave me."

Selina and Artie both paused for a beat as the words from their friend hit home. Selina knew that Jenna was now almost totally gone so it would be too great a risk to bring her with them, and Artie understood that Jenna was saying the mission had failed and they needed to get back to the people they'd left behind fast.

Despite the logic, it wasn't Jenna who convinced them.

Outside, there rose a swelling cacophony of calls from their enemies as all of the creatures outside the walls screamed 'ULT, ULT, ULT,' likely in response to word from the Ult-mind of what had just happened. All those voices were united in one thought, of finding and killing the ones who'd tried to hurt them, and every voice calling 'ULT, ULT, ULT,' was filled with rage.

Which included the new voice screaming 'ULT, ULT, ULT' from just outside the doors of The Beast.

27

Selina slammed the locks into place and dragged Artie with her, back and away from where Jenna would be coming through. There were just the wooden doors now standing between Jenna and what were now her targets. The doors rattled back and forth as Jenna probed from outside, 'ULT, ULT, ULT,' echoing out as they did. Selina drew her machete and prepared herself for the eruption.

"GET US MOVING DAVIS," she screamed over her shoulder, and without further prompting, The Beast lurched forwards away from the Hub and Jenna, moving with a ponderous weight which made those inside feel completely exposed and vulnerable. Speed hadn't needed to be a central factor in their transport before but the argument for it was now growing.

"She's not following us," said Artie as he swung the scope viewer around to track any and all threats. Outside, he'd registered that Jenna wasn't advancing as The Beast had started moving. Instead, she was repeating that strange Ult mantra while her appendage reached and grasped around her, reminding Artie of a snake's tongue testing the air.

"If she's under the control of the Ult-mind then she won't be able to do anything about what's going on, but if she's turned all of the way through the process and become an Ult, she can't see us. Davis, keep us heading out the way we came in," shouted Selina taking command of the others. The Beast continued moving slowly away but the journey was going to get much worse before it got any better.

As Davis drove, there was no visual sign that there was any problem but soon it was clear by the volume of the 'ULT' cry and the growing noise of breaking glass and brick, that all of the creatures which had been arranged outside the walls of

Hope were now pouring back into the city at the panicked call of their master.

Davis saw the first of them as the road curved off to the right and they were all moving rapidly by extending out their grasping arms and slamming them into the ground ahead of themselves before dragging themselves along. Moving far faster than they'd ever been seen to do before, the Ult formed a mighty river of flesh as more and more followed behind those in front and despite The Beast being a big, heavy lump, she was still only surrounded by a great deal of potentially fragile wood.

"We're in trouble guys," yelled Davis and began to steer towards an approaching side road.

Checking through the other scope, Selina agreed with his assessment.

"We can't stand up to that much force. Jesus, if they grab onto us by sheer dumb luck of being nearby, they'll rip the shell to pieces."

Davis pushed as much acceleration as he could muster from The Beast while Artie took a peek at their situation, and the Ult just kept on surging towards them.

They didn't reach the side road before the first of the Ult reached them.

Instead, Davis had brought The Beast in as close as he could to the wall of a nearby building and slammed the vehicle to a shuddering stop. The framework of The Beast was still rattling when he shouted at the others.

"Both of you guys get up here in the cab, it's the strongest part of the old girl. NOW."

Without there being any kind of pause, both Selina and Artie scrabbled their way alongside Davis into the cramped quarters of the cab and waited. Outside, the Ult thundered past where Davis had parked and didn't spare any time looking for anything as they went. The sheer volume of meat that was moving down the roadway was causing the Ult to bump and jostle each other but also anything that they happened to be near as they went. The Beast shook under the impacts of the creatures, the air filling with a fetid cloud of filth and rot as they passed, and with each impact, everyone felt as if that was going to be the one to destroy their chances. That was until, with as much speed as it had started, the attacking wave of Ult surged by them.

"I think they missed us," said Davis, without any hint that there'd been any danger at all.

"How did you manage that then?" asked Artie as he unfolded himself steadily and eased back into the open space at the back of The Beast.

"They'd have hit us head on and would've been reaching out to find purchase to keep moving. We'd have been ripped apart just because we were in their way. Over here out of the way, it meant we were only presenting half the area to risk being breached and part of that was the strongest part of The Beast, up here."

Selina nodded her understanding and grinned, slapped him on the back and headed back into the rear of the vehicle with Artie to hunt for any damage which needed repair. They were moving again after ten minutes.

The continuing call of the Ult was now split between the creatures which had passed them by and those who were somewhere ahead of them, but as The Beast continued to trundle forwards over the now pock marked and cratered road, those Ult ahead of them remained as yet unseen.

"Where are they?" asked Artie as he scanned around for any sign of their enemies. Davis grunted his opinion but kept pushing onwards. Wherever they were, The Beast was going to have to get past them somehow.

All around them, along with every other threat to their safety, night was also beginning its approach.

Finally, they rounded the final curve in the roadway to fully reveal the huge gated access point to the outside world and Davis slowed to a stop again with his eyes pressed hard to his viewer. He said nothing as Selina and Artie swapped worried looks.

"You OK Davis?"Selina asked him as Artie peered through the other scope.

Davis didn't say anything but Artie added a whimpered "Fuck," before slipping away from what he'd seen.

Selina had to know.

Out ahead of them, the massive gates of Hope were now shattered and gone. Fragments remained at the higher levels but almost all of the material which had been used to create the huge structures had been spread over a wide area of the gaping entrance way. The whole area was now swarming with the remaining Ult and they were clumped together in a writhing mass of deformed flesh which seemed to be one whole rather than any singular individual.

"Looks like they want to keep us in here then," mused Selina.

"At least they can't see us," added Artie. "That'll buy us some more time to try and come up with a plan."

They all stopped to consider their options in the face of the new threat.

The collection of Ult were totally blocking the only way out of Hope so they were left with the options of either giving up and going to create their own exit somewhere else, waiting to see if the Ult got board of just being there and were sent somewhere else, or making them leave the area so The Beast could sneak past. None of them really seemed that plausible to start with but each of the three knew that they had to do the best they could with the options they had available.

Selina grabbed Artie and between the two of them, they began to take an inventory of what they had with which they could add to the tools to complete their escape while Davis kept his attention through the scope.

The total list didn't make for great reading.

A small pile of sticks of dynamite, the heavy ropes and chains they'd used to contain Jenna, and spare ammunition for the guns they were all carrying. All in all, not much to make anyone feel excited.

"We're going to need some pretty big ideas," pointed out Selina, knowing that they were really in deep shit this time.

28

Far across the city, buried deeply within her own body and now marooned away from the controls of herself, Jenna screamed silently into the emptiness of her own mind.

The Ult-mind had surged into her as the device she'd thrown had exploded and she understood now that the constant mental avoidance it had been engaging in had been a ploy to get them all inside the walls of Hope. The Ult-mind had been able to ever so lightly drift it's thoughts around Jenna so that she hadn't been able to sense its touch but the Ult-mind had been able to keep her pinpointed as she'd travelled. It hadn't dared to risk a full contact after the last linking had resulted in Jenna being able to peer back into it so instead, just needed to know where she was. As soon as the explosions erupted, Jenna had blasted a call of utter human resistance and that scream had been enough to reach out and illustrate to the Ult-mind that she was doing something big.

In response, it had forced her transformation on her harder and harder as she'd been doing all she could to escape the Hub and get back to The Beast, but it had stopped short of taking her humanity fully. As she'd reached what should have been her sanctuary, she'd been trapped inside her new Ult form.

All around her dwindling humanity, the vast energy of the Ult-mind swam and pulsed as it controlled all of the others but also while it bucked and reared at the very edges of Jenna's own mind. The control and strength that Jenna had experienced before from the Ult-mind had made her understand in broad strokes what it was that her enemy was capable of, but as her transformation had moved on to the point of almost being complete, she could see so much clearer that she'd been incredibly lucky to have seen anything from it at all. Now, that mind just engulfed everything that she was and exuded so much raw power that it felt as if it would be able to control the smaller creatures across an absolutely enormous area.

Despite the dim environment of her mindscape, Jenna could see her surroundings as swirling energies which overlapped and coursed all around her like currents in water but they were all on a perceived flat surface. She was watching as the painting of her mind's eye writhed across her thoughts. The Ult-mind was so alien to her that she didn't have the palette of faculties to fully comprehend everything around her. Whereas she'd been able to see clearly when she'd first linked up, now, as her human self drained further and further away, that link just made no sense, beyond the sensation of seeing that there was a mind behind what was taking place. Whatever the Ult-mind was, it was possessed of such a force of thought that she didn't have the language to fully translate.

Wave after wave beat against her thought self; out at those far reaches of what was left of her, and through those waves and shapes, she swore that she could recognise individual perspectives at work.

The maelstrom outside wasn't just the Ult-mind at work.

Jenna was able to see the tiny singular minds in action around the massive central force, but far from the way that she'd been able to see when they'd fought at the farm. She was watching on at the complete Ult vision of what she could expect to see when human her was finally gone.

Jenna watched on from her trap within the void and began to try anything she could to be able to get her body back under her control. Pushing her mind at different areas of the bubble within the maelstrom, each time she found that the membrane which held her contained was able to absorb what she was doing far more easily than she expected and it soon became very clear that it was far stronger than anything she'd ever be able to throw at it. Each strike out, each gentle prod, everything just resulted in the same sensation of resignation at the futility of what was happening.

Outside, the forces of thought swirled, and eddied, and continued to buffet up against what was keeping Jenna from total absorption, and Jenna was forced to re-evaluate her attempts at escape. Whereas previously she'd been trying to force her way out on her own terms, via brute force, it struck her that now it was worth trying to meet those striking forces half way.

Forcing her mind towards the area where most impacts were landing, she slammed her mind forward and against that dividing membrane at the same time as the force on the other side lashed out and in that tiny second, the bubble surrounding her burst. In an instant, she was free to navigate through the river of the shared Ult consciousness. Panic filled her mind at the idea that the Ult-mind would now just gobble her up from the vast darkness around her but as the seconds ticked, there was no advance. The giant mind didn't even seem to be paying the slightest attention to the singular thoughts of what was left of human Jenna, and that realisation somehow left her feeling even more isolated.

"So should I just click my heels together three times?" Jenna mused to herself. No words drifted from the void to her but even without them, through a warping and stretching of consciousness which crackled around her thoughts, her mind was dragged hard from within the Ult and was deposited back in what was left of her body. In response to the sudden nature of the landing, Jenna collapsed backwards, leaving what could only loosely be called her legs dangling in mid-air.

She was back in her body and found that it hadn't moved from the position where she'd sent The Beast off without her. It took only a tiny effort to push herself back upright with that giant limb on top of her body, and once righted, she examined her surroundings.

The roadway that led past the Hub station had an enormous swarming mass of Ult clambering over one another far off away from where she stood and her Ult enhanced eyesight explained what was happening. The mass of Ult shone as diffuse blue shapes with sparks of glowing energy running through their bodies in a similar fashion to how she'd been able to pick out the nervous systems of the humans she'd been with. There was nothing to make out from anything else that was built all around her and her human vision was dwindling down to almost complete darkness.

On a different day, the view of the shapes and colours would have been beautiful. To just stand and take in the poetry of the way the Ult saw the world would have been something she could have enjoyed had it not come with such a high cost.

Edging closer to the mass, Jenna became aware of several Ult littering the open roadway but showing no signs of life at all. There was just a darkness all around them and the bodies just lay slumped to the ground like they were puppets with their strings cut. Each one appeared as a deflated lump of meat with no life within, exactly like the body of the Ult had been in the farm when she'd first been affected by the cure.

Had someone done the same thing to it as she had when this whole thing started?

There were many more Ult corpses so whoever had done it had been highly effective. She couldn't help herself but imagine that it had been Selina mowing them down, her machete swinging wildly as she struck them down, but her imagination was broken by the arrival of another drained body as it landed near the others and skidded to a graceless standstill.

Then another joined it.

Jenna couldn't believe what she was seeing. These Ult were dead but where had they been to fall to here? If they were being attacked and killed off, who was doing it? Again, she wanted to believe it could have been Selina doing the deed somehow but as she scanned around as much as she was able, all she could see was the mass of Ult surrounding the area that Jenna and her team had attacked. Another Ult body landed near her, but now, the pieces fell into place and Jenna understood.

It had become all too clear.

The Ult-mind was feeding off the smaller creatures and was discarding the bodies like empty cans.

Risking a closer look, Jenna waddled forwards and did her best to peak through any break in the mass that might present itself. Another body landed near her with a splitting squash and fluid from it slicked the area around where it landed, but as Jenna turned her attention back to the mass, she caught a glimpse of a giant Ult appendage swinging back and forth before it speared into the mound of smaller Ult, lifted another one from the mass, and held it aloft. The colours within the small one stuttered for the smallest time before the whole gripping hand of the larger one burst alive as it ingested the power running through its victim.

Jenna couldn't break the idea that she was watching the life being removed from another creature through what would have to pass as an Ult straw.

Gulp by gulp, the energy from the smaller Ult travelled down the appendage and away, beyond where she could make out, and no doubt underground to where the Ult-mind had been hiding. The latest body was discarded into the roadway the same as the others but this one slammed hard into the wall above where Jenna was standing and showered her in both spilled Ult fluid but also dust and falling pieces of brickwork.

It exploded her rage at the monstrosity of what she was witnessing.

The Ult-mind was destroying life on Earth but it was willing to obliterate its own kind to get the job done. She wasn't going to just stand and watch.

"FUCK YOU!" she yelled with as much force as she could muster, not caring that it wouldn't be heard but knowing that it felt good, and she began to stump away from the filth to try and catch up with The Beast.

Deep inside the Ult-mind, Jenna's scream of defiance may not have been heard in the strictest sense of the word but, in the same way as after the first attack, the mental explosion of humanity screeched into the core of the monster, and made it focus hard, right at her.

Jenna didn't wait to see what was going to happen next in the real world or within her mind. If the Ult-mind was going to come for her, she certainly wasn't going to just wait for it. Instead, she'd turned and began to struggle away as fast as her corrupted body was able. Inside her head, she could feel the Ult-mind approaching her fast, like a tidal wave that you can't outrun but you still have to try. Despite herself, Jenna couldn't help but wish that Enterprise cloud was out there somewhere ready to scoop her up and carry her to safety, but as she waddled, the enormous mind at the core of the Ult swept over her and reached needles of will into her brain.

Jenna shuddered to a halt as her body stopped responding. Behind her, the sounds of the Ult swarming around the pit of the Ult-mind just continued without any break and Jenna realised that the rest of the Ult weren't needed to stop her. Her vision began to darken around the edges as that huge brain of her enemy forced itself deeper and deeper inside her mind.

Then stopped.

Jenna couldn't move anything of her body but she wasn't ripped away from herself in the way that she had been before. Her mind swam with colours and shapes, overlapping and dancing before her eyes, but she was always still there at the very centre of everything. She was still her human self in control, just unable to move.

She pictured Chang.

He'd had something similar at the end, being unable to control his body fully but still being at the wheel.

She could feel all too deeply just how much she missed him.

More and more images floated through her mind as she considered all of the people that she'd lost along the way and with each one, even Scott, who'd managed to split their home apart with his obsession, she felt more and more anger.

Her Ult limb swept out ahead of her in a wide arc and kept snapping out as if to grip at something. More and more fury burned into her and she clung tightly to the pictures in her mind of Selina, of Davis, and Artie, of The Beast and what they were all fighting for, and she screamed as much force through her body as she could to break whatever hold the Ult-mind had on her. Her limb continued to flail, but with a shuddering change in her mind's eye, it felt as if the Ult-mind had crushed what little resistance she'd been able to muster and was now making her see what it wanted her to.

The Beast was the last image she'd created for herself and to prove its control of her, the Ult-mind had created another picture of the vehicle for her to examine. Jenna sagged as she pictured The Beast now, with that new picture serving as the proof that the Ult-mind was taking her own thoughts from her now. Human Jenna obviously didn't have long left.

The Ult-mind forced it's will down into Jenna's mind and made her see another Beast hanging before her eyes.

Then another.

And another.

Over and over, more and more pictures of The Beast snapped into her mind and despite the blurry and fragmented nature of what the Ult-mind had been able to affect, it was all too clear that Jenna's mind was open to her enemy.

Whatever this creature was, it had certainly learned and perfected levels of cruelty that just crushed Jenna, the multitude reminders of something she held so dear. Had it learned that from her?

Until it wasn't just a show of cruelty, and Jenna could see the much greater truth.

She screamed with as much force as she was able to muster.

29

“Guys. We’ve got a really big problem.”

Davis had shouted from the cab of The Beast as he’d been preparing to get the vehicle moving again and the clear panic in his voice had told the others that whatever he was talking about, he meant it.

“What’s up?” asked Selina, who was next to him in a flash.

Davis had his eyes fixed through the scope in the cab but he signalled to the other for her to see for herself.

“Look.”

Selina did but Davis was already giving The Beast as much power as he could to get the big rig turned round and moving.

Selina kept her view trained on the mass of Ult which were crowding through the route out of Hope and it took her a beat to pick out what Davis meant. One by one, all at different points throughout the swarming mass, the attention of the Ult was swinging their way.

“They can see us?” Selina couldn’t believe what she was seeing.

“Looks that way and I’m not willing to hang around to confirm it,” said Davis.

“Any ideas on how to get away from them now we can be seen?”

“We’d better come up with something pretty quickly; they’re starting to follow us.”

As The Beast heaved itself back the way it had come, Selina watched on as, one by one, Ult began to peel out of the collection of alien bodies and stump their own way down the roadway in pursuit of The Beast. There didn’t appear to be any rushed urgency as the earlier wave of creatures they’d seen had though. Instead, these Ult were just content to be moving towards their prey, relentless in the knowledge that there was nowhere for them to go.

Inside The Beast, panic gripped everyone. They needed options.

"Davis, keep us heading straight through Hope and aim for the wall on the other side of the town," shouted Selina as she continued to check on the Ult following them.

"And when we get there? Are we just going to blow a hole in the wall?" Davis didn't sound convinced.

"That's exactly what we're going to do. Not subtle but all we've got," replied Selina.

"Fuck subtle, we just need to get away from this place. If they can see us we're never going to survive inside here."

"I'll prime the explosives," shouted Artie from the back cabin as he was already sifting through all of the remaining odds and ends in search of everything he needed.

"How long before we get to the wall?"

"Could be about six minutes but I'd suggest that you aim to be ready sooner," yelled Davis as The Beast wobbled on the roadways which had been made rough and pitted by the previous Ult. Outside The Beast, Davis had recognised that they were fast approaching the Hub where they'd left Jenna on their hurried escape earlier so understood that it was very likely that they'd be crashing into resistance as they passed.

Outside the Hub, with the sound of the seething mass of Ult flesh still rolling behind her, Jenna not only still remained immobile as she fought against the power of the Ult-mind, but she still remained trapped in her body, with a clear view of The Beast heading away from its hiding spot. She wasn't clear on how, but she could see that the Ult had been able to affect another evolutionary step to 'see' in a way similar to humans. There were now scores of the hideous creatures which had now made the step forwards to totally negate a massive weakness that they had, but at the same time, also wiping out the central core of how the human race had been going about their survival.

Screwing up what was left of her face in concentration; Jenna tried again and again to force that awful Ult-mind away from her but with each attempt she was left with no results beyond a growing headache. Eventually, she was forced to admit defeat and rest. She could still see The Beast on its retreat, and even though the view was corrupted, from the multitude of scattered and broken images around the vehicle, she could make out that it wouldn't be long until it passed by ahead of her.

She hadn't even recognised that the tears had started to fall until her face was soaked with their passing. She couldn't break free, she couldn't strike out, she couldn't help her friends in any way, and, as she worked through any and all possible ideas which came to mind, it was likely that because of her addition to the Ult, she'd somehow been the one to grant them human eyesight. Her tears flowed freely and the sound of her sobs bounced back from the bare walls all around her, slapping at her by way of constant rebuke. She hadn't meant to be what gave the enemy the advantage that was going to kill off her whole race but here she was. She was sure that there'd been a story like that with Enterprise cloud way back when, and that tiny comprehension of her still strong willingness to reach for the familiarity of long distant fiction as a core of who she was made her burble a small laugh at the wasteful truth of her humanity. There she was, standing before the wave of destruction that was the Ult, creatures she was being beaten and broken by, and all she could cling to was that imagined cloud.

There really wasn't anything else to do but laugh.

At least she'd stopped crying, so that could count as the tiniest victory.

Looking up, she again let her mind just wander and created Enterprise cloud again, hovering just above the buildings of Hope and looming over everything below. The giant shape became the first arrival of what promised to be a vast armada and Jenna let the warmth of those thoughts wrap her tightly. One by one, weapons systems within the cloud ship began firing down at targets it had selected, and the sound of energy sizzling the air while distant explosions went off, filled her head. She wasn't going to just let the Ult take over the whole planet if she could stop them, even if it was just a day dream.

The scream of 'ULT, ULT, ULT,' blossomed behind her and reminded her that despite the fuzzy feelings a victory would have given her, it wasn't real. She tried to turn towards the Ult call to understand what had set them off, but refused to give up on her cloud saviour, and held it in mind anyway.

Yet more defiance.

Despite every effort she made, she still couldn't break free of the control of the Ult-mind, that metronomic call of 'ULT, ULT, ULT,' kept pulsing away behind her, but that too was soon joined more and more by an increasing cloud of that squirming of flesh that she'd been able to hear before.

'ULT, ULT, ULT.'

Then there was a breaking of stone and a rumbling of falling brickwork.

'ULT, ULT, ULT.'

Glass shattered and there came a crackling sound of buzzing power that put what few teeth Jenna had left on edge.

'ULT, ULT, ULT.'

She still couldn't move, but the shaking that tore through the ground made her fall limply to the side, forcing her to roll over onto her back. Above her, Jenna was treated to an awful view of the giant mass which was now a single, enormous Ult making its way slowly towards her and causing the ground to shudder under the weight of its motion. What had previously been a seething crowd had melted and reformed into one giant creature leaving behind just the discarded corpses of the drained Ult and the opening in the ground which held the Ult-mind.

'ULT, ULT, ULT.'

Those repeated calls echoed from buildings everywhere and drowned anything Jenna would have been able to scream in her defence and with each lumbering motion, the giant Ult edged forwards until it shuffled itself past Jenna, heading to a position where it would be able to intercept The Beast.

"AAAAAARRRRRRGGGGGGGHHHHHHHH," was all Jenna could do. She screamed and screamed and tried again and again to sever the Ult-mind from her own but there was still nothing there for her to be able to grip onto. That alien mind was too powerful to crawl from and again, Jenna was forced back to the futility of what was about to happen.

Why was she being just held as she was?

Did the Ult-mind just want to inflict as much suffering as it was able?

All the other smaller Ult had been gobbled up into the new whole so why not her?

Was this going to be her remaining life? Just stuck here until she withered away?

With no ability to move, she was left with nothing but time.

Enterprise cloud was all she had to divert her attention from her friends impending deaths. It was going to serve as the final spark of her humanity and she'd be damned if she was going to let that simple image leave her. In her mind's eye, the cloud reappeared and began firing again, aiming at targets indiscriminately.

'ULT, ULT, ULT,' rose up from far across Hope with a renewed power and aggression and Jenna could feel that the ground was beginning to shudder again. Inside her head she watched as the viewpoints she shared with the Ult swam together and overlapped until finally the resolved down to leave just two. One picture was ahead of her, clearly coming from the giant which had just passed her by, but the other exposed an open roadway and at the edge of the picture, The Beast. It was clear to her that the Ult-mind had made the same move with the other advancing force as it had with the one here, bringing them all together as one form.

'ULT, ULT, ULT,' erupted ahead of her and she could feel the very core of her body twisting as she joined the call herself, the sound being created from somewhere within her rather than her human mouth. That new organ she'd grown in her neck must have moved.

Still, she was helpless.

Ahead of her, Jenna was trapped watching the giant Ult move forwards. Its massive bulk swayed as it advanced and its mighty rubbery appendage swung forwards and it took a firm grip on the corner of the nearest building. With little to no effort that Jenna could make out, the giant Ult wrenched a huge mound of the building away, sending bricks and dust loose all around it, and drew it back behind itself.

It was going to crush The Beast under tons of masonry as the old engine appeared. It wasn't going to do anything which could even risk a failure against her friends, despite being more than able to obliterate them all on its own. The Beast image showed that it was getting closer and closer and all she could do was watch on.

The Ult held its position for a heartbeat, before accelerating that rocky weapon forward at remarkable speed and all Jenna could do was close her eyes, and close her mind off from the impending horror. The shared Ult images, though, remained playing behind her eyelids, impervious to any and all attempt she could make to push them away. She was going to watch on as her friends died whether she liked it or not.

The giant Ult didn't follow through though.

Jenna had expected that massive limb to bring the brickwork and rubble down like a massive hammer but instead, it released it much earlier and hurled it into the sky out over the buildings ahead of it. On the roadway below, The Beast was still moving but didn't appear into Jenna's view where she was.

The giant Ult ripped free another hunk of building and again drew its limb back before hurling the object into the sky.

'ULT, ULT, ULT.'

What was it doing?

Was The Beast moving that way and she hadn't seen it?

'ULT, ULT, ULT.'

Her mind's eye gave her a repeated glimpse of the view after The Beast and another huge mound of building material being launched into the air in what she felt looked to be the same area the other giant Ult was approaching from.

Were there other people coming to help them?

Jenna's soul rose in barely dared optimism that out beyond the walls of Hope, under the darkening skies of a day which had been about to deliver the final killing blow to her whole world, a previously unconsidered wave of marauding warriors were about to crash over the Ult and tear the very heart from them. She couldn't see anything from her position but the Ult must have been able to register something, even if she couldn't pinpoint it on the pictures that she was having beamed directly into her mind.

She imagined thousands of armoured people, weapons raised beneath a cheer of pure defiance, surging down towards the city walls while the Ult struggled to defend themselves, and smiled. Enterprise cloud returned above them and opened up with all of her weapons again.

"Where's it going now?" shouted Selina while she was bounced around inside The Beast as it traversed the pitted ground of the roadway. She signalled for Artie to check through the scope for another opinion.

Outside The Beast, the swarming mass of Ult had melted and merged into a single brutish horror which had begun to follow them as they'd beat a hasty retreat. They'd been able to see them and that meant that there was no time for deep scientific exploration, it just meant run.

Artie clamped himself to the scope and watched on as the Mega-Ult which had previously been following them, was now gathering a pile of brickwork from a nearby building before hurling it far away into the distance.

"Did it throw something?" asked Artie, not sure what he was supposed to be looking at.

"It did," replied Selina and shouldered him out of the way to watch again.

"But it didn't aim at us, did it?" Selina spoke and Artie confirmed.

Outside, an eruption of sound engulfed everything. The ground heaved like an earthquake had hit and the sounds of falling buildings swelled from the rear.

"What the fuck was that?" yelled Davis from the cockpit.

"It just changed direction and smashed through the warehouse we just passed. I can't see anything now, too much dust, but it looks like it's got a new target." Selina didn't want to sound too confident but she had a flicker of hope. Davis didn't let up on the speed, he didn't dare risk it.

'ULT, ULT, ULT,' continued to boom from outside but it was being joined by more and more destruction as structure after structure was demolished.

Something was drawing the attention of the Ult.

The next question was, who or what was it?

30

Jenna didn't understand what she'd watched unfold.

The Mega-Ult had continued to tear huge pieces of the surrounding buildings loose before sending them soaring through the air away from the Hub area of Hope, but it hadn't stopped there. With that all too familiar scream of 'ULT, ULT, ULT,' booming, it had accelerated into the far walls of old buildings, tearing them down as it barrelled onwards, fixated on something far beyond. She'd tried to comprehend what her shared mental pictures were showing her but they both appeared to have similar views of destruction and brutality.

She still couldn't move but she was able to see now that the Mega-Ult had obliterated everything which it had come into contact with during its advance. There were mountains of rubble, jutting metal beams, shattered glass and plumes upon plumes of thick, choking dust as proof of the creatures passing, and the wreckage had fallen everywhere around the whole area.

Mustering all of her energy again, knowing that taking any chance to escape was a must, Jenna slammed her will to move outwards, and for a second, she was pushing herself forwards. Her huge appendage slammed into the ground and she was pushed back into an upright position. The Ult-mind was still there, gripping tightly to everything in her mind, but for whatever reason, it had released her mobility.

She didn't waste any time trying to understand why she was free. With as much speed as she was able to create, Jenna began moving away from the hole where the Ult-mind was and followed behind the Mega-Ult which had just passed her by.

Her shared vision from the two Mega-Ult presented very little clue to any wider explanation for their sudden change in behaviour. All she was treated to was shuddering views of dust clouds and of falling debris as the monsters continued to smash through anything in their path and towards whatever new threat that they'd uncovered.

Reaching the corner of the roadway into the Hub, Jenna was able to see The Beast still moving determinedly towards her and the ragged vehicle just made her human heart soar. Stepping out into the open roadway between the tons of shattered rubble, Jenna swung her Ult appendage around to show her friends that the Ult soldier they were barrelling towards was actually still on their side.

The Beast didn't change its course.

'ULT, ULT, ULT,' roared in unison from far away as Jenna made out the huge creatures battering their way through the outer wall of Hope.

Jenna continued waving, occasionally pointing to what was left of her human form, the shrinking stump which had been her head, now devoid of all hair and appearing to be dragged deeper into the Ult body. She needed them to see her as her. Or what was left of her.

The Beast kept coming straight at her.

'ULT, ULT, ULT,' continued roaring.

And through the Ult-mind, Jenna caught the tiniest glimpse of what the two Mega-Ult were fighting.

The Beast was still moving without showing any sign of slowing down or even changing direction.

The Mega-Ult were tearing more and more material free from around them as they sent their missiles soaring into the sky at their targets.

The Beast was almost on top of her and still wasn't slowing.

It was going to hit her.

They didn't know that she wasn't a threat to them. They didn't know that she was still Jenna.

"Keep your foot down, Davis," yelled Selina as she braced herself for the impact of the Ult before them. "If they can see us we'll just have to be more forceful to get through."

'ULT, ULT, ULT,' swept over them, as did the ever present sound of material destruction being made as Hope was torn to pieces.

It wouldn't be much longer before Hope was totally lost.

Jenna waited as long as she could trying to attract her friends attention, waiting until the last possible second before reaching her Ult appendage out towards the nearest wall so she could drag herself out of the path. She wasn't completely successful, though, as the wing of The Beast slammed into her side as it passed, sending waves of pain through her body but also waves of blue energy through her now powerful Ult shielding. She was slammed into the wall and then over the wreckage of the buildings which were strewn everywhere and finished in a limp pile of misshapen flesh back towards where she'd come from.

The Beast had registered the collision hard, absorbing the force which had rattled everyone onboard, but Davis had kept the old girl moving forwards as best he could, but his efforts were quickly overcome by an awful grinding sound from outside.

"I can't keep her straight," he yelled while straining hard to keep the steering column turned against the new force pulling The Beast off course. With the wreckage and fallen brickwork mounds now rapidly approaching, he did the only thing he could to avoid a catastrophic accident, and slammed on the brakes hard. Everyone onboard silently crossed their fingers that it was going to be enough.

The crash which rattled around and through the broken town was far louder than it seemed to have been possible. Metal and wood on The Beast cracked and splintered apart as it crashed into a pile of bricks and came to a lopsided stop with the cab partially buried.

'ULT, ULT, ULT," and more destruction were still far away but sounded far too clear, showing that the fight was still very much at hand.

From her position on the rubble strewn roadway, Jenna was able to see that The Beast was now far from being capable of travel. The front wheel she could see was bent out at an awful angle and the bodywork was crumpled and broken in too many places to be able to fully hide anyone who was inside. She was able to make out that familiar glowing humanity of a nervous system from someone inside the cab, through a crack which had been opened up by the impact it had had with her.

Pushing herself back upright, Jenna checked on the shared views from the Mega-Ult but before heading to aid her friends, she grasped a clear picture of what was happening outside.

What was left of her mouth just fell open.

Both of the fuzzy points of view which she was sharing with the Mega-Ult had the two giants striking out against enemies who were swarming down from the hills around them, all with swords held high and some even being on horseback. Great collections of stone were being launched at the people as they advanced, between which the Mega-Ult swatted and slapped out with their huge arms as the crowds closed on them, but their missiles were also being launched skywards.

At the giant cloud which was firing kinds of energy weapons at the surface.

Jenna couldn't believe that the Mega-Ult were fighting Enterprise cloud.

She dared to risk a look in that direction herself but there was nothing to see. There was still a huge pall of dust cloaking the view but even with that considered, she should have been able to see something where the Mega-Ult were attacking.

A creak from The Beast brought her back to what was in front of her.

Hurrying forwards as much as her Ult body could muster, Jenna approached The Beast and tried to call out to those inside but only a shrivelled squeak of a word left her lips. She tried again; and again, but there was nearly nothing coming from her, until her body shuddered and from buried within her somewhere, her Ult-self barked out a call to those in The Beast.

'ULT, ULT, ULT,' boomed deeply, that all too familiar monotone of dead sound which had sent fear through the human race for years.

From another crack in the trailer section of The Beast, a gun began firing at her by way of retort.

The bullets all stung at Jenna and she instinctively raised her appendage across her human remnant face as they impacted the shield which hung all around her. Her own view was filled with a cascading torrent of blue flame as she was hit again and again.

Eventually the firing stopped.

Jenna needed to show them all that it was still her despite the appearance. Again, she began to point at her human head to highlight that she wasn't all the way gone, knowing that her friends would have been watching on for potential threat movements to open up with a fresh attack.

Nothing happened.

She continued to gesticulate wildly and after about ten further seconds, which felt as if it could have been at least a month, the rear doors of The Beast creaked and cracked open, and Selina jumped down, her machete drawn and raised for battle.

Jenna beamed and was just about to rush forwards but was clear minded enough not to risk spooking anyone.

"Jen?"

Selina was wound as tight as a drum, the threat she felt being all too clear, but that single word, that single timid, single fluttering, but single hopeful word, brought tears to Jenna's eyes. She switched those tears quickly to a small chuckle as she responded, imagining what Selina must have thought was taking place when the Ult warrior before her responded to her query with a lumpy approximation of a thumbs up.

Selina's shoulders sagged and her machete fell to her side to show that the message had been understood.

Davis and Artie slowly climbed out of The Beast and stood open mouthed as Selina explained that they were still with Jenna.

"Oh God, Jen. I'm so sorry," started Davis and he was quickly by her side. He'd recognised the mound on the Ult form which had Jenna's face and the expression on his face blurred so quickly from his initial concern to a melancholy happiness at the recognition of his friend. He smiled weakly as he reached out a gloved hand and slowly ran a finger across Jenna's forehead. Her Ult shielding prevented any actual contact between the two of them but Jenna was treated to a small sparkle of energy flare and for that moment, it was just as good.

Jenna's eyes welled with tears as he did so, as did Davis's. Selina and Artie had joined them and they too let their emotions run free. There didn't seem any reason to hold them all together now. The sounds of the two Mega-Ult continuing with their battles with figments remained as a constant reminder of the shattered world around them but there was just that very human shared emotion for them to feel, the Ult be damned.

"I'm sorry I tried to run you over," chided Davis. "Though your disguise was top drawer so what did you expect?"

Jenna wheezed a tiny laugh at the comment, which in turn set off the others. It was all just more proof to them all that despite her appearance, there was still a pretty important chunk of humanity inside Jenna.

Until she roared out that all too familiar call of 'ULT, ULT, ULT'.

The others all stumbled away from her and Selina was brandishing her machete in an instant.

"What's going on Jen?" she asked as she remained coiled to move.

Inside her head, Jen had been bathing in the warm glow of her friends and for that tiny period of time, she'd been ignoring the ever present weight out at the edges of her consciousness, of the Ult-mind. She'd been released from its hold on her and had just assumed that it was off dealing with the enemy at the gates, but that call from her Ult voice hadn't come from her. She hadn't wanted to reach out to her enemies; it had come from the Ult-mind.

Checking on the shared pictures of the creatures, Jenna could make out now that they no longer held Enterprise cloud and the screaming armies of people they'd been fighting against. Instead, the world the Mega-Ult were seeing was just the same as everyone else could make out, and with the reality of the empty sky and battlefield, they were being called back to their master.

"*They're coming back. The big ones,*" crackled Jenna as she winced against the energy rushing against her mind.

"*We need to get The Beast moving, fast.*" Her voice was nothing more than a shattered whisper but she was clear enough to be understood, before she began to stump her way towards the damaged vehicle.

"I think she's pretty much trapped under the rubble," called Selina as she followed, but before there was any further chance of discussion, Jenna reached her massive Ult appendage under the rear of The Beast, slithering forwards until her whole limb was obscured by the big vehicle, and without further fanfare, strained at the effort required and heaved The Beast free of the debris.

"Well someone's been eating their vegetables," commented Artie as Jenna withdrew her arm.

'ULT, ULT, ULT,' boomed from the enormous mountains of hideous flesh which were the Mega-Ult as they tore their way through the high walls of Hope and made their way directly towards the small group of humans who they thought were being supported by a huge new army.

"*You need to get her moving now*," wheezed Jenna as she winced and spasmed through her whole body under the mental onslaught of the Ult-mind.

Davis was inside making sure that the engine of the old girl was still primed for action, which to his amazement it was, while the others did their very best to examine the outside of The Beast for any problems.

It didn't take them long to find a big one.

"When we hit you Jen, it looks like that wheel was ripped away from the axle. We can't fix her here." Selina sounded flat with her description, like she was doing everything she could to just keep the reality away from them all. Artie rushed round from what he'd been looking at on the opposite side and Davis swore from inside the cab.

"*Can't you just rip it off and make do?*"

"I won't be able to steer properly so we'd have no speed. It might be a small injury, but The Beast will need to stay put until we can risk coming back to get her properly." Davis was matter of fact.

They needed alternatives.

"Looks like we need to hide or run then," said Artie with a determination to his voice which was harder than the others.

'ULT, ULT, ULT,' grew like a storm as the Mega-Ult closed on them and Jenna's viewpoint was now clear that they were focusing on them. The wreckage of The Beast and the four of them was central to both pictures.

There was no good option left open to them.

Everything was done.

They couldn't get The Beast moving to affect any kind of escape but even if they'd been able to, the Ult were not only able to see them, but they'd be able to chase them down. They could try and run but if the Ult were able to beat The Beast for speed, humans on foot had no chance, so they were only really left with hide. Each of them considered their chances and how they'd best be able to escape but it all fell down far too quickly.

The Mega-Ult were, thanks to Jenna's input to their shared function, able to see like a human as well as like the Ult that were their constituent parts, so would be able to track and find them, but even more simply, the two giants would be able to just rip the buildings of Hope to pieces faster than the team would be able to use them for any form of sanctuary. With Jenna a part of the shared abilities of these creatures, they were able to see everything perfectly so the single tactical advantage that they'd had to hide from detection had been lost, leaving behind nothing but a yawning gap which was going to take some serious imagination to fill.

"Any ideas then team?" shouted Artie.

"We can't get away from here so I reckon we try to hide. Whatever they were fighting against out there seems to have been beaten so I'd suggest that we find ourselves somewhere we can lock ourselves in for the short term," replied Selina as she was already beginning to edge back towards the Hub buildings.

"*Wait!*"

Jenna rasped the word through her dry throat but the others all turned to face her.

"*There wasn't anything out there to fight. They were fighting nothing but thought that they were under attack.*"

"OK. How do you know that?"

"*I can see what they see. I think that they can see us all now because I'm a part of them so they've spread my human eyesight somehow like I developed all of their traits.*" Jenna wafted her limb about herself by way of proof before continuing.

"*When I watched their views, they were out there fighting against something that I'd made up, a cloud that looked like a spaceship. I'd imagined it as being the final act before I was basically eaten by them,*" she stopped and dragged in as much breath as she was able to before starting up again.

"But the Ult didn't understand what the difference was between the real view of the world and my daydream. Their new

eyesight doesn't make sense to them yet so when they used my human system, they just thought that everything was real."

Jenna finished her description just in time before a massive hacking cough ran through her Ult body, causing her to double over to her side to allow for a column of sticky and lumpy material to pour from her into a viscous puddle on the dusty ground.

'ULT, ULT, ULT,' was now almost upon them.

"Get inside the Hub then find a way back through any building or street you can to the holes that those things made in the walls, I know what I can do to keep you safe," gasped Jenna as she straightened herself back up, The gasps that came from the others tried to break her thoughts but she pushed on as hard as she was able despite picking out that one of the lumps which she'd expelled had been her left eye.

"*Ult-mind let me move because it thought it had bigger problems. It doesn't want to risk that complete link again but I don't think it matters now. I'm a part of it, fully and never coming out, so I'm going to give it some enemies to fight and hide you, all with my tiny human mind*."

'ULT, ULT, ULT,' surfed towards them on the wave of destruction and there was nothing more that could have been said.

"*NOW GO!*" screamed Jenna quietly, waving her limb towards the Hub.

They did.

There wasn't any fanfare or drawn out hugs of farewell. There couldn't have been lingering glances and shed tears as the three of them scrambled up and over the debris mounds and sprinted hard for the Hub. Jenna, though, was left to sob at what she'd lost. The deepest feeling of what was the core of who she truly was and who she'd always wanted to be, was the strength of the bonds that she had with her friends.

The backs of her friends surged from her and with each step, it burned her deeper and deeper that after all of the struggles, all of the hardships that she'd been forced to endure over the years, it was here, at the end, as she was slowly engulfed by the Ult-mind, that she knew her own humanity for what it was. She could feel its purity right there in the very centre of who she was, of who she'd always been but had forgotten over time.

She was going to save her friends.

31

Inside her mind, Jenna planted her feet against the enormous weight of the Ult-mind and began to get creative.

First, Enterprise cloud was back in the sky above the Mega-Ult, more weapons blisters than it had ever had before now incinerating the ground below. That was quickly followed by a giant, city stomping lizard rearing up from far out to her left which was sprinting through Hope, obliterating anything in its path. Next, she imagined walls of flame blooming everywhere around and incinerating everything, before finally, she pictured in her head that The Beast and her retreating friends were gone from the town.

The effects were almost immediate.

The two Mega-Ult instinctively reached out to rip huge handfuls of brickwork from anything they could before hurling them up and through Enterprise cloud, but the approach of a new target made them hesitate briefly before one began hurling missiles at it instead of the ship above. The flames that followed caused them to swat out between launching their rocks in a pitiful attempt to beat the newest threat back and underneath all of this, there was just no way for them to even register that the humans they'd been chasing were now long gone.

Jenna watched on through her shared mind's eye and for a small but wicked heartbeat, she marvelled at the effect that just her imagination was having on the species of unstoppable killers which had been waging war on her whole planet. Flames and energy weapons and atomic lizard power all engulfed the Mega-Ult and that left her with the final part of her plan.

Reaching out with her limb, she tore away the cab housing from The Beast, quickly followed by the rest of the trailer coverage. With another massive effort, she dragged the nose of the vehicle to point directly at the hole in the ground where the

Ult-mind was ensconced, before reaching out to one of the piles of building wreckage and wrenching free a twenty foot long metal strut which had once been a part of the roof of a nearby warehouse. With ungainly movements, Jenna positioned the metal like a lance along the nose of The Beast before heaving her grotesque form on the vehicle as well.

The giant engine of The Beast was still sputtering along so Jenna knew that she didn't have anything really complicated to do. All she had to do was keep her moving in the right direction and everything should be handled at last.

Holding that combination of warring pictures in her mind while starting The Beast moving was proving to be harder than she could have imagined as the power of the Ult-mind twitched at the outer limits of her consciousness.

'ULT, ULT, ULT," came from back behind her and she could see that the two Mega-Ult were still fighting hard against enemies which existed only in the dwindling centre of a single human mind and that continued knowledge of what they were going to fall to fed the flames of resistance.

The Beast lurched slowly onwards, a grinding and tearing coming from the destroyed wheel fitting as it moved, but it didn't matter to Jenna. The remaining wheels kept turning and what was left of the old traction engine just limped forwards.

Twenty metres to go.

Jenna held the fire in her mind to keep the enemy busy but beyond that, she reached back to what had been her home. That ramshackle farm had been asked to do something far beyond what had been its original purpose but it had done just that. It had protected everyone who stayed there and had been treated as nothing more than an object. There'd been repairs to defences when they'd been needed but no-one had ever really cared for .... her.

Fifteen metres to go.

Chang had listened to her when she'd talked about looking after the house beyond just the function. He'd seen what she had and deep down, the fact that it had been him to stay behind and set off the explosives to let everyone else get away now screamed at her that he'd *really* understood what she'd been saying all along.

Ten metres to go.

She wanted to relish the clear air and breathe easily knowing that there wasn't anything out there which was going to destroy all of human life on Earth, secure in the knowledge that she'd been protected by the efforts of everyone working together, but thanks to another human frailty, made flesh by Scott, she was the one who was going to have to stay behind so everyone else could live.

Five metres to go.

Oddly, Halloween all those years ago drifted to the front of her mind without the tiniest help. Jenna was her child self again, running through the dark streets with all of the other kids out trick or treating. Her sister was with her, as was her dad and despite the lost details from her memories; she filled the missing features with her imagination. They were all enjoying the thought of being both scared and scary, but from this distance though the years, she understood that she'd been scared for long enough and now, it was the Ult's turn to know that fear. She was wearing a different costume now which her sister would have loved back then, and the smile on her dad's face at the two girls enjoying their adventures was just the perfect memory to hold onto as The Beast finally reached the edge, and toppled in.

Jenna didn't have to do anything else.

She held tightly to her family in her mind and gripped herself tightly to The Beast as it fell, knowing this was the end. In a final act of rebellion against her position, she emptied her head of everything but her family, dropping the images of her imagined attacking force. The shared views blanked clear of the phantoms which Jenna had called up and exposed the truth to the Ult-mind without giving it the chance to defend itself.

The Beast arrowed down towards the giant mass which was the Ult-mind, with Jenna keeping a tight grip on her makeshift lance. She wasn't going to miss this time.

A small collection of stones, broken free as The Beast had reached the edge, hit onto the flesh of the Ult-mind, which in turn, sent out waves of energy across its surface, showing that its shielding was still in place, but as The Beast hammered into it, the lance that Jenna had wedged into place passed through that shield and plunged deeply into the mound of meat, opening up a giant tear in its side. Jenna's grip of the lance had allowed it to pass through the electrical defences easily where their previous effort with the dead lumps of flesh had failed. Jenna had kept a grip on the lance and had allowed it to do the same kind of damage to her at the other end, ripping back and into her swollen Ult body to almost tear her in half but it was The Beast which really delivered the killing blow.

The shattering impact of the old traction engine had been enough to split the whole thing apart and the gallons of water which had been inside had spilled out, dowsing everywhere around it, and falling directly into the newly opened wound of the Ult-mind.

The Beast came to rest embedded in the flabby flesh of the Ult-mind, its broken and twisted frame ripping through with an almost casual ease. The effect of the water from the engine was practically instantaneous.

The Ult-mind shuddered once, a shivering of the energy overloading through its whole body, which in turn signalling a much more subdued end than anyone would have imagined this creature would have required.

The mind at the core of this whole invasive force just winked out under the short circuit effect of the water and in that very instant, the gargantuan force controlling all of the Ult, which had been driving the constant retreat of the human race, and that which had been screaming at the boundaries of Jenna's mind, ended.

Jenna could only smile to herself and rejoice that despite everything that had happened to her, she'd held tightly to the last scraps of what made her human, and despite that part being now just a flickering spark in her Ult form, it had been enough. It was, at long last, over, and while she relaxed into the darkness surrounding her, Jenna, who'd clung so tightly to what it was that had meant to live as a human being, finally winked out, and died as one.

32

Climbing through a nearby building with as much speed as could be mustered after what had been happening to them up to that point, Selina, Davis and Artie risked a look through a nearby window to take stock of the situation they'd left Jenna in. They were all breathing hard and sweat was pouring from them to create cascades all over their bodies.

"What's she trying to do?" asked Davis, pressing himself close to the glass to confirm what he was seeing. Below them, The Beast had already begun its slow advance towards the hole in the ground where they'd attacked the Ult-mind.

"She's not going to be able to get The Beast to do anything useful. Is she trying to move her out of the path of the big ones?"

Artie just shrugged but pushed himself back from the window as he recognised the approaching mayhem of the two Mega-Ult which had been flailing wildly, launching brickwork missiles, and generally destroying as they moved.

Their silence hung around them as they all examined what was unfolding.

"Give 'em Hell, Jen," whispered Selina from her position next to Davis and placed an arm on his shoulder, providing him the support she knew he was going to need but also claiming what she needed from him in return.

Davis' posture stiffened under her hand and she recognised that he'd understood too.

From their vantage point, high above where the final stand was being made, the others had seen the final seconds of The Beast's journey and the eventual fall which took it and Jenna into the darkness, but they had no clue what had happened after that.

There'd been no eruption of sound and light. There hadn't been a crushing blast wave escaping from the space underground, nor had there been any wrenching earthquake shaking the buildings. Jenna had taken The Beast over the edge but there'd been nothing more. They all traded looks and held their breaths.

Their first hint of an effect came soon enough.

'ULT, ULT, U.....' had been booming out as the enemy had thrashed around destroying everything they could, but that was only until the two Mega-Ult simply stopped moving, before they collapsed to the ground like their strings had been cut. There'd been no graceful collapse or tottering downfall. The two giants hadn't given any sign of trying to resist the effects of any outside forces, or of being under any kind of attack before the end. Instead, they just stopped, and fell.

Clouds of dust and smoke rose in plumes under the force of the broken Mega-Ult, and for almost ten minutes, there was just nothing outside which gave any hint of life signs. At long last, the air stilled all around them as the giants settled to a complete stop, leaving behind only the barest wisp of breeze to casually pass through the wreckage of Hope, now unflustered by all the events which had been unfolding.

Artie had wanted to get a closer look, suggesting that he was keen to find out any and all information that he could from the two corpses, but also to make doubly certain that they were indeed dead. Selina and Davis dared to hope that there could have been some way that Jenna had survived, but before they could decide what was likely going to be the best course of action, the giant masses began to expel torrents of dark and steaming liquid all over the area around them. The oily filth spread and stuck to everything it touched and the smell was very quickly upon them, making all three of them gag and heave.

Artie was less keen on getting a closer look of that.

Eventually, Selina made the unilateral decision to barricade themselves into a nearby room without windows and wait the night out. They just couldn't risk the journey to hunt for Jenna. Selina hated herself for it but everyone agreed that any search would have been just too dangerous. Outside, it was moving rapidly now towards full darkness and they all understood that they'd need every possible advantage to evade any wandering

Ult that may still be moving around, but as it turned out, they hadn't needed to worry.

Selina had taken the first watch of the night while the others slept. The room they'd chosen was little more than a storage cupboard but it was big enough to fit them in with as much comfort as they could really hope for and still be tightly defensible. The door was locked and had pieces of the plastic sheeting that they all still wore jammed tightly into place to completely obscure any sign that there may have been anyone inside. By the time the first switch in watches rolled around, Selina had heard nothing beyond the door at any point which suggested that they were in the vicinity of another life form. Davis took over and again sat in relative silence as nothing more happened. He was happy to report that he'd heard the building creaking on occasion when it was time for Artie to take his place. He was also pretty sure that he'd been able to pick out the sound of rain but he just couldn't be sure. Artie watched the remainder of the night slip by, but again, without any sign of life outside at all, possible threat or anything else.

Cracking the door open ever so slightly, Davis risked furtive glances through the tiny space and found there to be nothing visible. Inch by inch, he pushed the door further open and continued to scan for any signs of anything which may have changed since they'd locked themselves in. All three of them had left their bunker slowly before finally accepting that there was no further threat nearby, meaning they all felt slightly more at ease but no-one was free of fear.

Checking through the windows, there were fresh gatherings of water on flat roofs and on the ground, showing that there had indeed been rain during the night, but that whatever water had come down had been pretty powerless to wipe clean the enormous areas of sludgy gloop which had been expelled from the Mega-Ult. The giant carcasses had continued to deflate overnight and the viscous material inside had continued to drain out of them but it had now become pools of sticky filth. It was so thick now that a section of a nearby building had fallen free overnight and landed in an area of it, only to be held rigidly in place at a perverse angle.

"I wonder if we can use any of that stuff as a sealant of some kind?" mused Artie as he peered down at the mess below.

"One step at a time," said Selina calmly. They couldn't get ahead of themselves.

The mounds of the Mega-Ult had split apart in some areas and their insides had been exposed to the elements. They'd previously been the cause of the greatest horror the human race had ever encountered but in the cold light of a clear day, the hulks looked more like the bodies of whales which had been washed up on shore. There was no way to say if they were going to swell up and rupture though, so time was certainly against them.

After an age of checks and risked glances, of hearts racing at any possible sound, of cautious movement through the wreckage of Hope, Selina, Davis and Artie were able to find a safe way through the debris and into the hole where Jenna had fallen. There was still no other sign of Ult anywhere along their journey so, for the first time in far too long, they all began to kindle the very smallest hope of success.

Deep in the underground, the three were descending into the inky nothingness of the lair of the Ult-mind. The air felt thick with swirling rot and the odour coming from far below them turned all of their stomachs. In the low light, there was still a constant threat everywhere around them but they pushed on regardless, hoping for a miracle.

Despite their best efforts, they couldn't find one.

As their eyes adjusted to the available light while they moved uneasily around, the scale of the location unfolded before them. The huge mass of the Ult-mind bore a striking similarity to the creatures lying dead above ground. It wasn't as big as the Mega-Ult but it was far beyond the singular creatures. It too was a shapeless mass of flesh, a deep grey hide covering its inner workings but after Jenna, it appeared more like a circus tent which was slowly falling in on itself.

Selina held her machete primed and ready while edging towards the creature, but there, out close to the nearest edge of the mass, was what was left of The Beast, standing proudly in place like the sword in the stone. There were jagged edges and broken metal forming macabre shapes of the old engine, but she'd struck true.

And as they all closed in, they could see that Jenna had struck true as well.

Her split body lay in the broken engine and hung as if to display her final act in death. The three friends gathered closer in to pay their respects to their fallen comrade. To anyone else who could have come upon this scene, it would have appeared that there were the ruined remains of a single Ult mangled within the parts of The Beast but to Selina, Davis and Artie, they were able to recognise Jenna.

"She looks so peaceful," said Artie.

Davis stepped forward and reached out to run his hand ever so lightly across what was left of Jenna's human head and face within the mass of the Ult form she'd been mutated into. Even through his glove, he could feel that she was icy cold.

What more could be said?

"Should we take her with us?" asked Davis, his voice cracking.

"We'll come back to get her when we're more able to take her home. She deserves to be carried by more than just us." Selina was smiling as she spoke but she didn't feel the smile anywhere else. She nodded skywards and the three of them turned their backs on their friend and began their return journey. They fully intended to bring her home but there could never be the guarantee that they'd be able to.

If nothing else, Jenna was going to be remembered by everyone who they could tell.

At the surface, the sky was still a beautiful, clear, pale blue, and a breeze of unusual lightness danced its way through the devastation.

Was this really over?

Did this mean that they'd defeated the Ult?

If they had, how were they going to start everything over again?

Selina led the way and the long journey back towards the Way Station spread out before them, but no words were spoken as they walked. Davis and Artie both held their heads down as they walked in silent recognition of the loss of so many, but of Jenna most of all, though Selina was smiling again.

The others couldn't see her smile, she was leading after all, but for Selina, she was thinking about what her friend Jenna had been saying about doing more than just surviving. She was filled with a new appreciation for the life that she had and for all of the very silly and inconsequential things which may only matter to a single person, but which make life that much more valuable.

Maybe they were in a position now to put the horrors of the Ult behind them and start living more than surviving.

It seemed to be the most human thing to do.

About the Author

Owen is a fan of all forms of storytelling and enjoys books, film and TV, as long as there's something compelling going on. He's worked in different roles over the years but has always had the spark of creativity lurking in the back of his mind. A Welsh rugby supporter, he lives in South Wales with his wife Joanne and their guardian cat, Sausage.

https://www.facebook.com/OwenElgie/

https://twitter.com/OwenElgie

https://owenelgie.wordpress.com/